MURDER AT RAVEN'S GATE

LOUISE MARLEY

Storm
PUBLISHING

Ebook ISBN: 978-1-83700-215-3
Paperback ISBN: 978-1-83700-217-7

Cover design: Ghost
Cover images: Adobe Stock, Shutterstock

Published by Storm Publishing.
For further information, visit:
www.stormpublishing.co

An English Village Mystery

Murder at Raven's Edge

Murder at Ravenswood House

Murder at Raven's Hollow

Murder at Castle Vyne

For Betsy and Harriet

ONE

MARCH

Friday

The carved stone arch brooded in the heart of the King's Forest, abandoned but never forgotten. For centuries it had been a place of reverence and respect, a refuge and a sanctuary, a *home*. Now, however...

'*This* is "the Gateway to the Dead"?' The man glared at the crumbling ruin in front of him. 'Now you're just making stuff up.'

Detective Sergeant Harriet March sighed. The entire history of Raven's Edge was made up but it didn't stop people flocking here for their Magik Meg T-shirts and Raven Queen mugs. Some mornings she wished it would, because then there wouldn't be such a queue at The Crooked Broomstick, and she could buy her breakfast in peace.

'Is it safe?' The man tilted his head. 'It looks as though the forest is holding it up.'

Or the gateway was holding the encroaching forest back, Harriet thought. But then she'd grown up in Raven's Edge and, well, sometimes it was best not to think about the forest, in case one day it started thinking about you.

Her stomach rumbled and she glanced at her watch. If the

ghosts that haunted this part of the forest were going to make an appearance, they'd better hurry up. She'd booked a table at Pizza at Cosimo's for nine, and would not be pleased if it was given to somebody else.

'The Gateway to the Dead was originally part of Buckley Abbey,' the tour guide was saying. His name was Oscar, he was knowledgeable and enthusiastic, but he couldn't have been more than eighteen. 'The rest of the abbey was demolished following the Dissolution of the Monasteries in the sixteenth century. The land the abbey stood on was bought by the wealthy Weston family, who still own the nearby Blackheath Hall. They kept what was left of the abbey as a romantic ruin.'

The tour group's attention obediently turned to the shadowy woodland on the other side of the clearing.

Was Blackheath Hall still there? Harriet wondered. Hidden behind the trees like Sleeping Beauty's palace? Or had it been swallowed by the forest like the abbey, leaving barely an outline of rubble to show where it'd been?

'Why's it called the Gateway to the Dead?' the same man asked.

'A battle took place in this clearing during the Civil War,' Oscar said. 'The dead from both sides were buried where they fell. Hence, "Gateway to the Dead".'

The man's partner, who'd been about to walk through the gateway, immediately took a step back. And then another to be certain. 'The bodies are still out there?'

'No, there was a big archaeological dig just over forty years ago. Any skeletons they found were re-buried in the village churchyard.'

Oscar moved back to allow the tour group to peer through the arch and into the wide clearing where so many men had died, but no one was brave enough to step through into the darkness beyond. The gateway and the tree-lined road leading into the clearing were illuminated until late in the evening for the tourists. Everything beyond that relied on natural light.

And in Raven's Edge, natural light was not always forthcoming.

Everyone immediately began taking photos.

Harriet, tired of waiting, sidled up to Oscar. 'Will your next ghost be a soldier?' The ghost of Magik Meg had jumped out at her by the village pond (complete with pond weed and rattling chains), and she did not want a repeat performance.

'Harriet,' her date sighed. 'Remember our talk about spoilers?'

'I'm not great with surprises,' she grumbled.

'That *is* the point of a ghost tour.'

Oscar seemed to be debating taking sides, but one glance at Harriet's expression and he must have thought better of it.

He indicated his Parliamentarian soldier's costume: a buff-coloured jacket, with a metal breastplate on top, worn over matching trousers and boots, topped with a metal 'pot' helmet. 'I'm playing the part of Major Lord John Weston,' he said, 'and, to end the evening, I've arranged a sword fight with my mate Stuart, who's playing the Marquess of Blackheath. "Brother against brother", you know? That's what the English Civil War was all about. Their ghosts still haunt this clearing.'

From what Harriet remembered of her (admittedly sketchy) history lessons, the Civil War had been about King Charles I getting too big for his boots, but then someone asked Oscar a question, so she moved away, feeling uneasy. Was it in the best taste to recreate a sword fight on top of what had once been a mass grave?

Her date had wandered over to peer through the ancient stone arch like everyone else, his pale blond hair gleaming in the moonlight. As she approached, he reached out his hand and pulled her into his arms. In theory, it was what she'd been hoping for since she'd asked him out on this date, yet it still felt awkward. But they were standing beneath a centuries-old ruin. He must think it romantic, but she'd tensed, waiting for the next 'ghost' to jump out.

There was a good reason why she didn't like surprises. Even now, her police training was refusing to switch off. The last ghost should consider herself lucky she hadn't ended up pressed against the wall with her arm in a lock, pond weed and all.

Harriet sighed. With hindsight, a ghost tour had been a poor choice for a first date – but she could hardly invite a barista out for coffee.

Assuming Misha was now going to kiss her, she tried to relax. Fortunately, before she closed her eyes like a fool, she noticed he'd been distracted by something happening on the other side of the gateway.

'That's... spooky,' he said.

She followed his gaze. There must be a stream nearby, or perhaps the ground was marshy, because thin columns of mist were moving slowly across the field.

Logic told her this was a natural phenomenon, caused by water vapour cooling in the air, but the mist still resembled ghostly soldiers squaring up to each other.

Was this how the legend had started? From an entirely natural phenomenon?

Oscar launched into his act, brandishing a sword above his head and shouting, 'For God and Parliament!' before striding off through the gateway.

For a moment it seemed as though he would vanish into the mist...

And then the mist parted to let him through.

That was... odd.

'Did you *see* that?' Misha said.

'It's a special effect. Dry ice or something.'

Because anything else...

His fingers threaded through hers and squeezed reassuringly.

Harriet didn't squeeze back. If there was any saving to be done, it'd be done by her.

'What *is* he doing?' she muttered, watching Oscar slash his way across the field, occasionally pausing to untangle his sword from a bramble bush or yank it out from the mud.

Misha shook his head. 'Twenty quid that kid will stab himself in the foot before the night's over.'

She glanced at her watch. 'Shouldn't the other ghost have joined him by now?'

'Who cares?' Misha was back to smiling at her, his blue eyes softening.

Sometimes she could be slow on picking up romantic signals, but she caught that one clearly enough. Particularly when his head tilted, he bent towards her, and—

From beyond the arch she heard another loud, 'For God and —!' before it was abruptly cut off by a yell. She turned her head in time to see the mist fading into the trees and the forest settling down to a contented silence.

There was no sign of Oscar.

What on earth—

Misha's kiss hit her ear.

She stepped away from him, distracted. 'What just happened?'

He gave a rueful smile. 'I tried to kiss you, but you moved.'

'Oscar was stood right *there*,' she said. 'I saw him. We all did. There was a shout and now he's disappeared.'

'Maybe the forest ate him?' Then, when she glared at him, he threw up his hands and said, 'It's a ghost tour. Things like that are supposed to happen.'

'I don't think so.' Seven years of working as a police officer and the back of her neck had already started to prickle. 'Something's not right.'

'It'll be fine.' He reached for her again.

She stepped back smartly. 'I'll check it out,' she said. 'You lot' – here she glared at the rest of the tour, who were beginning to edge curiously towards the clearing – 'stay *here*.'

Switching on her phone torch, she walked confidently through the gateway. A tendril of ivy slid over her shoulder as she went, tangling into her curls as though coaxing her to return.

She irritably brushed it aside. 'Stop that.'

The mist had retreated behind the trees, and the forest was perfectly still, but it was hard to shake the feeling something was watching.

Waiting.

It was remarkably easy to imagine the scene as it must have appeared centuries ago. A brutal battle; smoke and fire; the clash of swords; firing of muskets and cannon; shouts of the wounded and moans of the dying. And those poor soldiers, cursed to keep fighting through the centuries, haunting the forest surrounding Raven's Edge.

Yes, everyone who'd grown up in the village knew *that* story.

But it *was* only a story. The dead did *not* return to haunt the living. Ghosts did not exist. There was no one else in this clearing apart from her and Oscar.

In theory…

'Oscar!' she shouted, lengthening her stride as she approached the halfway point, sweeping the beam of her phone torch in a wide arc. She saw nothing but long grass, brambles and nettles. Where *was* he?

Despite living here her entire life, she'd never walked this far past the gateway. The ground was uneven with unusual holes and hollows, dips and trenches, all partially concealed by the undergrowth. Had Oscar fallen into one of them? How deep were they?

She allowed the beam of her torch to play along one crumbling edge.

What were they?

The remains of those fallen soldiers had been moved to the village churchyard decades ago. Had no one bothered to fill in the holes? Were these empty *graves?*

No, of course not! They would've made good the site. She was being ridiculous.

'Oscar!'

She'd reached the other side quicker than she'd expected. She ignored an overgrown path leading up a slope and into the woods, turning around to make her way back, slower this time.

'*Oscar!*' Honestly, it was as though he'd disappeared into—

'*Harriet?* Is that you?'

She lowered the beam of her torch, revealing Oscar lying along the length of the nearest hole, his lantern smashed beside him.

'Before you ask, the only thing that hurts is my pride,' he said, sitting up and rubbing the back of his head. 'Please tell me no one's filming this.'

'I think it's too dark.' She glanced back, where the ghost tour was huddled beneath the gateway, waiting for the show to recommence. 'What happened?'

'I fell into a rabbit hole and must have knocked myself out. Can you believe it? What bad luck, eh?'

'A *rabbit* hole?' Harriet ran the beam of her torch along the length of the hole. *That* deep? Since when had rabbits started using shovels?

Big shovels.

Enough of this.

Sliding her phone into her pocket, she jumped into the hole, caught hold of Oscar beneath each arm and abruptly yanked him to his feet.

'Whoa,' he said, swaying slightly. 'You're quite strong for a little thing...'

'*Years* of practice,' she told him briskly. Although the hauling usually ended with the other person being dragged off to a waiting patrol car, but she wouldn't mention that. She'd been working on her tact. 'You're *sure* you're OK? No broken bones, no twisted... whatever?'

With hindsight, perhaps she should have checked that *before* the hauling.

'Sure, I only—'

'Great.' She slapped him cheerfully on the back. 'Let's get you out of here.' As he showed no sign of moving, she helpfully pushed him towards the edge of the hole to encourage him out. 'Your audience awaits.'

That got him moving.

'Really?' He smiled uncertainly. She was reminded of how young he was. But he obediently grabbed his broken lantern and clambered up and out of the hole. When the tour group broke into spontaneous applause, he raised his hand sheepishly.

As usual, Harriet was left to rescue herself.

It took a bit of scrambling and her new jeans – worn in honour of her first date in over a year – got covered in mud.

Instead of heading towards the Gateway to the Dead, Oscar was staring around the clearing, slightly confused. 'Where do you think Stuart is?'

Skipped the fight scene and headed straight to the pub, if he had any sense. It was too cold to hang around a damp, misty forest playing at ghosts.

'Maybe he's running late?' she suggested, grabbing Oscar before he stepped into another hole. She'd send someone from the station to check them out tomorrow. DC Dakota Lawrence was always grumbling that she never left the office. Here was her perfect opportunity.

'Why don't we go to the pub?' she told Oscar. 'You can tell the group more ghost stories and answer any questions.'

And it'd be warm and there'd be food.

Her stomach rumbled an agreement.

'We usually end up at The Lucky Cavalier anyway,' he said. 'If I bring enough people, the landlord gives me a free meal.'

Nice. No wonder he was keen to come all the way past the village boundary.

She followed as he carefully detoured around another large hole, and then almost walked into the back of him as he stopped abruptly.

'*Stuart?*' he said in disbelief.

That didn't sound good.

She stepped past him, shining her torch into the hole ahead. It had partly collapsed, half-burying a man dressed as a Royalist soldier, in a blue tunic and frilly white shirt – although it was no longer white. He was lying face down and, as she moved her torch, something glinted in the light. Something metallic. It looked like some kind of prong. And it was sticking straight out of his back.

Oh, no...

She yanked Oscar back before he could jump in beside the body.

'Don't!'

'Are you *crazy?*' Oscar shot her the same look he might have given her if she'd suggested not helping a drowning man. 'That's Stuart. He's *hurt!*'

'*I'll* do it,' she said. 'I'm a police officer.'

Once she was sure he was going to stay put, she jumped into the hole. It was deeper than the last one, almost hip height. The soil was wet and muddy, and water had pooled at one end. She almost slipped. Had it been freshly dug?

Trying not to dwell on the ramifications of *that*, she leant over the body, endeavouring not to touch anything that might end up being evidence. His head, shoulders and one arm were the only parts of him not covered with dirt. Gently, she brushed it from his neck to check for a pulse.

As she'd suspected, there was none. His clothes and hair were damp from the mist, although his skin was warm to her touch. He'd not been dead for long.

Poor Stuart.

She lifted her head. Oscar was standing on the edge of the hole, wringing his hands.

'I'm sorry,' she said. 'Your friend is dead.'

He stared at her. 'Of course Stuart's not *dead*! I was talking to him on the phone less than an hour ago. We have to call an ambulance.' He looked around, perhaps hoping for someone with more authority to agree with him.

'I've called the emergency services.' Misha was already striding towards them, holding up his phone as though providing proof. 'They're going to send a paramedic.'

'Thank you,' Oscar said, giving her a sideways glare.

As a police officer, it wasn't anything she wasn't used to.

Unsurprisingly, he was now going into shock: breathing quickly and shallowly, bending over as though he was going to be sick.

Fortunately, Misha understood very quickly what was required of him. Putting his arm around Oscar's shoulders, he led him back towards the gateway.

'Is there anyone you'd like me to call for you, Oscar?' she heard Misha say, leaving her free to phone her boss.

Ben answered immediately. 'Taylor.'

He couldn't have looked at his screen or he'd have known it was her.

Had she interrupted him working late?

'Hi, boss,' she said. 'There's been an... er, incident...'

'What sort of incident?' Ben sounded amused. 'I thought you were having a romantic evening with Misha Sokolov from The Crooked Broomstick?'

'How did—?' She broke off. Honestly, the officers in the Murder Investigation Team were worse than a bunch of little old ladies when it came to gossip.

'I'll message you the details,' she said, 'but you need to come right away.'

'Location?'

'We're at the... er... ah...'

Was she going to have to say it out loud?

'We're at the Gateway to the Dead.'

Ben was silent, and then, 'You took *Misha* on a *date* to the *Gateway to the Dead?*'

'We were on the ghost tour and—'

'Harriet, you and I need to have a little chat about dating conventions.'

He disconnected before she could think up a comeback.

Still, as the first officer on the scene, there was a whole bunch of other people she needed to contact. It was standard procedure after an unexplained death. Although that strange metal prong sticking out of Stuart's back meant his death was hardly going to be 'unexplained'.

Harriet sighed. She could almost hear the forensic pathologist's voice in her head: 'Never make assumptions, DS March...'

TWO

Ben Taylor had been watching television when Harriet had phoned but he couldn't have told her what had been on, because, in reality, he'd been clock-watching, waiting for his girlfriend Milla to call before he went to bed. His sitting room was far too quiet and empty without her, and he always worried when she was out on a job with Kieran Drake, although he'd never have told her so. Milla was a free spirit who never dealt well with anyone telling her what to do.

He'd have liked to have got up from his seat and done something more constructive, but his black cat, Binx, had settled around his shoulders like a fur stole (a trick Milla had taught him) and showed no sign of wanting to move – unless someone opened a tin of tuna in his immediate vicinity.

At least Ben could still reach the remote control and, fortunately, his phone. Binx was not at all pleased when Ben tried to gently remove him, and stuck his claws into Ben's sweater before stalking off to sulk on the windowsill.

Ben drove to the police station but left his car there to walk through the village and onto the overgrown lane that had once been the original driveway to Blackheath Hall – coincidentally, where Milla was working tonight. Growing up in Raven's Edge, he knew the history of the Gateway to the Dead. Everyone did. It was one of the village's most famous landmarks, and was usually photographed from about halfway down the approach to the house, neatly framed by the long avenue of beech trees, planted in Victorian times to create a romantic effect, particularly in autumn.

The Civil War soldiers that were rumoured to haunt the area, however, were a whimsical invention for the tourists, like most of the folklore of Raven's Edge.

As Ben approached the ruined arch, accompanied by a grumpy DC Sam King (who'd planned a much different evening, starting with chatting up Nina, the waitress at The Drop pub), he found Harriet interviewing a blond teenager with no sign of her date. He sighed. That didn't bode well, although he'd never quite understood her crush on Misha Sokolov. OK, the man owned The Crooked Broomstick and made the most delicious cookies in the southern counties, but he'd never seemed the right match for Harriet.

But who was he to give relationship advice?

The local council now owned what was left of Buckley Abbey (basically, just the archway) and illuminated it until eleven at night. There were also streetlamps on the road leading to it, but it was overgrown and no longer suitable for motor vehicles. In addition to the existing abbey lights, portable floodlights had been set up to allow the crime-scene investigators to work.

He spotted Misha, compiling the names and addresses of the witnesses, currently collected in a grumpy huddle beneath the arch. Ben directed Sam to take over from him, so the civilians could go home. Apparently over their shock, they were becoming a little too curious and getting in everyone's way, and at this point in the investigation Ben would rather keep photos of the crime scene off social media.

As the civilians left, DC Freddie Kuang from Calahurst Police Station tied police tape across the lane – just in time, because the local press were beginning to turn up, grumbling about there being nowhere to park.

Harriet was on the other side of the arch, amongst the few desultory broken stones that were all that was left of the abbey. She was standing beside a blond youth, the same height as her despite him sitting on a broken pillar. He was wearing strange, faun-coloured clothes, which took Ben a moment to recognise as a Civil War costume, and swinging a soldier's helmet from his fingers.

'Hi, boss,' she said. 'This is Oscar Montgomery. He runs the Raven's Edge ghost tours. He's identified the victim as his friend, Stuart Huntingdon. They were due to have staged a sword fight in the clearing.'

Oscar, Ben belatedly noticed, had what was presumably a replica sword in a scabbard dangling from his belt.

'I'm sorry for your loss,' Ben said.

Obviously in shock and terribly upset, Oscar barely lifted his head to acknowledge him. If *he* were the murderer, he was a very good actor.

Beyond the gateway was a large, overgrown clearing. About halfway across was a familiar white tent – to protect the body from the elements and prying eyes, and to allow the investigative team to work undisturbed.

Ben bent beneath the barrier tape and approached the tent. He was impressed they'd found land flat enough to pitch it on. The clearing was full of holes. Some small, some large, as well as a few trenches crumbling in on themselves. He vaguely remembered the site had been the scene of an archaeology investigation, but surely the archaeologists would have restored it to its former condition?

He ducked into the tent. On the other side was the Force forensic pathologist, Caroline Warner, who was also his ex-wife. Their divorce had been sticky, but in the last twelve months they'd declared a truce for the sake of their daughter, Sophie. It helped that Caroline had moved here from London, to share childcare more easily, and they'd both begun dating other people.

'Hi, Caroline,' he said. 'What have we got?'

She grunted something that could have been 'Hello', or perhaps she was clearing her throat.

The tent completely enclosed another trench, which was unexpected.

He peered into the hole. 'Was he being buried or dug up?'

The woman kneeling at the bottom of the trench glanced up at him. As she was wearing coveralls, now distinctly muddy, it took him a moment to recognise Lucia Serrano, the forensic archaeologist.

'Buried, I believe,' Lucia said in her soft Spanish accent. 'I'm now digging him up. It could take a while though.'

'Meaning I can't work until he's out,' Caroline grumbled. 'Waste of time me being here actually.'

In the trench, Lucia cringed. 'I'm sorry, I have to—'

'Go slowly, take care, I know.' Caroline sighed. 'I'm sorry. I'm being unprofessional. I was out on a date, a nice little wine bar in Norchester. Sorry,' she said again. 'None of you want to hear about my personal life.'

Ben thought that, actually, they *did* all want to hear about her personal life, especially him. Had their seven-year-old daughter, Sophie, met this new man? What was he like? What did he do?

With an effort, he turned to Lucia. 'So—'

'What have we got?' She completed the sentence with a grin. 'White male, early twenties to mid-thirties – Caroline can give you more details. The hole was already here but freshly dug, and someone's tried to bury him in it. There are signs that he might have been dragged into it from a few metres away.'

'Killed here or elsewhere?'

'Here, we think. There's no obvious pool of blood, only the traces CSI picked up with their lights. We'll know more when we get him out.'

Ben glanced back to Caroline, but she was looking at her phone and smiling, paying them no attention whatsoever.

Why had no one mentioned the rusty prong sticking out of the victim?

He pointed to it. 'Murder weapon?'

Caroline glanced up from her phone long enough to shrug. 'I won't know until I get him back in my lab for a full post-mortem. And we can't load him into the van until he's out of that trench.'

'It could take a while,' Lucia repeated, apologising again.

Being stabbed with a two-foot prong would be bad for anyone's health, but at least Caroline hadn't given Ben her usual speech on making assumptions.

'What is it?' he asked, crouching at the side of the trench to examine the weapon more carefully. Whatever it was, it had rusted and there were soil flakes stuck to it. 'Some kind of gardening tool?' It was too small to be a hoe, and was definitely not a pitchfork.

'I've not been able to examine the victim,' Caroline said, without looking up this time. 'But my guess is that he was stabbed with the business end of a medieval pike. It would've had a length of wood at the non-pointy end but presumably that's rotted away.'

Both ends appeared pointy to Ben but, 'You think the pike could've already been here? Buried in the trench?' That could mean manslaughter rather than murder, but he could see Caroline was warming up to say, 'Isn't that *your* job?' so he backed out of the tent with, 'Thank you very much. Keep me informed.'

Caroline rolled her eyes.

Lucia grinned and gave a little wave of her fingers.

He inclined his head and walked back towards the archway, pausing only to ask one of the CSIs to liaise with Caroline to arrange for soil samples from the pike to be sent off for analysis.

As he ducked beneath the barrier tape, now stretching across the arch but, bizarrely, not on either side of it (so anyone could walk around), he almost collided with a middle-aged woman on the other side.

She had a sleek blonde bob, wore a long raincoat, similar in style to the ones DCI Doug Cameron favoured, and a scarf that was probably designer because the bold blue pattern seemed familiar. Harriet would have known, but Harriet was talking to—

Except she wasn't. Harriet was trying to get his attention,

waving her hands, pulling a face and pointing to the woman – who must be either Oscar's mother or Stuart's.

'Good evening, ma'am. I'm DI Ben Taylor. How may I help—?'

The woman prodded him in the chest. 'How dare you treat poor Oscar like a criminal? Can't you see my son's in shock?'

Oscar's mother.

She was right. The lad couldn't have been more than eighteen and he looked as though he might keel over at any moment. He'd found his friend's body. He'd never get over that.

'I'm sorry,' Ben said. 'Take him home. Let him get some rest, but I'll need someone to call on him tomorrow to take a formal statement.'

Mrs Montgomery glared at him, and then her expression unexpectedly softened. 'I understand. You want to catch whoever did this. Come round whenever you like. I'll make sure we're both in. Would you like the details of Stuart's next-of-kin?'

'That would be helpful.' He beckoned Sam forward. 'DC King will—'

Another teenager, dark-haired and wearing jeans and an anorak, barged between them, treading on Ben's foot and making straight for Oscar. 'Hiya! Sorry I'm late. What's going on?' He turned back towards Ben, looking him up and down suspiciously. 'Who's this guy?'

Oscar turned paler if that were possible, his eyes round, his mouth literally dropping open. '*Stuart?*' he croaked.

'You got a cold coming on?' The other teenager clapped him on the shoulder. 'You sound weird. What's with all these lights? Are they making a film? Are we in it? Cool! Where do you want me to stand?'

'*Stuart!*' Oscar flung his arms around him, squeezing hard.

'S'OK' – Stuart patted his shoulder cautiously – 'I missed you, too. The dry cleaners closed before I could pick up my costume and then I met this really cool girl—' He broke off, suddenly aware of the audience. 'What *is* going on?'

'You were *dead*, mate. You were *dead*!'

Oscar promptly burst into tears.

Mrs Montgomery's glare turned flinty, but this time her ire was directed at Stuart, who seemed more baffled by the minute.

And Ben wished he was anywhere other than here.

It was going to be a *very* long night.

THREE

Earlier that day

Mid-afternoon and private detective Milla Graham and her boss, Kieran Drake, were walking down an avenue of skeletal beech trees that seemed to stretch forever. Perhaps planned as an elegant approach to some grand manor house, many of the trees had died over the years, leaving those that remained leaning into each other for support, creating a gloomy tunnel.

The weather was cold and grey, with drizzle so faint it was more like mist. The further they walked from the main road, the colder, quieter and mistier it became.

Milla turned up the collar of her red wool coat, wishing she'd brought an umbrella or, better still, her car. Not that it would have got very far down this narrow lane. Somewhere beneath her feet there must have been tarmac, but the rotting leaves were spread so thickly it was impossible to tell. The lane couldn't have been used by vehicles for decades.

'The sun was shining when we left The Square,' she grumbled, grateful that at least she'd worn her winter coat instead of her new jacket.

Drake shrugged. 'Welcome to Raven's Edge.'

He didn't have to explain the microclimate of the village to her. She'd lived here for almost a year.

'Technically we're not *in* Raven's Edge,' she said. 'We crossed the boundary when we passed The Witch's Brew.'

The boundary into where, she wasn't sure. The road leading from the west side of the village led past her father's house and eventually onto the moor, presumably – she'd never been that far. There wasn't any point. There was nothing there.

She was starting to believe there was nothing here either.

Drake glanced sideways, perhaps wondering why she'd lapsed into silence, and caught her staring at him. His shaggy black hair was a mess, as usual, and he hadn't bothered to shave. His only concession to the weather was a battered jacket. He must have been frozen. On his feet were his habitual Chucks – except these ones were black. Had his favourite red ones finally fallen to bits?

It had been a long walk from the village, so she wasn't surprised to see him limping – he often did when he was tired.

'Are we there yet?' she said.

He laughed. 'Don't you *know* where we are? Didn't you once tell me you could find your way around the forest blindfold?'

'We're not in the forest, we're on private land.'

'Very good. This is council-owned land, but it was once privately owned.'

'And presumably this is the tradesmen's entrance?'

'It's a road not often taken, that's for sure.' He kicked a branch aside. 'We're not taking the main drive. This is what is known as a subtle approach.'

'A subtle approach?' she repeated. Couldn't he just come to the point?

He winked. 'We don't want the bad guys to know we're coming.'

OK... Hopefully *not* the people they were working for, although they often were.

She and Drake were fixers, finders and investigators for hire –

by some of the most powerful people in the King's Forest District –
including her own father.

Despite Drake's insistence that everything they did was
completely within the law, she'd realised very early on that he
often treated rules as optional.

Much like her.

Milla checked her watch. How long had it been since they'd
turned off the main road? Surely they should have arrived by—

Oh...

Ahead, neatly framed by the trees and partly covered in ivy,
which was why she hadn't spotted it immediately, was a ruined
stone arch.

No, not an arch – this was the famous 'Gateway to the Dead',
all that remained of the ruined Buckley Abbey. She'd never been
here before, but it wasn't hard to recognise it from the postcards for
sale in the village.

Why on earth were they *here*?

She slipped out her phone to take a photo.

Drake frowned. 'We're not tourists.'

'I wanted to show Ben. It's such a great aesthetic, the gate
looming out of the mist like this. It's like the entrance to the Under-
world. Super spooky!'

His frown deepened. 'What mist?'

She lowered her phone. 'Well, that... Oh...' The sky was over-
cast, the drizzle had left little beads of moisture on her coat, and
her usually sleek black plait was starting to turn frizzy. But there
was no longer any mist. How strange.

She glanced at the photo she'd just taken. It was pretty enough
– a bit dark and gloomy – but there was definitely no mist.

Milla glanced up at the arch. She hadn't imagined it, she knew
she hadn't, but she shoved the phone back into her pocket and
hurried after Drake.

As they moved closer to the arch, she could see it had once
been one end of a substantial sandstone building. Beyond it were
blocks of broken stone, some in neat lines where the walls had once

stood, others in sad little heaps, methodically collected for building materials perhaps but never taken away, and in the clearing beyond, lots of strange-looking holes.

She pointed them out. 'What are they?'

'Well, Buckley Abbey was one of the wealthiest in the country and, rumour has it, when the monks were forced to flee, they left their treasury behind, hidden in a secret vault – presumably intending to return for it.'

'Buried treasure? Seriously? People actually believe that?'

Drake laughed.

'You're winding me up, aren't you?'

'Not at all, although some say the Weston family got to it first – which is why they were so rich. They owned all the land here after the Dissolution of the Monasteries – until the council bought the ruined abbey forty years ago.'

'Typical.'

Heavy-duty lights had been set into the ground, presumably to illuminate the arch after dark, and a large, faded board to one side displayed a diagram showing how the abbey had originally looked, along with a few paragraphs about the Civil War battle a hundred years after its destruction.

On the other side of the arch, warning signs said things like:

PRIVATE PROPERTY

KEEP OUT

TRESPASSERS WILL BE PROSECUTED

'It's almost like they don't want us to go any further,' Milla said.

'We have permission from the owner.' Drake set off across the clearing, following a faint path through the long grass. 'Watch out for the holes!'

That was easier said than done as some of the holes had collapsed, leaving little hollows grown over with brambles and weeds. But Milla followed Drake into the woods on the far side of the arch, where a distinct footpath led up a slope.

The path twisted between the trees, coming out at a wrought-iron gate set in a high stone wall, an extensive garden on the other side. The most curious thing, however, was that large sections of the wall were missing.

What was the point of the gate?

'I never knew this house was here,' Milla said, as Drake held the gate open for her. 'It's completely hidden.'

'Not many people do, which suits the current occupants just fine.'

It was surreal walking between tumbledown walls, roofless outbuildings open to the sky, and twisting stone staircases that no longer went anywhere. An attempt had been made to pretty up the ruined walls with climbing plants and flowerpots, but the plants had withered and the pots were broken.

Although it was now wildly overgrown, someone had once loved this garden. Milla could see glimpses of bright pink camellias, purple hellebores and masses of yellow daffodils.

The path led through the garden and into a weed-strewn courtyard directly in front of the house. Opposite was the remains of a formal gatehouse set into the stone wall. There were towers on either side, although the top of one had crumbled away. On the other side of the gatehouse was a modern tarmac drive, albeit severely potholed.

What was it Drake had said?

'We don't want them to know we're coming.'

Who were 'we' and why would they be watching the main drive?

Drake walked up a flight of stone steps to a studded oak door in the centre of the main house and used the massive bronze knocker. It was in the shape of a lion's head, with a starburst mane and a huge ring held in its jaw, which Drake crashed against the metal plate behind it.

Milla winced. The size of the thing meant he could have easily crushed his fingers; even standing at the bottom of the stone steps, she could hear it echo throughout the house.

'That's some door knocker,' she said.

'It's a sanctuary ring,' he said, 'probably "liberated" from the abbey and never intended to be used like this. Those claiming sanctuary would have grabbed the ring. The monks keeping watch would have then let them in.'

Maybe the door was originally from the abbey as well. It looked old enough.

Drake came back down the steps to wait beside her. 'This might take some time. Lady Peony Weston is in her sixties and a little eccentric. Three years ago, she accused her staff of spying for her cousin, the Marquess, and sacked the lot of them. Now she and her older sister Lady Rose live here alone, never leaving the house. The only person they see is the cleaner who visits once a week; Lady Peony watches her like a hawk.'

Slightly paranoid then, thought Milla.

With good reason?

Was that why they were here?

The door creaked slowly open. Drake smiled effortlessly, completely changing his appearance from evil elf king to friendly neighbourhood investigator. She'd often seen him do this, but that didn't make it any less impressive. He'd adjust his accent, too, whatever it took to make prospective clients believe he was one of them.

But as Milla stepped forward she heard something strange behind them. A kind of metallic chink that took a moment for her to identify as a bridle.

She turned automatically, expecting to see a horse walk into the courtyard.

But there was nothing, only mist rapidly fading back into the forest.

· · ·

Lady Peony Weston wasn't your average 'little old lady'. For a start, she was a good eight inches taller than Milla and had bubblegum-pink hair piled on top of her head, although it looked as though it had been fastened in place by anything to hand. Flouncy broderie anglaise petticoats skimmed the tops of brown riding boots, topped with a dark-red tartan dress and an overlarge moth-eaten RAF jacket slung around her shoulders. According to the insignia, Lady Peony was a Wing Commander.

Milla thought this unlikely but smiled in what she hoped was a friendly way.

She might need to work on that because Lady Peony looked her up and down and frowned. 'You look familiar.'

'I don't believe we've met—'

'You're a Graham. I'd recognise those eyes anywhere.'

Milla's silvery grey eyes, a startling contrast with her brown skin and long black hair, had caused people to comment before, not always kindly.

She got ready to utter her usual putdown but Lady Peony was grinning.

'Dermot Graham's long-lost daughter? I've heard about your exploits. Your father always ran your grandmother ragged. It must be doing him good to get a dose of his own medicine.' Peony turned and walked into a cavernous hall, leaving them both standing on the doorstep.

OK...

Drake raised an eyebrow as if to ask, 'What was *that* all about?' but Milla followed Peony into the gloomy house, leaving Drake to close the massive door. Mismatched planks showed where it had been repaired over the centuries.

An icy draught followed her across a two-storey hall overlooked by a gallery, with a wide wooden staircase to the left. Directly above was the kind of medieval chandelier you could swing on, but fitted with modern light bulbs. Doors led to other rooms on both storeys, while Lady Peony was heading towards a massive stone fireplace directly opposite. Milla couldn't blame her. As she approached, she felt the heat from its crackling flames.

Lady Peony flopped onto a sagging couch covered with multi-coloured throws and blankets. She pulled one around her shoulders and another over her lap. She could have been sitting in a nest.

'Take a seat,' she said, waving regally at the sofa opposite, also tangled with blankets.

Milla went to stand in front of the fire, deciding it would appear more professional. It was also beautifully toasty.

'You'll scorch yourself,' Peony said, as though she didn't care either way. 'Better to acclimatise. Most of the rooms here are kept shut up. You'll need warmer clothes.' Milla's jeans and red wool coat were given a disparaging glance. 'Honestly, young people today. You're too used to modern houses.'

'I live on The Square,' Milla said, ignoring the slight shake of Drake's head that usually meant 'shut up'. Everyone knew the pretty half-timbered houses around the village square dated from Tudor times.

Peony ignored her, carelessly sloshing what appeared to be neat whisky into a handleless porcelain cup. 'The secret is layers, girl. Lots of layers.'

The secret was central heating, but Milla kept her mouth shut. If the rest of the house was like this, she had every intention of keeping her coat on.

Drake, unbothered by the chill, sat on the sofa opposite Peony, who held up her bottle of whisky.

He shook his head. 'We need to start work. If you could spare the time to detail your experiences and give us a tour of the house, we'll crack on with it.'

'You mean this stupid ghost?'

'*Ghost?*' repeated Milla. Was that why they were here? To take advantage of a deluded old lady?

Peony rolled her eyes. 'Obviously it's not a *real* ghost,' she said. 'Sorry to disappoint you, darling. If a ghost is banging on our door after dark, it means something more corporeal wants our house. It might not look much, but I expect it's worth a pretty penny on the market with all the land included.'

Milla looked to Drake. 'A *fake* haunting?'

'Designed to scare Lady Peony and her sister from the house.'

'I grew up here,' Peony said. 'My ancestors have lived in this house for five hundred years before me. They *built* this house. I've no intention of moving out.' She took another glug of whisky. How much had she drunk today?

'Lady Peony and her sister, Lady Rose, can only have use of this house while they remain unmarried, in good health and in residence,' Drake said. 'As soon as they move out, ownership reverts to their cousin, Giles Weston, the current Marquess of Blackheath.'

'Well, that's your suspect right there,' Milla said.

'Perhaps, but we'd have to *prove* it.'

Drake, she remembered, had been a detective sergeant before he'd been invalided out of the police.

'If I'd been born a boy, the house would have come to me,' Peony growled.

Aristocratic titles, and the vast estates that went with them, were often passed from father to son – or the nearest male relative if there was no son – leaving nothing for the remainder of the family. No wonder Peony felt bitter. Losing your home would do that to anyone.

Drake rose to his feet. 'The sooner we start, the sooner we can catch whoever's responsible, and the sooner you'll be left in peace.'

'I'm all for that.' Peony raised her cup in a toast, carelessly discarding her blanket on the floor as she stood up.

Drake surveyed the hall, his sharp green eyes missing nothing as he catalogued all the doors and the gallery above.

There were plenty of nooks for a fake ghost to direct a haunting from. Had they used hidden cameras or speakers? Trickery with mirrors? Milla slowly turned on the spot. She couldn't see any reflective surfaces, little lights that would reveal the location of technical equipment, or wires where they shouldn't be. Just how would you go about faking a haunting?

Drake was asking Peony if his surveillance equipment had arrived.

'A large van, loaded with boxes, arrived this morning,' Peony told him. 'I had the man stack them in my father's study.' She indicated a door to the left of the fireplace.

If someone was watching the house, surely they'd have seen the delivery van arrive?

Drake was too busy looking at Lady Peony to answer her enquiring gaze.

'I'll see to that,' he said. 'Meanwhile, Lady Peony, if you could tell Milla about the disturbances, then you can give both of us a tour.'

Milla would have preferred to have stayed beside the fire, gently warming herself, but Peony had put down her mug and was beckoning her over – a little too imperiously. She reminded Milla of her grandmother, Brianna Graham, who considered herself the Queen of Raven's Edge.

Best to make it clear she wasn't the kind of person to be easily summoned.

As Drake disappeared into the study she moved away from the fireplace, towards a painting that had caught her eye.

It was the type of group picture you saw in homes all across the country – except this one had been painted in oils and the people in it were dressed for a ball. A mother, a father and their two teenage daughters, perhaps from the 1980s, judging by the fashions. The mother was wearing a diamond tiara, necklace and bracelets. Peony was easily recognisable by her pink hair, cut into a short, geometric bob. The other girl, presumably Lady Rose, seemed older but was smaller, her smile less confident, her hair long and dark brown. Was this Peony's natural colour?

'How's Lady Rose?' Milla asked as Peony stood beside her. 'This business must be very hard on her.'

Peony glanced dismissively at the painting and then regarded Milla a little too keenly. 'Yes, it's not nice to know someone wants to frighten you out of your home. I'll introduce you when we go upstairs. My sister is in her seventies and suffers with dementia. I've not told her the truth. It will only confuse her. She believes you're relatives, come to visit.'

'We'll be very discreet.'

'Hmm. Well, in the meantime' – she winked – 'let me introduce you to the ghost.'

Milla followed Peony back to the main entrance, where she stopped and pointed to a little brass plaque set into the floorboards. It was so grubby, Milla must have walked straight over it without even noticing.

She crouched to read the words, using one finger to wipe away the dust.

Major Lord John Weston (1615–1645)
Brother shall deliver up the brother to death

'Who was he?' she asked.

'Major Weston was the brother of my nine times great-grandfather, the fifth Marquess. During the Civil War, they were on opposing sides. The village was under siege, so one evening the Major turned up to ask the Marquess to surrender to spare further bloodshed. Instead, the Marquess shot him in cold blood, right *there*, if the story is to be believed.'

Peony indicated a dark stain on the floorboard beside the plaque.

'Is that... *blood*?'

Peony laughed. 'After three hundred and eighty-one years? No, darling. That's Victorian theatre. In Major Weston's time these would have been flagstones. Perhaps his blood *is* still there, hidden beneath these floorboards. Who knows?'

'Why do you believe he's the one haunting the house, rather than some other random ghost?'

'The legend of Major Weston says that his ghost knocks on the door after dark, until someone lets him in.'

'You've heard this knock?'

'Yes, otherwise I wouldn't have hired Mr Drake.'

'And you opened the door?'

'Once or twice, before I realised it was a trick. There was never anyone there.'

'Do you believe in ghosts?'

'Of course not! Plenty of people have died in this house over the centuries but I've not seen a single one return as a spirit. More's the pity. I could do with the company. But now the joke has worn thin and the whole business has become tiresome. They can knock on the door all they like, bore themselves silly, see if I care. Trust me, it'd take more than a ghost to get me out of *my* house – even if they were here first.'

Milla almost felt sorry for the ghost.

FOUR

As promised, Lady Peony gave them a tour of Blackheath Hall, finishing at Lady Rose's bedroom, which was behind one of the doors leading onto the gallery. The room was huge, with a four-poster bed set on a platform to one side which made Lady Rose seem small by comparison, even though she was tall, like her sister.

Rose was lying on top of the bed covers, propped up by cushions, surrounded by old books and watching a rerun of *Pride and Prejudice* on a crackly old television. The resemblance to Peony was obvious – they both had the same prominent nose – although Rose's hair was a more conventional white and cut short, albeit not terribly neatly. Perhaps she'd done it herself?

'You didn't tell me we were having guests!' Rose cried delightedly as they entered. 'How lovely! We never have visitors.'

'Yes, I did.' Peony sighed. 'I told you yesterday, and I reminded you this morning.'

Rose clapped her hands. 'Introductions, please!'

Peony went into a kind of performance they'd evidently run through before, sweeping a low curtsey before saying, 'Lady Rose Weston, it is my utmost pleasure to introduce to you Mr Kieran Drake and Miss Camilla Graham.'

Drake inclined his head, slightly bemused. Milla wondered if she was supposed to curtsey too but shook Rose's frail hand instead, although she had to step onto the platform and lean across the bed to do so.

Rose had mischievous blue eyes, a dimple in one cheek, and wore a bright yellow cocktail dress, accessorised with a glittering array of costume jewellery, including thick diamanté bracelets around her thin wrists. She could have been going to a society party – forty years ago.

Briefly, she squeezed Milla's hand before releasing her. 'How delightful to meet you, Miss Graham. One of the Graham family of King's Rest?'

Milla's family home had burned down nearly twenty years ago, but she nodded.

Peony, meanwhile, was straightening Rose's sheets and collecting most of the books, dropping them heavily onto the night-stand. 'One book a day, Rose. *One* book a day. Else I'll come in here and find you buried beneath the weight of them – that's if I find you at all.'

Rose giggled, beaming at Milla in a conspiratorial way, ignoring Drake completely. 'Would you like a cup of tea? It'd be no trouble. Please say you'll stay for a chat? I never meet anyone new.'

'I've promised Kieran and Camilla that I'll give them a tour,' Peony said. 'I'll make us all tea later.'

Lady Rose reached up to stroke her sister's cheek. 'Peony,' she said reprovingly. 'You know I've always hated being left alone.'

Peony took hold of her hand and kissed the back of it. 'I'll return with your tea when I've finished the tour.'

Rose nodded enthusiastically. 'Ooh, yes! Don't forget the mausoleum!'

'I might save that until tomorrow. Mausoleums aren't to *every-one's* taste, you know.'

Rose sighed. 'We had such wonderful parties in there! Do you remember the wedding? We danced all night...'

Milla wondered if she'd heard correctly. Parties? In a *mausoleum?*

'We did, didn't we?' Peony said softly, but Rose's gaze had turned vacant, staring right through them, her attention sliding back to the television as though they were no longer there.

How horrible it must be, Milla thought sadly, to watch someone you love become a little less 'them' every day.

'I'll have to introduce you again tomorrow,' Peony said in a low voice, ushering them out and softly closing the door on her sister. Her cheerful expression dropped like a mask the moment the door shut, leaving her tight-lipped and frowning. 'You can see why I don't want my sister upset.'

'Hopefully we'll have this business cleared up tonight,' Drake said.

Lady Peony humphed disbelievingly but said nothing, leading them back downstairs.

Milla was inclined to share her doubt. What if the ghost didn't show tonight? Or the next night? They could be here for *weeks*.

Was this what Drake was hoping for? The longer they were here, the more money he could charge...

Why had she *ever* agreed to work with him? She could have been working for her father, as the editor for his newest magazine. He'd already offered her the job, several times.

'You didn't mention a mausoleum, Lady Peony,' Drake was saying. 'That's not on my plan of the estate.'

'To be honest, I forgot. It's beyond the formal garden. Easily missed. Looks like a gothic summer house.'

That didn't sound 'easily missed' at all. Milla, remembering the tangled jungle they'd walked through, wondered how any of it could be considered 'formal'.

'I've no idea where the key is, probably still stuck in the door and turning rusty, but my sister is right. We did have some fabulous parties there when we were young.' Peony winked. 'No one to complain about the noise.'

As she led them down the stairs, she added, 'There are ten bedrooms in all, including the state rooms – or the "in a state" rooms, as my sister used to call them. On the second floor is the nursery and former servants' quarters and, above that, is an attic used for storage. You're welcome to explore up there but I wouldn't recommend going above the gallery floor. That part of the house is no longer safe. It's a miracle the place is still standing.'

Then why on earth did they live here?

Because it was their home.

As they walked across the great hall, Peony asked, 'Would you like to choose one of the bedrooms for your own use? Everything's covered in dust sheets but completely clean.'

'That's kind,' Drake said, 'but we're not here to sleep. We'll be working.'

'Throughout the night? Will you sleep during the day?'

'I'm not planning on sleeping at all,' Drake replied. 'I'll have caught this ghost before midnight – providing he shows up.'

'My, you *are* confident.'

She didn't make it sound like a good thing.

Milla grimaced. Drake was too busy rummaging in his kit bag for his tools to realise his cocky attitude was grating on Peony, but surely she'd be pleased to have this pretend haunting solved as soon as possible?

'Then I shall leave you to it,' Peony said, her tone much cooler. 'You may have free range of the house. We're usually in bed by ten.'

'We'll try not to disturb you,' Milla said.

'You won't. I sleep like a log.'

'But won't the ghost...?'

'He likes an early night too. If he's going to knock, it's usually at 9.00 pm, as punctual as clockwork. I suppose that must have been when he was murdered, the poor man.'

It almost sounded as though Peony *believed* in the ghost.

'Some people say the knock is a portent,' Peony added carelessly, swathing herself in blankets before flopping back onto the sofa and picking up a book.

As Drake was busy fiddling with something electronic, Milla thought she should answer. 'A portent?'

Peony grinned wickedly. 'Of imminent death.'

Milla helped Drake install motion sensor cameras around the great hall and then outside, trained on the main door. This basically meant her holding the ladder and passing up screws. Not quite how she'd imagined spending her afternoon.

After making them some very pungent cheese sandwiches for tea, Peony abandoned the sofa but took several of the blankets, disappearing upstairs to watch television with her sister. Milla ate her sandwich sitting on the bottom rung of the ladder. Drake took a large sausage roll from his jacket pocket and wolfed it down, so Milla ate his sandwich, too.

'Do you think Lady Peony might be faking the haunting herself?' she asked him once he'd gone back up the ladder.

'Why would she do that?'

'If she's lonely, she might want company?'

'Us?' He laughed. 'Even she can't be that lonely.'

'That leaves her cousin, Giles. Would he really terrify a couple of old ladies to get his hands on this house?'

'Families have done worse.'

'Could it be kids from the village, playing tricks?'

'This isn't the 1970s.' Drake took a screw from the corner of his mouth, where he'd stuck it like a cigarette, and drilled it into the wall, holding out his hand for another one. She passed it to him. 'Kids these days have better things to do.'

'It *is* a classic child's trick,' she said, 'knocking on the door and running away. A child would find it easy to hide in the garden.'

'You could hide a bus in *that* garden. Here, hold this.' He passed down the drill. 'But it's good that you're thinking it through, Princess.'

She rolled her eyes. 'Patronising, much?'

'Even the liveable part of this house is inhabited by rats, mice and birds – possibly bats too,' he said, 'which would explain the creepy scratching and tapping noises we heard as we moved around upstairs. Anyone could gain access to the courtyard through the breaches in the wall without walking through the main gate, or by taking the route past the Gateway to the Dead and into the garden, as we did.'

'Do you seriously believe you'll catch the person responsible in one night?'

'I *am* Kieran Drake.'

The words were delivered ironically but now his attitude was beginning to annoy her, too.

'If someone's watching the house, they've seen us *and* your equipment arrive,' she said. 'Most people know who you are and what you do, and what you're likely to be doing here. We might have frightened the "ghost" away – but there'll be nothing to stop him returning once we've left.'

'Wanna bet?'

Milla would have happily taken him up on that, but Lady Peony came downstairs to ask if they wanted a cup of tea. It felt awkward, having an elderly lady wait on her like a servant, so Milla offered to make it and take it upstairs to Rose's bedroom. By the time she was downstairs, Drake had finished fixing the cameras to the walls and was linking them to his laptop and an app they already had installed on their phones.

They sat down to wait.

For the first few hours, it was so quiet Milla almost forgot why they were there. Every hour they took it in turns to leave the other to watch the cameras before checking each room in the house. Every room, apart from the study and the kitchen, was the same – empty and quiet, with all the furniture covered in dust sheets. It was no wonder the house attracted ghost stories, and the ever-present scuttling sounds coming from the walls didn't help.

As Milla completed her check, she received a message from Ben saying he'd been called out to 'an incident' at the Gateway to the Dead. As he was the head of the local Murder Investigation Team, she could guess what the 'incident' was. The site had been deserted when she and Drake walked through the arch, but that kind of place probably attracted all kinds of undesirables after dark.

It seemed they would both be working overnight.

She checked the back door was locked, then paused by the servants' staircase, the one that led up to the gallery and into the attic. There was no bulb in the light fitting, but she could see the wooden steps had rotted through, with several missing altogether. No one would be using *that* any time soon.

She returned to the hall in time to hear Drake curse as one of the cameras fizzled out in a burst of static, leaving a blank square on his laptop screen.

He slapped it.

Even Milla knew that wouldn't work.

They stared at each other uneasily.

Milla, ignoring the creeping sensation tingling along her spine, raised an eyebrow.

'No,' he said. 'It's not the ghost, because ghosts don't exist.'

'It's five minutes to nine. He's nothing if not punctual.'

'There *is* no ghost.'

She side-eyed the screen. 'Sure about that?'

He groaned theatrically. 'Fine, I'll go and check on it.'

'Excellent idea.'

His eyes narrowed. 'You're enjoying this far too much. How about *you* go and fix it?'

She sat back on the sofa. 'I'm quite comfortable here, thank you very much. Better hurry though. The Major's due to turn up in less than a minute. You'll want to catch his best side on camera.'

He fixed her with a look. 'I've been doing this since before you were born, Princess.'

As he was less than ten years older than her, she sincerely doubted it.

But as he reached the door, a loud crash had him instinctively stepping back.

Milla sat up. She hadn't actually believed—

The crash sounded again, reverberating around the hall. Even the floorboards trembled beneath her feet. How could it be so *loud*, as though it was in this very room?

She remembered the enormous knocker on the door. Perhaps they should have taken it down. Would the ghost be able to knock without a knocker?

No! Because it wasn't a ghost!

Drake must have come to the same conclusion because he slowly smiled. 'We're on!'

'Wait...' Was it the smartest move to pull open the door when anyone – or any*thing* – could be on the other side? She sprang out of the chair, running towards him. 'Drake, no!'

Too late. He'd grabbed the handle and wrenched open the door.

As expected, there was no ghost.

Instead, a tall figure loomed out of the mist. He was wearing buff-coloured clothes, his face hidden by vertical bars across a metal helmet.

Drake snorted. 'What are *you* supposed to be, mate? A sheet over your head would look more realistic.'

The man didn't laugh. He casually raised his hand. There was a loud 'bang', a puff of smoke and a strong scent of burning, and then he stepped silently back, becoming as one with the mist behind him.

Drake didn't move. Was he in shock? He looked down at his chest, trying to say something, then slowly sank onto the steps, like a puppet with its strings cut.

Milla ran forward, dropping to her knees beside him, half catching him as he toppled sideways.

Was he *dead*?

She rolled him onto his back, yanking open his jacket. The shirt underneath was a faded green, but it wasn't hard to see a dark red stain on the side of his chest, blooming outwards like a flower.

This wasn't real.

It *couldn't* be real.

'Drake?' she said, trying to sound calm. If he was conscious, she didn't want to panic him. 'Drake!'

'Leave me,' he said, teeth gritted, face screwed up from the pain. 'Get back inside. Shut the door. Call the police. Call *Ben*.'

'Bother that.' She pulled her phone from her pocket. 'I'm calling for an ambulance.'

'Listen to me.' He grabbed her wrist. 'He might come back. He *will* come back. Get inside. Forget about me.'

He was speaking in short bursts, his breath shallow. Unhealthily pale to start with, the colour was leaching from his face in front of her eyes.

This was bad.

Shoving her panic down so far inside her she could no longer feel it, no longer feel *anything*, she attempted to distract him. 'You're *such* a drama queen.'

He huffed a laugh, then swore as she grabbed him beneath the arms and dragged him up the steps. 'You're going to kill me, Milla!'

'Probably,' she agreed, 'but not today.'

Kicking the door shut, she turned the key, slid back two hefty bolts, and then sat on the floor beside him to phone for an ambulance.

FIVE
SIXTEEN YEARS PREVIOUSLY

Kieran Drake walked along the harbour at Port Rell, to the ratty little shed at the end, and, as always, cringed at the hand-painted sign over the door.

Francis Drake & Sons
Private Investigation

His father had painted the sign himself about twenty years ago and it showed. The paint had begun peeling before it was even dry and the letters had become more squashed as Francis Drake began flamboyantly, without any kind of plan, and then ran out of space – which was pretty much how he approached everything. But the real sticking point was 'sons' because (1) Kieran had no intention of following his father into what he considered the seedy and immoral world of private investigation, and (2) he'd always been an only child, thanks to his mother hightailing it off to Scotland at the first opportunity. She hadn't run off with someone else, which had been particularly galling for both of them. She'd just left, without taking anything more than one small suitcase. She hadn't even taken two-year-old Kieran, something he found increasingly hurtful with each passing year.

Occasionally, Kieran had wondered if, in fact, his father had murdered her and dumped her body at sea, but when he'd mentioned this to Grandma Esme, she'd rolled her eyes and told him not to be ridiculous. His mother was perfectly safe and well, and working in Edinburgh for a major international bank.

So his mother was still in contact with *one* member of her family.

Telling himself the sooner he got it over with, the better for everyone, Kieran pushed open the door. The office really *was* a shed – a tin shed, perhaps once used as a boat house or for storing fishing equipment. It still had a particular smell; it had certainly never been intended to use as an office. Despite that, Francis Drake was sitting in a chair with his eyes closed and his feet up on the desk, nursing a cardboard mug with the familiar blue yacht logo of the local coffee shop. The remains of a sausage roll – flaking pastry and grease stains – decorated the official-looking paperwork in front of him.

Kieran hoped it wasn't his tax return.

It probably was.

The other desk, where Francis's assistant, Terry, usually worked, was empty. Normally this would mean Terry was out on a job, but the desk was suspiciously clear of the usual office debris.

Kieran sighed. He'd liked Terry. He worked hard and he was honest. Obviously, he had nothing in common with Francis. The mystery was why he'd stayed and put up with his father's crap for so long.

Still, no longer Kieran's problem.

'Hi, Dad,' he said, perching on the edge of Terry's desk. It was dusty, so Terry must have left about a week ago. Why hadn't Francis said anything?

Francis opened one eye. It was bloodshot. Had he spent last night at The Smuggler's Inn? It would explain the coffee.

'What do you want?' his father growled. 'Shouldn't you be at college?'

Kieran felt his cheeks redden. He'd never been much good at

lying and the good thing about his father having absolutely no interest in what he did meant he hadn't had to explain that his last exam had been a month ago and, since then, he'd been applying for jobs.

Now he'd got one.

'I've finished college,' he said.

Francis closed his eyes again. 'Good, you can come and work for me.'

Kieran bit down on a derisory laugh. Be a private detective? *Over his dead body.*

'I *have* a job,' he said, unable to keep the note of pride from his voice. The interview had been almost a month ago, but the acceptance letter had arrived last week.

It had taken this long for him to pluck up the courage to tell Francis.

His grandmother had suggested not telling him at all, but Kieran had thought hard about how it might feel to have two family members run out on you without any explanation, and so here he was.

Grandma Esme had already told him he was a fool.

He was starting to agree with her.

'I hope you've packed your bags,' she'd said, 'because he'll chuck you out.'

'A job?' His father sneered. 'Working at the local grocery store? You can do better than that.'

The grocery store had been two summers ago, but he was hurt that his father thought so little of his abilities. He could have gone to university, if only... but there was no use thinking about that. If there was no money for rent, there was no money for further education.

But he didn't say any of this. Francis Drake had been drinking heavily and it had not improved his mood.

Kieran slid off the corner of the desk and took a step towards the door to be on the safe side. His father didn't even notice.

'I applied to join the county constabulary,' he said.

Francis barked a laugh. '*My* son? They'd never have you.'

Something that had also occurred to him. As a police officer, he'd be in a position of trust. There could be nothing in his past, or that of his friends and family, that might leave him open to blackmail or extortion.

Francis Drake's interpretation of the law often differed from the local constabulary. Understandably, they didn't get on.

But Kieran's acceptance letter was already packed in his suitcase and waiting in Grandma Esme's sitting room, just in case.

'My probationary period starts next month,' he said.

Francis sat up slowly. 'You're serious? You'd rather work for that bunch of crooks than your own family?'

As Grandma Esme would have said, 'Pot, meet Kettle.'

But he took another step back, feeling the door handle behind him digging into his back.

Francis leapt up, slamming his palms on the desk. The whole shed seemed to shake. 'You ungrateful weasel!' he roared.

His reaction wasn't entirely unexpected.

'If you go, you go! No crawling back. You understand? That's it!'

'Fine,' Kieran snapped, surprising both himself and his father. 'I've already packed.'

Perhaps he shouldn't have admitted that.

Francis sat back down. 'I blame your grandmother,' he said. 'Putting fancy ideas in your head. You even talk like her.'

Was he wrong to believe he was worth something? That he was smart, capable, and that people *liked* him? That he deserved more than a life working for his father, spying on unhappy spouses and trying to catch poorly paid staff pinching pennies? That he could choose his own employment, his own home, his own friends?

Francis Drake used the side of his hand to sweep the crumbs from his desk. 'You'll be back,' he said. 'You pretend to be like her, with all those airs and graces, but you're just like me. A chancer, a hustler, a grafter. You'll be back in a month.'

It sounded like a curse.

As Kieran left, closing the door behind him, he leant against it for a few moments, breathing in the familiar scents of Port Rell: seaweed and saltwater, mixed with fried onions and burgers from the beach cafés.

He'd miss the little seaside village he'd grown up in.

He wouldn't miss his father.

Come back?

Never.

SIX

PRESENT DAY

Friday

Milla was put through to the ambulance service very quickly. They told her what to do – apply pressure to the wound to stop the bleeding (which caused Drake to scream and then black out) – and promised a paramedic would be with her promptly, along with the police.

She left the phone on the floor, because she'd also been told to keep the line open, and concentrated on Drake. She'd used what appeared to be one of the cleanest throws from the sofa to press against the wound, which fortunately appeared to be on his upper arm rather than his chest. He still had a marble-sized hole that wouldn't stop bleeding. What *had* he been shot with?

'Did you get him? Did you get the ghost?' There was a clatter from upstairs as Lady Peony ran along the gallery and launched herself down the stairs. Rather than a nightdress, she was still wearing the tartan dress and RAF jacket.

Milla didn't care. All she cared about was Drake.

Where was that paramedic?

'Is that him? Oh... It's Mr Drake! Has he been *shot*? Oh, no! *No!*'

Milla ignored her. Right now, Drake was more important.

She watched his chest move up and down. He was breathing. That was good. His colour was terrible, almost grey – not so good – and he was sweating. Presumably that wasn't good either.

Oh, hell...

After watching silently for a few moments, Peony announced, in a slightly wobbly voice, 'I'll fetch towels and hot water,' and strode off to the kitchen.

How was *that* going to help?

Perhaps the towels might come in useful, but at least Peony was keeping a clear head and not panicking. Milla didn't think she could have coped with that. She didn't think she could have coped with *this*, yet here they were.

In the distance, she heard sirens.

Were they for Drake?

'Peony!' she shouted. 'I'm going to need you to open the front door.'

Peony popped her head back into the hall. 'Darling, I'm not sure that's a good—'

'For the *paramedic*.'

'Oh... Yes. Right.' Peony looked across the hall towards the big old door, but didn't move from the kitchen.

'*Now*, Peony!'

The elderly woman walked slowly across the hall, twisting the towel she held between her fingers.

Milla understood her reluctance. She'd do it herself, but she had to keep this pressure on, and—

She was an idiot!

'Peony, check the laptop. Drake installed cameras outside. They'll show you if anyone is out there.'

'Good idea!' Peony threw herself down onto the sofa and twisted the laptop towards her. Moving it caused the screen to light up, for which Milla was grateful. She wasn't sure how computer-literate Peony was.

'The screen is blank,' Peony announced. 'Your camera must be broken.'

The knocker crashed down on the door making them both jump, although it wasn't nearly as loud as before.

'Police!' shouted a disembodied voice.

'Phew, that's a relief!' Peony got up and moved towards the door. She was quite nimble for an old lady – but was sixty-something that 'old' after all?

Milla had a horrible sense of déjà vu. 'Wait!'

Anyone could say they were the police.

It was too late. Peony had opened the door.

On the other side were two men wearing Kevlar vests.

Milla recognised one and almost cried with relief. 'Sergeant Rackham!'

He frowned. 'Miss Graham? We had a report that someone had been shot.'

'I called for an *ambulance*. Do *you* know any first aid?'

But PS Rackham had already turned away, barking into his radio. 'Clear.'

Running across the courtyard were two more people, a man and a woman, both wearing green, and Milla realised the paramedics had been waiting for the police officers to assure them the scene was safe. She moved out of their way, and it soon felt like the hall was full of people, as the paramedics tried to stabilise Drake to transport him to hospital, and PS Rackham's team began searching the house and garden for the gunman.

Peony muttered something like, 'I'd better put the kettle on,' and disappeared back into the kitchen.

Milla thought everyone was far too busy to be bothered about tea or coffee.

After what seemed like forever, Drake was loaded into the ambulance, the doors slammed and it drove off across the courtyard and through the gatehouse, blue lights silently flashing.

He'd been so pale...

She rubbed the back of her hand across her eyes. What should she do now? She knew what she *wanted* to do – get in the ambulance with Drake. But because she wasn't a relative, they wouldn't let her. She'd tried phoning Esme, his secretary, but she wasn't answering her phone, so Milla left a message.

Should she phone Ben? He'd said he was working by the Gateway to the Dead, but she could hardly disturb him while he was on duty. It wouldn't be fair. PS Rackham would soon pass the news on to him.

She had to deal with this by herself. The paramedics had suggested following in her own car, but she and Drake had arrived here on foot. Her car was parked outside her house in the centre of the village, a twenty-minute walk away.

She could call a taxi? But what if it was busy? There was only one taxi in Raven's Edge. It was that kind of place.

As she took out her phone, she heard footsteps behind her.

Had the police finished their search of the grounds? Had they found the gunman? As she turned, PS Rackham walked around the corner of the house, accompanied by a man and woman of mismatched heights, dressed casually.

'Ben? *Ben!*' She ran the short distance across the courtyard and threw herself into his arms.

He hugged her back. 'Sam heard the call go out on the radio and Rackham's just explained what happened. The gunman has left the scene. You're safe now.'

All the emotion she thought she'd shoved safely out of the way was now a returning tide, threatening to overwhelm her. It was as though she'd forgotten how to breathe properly, and she had to swallow a few times before she could speak without bursting into tears.

It didn't help that both DS Harriet March and PS Rackham were listening to every word, although at least Harriet was polite enough to pretend not to.

'They shot him!' Milla said, even though Ben knew this already. 'A man, wearing a Civil War costume, pretending to be a ghost, shot Drake.'

'You're safe now,' he repeated, rubbing her back in a soothing motion.

Did he think she was only worried about *herself*?

'Drake *isn't*.' She tried to push her way out of Ben's embrace, but he held her too tightly. 'He's on his way to hospital in an ambulance and they wouldn't... they wouldn't let me go with him.'

'They'd have expected you to follow behind,' Harriet said in her usual matter-of-fact tone. 'Emergency ambulances aren't designed to carry passengers, unless the patient is dependent on you. You'd have got in their way.'

Milla didn't miss the way Ben glared at Harriet over the top of her head, but the other woman was right.

'I was about to call a taxi.' Milla gave Ben a final, firm push. He released her but watched her lift her phone as though he'd really like to swipe it out of her hand and do it for her.

Sometimes his protectiveness was sweet. Separated from her family at an early age, she'd never had anyone truly care about her until very recently. Other times, like *now*, it was incredibly annoying.

As though unable to wait any longer, he said, 'I'll take you.'

The two other officers' heads swivelled in his direction, almost comically.

'I'm going to check on my team,' PS Rackham said, obviously grateful to have an excuse to leave them to it.

Harriet was also edging away.

'You can't abandon an investigation to take me to hospital,' Milla said.

'Harriet can take over here and Sam is finishing up at the gateway. They don't need me.'

'Where's your car?'

'At the station, but it won't take five minutes to get it.'

Milla saw Harriet pull a face at the blatant lie, but she was smart enough to keep her mouth shut.

'It'll take *twenty*,' Milla said.

'*Fine,*' Ben snapped. 'Call a taxi. They can take us to the police station and we can go the rest of the way in my car.'

'What's wrong with *my* car?'

'You're in shock. You're not in any fit state to drive—'

'Let *me* call a taxi,' Harriet said quickly, hitting speed dial on her phone, raising it to her ear and sidestepping out of earshot.

Ben took a deep breath, exhaled, and then took Milla's hand in his. 'I'm sorry,' he said. 'My training means I become very task focused and bark orders at people.'

Harriet muttered something that sounded like, 'Not that we ever take much notice...'

Milla briefly closed her eyes. This wasn't Ben's fault. None of this was Ben's fault. He wasn't the enemy. They were standing here yelling at each other when the real victim was Drake.

'I'm sorry,' she said. 'I panicked. I'm out of my comfort zone. I didn't know what to do. Drake was hurt and I don't even know any basic first aid.'

'You did brilliantly. Drake is on his way to hospital. He'll receive the best care. We'll be with him soon. Don't worry.'

'Don't *worry?*' Her voice broke on the last word. She bit her lip, struggling to keep control.

'Dakota is on her way,' Harriet said gently. 'She'll take you back to Raven's Edge or to the hospital, whichever you prefer.' She patted Milla's shoulder and walked towards the house, leaving them alone in a little puddle of moonlight.

'Drake will be fine,' Ben said firmly. 'He always is.'

'I know. You're right. It's just...' As though sleepwalking, Milla stepped back into his arms, allowing him to hold her close, burying her face in his coat, feeling his hand stroke the back of her head. 'Thank you.'

Drake will be fine.

Because that was his reputation.

But Milla still couldn't block out that little voice whispering in her head.

What about this time?

SEVEN

Saturday

Drake regained consciousness to find himself lying in a hospital bed with DI Ben Taylor sitting in a chair beside him. Ugh, not *quite* what he wanted to wake up to. He couldn't even feign sleep, because the moment he'd opened his eyes, Taylor's attention zeroed in like a bird of prey.

Drake waited for Taylor to speak first.

He didn't.

Fine.

'I must be sick if you're here, petal.'

'But you're not dead,' Taylor said, as though that was a great disappointment to him.

'Bloody feels like it,' came out before he could stop it.

Taylor, ever the good guy, frowned in consternation. 'Would you like a drink of water?'

Be waited on by the local detective inspector? Tempting, but ultimately humiliating. Drake ignored the question and took stock of his surroundings. Norchester General, by the look of it. There was a nice view of the castle from the window – and the sun was shining in a cerulean blue sky, so he'd been unconscious the entire night and well into the day. He was the only patient and appeared to have his own bathroom, so it must be a private room. Who'd swung that for him? Drew Elliot? Dermot Graham? Probably Graham – Milla, who was his daughter, would have told him about the shooting. Or even Milla herself? He kept forgetting she was rich.

Still, he wasn't complaining.

Other than having to suffer the harbinger of doom beside his bed.

'Don't let me keep you,' he told Taylor. 'I'm sure you have other places to be, bad guys to chase, damsels to save, doughnuts to eat.'

Taylor's dour expression didn't change. 'I need to ask you a few questions.'

'If you call Esme, she'll book you an appointment. Six weeks OK for you?'

He closed his eyes, but he'd pushed the DI too far. A sudden sharp pain in the back of his hand had him cursing and yanking it away, which only made the pain worse. His eyes flew open to see the DI sitting back in his seat, completely unconcerned and slightly smug.

'What the hell did you *do*?' He stared at his hand and saw an IV cannula in it, linked to a couple of bags of liquid suspended from a pole. One was dark red.

A blood transfusion?

He shivered, remembering the last time he'd needed one of those.

How much blood had he lost?

'I may have accidentally flicked your cannula while I was tucking you back in,' Taylor said blithely. 'Sorry.'

'When I get out of this bloody bed,' Drake began icily, 'I'm going to rip your—'

Milla walked through the door with two cardboard cups of coffee and both men immediately assumed politely interested expressions. She handed one coffee to Taylor, but it turned out that the other was for herself.

That hurt Drake more than the cannula.

'You're awake!' She beamed. 'That's wonderful! How are you feeling?'

'Like...' Belatedly he remembered to modify his language. 'Like hell.'

'I'm not surprised. You've been shot!'

'Really? I hadn't noticed.'

She smiled sympathetically. 'You must be in a lot of pain. You're not usually this grumpy. Would you like me to ring for the nurse and ask for more painkillers?'

Yes.

'I *need* coffee.' He pointedly regarded the mug in her hand.

She held it closer – as if he was in any condition to snatch it. 'You can't have one.'

Why was she talking to him like he was a two-year-old?

'You've been in surgery,' she added. 'You're only allowed to have water until the nurse says it's OK.'

'Then fetch me the damn nurse!'

Her mouth tightened.

DI Taylor sighed, leaning forward to press the call button at the side of the bed. 'Be nice,' he told Drake, 'or we're leaving.'

'*Promise?*' Drake snarled.

Milla said nothing but the hurt was clear in her eyes.

Damn, damn, damn.

He tried breathing with the pain but that made no difference. Why had he thought it would? Why did it *hurt* so much? What the hell had he been shot with? A cannonball?

'You'd better go,' he said, closing his eyes. 'I'm not fit for company.'

'My, we *are* feeling sorry for ourselves,' a new voice said.

He opened his eyes in time to see a woman in blue scrubs bustling up to him. 'Time for your painkillers, Kieran.'

Another one talking to him as though he was a toddler. The only person who still called him Kieran was his grandmother.

'Thank G—' She raised a stern eyebrow, reminding him of Esme. 'Thank goodness for that,' he amended.

'Hmm...' She handed him two tablets in a tiny paper cup and a plastic beaker of water. 'Take these, you'll feel better in no time.'

'Excellent, when can I leave?'

'When the doctor says you can. You've lost a lot of blood, and you were shot with a lead ball. It was old, so it wasn't very clean and there's a risk of infection. Fortunately, it didn't penetrate deep enough to hit bone, just made a mess of your upper arm.'

Looking pretty had never been a particular ambition but, remembering the last time he'd been shot, he felt a stab of fear and wriggled his fingers experimentally. They were fine. Not even numb. That was a relief. He'd had a lucky escape.

'I'll be back to check on you properly in fifteen minutes. You two,' she added to Milla and Taylor, 'don't tire him out. I need you gone in ten.'

'No problem,' Taylor said as she left, without taking his eyes from Drake.

Beside him, Milla grimaced.

Drake had a horrible sense of foreboding. Why *was* DI Taylor here? Joking aside, *didn't* he have better things to do? Unless Milla had let something drop...

As though reading his mind, Taylor smirked.

What had she told him?

'I've seen the film footage, so don't bother trying to think up some convoluted story. I know how you were shot and by whom. And, more importantly, exactly why you were at Blackheath Hall in the first place.'

No... No, she wouldn't. She *wouldn't*.

'Milla?'

'I gave him access to the app,' Milla said. 'I thought... I thought you were going to die.'

That's why she'd looked guilty. She'd thrown him to the wolves.

Thanks, Camilla.

Would Drew's patronage extend to a good lawyer?

'The footage confirmed Milla's statement,' Taylor said. 'A man in a Civil War costume knocked on the front door to Blackheath Hall, shot you with an antique pistol and then faded away into nothing.'

'You make it sound like he was a ghost,' Drake said flippantly. If he went with the flow, maybe Taylor wouldn't realise exactly what had been going down last night. 'He was real, trust me.'

'If the aim was to frighten Lady Peony Weston out of her house, why shoot you and not her?'

'Same result.' Drake shrugged. He tried to sit up, feeling too vulnerable half-reclined. 'Whoever got shot, it would scare Peony into leaving.'

'Better you than an old lady,' Taylor said thoughtfully.

'*You* might think that. I beg to differ.'

Taylor rolled his eyes; Milla was scandalised. Didn't they realise he was joking, albeit in poor taste? He quit trying to sit up and flopped back against the pillows. Whatever painkillers the nurse had given him, they were *not* working. He was in absolute agony. Why wouldn't they go away and leave him alone?

Maybe he should throw the DI a bone and give him something else to think about.

'If Lady Peony *was* the target,' he said, 'they could've still shot me, barged their way into the house and shot Milla to get to Lady Peony – but they didn't. Although they'd have had to be very fast at reloading a flintlock. Those old pistols take at least twenty seconds, even for an expert.'

Predictably, Taylor turned pale at this. 'If you've deliberately put Milla in danger—'

'Ben,' Milla warned and the detective shut up, although he folded his arms and continued to glower at Drake. 'Why don't the two of you try working *together* instead of against each other? For starters' – here she glared at Drake – 'why not admit who you're really working for, because it's certainly not Lady Peony.'

'Who would that be then?' Drake snapped, not believing for one minute that Milla would say 'Drew Elliott' in front of Taylor – but then she did and Taylor suddenly became very interested in the conversation. It was amazing he didn't take out a notebook to jot everything down.

'How did you—' Drake began.

'You're *really* going to ask me that?' Now it was Milla's turn to roll her eyes. 'When it comes to your precious clients, whatever the question, the answer is *always* Drew Elliott. So, not hard to work out! And if it's not Drew, it's usually my father.'

DI Taylor had an all-his-Christmases-come-at-once expression and, oh look, he *had* taken out his notebook.

Drake closed his eyes. It was a pity that 'ghost' hadn't done a better job and finished him. 'Why don't you both *bugger off?*'

Taylor smiled. 'Not now I have you at my mercy, *petal*.'

He deserved that.

There then followed an excruciatingly embarrassing interview with DI Taylor wanting to know exactly *why* Drew Elliott (a local entrepreneur, who didn't always operate *entirely* within the law) was interested in Lady Peony moving out of Blackheath Hall.

Was the man serious? And he called himself a detective.

'Why do *you* think Drew Elliott's interested in a big old house, surrounded by acres of prime building land, well outside the boundaries of Raven's Edge, and therefore not constrained by any planning regulations whatsoever? Go on, take a wild guess.'

Taylor's expression turned stony. 'I'm going to offer you a choice, Mr Drake. Apologise to Lady Peony, refund *all* her money and quit the case – or be arrested for fraud. In the meantime, we'll try to persuade Lady Peony and Lady Rose to move to a safer environment until we can ascertain they're no longer at any risk.'

'Good luck with *that*. Peony will never leave Blackheath Hall. Her sister and that old wreck are all she cares about. You'd have to drag them out.'

'Hopefully it won't come to that. I've posted a police presence at the house to deter any more attempts, but if you were the target, do you have any idea who'd want to kill you?'

'Would you like a list?' Drake asked sarcastically, but it gave him a strange feeling, knowing someone out there wanted him dead – and was willing to go to the trouble of disguising themselves to do it.

Most of his 'acquaintances' would happily look him in the eye while they did it.

And that wasn't reassuring either.

Taylor's reply was completely deadpan. 'If you think it would help. Could it be someone from your past?'

He'd certainly upset more than a few people over the years.

'I didn't get a clear look at the gunman,' he replied truthfully. 'They were wearing a soldier's helmet with bars across the face, there was no outside lighting and it was dark.'

Why was there no outside lighting?

The same reason the camera had stopped working.

The gunman hadn't wanted to be seen.

They'd known about the camera, they'd known which light to knock out. They obviously knew about the house but not the additional cameras, which had caught them.

DI Taylor was still talking. Drake forced himself to concentrate, even though it was getting harder, as though his brain was turning to marshmallow, and he was feeling very tired. Did that mean the painkillers were finally kicking in?

'According to the footage I saw,' Taylor was saying, 'the gunman was wearing the uniform of a Parliamentarian soldier. There was another incident in the village around the same time. Following a ghost tour, a man dressed as a Royalist soldier was found half-buried beside the Gateway to the Dead.'

'Milla and I passed through the gateway on the way to Blackheath Hall,' Drake said. 'At about 3.00 pm, we crossed the clearing, walked through the woodland on the other side, and entered the grounds of Blackheath Hall that way.'

'You didn't see anything... unusual?'

Drake glanced at Milla. What had she told Taylor?

'There was no one else there, dead or alive, only us.'

Taylor stared at him, apparently unsure whether to believe him. '*Two* Civil War soldiers? It's a remarkable coincidence.'

No good cop believed in coincidences.

And there was the snagging point. While Drake could accept that several people might want him dead – he was *far* more likely to be the intended victim than Lady Peony – why go to the bother to dress as a Civil War soldier to do the deed? They'd have to hire or buy a costume, which would leave a trail...

'Who was the victim?' he asked.

'No idea,' Taylor said. 'We're yet to identify him. He had no wallet or phone. No ID at all. He was originally misidentified as Stuart Huntingdon, a local teenager connected with the ghost tours, but Huntingdon has no links with Blackheath Hall. We showed the victim's photo to Lady Peony and she didn't recognise him either.'

'I have no connection with Blackheath Hall,' Drake said. 'Yesterday was only the second time I'd visited. My family are from Port Rell, not Raven's Edge, and we're not related in any way to the Westons.'

Taylor shut his notebook. 'I have no theories either. Who even remembers that Blackheath Hall is hidden so deep in the forest? Most people only know about the Gateway to the Dead and the avenue of trees that leads to it, not that two little old ladies still live there.'

'Unless...'

Taylor's gaze sharpened. 'Unless?'

'If you wanted to approach the house without drawing attention, and leave by the same route, why not put on a costume and pretend to be involved with the ghost tour?'

'Damn.' DI Taylor sat back and regarded him with an expression that on anyone else might have been called admiration. 'You could be right.'

Drake closed his eyes. *Bone thrown.*

With any luck, it'd take a few more hours before Taylor worked out that the timings of the two events didn't match up.

By then, Drake would be long gone.

Trust this idiot to investigate his attempted murder?

Not likely!

It's what Drake had trained for after all.

EIGHT

TEN YEARS PREVIOUSLY

Six years after joining the Force as a naïve eighteen-year-old probationer, Kieran Drake walked into Raven's Edge Police Station and introduced himself to the civilian receptionist as their newly minted detective sergeant. He was late for the morning briefing – he'd underestimated the amount of tourist traffic on the roads through the King's Forest District – but no one was bothered. They seemed a bit *too* laid back in Raven's Edge. Surely there was as much crime here as anywhere else?

The police station was a seventeenth century former court-house, neatly divided into CID on the top floor with Uniform at street level. His new boss was Detective Inspector Jake Davenport, who didn't appear to be much older than Kieran, perhaps because he was one of those chosen few to be fast-tracked through the ranks with a series of 'easy' posts.

Kieran had heard rumours before he'd arrived; that Davenport didn't want to be there, was happy to delegate everything, and disappeared into his tiny office, with the blind down, at every opportunity. Most inspectors Kieran had worked for wanted to micromanage everything, aware that the buck *always* stopped with them.

'What's *his* story?' Kieran asked the other detective sergeant, as he slid into the empty seat beside him.

'He's learnt too late that he's in the wrong job,' the man replied, 'and he hates every minute of it. He can't wait to leave at the end of the day.'

'Why apply in the first place?'

'Like the rest of us, I expect he thought he'd be helping society, giving something back, that kind of thing.'

They both snorted silently.

'Human nature has come as a bit of a shock to him,' the DS said.

Kieran wondered where Davenport had grown up. Brigadoon? Even coming from a cosy little seaside village like Port Rell, Kieran was well aware of the frailties of human nature. Most people *wanted* to be good, but when it actually came down to it...

'He wants to be a *writer*,' the DS added when Kieran remained quiet. 'When he disappears into that office of his, I reckon he's working on a book.'

Kieran went with it, rather than reveal his own half-formed thoughts. 'Let's hope we're not going to be in it.'

They both sniggered, not so quietly this time, drawing the attention of the man they were mocking. As the DI's dark eyes narrowed, Kieran realised Davenport was smart enough to recognise their derision.

'We've had some intel about a nasty little gang,' he was saying, his gaze falling on Kieran again, 'travelling from village to village throughout the county, holding bogus psychic readings and preying on the recently bereaved and vulnerable.'

'How do we know the readings aren't genuine?' a female DC asked. She was sitting at the front, doing everything up to and including fluttering her eyelashes to obtain the boss's attention.

Kieran could have told her she was wasting her time.

Davenport regarded her patiently over the top of his spectacles. 'Do *you* believe people can talk to the dead?'

'No, of course not!' Her cheeks coloured and she lowered her head. 'Sorry, sir. People must be told the truth.'

It was the wrong answer. The punters should be allowed to believe whatever they wanted to, provided it didn't hurt anyone else. The police were not there to judge, but to act in accordance with the law – and ensure everyone else did.

The last DI Kieran had worked for would've completely demolished her – in public, too. Davenport... Kieran frowned. It was hard to get a handle on the man. He hoped he wasn't soft. Kieran didn't want to work for a team that would happily walk all over their boss. Was that why Davenport had been posted to Raven's Edge? To keep him out of the way of the real investigators?

'We've found out there's a young woman with them on stage,' Davenport continued, 'who connects members of the audience to a dead friend or relative. She comes across as authentic and caring, and appears to know things about the person she's talking to that no one else would. It's definitely some kind of swindle. The question is: what sort? I suspect the gang have done their research beforehand and the woman's wearing an earpiece, or perhaps they have people planted in the audience. We'll need to gather evidence to prove they're up to no good.'

No kidding. Kieran's mouth twitched. Where had HQ *found* this guy?

Again, Davenport's dark-brown gaze snagged on him, regarding him thoughtfully.

It was as though the man could read his mind.

'At the moment, it's hard to understand what this gang is trying to achieve—'

'Money?' chipped in another DC: young, hopeful, *stupid*.

Predictably everyone laughed, but it was good-natured.

Kieran began to get a sinking feeling. Was Raven's Edge 'that' station, the one where all the misfits were sent, where they could cause the least amount of trouble? Because that would *also* imply—

'Pay attention,' Davenport said, although the reproof was gentle. 'No money's changed hands. The so-called psychic doesn't do personal readings. She'll only work in front of an audience – witnesses, if you like – usually in a community centre or town hall, sometimes in a museum, if there is one. She makes a big point of telling everyone that she doesn't charge for her services. Apart from refreshments, the performance is free and open to anyone. Needless to say, these shows "sell out" very quickly. Even if you don't believe in that kind of thing' – he glanced at the female DC who'd spoken earlier – 'it's still entertainment.'

The other DS bent his head to whisper to Kieran, 'Wait till these guys discover the internet.'

Unsettled, Kieran didn't respond. Davenport was right to be concerned. These people weren't doing this out of the goodness of their hearts.

'There must be something in it for them,' he said. 'There's a scam in play.'

That DI Davenport did hear. 'My thoughts exactly, DS Drake,' he said. 'Not least because the person organising everything – booking the venues, printing out the programmes, advertising the tickets – is *this* man.'

A familiar face appeared on the screen: dark-skinned with close-cropped hair and laughing brown eyes. The man even had dimples. He was an attractive man, a trustworthy man, the kind of man who'd be everyone's mate.

Damn.

A low murmuring broke out amongst the other officers in the room.

'Arlo Fisher,' Kieran said. Why hadn't he realised he'd be seeing that face again? Raven's Edge wasn't that far from Port Rell. The man's territory probably reached all the way to Norchester, and that wasn't a reassuring thought.

'You know him?'

I grew up with him.

He could hardly admit that.

Or the rest.

He lived next door.

We went to the same school.

I dated his sister.

Leading to a trip to A&E with a broken hand when Fisher had 'accidentally' stamped on it. This had happened after Kieran's face had made contact with Fisher's fist, shortly followed by the school wall.

His father had signed him up to boxing classes that very night.

Hardly aware he was doing so, Kieran flexed the fingers of his left hand.

Oh, yes, he knew Arlo Fisher. The man who'd had every advantage, every opportunity – and ended up a career criminal.

But he smiled casually and shook his head. 'Only by reputation.'

'Don't we all, but hopefully we can gather enough evidence to put this man behind bars permanently.'

Good luck with *that*, Kieran thought.

But throughout the remainder of the briefing, DI Davenport's gaze rested on him a little too often.

NINE

PRESENT DAY

Saturday

After staying late at Blackheath Hall to organise protection for Lady Peony Weston, Harriet sent a message to Misha apologising for the way their evening had turned out, and another to Ben, informing him she'd be late for work. When she woke, she hadn't heard from Misha, but Ben suggested he buy her a late breakfast at The Witch's Brew so they could catch up.

She certainly wasn't going to say no to that.

Caesar, her little white chihuahua, was waiting for her by her bedroom door, looking at her resentfully, even though she'd got up at six to allow him to do his business in the garden before collapsing back into bed.

'Walkies?' She waved his lead encouragingly.

Caesar huffed and turned his head away. For a dog, he was rather too good at sulking.

'You'd rather spend the day with Gabriel than me?'

Caesar raised his head and yipped hopefully.

'Seriously? You prefer *that* idiot?'

It had always been a huge mystery to her that Caesar would rather spend his time with her landlord, who co-owned the florist's beneath her apartment and was delighted to let Caesar snooze beneath his desk whenever she had to work away from the station.

'I bet he sneaks you treats,' she muttered.

'Yip.'

'Thought so. To think, I was going to take you to The Witch's Brew and buy you a sausage...'

It was the magic word. As soon as she said it, Caesar began dancing on the spot.

Harriet laughed, scooped him up into her arms and kissed the top of his head. 'You are such a faker.'

The wooden staircase to her apartment was uneven and rickety, so she carried Caesar down and then walked through the shop. They both ended up covered in petals, because Gabriel's partner, Amelia, was constructing an enormous arch of spring flowers across the entrance. Except, this being Foxglove & Hemlock, famous for their gothic arrangements, the arch consisted of black tulips, purple hellebores and ranunculuses, brightened by white narcissus and edged with olive leaves.

'What do you think, Harriet?' Amelia called. 'It's for our wedding exhibition at the weekend.'

Very... purpley?

'Very spring-like,' she said out loud.

Amelia beamed. 'That's what we're going for!'

It took twice as long as usual to walk through Raven's Edge because everyone bent to make a fuss of Caesar – and also to say good morning to Harriet, but maybe as an afterthought.

'It's lucky I don't get jealous,' she told the dog, but he was too busy happily trotting beside her to reply.

Other than The Crooked Broomstick, which was where she bought her breakfast cookies, Harriet's favourite café was The Witch's Brew at the other end of the village. Once home to the local 'witch', the squat little cottage was completely covered in Virginia creeper, which looked fabulous in autumn but not so great in March, when the cottage appeared to be brooding behind a cage of dead twigs.

Ben was sitting at their usual table beside the window, reading the menu. He handed it to Harriet and then bent to pet Caesar, who promptly rolled onto his back for a belly rub.

'Can't you try to be a little harder to get?' Harriet asked the dog, who merely beamed ecstatically at Ben, eyes half closed, tongue lolling. When Kat came over to also pet the dog, Harriet sighed. 'I'm starting to think everyone likes him more than me.'

'They do,' Ben agreed.

She swatted his arm with the menu, then ordered an English breakfast and handed the menu back to Kat.

'The same for me,' he told her, 'and a large cafetière of extra-strong coffee to wake me up.'

'Didn't you get much sleep either?' Harriet asked as Kat returned to the kitchen.

'I stayed at the hospital with Milla, waiting for Kieran Drake to come out of surgery and regain consciousness.'

'Oh.' There was a distinct pause before she remembered to ask, 'How is he?'

Despite Drake once having Harriet's job – years before she joined the police – none of the team at Raven's Edge liked him very much, due to his casual interpretation of the law.

'He lost a lot of blood – he had to have a transfusion – but the surgery went well. He was shot with a lead ball, which made a mess, as you can imagine. The ball has been passed on to ballistics, not that they'll be able to tell us more than, "It's a lead ball."'

'Why on earth was he shot with that?'

'Either it was all the gunman had to hand, or it was deliberately intended to resemble a harmless replica and therefore part of a costume.'

'Like those re-enactments? We used to have them here in the village, next to the Gateway to the Dead, but the tourists were always more interested in the spooky made-up stuff than the historically accurate battles and explosions.' She gave a mock sigh. 'I miss the explosions.'

Ben laughed. 'When Drake regained consciousness, he

suggested the gunman might have been in costume to blend in with the "ghosts" on Oscar Montgomery's tour.'

'You think the kind of enemies that Drake has would bother to put on a costume?'

'Being a private investigator is obviously dangerous work.'

Harriet was unsure if Ben was being sarcastic. 'The way he does it, yes.' Too late, she remembered that Milla was now Drake's assistant. 'Although he used to be a cop,' she said quickly to hide her mistake, but was saved from putting her foot in it further by their breakfast arriving.

She gave Ben her mushrooms, beans and black pudding. Ben handed her the ketchup.

She wrinkled her nose. 'What's this?'

'Ketchup. Your favourite? You smother it on everything.'

'Ketchup is for *lunch*, Ben. *Brown sauce* is for breakfast.'

'And mayonnaise?' he asked, amused.

'The devil's own invention,' she said, but then remembered how, not so long ago, and sitting at this very table, Milla's brother, Malcolm Graham, had offered her his potato wedges dipped in mayonnaise...

'You were saying?' Ben prompted. 'Drake used to be a cop?'

'Um, yes. I thought you knew that?'

'Why did he leave the Force? Was he fired for misconduct?'

It wouldn't have surprised her but, 'No, quite the opposite. He was shot on duty.' Was that why he sometimes limped? 'I don't know the details. No one talks about it.'

'Interesting that he decided to become a private detective. It's not at all like police work, despite what everyone thinks.'

'I suppose it was that or the security industry.'

As neither of them wanted to dwell on life after the Force, Ben poured his coffee and changed the subject. 'As you know, we have a John Doe, dressed as a Royalist soldier, left half-buried in either a new or an existing grave – Lucia is sending me a report about that today. The victim has no wallet, phone or ID. His costume appears to have been bought, perhaps online. None of the local fancy-dress-hire shops have anything that meets its description. There isn't much call for that kind of thing, apparently. Musketeers, yes; Cavaliers and Roundheads, no.'

Harriet recalled the rusted pike that had been left sticking out of the man's back. 'Do we have a cause of death?'

'I've not received anything from Caroline. She usually takes a couple of days to carry out a full post-mortem, as you know.'

Harriet was unable to resist saying, 'Not "stabbed with a pike"?'

He shook his head. 'Harriet...'

She grinned unrepentantly. 'It seemed obvious to me.'

He sighed and picked up his coffee.

'Do you have another of your headaches?' she asked. 'You look terrible.'

He smiled wryly. 'Thank you, Harriet. You always say the nicest things.'

'Well, you do. And wouldn't you rather work with someone who comes straight to the point, rather than waffle inconsequentially for hours?'

He muttered something that could've been 'It'd make a pleasant change' as he bent to give Caesar the last piece of his sausage.

Ben looked as tired as she felt. How had he managed to take the morning briefing?

'Didn't you get *any* sleep last night?'

'Not much. I went from the hospital to the station, to here.'

She watched him wash down a couple of paracetamol with the coffee. 'I think that' – she pointed to the cafetière – 'cancels out *that*,' – she gestured to the packet of paracetamol – 'but, whatever. It's your funeral.'

'Thank *you*, Harriet. In the meantime,' he added, 'I've ordered a fingertip search of the clearing between the Gateway to the Dead and the woodland around Blackheath Hall, and Dakota is going to look into those strange holes.'

Harriet snorted.

'Sorry, I could have phrased that better. Dakota is going to *research the unusual hollows* around the abbey ruins, which I suspect might be due to metal detectorists illegally hunting for Civil War souvenirs. The County Archaeology department carried out a large survey of the land back in the 1980s, but I assume the detectorists are hopeful they might have missed something. There's a local club. Dakota's trying to get us an appointment with the chairperson.'

From what Harriet remembered, the area around the ruin was overgrown with long grass, weeds and brambles. 'A fingertip search won't be easy.'

'It's always worth a go. If the man was a detectorist, where was his metal detector? What was he searching for? Civil War souvenirs? If he was digging something up, where's his shovel? How did the murderer bury him without one?'

'The tools could have been buried with him?'

'Lucia's found no trace of anything so far, but soil samples have been sent off to the lab to ascertain whether the pike was found on site or brought in from elsewhere.'

Harriet grimaced. 'Who walks around with a pike?'

'More to the point, who walks around with a shovel?'

'Then we have that other mystery man, this time dressed as a *Parliamentarian* soldier who banged on the door at Blackheath Hall and shot Drake,' she said.

'Drake says he didn't recognise him, but...'

'Drake has a lot of enemies.'

'I was going to say he lies a lot, but I didn't get much sense out of him this morning. In addition to being his usual antagonistic self, he was too groggy from the painkillers.'

'He won't talk to you,' Harriet said. 'You know what he's like. He takes a perverse delight in being unhelpful.'

'He can be helpful if he wants to be.'

'But it has to be *his* idea. And if he helps us, he'll want a favour.'

'He's already had his favour – I didn't charge him with

attempted fraud!'

'*Is* it possible the person who shot Drake also murdered the Royalist soldier?'

'Drake was shot,' Ben said, 'while the other victim was stabbed with the pike. It's not unfeasible though,' he added. 'Flintlocks – if that's what it was – are hard to reload quickly and why not stab someone with whatever you had lying around if it was easier? Equally, why not take your weapon with you for your second murder – especially if it was planned?'

'You're working from the theory that the attack on Drake *was* planned?'

'The assailant dressed like that for a reason,' Ben said. 'And the costumes are too much of a coincidence.'

Ben had never believed in coincidences.

However...

'They were *different* costumes,' said Harriet.

'From the same time period, worn close to the scene of a well-known Civil War battle.'

'What time did the victim by the gateway die, compared to the attack on Drake?' Harriet asked. 'Do we know?'

'Not officially. You know Caroline.'

'A guess then? About an hour?'

'The victim's body was still warm. It could have been as little as thirty minutes earlier.'

'How long does it take to walk between the two sites? Ten minutes? It's definitely possible, but that leaves us with the "why". *How* can the two events be connected?'

'The location,' Ben ticked it off on his fingers, 'the Civil War costumes, and the antique weapons.'

'But not the victims.'

'They might have been selected randomly because they had the misfortune to be in the vicinity of Blackheath Hall.' He grimaced. 'Although Drake was really keen to persuade me that the crimes were linked.'

'Which would immediately make you take the opposite view?'

'Correct. We shouldn't rule out *two* would-be murderers,' Ben said. 'As unlikely as it sounds.'

'So, back to our original question: who'd want to kill Drake – and will he retaliate?'

'It'd be interesting to find out who he calls from his hospital bed – apart from Esme.'

'He won't trust a phone line for that sort of conversation,' she said.

'In person, then,' Ben said. 'We could follow him?'

'He'd spot the tail.'

'*Would* he though?'

She liked the way the conversation was going but, 'Surveillance is Drake's main business. He excels at it.'

'That's why he'd never expect anyone to follow *him*.'

TEN

Drake had his own theory about who'd shot him – you didn't get to do his job without upsetting a lot of people – but he had no intention of telling DI Taylor. He'd sort out his own problems, thank you very much.

He discharged himself from hospital, losing an obvious police tail by ducking out the staff entrance and climbing into a taxi that had dropped off a pregnant woman and her very nervous partner at the maternity unit, directing the taxi to leave him in central Norchester, where he took off his sling and walked the rest of the way to an exclusive jewellery store called Wyndhurst – grimacing, as he always did, at the name.

'Wyndhurst' had been the original name of Port Rell three hundred years ago, but presumably no one in Norchester remembered that. It sounded very English, very traditional. Everyone would assume it was an old family firm. In some ways it was – except the original 'family business' had been something quite different.

The store was located in the centre of town, on the corner of what had once been a Roman crossroads. The paintwork was a subtle black and gold; anything glass or metal was super-shiny. The pieces for sale in the window were spectacular and the prices eye-wateringly high. From what he could see, standing here on the cobblestones like a Dickensian waif, his nose practically against the window, the décor inside was equally understated.

There was a discreet doorbell to ring – no one was allowed to just walk in off the street – and, doubling down on this, a young but mean-looking security guard watched over the main door. Well, he was younger than Drake, who was currently feeling every bit of his thirty-four years.

A security guard who took one look at Drake and refused to let him in.

They glared at each other through the glass door.

Drake's reputation *could* have preceded him but, more likely, he never wore anything that would make him appear to have access to a disposable income. That was the easiest way to make yourself a mark. Plus, his entire career had been built on blending in and making himself invisible.

Right now, amongst the neatly dressed inhabitants of Norchester, Drake did not blend in, nor was he invisible.

He *was* angry though, so he shoved at the door and, to the surprise of both of them, it flew open.

He was in.

'Don't be ridiculous, man,' Drake said, as the security guard first got in his face and then tried to restrain him – yet 'somehow' ended up with his face against a glass display table and his arm behind his back, much to his confusion.

A man in a smart suit, standing in the centre of the showroom, made a dive towards what was presumably a panic button beneath the counter, linked to the local police or a central security team, but an attractive Black woman in a close-fitting, cream-coloured dress held up her hand and sharply told everyone to calm down.

Like *that* was going to happen.

The moment Drake's grip loosened, the security guard tried to kick his legs from under him, so he pressed the man's face harder against the glass.

Glad he wasn't going to be the one cleaning off *those* smears.

'Drake!' the woman snapped. 'Drop!'

'When I'm having this much fun?'

But his arm felt as though someone was trying to reopen the wound with a red-hot poker, so he reluctantly released the security guard and stepped back, holding up his hands.

The woman watched him with a scowl, her arms folded. 'Kieran Drake,' she said, with exaggerated calm. 'Lovely to see you again. I assume you're not here to rob me, so how may I help? Something for the wife or girlfriend? Or both?'

He grinned. She knew perfectly well there was no wife or girlfriend. His brain was too fuddled from the painkillers for a comeback though, so he let it go.

Her frown deepened.

The security guard, unhappy with what he saw as her capitulation, took a step towards her, mouth opening in protest. The woman held up her hand again and he immediately stopped.

Drake, impressed, raised an eyebrow. She raised one back, hesitating for only a moment before saying, 'Come into my office, Kieran. Still drink your coffee black?' Before he could answer, she said to another member of staff, 'Lena, two black coffees and the first-aid kit to my office, please.'

First-aid kit?

She opened a door behind the counter marked 'private', which led into a short corridor with an office at the end of it. She indicated Drake should go through first, then shut and leant against it, effectively blocking his exit.

Drake noticed but pretended he hadn't, walking into a room presumably meant to entertain select clients, admiring the collection of heritage jewellery in the locked glass cases lining the wall, and the modern art interspersed between them. Original, but nothing too valuable. He was almost disappointed. Perhaps the lack of any art of true value was a security precaution but, more likely, the business wasn't performing as well as she liked it to appear.

He counted the exits (there was only the one, which he'd

walked through) and the windows – also just the one, with a view onto a small, neat courtyard below, with tables, chairs and solar lighting. Perhaps used for out-of-hours events for those special clients?

'You've done well for yourself, Bailey,' he said.

'While you, not so much.' She looked him up and down, deliberately making him feel conscious of his scruffy appearance. 'I heard you were shot,' she added. '*Again*. It's becoming quite a habit.'

Why did his chest feel uncomfortably tight?

'Twice in ten years is unfortunate, but hardly qualifies as a habit.'

'Is that why you're here? Because those days are long gone. I'm legitimate now.'

Funny how many of Drake's business acquaintances would tell him that – and then demand he do something dodgy for extra cash.

'What about Fisher?' he asked, pleased with the casual tone to his voice.

He didn't fool her. 'My brother and I are two very different people,' she said. 'As you know, he was all about the shortcuts to success. I haven't spoken to him in years. Not since...' She waved her hand in his general direction. He waited for her to elaborate, to admit to Fisher's role in him losing the job he'd loved, but instead she said, 'You're welcome to go after him. He means nothing to me. Kill him, if you like.'

Bloody hell!

Her own *brother*?

A tiny flicker of something that had once burned fiercely inside him died right there.

It was an effort to keep his expression neutral. Was *that* the opinion she had of him? That he would cold-heartedly murder someone over a grudge from almost a decade ago? He'd moved on. Hadn't she?

Lena brought in a tray with the coffee and the first-aid kit.

He frowned. What the hell was *that* for?

'Take off your jacket,' she said.

His eyebrow arched again.

She rolled her eyes. 'You've just got out of hospital, Kieran. Your face-off with Algie will have reopened the wound. I can see you're in pain. Have you no sense at all?'

Possibly not or he wouldn't be here, but he obediently slid out of his jacket. He was wearing a clean, long-sleeved T-shirt beneath (courtesy of Esme dropping it off earlier) but, despite the dark-grey colour, one sleeve was clearly spotted with blood. He carefully slid that off too, revealing a blood-soaked bandage.

They both grimaced.

How had she *known*?

To counter the awkwardness of him standing there shirtless – *not* that it wasn't anything she hadn't seen before – he said, '*Algie?*'

Bailey began rummaging through the bandages. 'Named after his grandfather, Algernon, who used to own the sweet shop on Sage Street? Took the whole family in when the dad walked out. You must remember the place? All us kids went there.'

He shrugged. Like her he'd grown up in Port Rell, but finances were tight, and he'd rarely made it as far as Norchester. The Fisher family, however, always had money.

When he bit off a curse as she checked the bandage around his upper arm, she glanced up but didn't say anything.

Instead of replacing the bandage, she wrapped a fresh one over the first.

'You need to get that checked professionally,' she said.

As if he had time for *that*.

'What did they shoot you with? They certainly made a mess.'

'You tell me,' he said. 'You seem to know quite a lot.'

She handed him his coffee, which was red hot, so that he was forced to juggle it from hand to hand until he was able to put it down on her desk.

'The gossip is that you were shot by the ghost of a Civil War soldier,' she said, with a remarkably straight face.

Terrific.

'I didn't come here to talk about me…' he lied, breaking off when he saw her eyebrow had gone up again. He pointed to the bandage. 'Not your handiwork, then?'

'No.'

'You knew it'd happened, and that I'd ended up in hospital?'

'I have an excellent communication network.'

'You mean we share the same informants,' he grumbled.

'You'd better give them a raise if you want exclusivity.'

'Touché.' He slid his T-shirt back on, *very* carefully, then his jacket. Did she seem disappointed? Not in the slightest. He sighed. Enough with the flirting, it was time to get to the point. 'What's your interest in Blackheath Hall?'

Her eyes narrowed. 'Who says I'm interested in Blackheath Hall?'

Jackpot.

'Why else would you be gathering information about what goes on there?'

'Maybe I'm interested in you.'

It would've been nice to believe her, but those days were long gone.

He tried again, not bothering to be subtle. 'What's your interest in Raven's Edge?'

'Perhaps I'm thinking of opening a branch there.'

'No, because you'd have competition from Vanders in Port Rell.'

'What do *you* know about the jewellery business?' she snapped.

Excellent; he was getting under her skin.

'Nothing, but I know people. An exclusive jewellery store like this would not do well in Raven's Edge. Cheap witchy pendants and silver rings set with semi-precious stones, however…'

But Bailey would never stoop to selling those. He took in her designer dress, discreet jewellery, immaculate hair and make-up… No, Bailey was doing very well here. She wouldn't do anything to upset that.

And yet...

He'd known her since they were teenagers. She'd always had a weakness for sparkly things.

Oh, no. She couldn't be *serious*.

'*Please* don't tell me you're still after that treasure? It doesn't exist.'

This time her laugh was genuine. 'Guess again,' she said, opening the door, where a glowering Algie was already waiting to show him out. 'I'm not my brother.'

'But there's *something* at Blackheath—'

'*Goodbye*, Kieran,' she said. '*Don't* come again.'

Algie grinned, showing some surprisingly bad teeth.

'So,' Drake began conversationally, as he was firmly escorted from the premises, 'you grew up above a sweet shop...?'

ELEVEN
TEN YEARS PREVIOUSLY

Arlo Fisher and his 'nasty little gang' arrived in Raven's Edge the following week. They'd been booked for two nights at the village museum, which was the only place large enough for the size of gathering they apparently expected.

Kieran was disappointed by the excitement the event was generating amongst the villagers. Even those who should know better, who happily admitted it must be some kind of trick – talking to the dead? *Really?* – were eager at the prospect of free entertainment.

CID were caught on the hop, underestimating the appeal and leaving booking tickets until the day before the first performance, by which time they'd all gone.

Fortunately, Kieran was able to blag three tickets from the elderly curator – one of the more useful talents he'd inherited from his father.

He and two DCs, all wearing casual clothing (carefully timed so they didn't arrive too early), walked into the museum and found the main hall full of people, the display cases pushed carelessly to the sides. Kieran could still see the handprints on the dusty glass and the darker patches on the wooden floor to show where they'd been.

Now mismatched chairs were set out in a wide semi-circle going all the way to the back wall, where a painting of the building's original owner, Sir John Buckley, seemed to be watching the proceedings with amusement.

Kieran wondered where the chairs had come from – the church hall? – but he took a seat at the back where he was unlikely to be noticed. What he didn't like was being at the very end of the row – a prime target for audience participation – although better him than one of his naïve young colleagues. DC Carina Field was already telling everyone within earshot that she hoped her grandfather would make contact. Kieran ensured she sat well away from the aisle, firmly wedged into her seat by the sour-faced Hestia Fox on one side and DC Carl Nicholls on the other. Carl was already showing promise as an investigative officer, which was why he'd picked him. Carl wouldn't have believed in the tooth fairy if it materialised in front of him and knocked out his two front incisors.

There was *no* sign of Arlo Fisher. It was unsurprising; he was a well-known face, for all the wrong reasons, and would be keeping a low profile to avoid attracting the attention of local law enforcement.

Too late for that, buddy, Kieran thought, folding his arms and leaning back in his chair.

About ten minutes before the show was about to start, classical music filtered quietly through the speakers. There was no stage or spotlight, only a single chair at the very front, facing the audience. Kieran only realised someone had occupied it when everyone burst into applause.

He shifted into a more upright position, glimpsing a young woman between all the heads. She wasn't very tall and had dark-blonde hair that she appeared to have cut herself in no particular style. When she turned to face the audience, he recognised her immediately.

Phyllis Halfpenny had grown up in the house next-door-but-one to his grandmother. A strange family, the three daughters all had old-fashioned names: Selma, Phyllis and Constance – named after their grandmother and great-aunts. Selma was the pretty one, little Connie was the smart one, and Phyllis was the 'weird' one that every family seemed to have.

Listening to her now, she hadn't grown any less weird.

'I see a woman...'

He almost groaned aloud. The clichés were going to come thick and fast tonight.

'Her name begins with an "A"...'

Or a 'B' or a 'C' depending how quickly someone in the audience volunteered themselves as a victim.

'Something to do with money?' she added.

Oh, it was *always* to do with money.

Sure enough, every hand shot up. How many of *their* relatives' names actually began with an 'A'?

Disappointed in his fellow residents, Kieran zoned out, wondering when the scam would come into play. Where was Fisher? She couldn't be on her own. Someone must be feeding her this stuff behind the scenes.

He was just turning in his seat to see if anyone was behind him when DC Carl Nicholls poked him in the ribs.

'Come on, boss. Try to look as if you're happy to be here and not waiting to escape at the first opportunity.'

He stifled a laugh, but Carl was right, he should have been paying attention. Phyllis had been working her way up the aisle, taking the hands of anyone who offered and giving them a reading. It varied from a message from their deceased relative to a cryptic telling of their future.

And then she was standing in front of him, holding out her hand, not a flicker of recognition on her face.

Damn, damn, damn.

As he froze, Carl leant past him and placed his hand into hers. 'Ignore my mate,' he grinned. 'Read me.'

Glancing sideways at Kieran, obviously confused, Phyllis took hold of Carl's hand, looked him straight in the eye and said, 'Don't chase what you can't have, what isn't yours and never will be.'

It sounded like something out of a fortune cookie, but the audience murmured a reverential 'Ooh...'

Carl winked at her. 'Could you be a little more specific?'

Kieran watched her close her eyes, frowning in an apparent effort to concentrate. She would have made a brilliant actress.

'There's a car hidden in the trees,' she said. 'Take it as a sign to walk away.'

'OK, so I'll look out for a car parked in the trees...' Despite his flippant tone, Carl seemed to be trying to pull his hand away. Phyllis held on tightly. 'Raven's Edge does have a *lot* of trees, you know...'

'Not here.' Her eyes flew open. 'Not here. Somewhere... else.'

'Where?'

'I'm sorry, it's fading. I... I don't know.'

Kieran was thoroughly creeped out. The way she'd stared at Carl, and her *eyes*. Her eyes had changed colour from hazel to almost... *gold*?

'What will happen' – Carl's voice sounded shaky – 'if I don't take it as a sign?'

She regarded him sadly. And if Kieran hadn't seen it himself, he'd never have believed it possible. It was a trick. It must be a trick. Coloured contact lenses or something, because her irises were fading from gold back to hazel.

'Beware the man who calls you his friend,' she told Carl, and released him suddenly, leaving Carl staring at his hand as though it no longer belonged to him.

How could she say that stuff? It was horrible. What if her victim had been a weaker personality? They could have been utterly floored by that.

'Oh, *please*,' he scoffed. 'What utter rot.'

Around him were gasps of disbelief.

'Boss...' Carl muttered. 'It's OK...'

For the first time, Phyllis smiled. 'Hello, Kieran Drake.'

Ah, so she *did* remember him.

He held his own hand out towards her. 'Go on, then,' he said, completely defying DI Davenport's orders, which had been to observe only. 'Read me. I dare you.'

She shook her head. 'It won't work on you. Your heart is closed.'

He had a heart? It was news to him.

He let his eyelids droop, turned his smile sultry and his voice deep.

(Well, it had worked a treat on the waitress at The Smuggler's Inn.)

'I'm sure *you* could open it...?' he suggested.

But she'd already begun to turn away. 'As your grandmother would have said, the road ahead will be difficult but you'll always have a choice.'

His blood chilled. His grandmother had told him that once, after she'd caught him following some misdemeanour and clipped him around the ear.

But his grandmother was still alive...

Phyllis had made a mistake.

He'd caught her out!

All attempt at seduction forgotten, he snapped, 'What the hell does *that* mean?'

Phyllis had already walked over to the other side of the aisle, where the audience was waiting eagerly.

He would've gone after her, but Carl gripped his arm and held him back. Forcibly.

'We're drawing attention, sir.'

Kieran stiffened at the man's touch and then forced himself to slump back into his seat, schooling his expression into something more pleasant than a glare of marked hostility. Fisher and Phyllis had grown up on the same street as him. Of *course* she knew the kind of thing his grandmother would have said to him and the words she'd use. And, as Phyllis's family still lived in the same cottage, *obviously* she knew Esme was still alive.

Phyllis had deliberately goaded him – and it'd taken a *DC* to tell him to get a grip? The entire point of him being here was to expose a scam.

And he'd just fallen for one.

TWELVE

PRESENT DAY

Saturday

Harriet peered around the corner of Norchester's most popular pub, The Centurion, and watched Kieran Drake barge his way into Wyndhurst Jewellers opposite. What on earth was he doing? Was he *robbing* the place?

Without taking her eyes from the altercation inside, she groped in her pocket for her phone, ready to speed-dial the local police. She watched him shove the poor security guard up against a glass display cabinet and get into a heated argument with a woman who appeared to be in charge; then they both disappeared through a door at the back of the shop, and everything returned to normal.

How... odd.

She waited a couple more minutes but, as Drake didn't emerge from whatever back room he'd gone into, she cautiously approached the jewellers and peered through the window.

The shop was designed to appeal to the high end of the market. There were no customers inside, only the staff – who were still talking about Drake's dramatic entrance, to judge from the hand waving.

But when their attention soon turned to her, she dropped her gaze to the trays in the window, as if she'd be interested in engagement rings with diamonds the size of her fingernail – bloody hell, was that the *price*? That was more than she'd paid for her beloved sports car, Little Red. And she'd only been able to afford that due to an inheritance.

On some rings the price ticket had been deliberately turned over.

'Can I help you?'

She jumped, half expecting to see Drake standing beside her, smirking at having caught her out, but an attractive man in a suit was smiling at her. She recognised him as one of the shop staff. He must think he had a prospective customer.

'We have more choice inside,' he said.

Did she *look* as though she could afford this stuff?

'To suit all budgets.'

Apparently not.

Should she be offended that he'd summed her up so quickly?

'Just looking, thanks,' she said cheerfully, before turning and walking briskly away, stepping around the corner into a modern shopping precinct and hopefully out of view.

The last thing she wanted was for Drake to emerge from the jewellers and find her standing outside. She'd deliberately picked DC Ash Chopra to tail Drake from the hospital because she knew he'd be hopeless and would be spotted right away. Sam had the job of waiting outside the hospital in his own car and then tailing Drake's taxi, following it down the hill and through the town's ancient gate without incident. She'd then picked up Drake as he'd arrived in the city centre – and nearly blown it by being distracted by pretty things.

Idiot!

She risked a glance around the corner and immediately saw Drake exiting the jewellers, mention something about sweetshops to the glowering security guard and then cross the road.

There was a split second when his step faltered and she thought he'd spotted her, but then he walked into a cosy café next to The Centurion pub, taking a seat at the back, close to the counter.

If he was stopping for lunch, he could be some time.

Did she have time to find her own lunch?

It wasn't worth the risk of losing him. To avoid detection – and temptation in the form of the delicious pastries in the window – she moved away from the café and found a bench to sit on, where she'd be partly hidden by an elderly gentleman reading a newspaper.

She checked her watch, wishing she'd brought sandwiches with her, but she hadn't believed she'd be this successful. Why had Drake gone into that particular jeweller? And where would he be heading next? Perhaps she should ask Sam to be on standby if they needed to follow a taxi again and—

'Harriet March? This is for you,' a female voice said.

Harriet looked up. A woman was standing in front of her, offering a cardboard cup and a large paper bag, both printed with the logo of the café Drake had just entered.

Oh, no...

Almost sending the poor woman flying, Harriet shot off the bench and ran across to the café, but Drake, as she'd suspected, was long gone.

'Damn, damn, damn!' She almost stamped her foot. 'That bloody man!'

'Er, miss?'

The barista had followed her like a lost chick and was holding up the cup and bag.

Harriet's first inclination was to tell her she could chuck both into the bin, but, what the hell, she was hungry. So she took them, peeping into the bag.

Instead of a nice bacon and cheese panini, as she'd hoped, it was filled with crisply fried mini doughnut rings.

She had to admit, they smelt delicious.

One to Drake.

'How much do I owe you?' she asked the barista.

'The gentleman paid,' she replied. 'He also told me to give you this.'

'This' turned out to be one of Drake's business cards. On one side it said:

Kieran Drake Investigations.

And on the other:

7/10
Not bad
Call me if you'd like some pointers

As Harriet returned to the bench to drink her coffee, she realised the entrance to the precinct where she'd hidden was reflected in the pub window – *that* was how he'd spotted her. But a quick search on her phone revealed that Wyndhurst Jewellers was owned by Bailey Fisher, sister to notorious career criminal Arlo Fisher, which could explain why Drake was paying them a visit.

So she'd learned something, and got a free coffee and bag of doughnuts. Not an entirely wasted hour or so. And now she could have a nice break before heading back to the office.

Her phone rang. It was Ben.

'Hi, Harriet. Are you still in Norchester? Want to join me for an interview?'

'OK,' she sighed.

But first she was going to drink her coffee.

Ben collected Harriet from outside the cathedral and was entertained by her self-deprecating story of how she'd ended up with a large bag of mini doughnuts – although he wouldn't have been half as amused if she hadn't also picked up the information about Drake.

'Maybe I *should* get Drake to give me some pointers,' Harriet added gloomily, as Ben parked his car in the DCI's space at Police Headquarters, safe in the knowledge that the DCI was at Raven's Edge, probably parked in his space. 'Honestly,' she said, 'I've been doing this job for years. How could I have been caught like that? I'm a *detective sergeant*, for heaven's sake!'

'You're out of practice. It's understandable.'

'You mean I should have asked Sam to do it, and you're right. It's just the higher we go, the less actual police work we get to do. I never thought it would be like this.'

Welcome to my world, he thought, but didn't say out loud. It was the same reason DCI Cameron was in the MIT office at Raven's Edge Police Station instead of behind his desk at Headquarters. They'd all rather be where the action was.

Harriet offered Ben another doughnut. He shook his head so she shoved the bag into the glove compartment.

'I hate it when Drake gets the better of us,' she grumbled.

She wasn't the only one but, as he was fed up with hearing about the man, he didn't say anything as they got out of the car and headed down the street.

It was the second time in one day that Drake had made a reference to cops and doughnuts, he reflected, which had never been an original joke in the first place.

Maybe he and Harriet weren't the only ones losing their touch.

Adam Buchanan, the chairman of the King's Forest Detectorists' Club, lived on one of Norchester's side streets in a Victorian red-brick terrace, although the front of his house had been painted white. He had a pretty, very neat front garden, with lots of daffodils, and an apple tree about to come into bloom – unusual for the centre of Norchester, where most residents had paved over their gardens to provide space to park their cars.

Harriet got to the doorbell first, still brushing doughnut sugar from her coat, and an elderly man answered, agreeing that yes, he was Adam Buchanan and how could he help them?

Harriet casually waved her warrant card in his general direction. Buchanan appeared interested rather than shifty and eagerly invited them inside, quickly shuffling off to switch on the kettle for coffee. This wasn't the reception they usually received. Perhaps Buchanan was lonely? He didn't appear to share the house with anyone else.

'Do you think *he* could stab someone in the back with a pike?' Harriet muttered, not quite quietly enough.

'Yes,' Ben said. The man seemed fit and it was easy to underestimate the elderly. But bury a body and dispose of the tools when there was no vehicle access to the Gateway to the Dead? 'Unlikely though.'

While Buchanan was in the kitchen, noisily opening cupboards and crashing crockery, they had a quick peep into the other downstairs rooms – a tiny dining room and an equally tiny sitting room, both painted white. In Ben's experience people would usually add colour with their furnishing, but Buchanan's was mostly brown and very bland.

'He doesn't seem much interested in decorating,' Harriet said, as they headed into the sitting room.

'Perhaps Mr Buchanan has other interests?' Ben pointed to the large glass display cabinet that filled most of the space.

Instead of sitting on the brown squashy sofa to wait for their coffee, they took a look at the cabinet. There were lots of old coins of varying size and colour, most from the early twentieth century but some going back as far as Elizabethan times, all displayed on a black velvet cloth. On a higher shelf were a few ancient rings, misshapen and heavily scratched, set with what might have once been precious stones which were now worn flat or cracked. The bottom shelf contained lots of bent metal pins, which, at first glance, didn't seem to be anything much at all.

Ben had recently taken his seven-year-old daughter to the museum in Raven's Edge, where he'd seen items like these arranged in a similar way. Norchester had once been a Roman fort and there was evidence of their occupation all over the King's

Forest. Were these fragments of Roman brooches? Some were green. Could they be corroded copper?

Buchanan returned with a tray containing three mugs of coffee and a plate of chocolate biscuits, and was delighted to see their interest in his collection.

'Everything in that case was unearthed with my metal detector,' he said proudly, setting the tray down and handing out the mugs. 'I've hit upon Roman coins and medieval jewellery in the past, but they ended up in the local museum. One of our members discovered a beautiful ring last year, believed to have belonged to a bishop. It was sold for twenty thousand pounds.'

Ben was trying to recall what he knew about the Treasure Act, where archaeological finds had to be handed over to the Crown, when Buchanan added, 'Of course, *he* didn't receive that. We have to report anything of value to the local Finds Liaison Officer. The coroner then holds an inquest. The piece goes for auction and we're given a reward, if we're lucky.' He tapped the display cabinet. 'These are low-value items that no one wanted, so I was allowed to keep them. Did you know, less than five percent of historical artefacts are discovered by archaeologists? The rest of it is found by people like us. Do we get any credit for that? Of course not!' Buchanan laughed good-naturedly all the same.

Ben sipped at the coffee, which was surprisingly good, and then smiled at the old man, whose enthusiasm was infectious. 'You enjoy history?'

'Oh, yes. I once considered archaeology as a career, but never had the patience for all that *painfully* slow excavating. Who's got time for *that*? It's why I love my metal detector – saves all that digging in the wrong place. Not that it's without drawbacks. Over the years, I must have dug up enough ring-pulls to fill this house!'

'Have you heard of Blackheath Hall?' Harriet asked.

'Oh, yes! It's just outside Raven's Edge. I visited there once in the eighties, when the old Marquess was alive. He was very proud of his garden and opened it every year for charity. It was wonderful. I've never forgotten it. Someone told me it's completely over-grown now.'

'There was a battle fought on the edge of the village, beside Blackheath Hall, during the Civil War,' Ben said. 'Have you ever searched the area with your metal detector?'

'Well, I wouldn't call it a *battle*. It was more of a light skirmish. The Parliamentarian troops had half-heartedly laid siege to the village and, being typical Brits, everyone was keen to give up and go home. But then the Marquess of Blackheath's younger brother turned up, strolled right up to the house where the Royalists had taken cover, and demanded to be let in. The door was opened, presumably by some not-too-bright loyal retainer and that was the end of the siege. Everyone piled in behind him. The village was won and the wall surrounding the house was partially demolished so the Hall could no longer be used as a military base. That was the end of the Marquess's brother, too, killed in the confusion.'

'But have you or any of your members used their metal detec-tors on the site?' Ben repeated. 'We've seen...' How to put this politely?

'Lots of big holes,' Harriet interjected.

'No, because that would be illegal,' Buchanan said primly. 'The abbey and the battlefield are a protected site, and the land and forest around it is owned by the Weston Family. No one can use a metal detector there without permission. We've written to Lady Peony, of course, and the current Marquess, but neither replied. I did wonder if Lady Peony had died. No one's seen her for decades.'

'Is there a big market for battle souvenirs?' Ben asked. Could that be what their victim was looking for? He must have known what he was doing was illegal, which was why he'd accessed the site after dark. 'Buttons and coins...' Ben deliberately let his gaze stray in the direction of the display cabinet.

Adam Buchanan laughed. 'If people are digging around the abbey and the battlefield, they're not wasting their time looking for *buttons*. They're after the treasure.'

THIRTEEN

'*Treasure?*' Ben and Harriet said as one, hardly knowing whether to believe what Adam Buchanan was telling them.

'The monks' treasury,' he replied. 'It was lost after King Henry VIII disbanded all the Roman Catholic monasteries and priories in the sixteenth century. The official record says that everything of value was confiscated by the Crown, but various historians believe the monks took some of it with them. Others believe the Weston family appropriated the treasury when they bought what remained of the abbey. No one was quite sure where their vast wealth came from and their meteoric rise to power dates from that point. Finally, a very few deluded souls are convinced the treasury, which would have only amounted to a few silver plates, chalices and crucifixes, is still hidden somewhere beneath the ruins.'

'And that's what those holes are?' Harriet said. 'People are literally digging for treasure?'

'What do you believe?' Ben asked him.

Adam Buchanan laughed. 'There's no lost treasure. Anyone who believes in it is a fool. The Marquess of Blackheath was rich before the Dissolution – rich enough to pay for a fortified manor house and his own private army – and rich after the Civil War, despite having to pay a fine to regain his estate.'

It might not exist, but it didn't mean people weren't looking for it. Who wouldn't like to find a bona fide treasure chest?

Ben took out his phone to show Buchanan a photo of the Royalist soldier they'd found half-buried in the clearing. He was lying in the mortuary, the mud cleaned off him, his dark hair and good looks similar enough to Stuart Huntington for his identity to be mistaken in the dark. Unlike Stuart, however, this man had been careless with his health, his features gaunt with hollow cheeks and dark shadows around his eyes.

'Do you recognise this man?'

'Oh dear,' Buchanan said, his good humour erased in an instant. 'Oh dear, oh dear. That's Kyle Hayward, the grandson of one of our founders. He *was* a member, but we had to ask him to leave because he was bringing the name of our club into disrepute. Kyle never cared about history. He was obsessed by the thought of that one big find that would make his name – and his fortune. I haven't spoken to him in years. Oh dear' – he lifted his glasses to wipe away a tear – 'it's such a shame. His grandfather will be so upset.'

Harriet wrote Hayward's grandfather's details down in her notebook and Ben slipped his phone back into his jacket pocket. They drank their coffee, politely admired Buchanan's finds to distract him from his distress, and then left to walk back to Ben's car at Police Headquarters.

'Theory?' Ben said, when they were well on their way back into town and unlikely to be overheard. 'I know you're dying to tell me.'

She grinned up at him. 'What do you reckon Kyle Hayward found something worth killing him for?'

'That's what worries me. And that the murderer might have the audacity to go back for more. We'd better keep a watch on the place, particularly as Lucia Serrano is still working there. She might be in danger.'

'Do you really believe in this treasure?'

'I believe Kyle Hayward found *something* of value. We still haven't located his metal detector or any of his other tools, and presumably he had some kind of bag to carry his equipment and his finds. The murderer must have taken them.'

'Evidence,' Harriet said, somewhat gleefully, 'unless the murderer's dumped them. Do you think he – or she – was interrupted when the ghost tour turned up?'

'Yes, they'd have done a better job of hiding the body otherwise. Their bad luck was our good luck. We might never have found Hayward's remains.'

'I was there. I didn't see anyone else. How could they have got past us? Unless they never left... That's not a comforting thought. Were they watching us, all that time? While I was searching for Oscar? Even when you turned up with Sam? That would take some nerve!'

'It was dark,' he reminded her, 'and don't forget, there's another path onto the battlefield clearing. They could have escaped that way.'

'The path that leads into the garden at Blackheath Hall.' She stared at him. 'Do you believe the same person could have shot Drake?'

'Possibly... but why didn't they shoot Kyle Hayward? Why knock on the door of Blackheath Hall – effectively announcing their presence – then attack someone else in front of witnesses?'

'A distraction from the other murder?'

Ben said nothing, waiting for Harriet to join the dots.

'Or they *wanted* to be seen! They wanted their attack on Drake to be blamed on the "ghost" of Major Lord John Weston, and they went to all the trouble of dressing up and knocking on the door at the exact time the legend said he would "appear" to ensure it would be.'

'Why risk the timing of that performance by killing someone else at a different location?'

'They wouldn't,' Harriet said. 'They knew nothing about the other murder and, although it pains me to say it, having two people wearing Civil War costume, involved in two separate incidents within the same short timeframe, *and* in the same area, could only be a coincidence.' She sighed. 'How often does *that* happen?'

'Almost never,' he agreed. 'Despite the costumes and the close proximity, there were *two* assailants.'

'Do you think the first assailant could have witnessed the attack on Drake? Or vice versa? Wouldn't that be a lucky break?'

'They'd have to admit to what they'd done.'

'I suppose so,' Harriet said. 'Ha! Drake was wrong!'

While he hated to rain on her parade... 'Was he?'

'You believe he deliberately lied? Why would he *do* that? Doesn't he *want* to catch the person who shot him?'

'Oh yes,' Ben said, as they walked through the entrance to Police Headquarters. 'But unfortunately, he doesn't trust us to do it for him.'

'Are we even sure he was the target?'

'No, but I find it interesting that he believes he was.'

When they returned to Raven's Edge, everyone in the MIT office had their heads down and were working suspiciously hard, mainly because DCI Doug Cameron was sitting at Ben's desk with the door open. He was drinking his usual black coffee (from The Crooked Broomstick, rather than the much-maligned machine downstairs) and tapping briskly at his laptop. Wearing one of his favourite designer suits, his black hair was cropped close to his head and his beard was a sculptured work of art. He could have been advertising expensive cologne rather than working as the Detective Chief Inspector in charge of the Murder Investigation Team.

'Ah, Benedict!' he said cheerfully, as they approached. 'Working part-time?'

Ben didn't reply, knowing full well his team would have already explained his absence. Harriet made herself scarce, muttering something about checking how the fingertip search was going. He suspected she was going to message Misha. If she planned to sneak down to The Crooked Broomstick to see him, he hoped she'd bring him back a coffee too.

'Ghosts?' the DCI repeated, his face expressionless, as Ben brought him up to date with the events of the last few hours, including Drake discharging himself to confront Bailey Fisher (sister to the notorious Arlo Fisher), the ID of the murder victim as Kyle Hayward and their interview with Adam Buchanan. 'Monks? *Treasure?*'

Ben braced himself for something scathing, but Cameron threw back his head and laughed. 'Well, it's never dull here in Raven's Edge!'

Perhaps if the village was a little more boring, he might occasionally have the use of his own office, Ben thought.

'Ghosts...' Cameron repeated, but his dark-brown eyes were narrowing into that razor-sharp focus that never boded well.

Before Cameron could suggest that they contact Giles Weston, the current Marquess and legal owner of Blackheath Hall, for interview, which would have been so basic as to be insulting, he asked, 'Sir, what do you know about Kieran Drake?'

'Ex-copper, bloody disgrace.'

Yes, but apart from that...

'Do we know why he left the Force?'

If Cameron was surprised by the question, he didn't show it. 'Under a cloud, I'm sure. What does it matter? Ah, you think it has bearing on his attempted murder? You're barking up the wrong tree, Benedict. It'll be some villain he's upset. We don't need to waste our resources on him. We already have a murder to be getting on with. Let him sort out his own mess.'

Ouch. Surely Drake had as much right to justice as anyone?

Although he appeared to have already started his own investigation.

'I'll tell you who might be able to help though,' Cameron said unexpectedly. 'Jake Davenport.'

'The thriller writer?'

Jake was one of the village's celebrities. He wrote historical thrillers, using one of his own ancestors, a highwayman, as the mystery-solving hero.

He was also married to Kat Davenport, who owned The Witch's Brew.

'Davenport left the Force about eight years ago,' Cameron was saying, 'but, before that, he was head of the CID here at Raven's Edge and Drake's superior officer. I suggest you speak with him if you want to find out more about the man.'

'OK, sir. Thank you.'

Cameron frowned. 'Where's DS March? I have a job for her.'

That didn't sound good.

'I'm not sure—'

'March!' Cameron bellowed. 'Get yourself in here, lass. I know you're out there.'

How often had Harriet joked that DCI Cameron had the hearing of a bat?

Sure enough, Harriet appeared in the doorway, shoving her phone back into her pocket, her expression mutinous at being summoned in such a way but, for once, smart enough to keep her mouth shut about it.

'Yes, sir?' she said.

Cameron came straight to the point. 'Those little old ladies at that big old house?'

That could describe several residents of the King's Forest, but Harriet replied promptly, 'Lady Peony and Lady Rose Weston at Blackheath Hall, sir?'

'We can't have officers on duty there indefinitely. We don't have the manpower, especially if the target is Kieran Drake. It's a waste of resources.'

A waste of resources, preventing two little old ladies from being attacked?

Ben shot Harriet a warning glare. Her mouth tightened but thankfully she kept it shut.

'I want you to return to Blackheath Hall and persuade Lady Peony to move out,' Cameron said. 'According to DCs Kershaw and Kuang, Lady Peony took a liking to you after she met you the other night, and might therefore be inclined to listen to your advice.'

More likely Pete and Freddie would do anything to avoid the job.

'What if the ladies don't want to move out?' Harriet asked.

'That's not an option,' Cameron said.

'Surely it's their choice?'

'Not when their *lives* are at stake, DS March.'

It was a good point, but Harriet still wasn't happy about it, something that was plain on her face because Cameron said, 'I have complete faith in your powers of persuasion,' and went back to tapping at his laptop with his long brown fingers.

They'd been dismissed.

Ben turned to leave but Harriet couldn't let it go. 'I'm a detective sergeant.'

Cameron sighed. 'We've had this conversation before, DS March. You do what you're told.'

'I'm a member of the Murder Investigation Team, not the — Ow!'

Ben had trod on her foot. She glared at him, eyes watering.

Cameron didn't even glance up. 'And the keyword there, March? *Team*. We work together. Lady Peony asked for you personally. You have rapport, you've built up trust, now use your powers of persuasion to move them out. The sooner you do that, the sooner you can return to your regular duties.'

They all knew there'd be no arguing with that, but Ben still held his breath.

'Yes, sir,' Harriet said.

FOURTEEN

TEN YEARS PREVIOUSLY

The Halfpenny family had lived in a little thatched cottage high on the cliff above Port Rell since 1696, when their ancestor, Jack Halfpenny, had been shipwrecked in the bay below. He'd been the only survivor, for which the villagers had eyed him askance for the rest of his life. Who but the devil himself could have survived such a storm?

After that dramatic start, the Halfpenny family tried very hard to keep their heads down, not cause trouble and blend in with everyone else, which – until Phyllis was born – they'd mostly achieved.

As Phyllis unlocked the front door to Smuggler's Cottage following her performance at Raven's Edge – and her run-in with Kieran Drake – all the memories came flooding back. It was humiliating to be forced to return to her childhood home like this. She was too broke to afford a place of her own, too broke to even afford a room at a B&B, and Fisher certainly wasn't going to pay for her accommodation. As far as he was concerned, she was four girl-friends ago and she'd have already been dumped if it hadn't been for her 'talent'.

Phyllis thought she *would* rather have been dumped, but he'd flatly told her he was never going to let her go.

Arlo Fisher wasn't the kind of man one argued with – more than once, anyway.

The best Phyllis could do to ease her conscience was to give her clients something of value to them. This might not be what they'd come for – or what Fisher *wanted* her to tell them – but it'd be the truth. Fisher was happy enough if the result was the same.

The thing about crooks was that they assumed everyone else was a crook too.

So she swallowed her pride, did as she was told, put on a 'show' and was sure to never ask anyone for money.

This was why she was back in the village she'd grown up in, broke and homeless, with her childhood friendship with Kieran in tatters. What wouldn't she give to go back to those carefree days, even if it meant watching Kieran pine over Bailey? The way he'd stared at her tonight, as though he didn't know her, as though he didn't even *like* her...

But then all he saw was a trickster.

As she let herself into Smuggler's Cottage, her ears ringing from the bitter cold wind outside, she heard her grandmother say, 'It's good to have you home, love.'

'Thank you,' she muttered, dropping her coat onto the end of the banister, 'but I'm not stopping for long. Just a couple of days.' There was no telling what Fisher would do to ensure she stayed with him. She was his 'golden goose'. How could she put her family in danger by making him aware how much she cared for them?

Arlo Fisher didn't care for anyone. It was an emotion he'd never been able to understand – except as a blackmail opportunity.

Pausing halfway down the stairs, her younger sister Connie had watched her come inside and was now regarding her curiously.

'Hi, Phyllis. It's great to see you again. Who were you talking to just now?'

'No one,' Phyllis lied. Sometimes it was easier to do that than convince people of the truth. She headed into the kitchen, her mother's favourite room, leaving the hall behind her empty. 'There's only me.'

FIFTEEN

PRESENT DAY

Saturday

Before heading back to Blackheath Hall, Harriet called into Spellbound for a takeaway sandwich and coffee, because she was too much of a wimp to face Misha and buy a cappuccino and chunky chocolate cookie from The Crooked Broomstick.

What if he didn't like her anymore?

While Phyllis Halfpenny, the strange but surprisingly efficient barista, made up her order, Harriet scrolled through her phone. Misha hadn't replied to any of the messages she'd sent him late last night or this morning. Had she upset him? It was likely. After finding Kyle Hayward's body, she would've gone into police mode and begun organising everyone. She always *tried* not to become too brusque, but maybe he didn't appreciate being bossed about. Wasn't it better to discover that now, before she became too attached to him?

Still, it wasn't a great feeling to be dumped after only one date.

It took a moment for her to realise Phyllis had slid Harriet's 'Queen of Everything' reusable cup across the counter and was saying, 'You get a free fortune telling with that?'

'Hell no,' Harriet said. 'I know exactly what fate has in store for me today, thank you very much.'

Grabbing the coffee and sliding the sandwich into her bag, she walked back across The Square to Foxglove & Hemlock, the florist's beneath her apartment, where she found Caesar snoozing on a comfy cushion beneath the manager's desk, as usual. The tiny dog was surrounded by a suspicious amount of crumbs and, although Gabriel tried to drop his woollen hat over it, she also spotted a glass jar of dog biscuits on the desk beside his laptop.

No wonder Caesar preferred Gabriel to her.

At least Gabriel had the sense to look sheepish.

Harriet tapped the jar. 'In moderation, Gabriel. Remember our chat?'

Gabriel saluted. 'Yes, ma'am.'

Yes, some men did *not* like being told what to do by a woman.

Deciding both she and the dog needed the exercise, Harriet walked with Caesar to Blackheath Hall, keeping her head down and her shoulders hunched as she passed The Crooked Broomstick, and taking care to keep her coffee out of sight.

She'd hardly walked to the other side of The Square when her phone pinged with a message from Misha, asking if she was OK. *Had* he seen her pass? Why hadn't he returned any of her messages until now? Skilfully weaving between a gaggle of tourists, she returned the message, apologising (again!) for running out on their date, and asking if he'd like to try again sometime?

She didn't receive anything back.

Maybe it was the lunchtime rush?

The café hadn't seemed particularly busy – not that she'd dared to look properly.

Maybe he didn't approve of women asking men out?

She sighed. Why was dating so damned difficult? So many unspoken rules. Thou shalt not take one's date on a ghost tour, for example. (Although, with hindsight, that would have been a helpful one.) She'd felt on edge all the time she'd been out with

Misha, as though she couldn't relax enough to be herself, and that probably wasn't a good sign.

Knowing the fingertip search was still in progress, Harriet walked past the lane that led to the Gateway to the Dead and carried on to Blackheath Hall's main drive instead. This was far shorter than the route she'd taken with Ben and led through a medieval gatehouse between two crumbling towers built into the surrounding wall.

Long before they got to that point, however, Caesar sat down and refused to walk any further, so she had to pick him up and carry him, which she suspected he much preferred.

If there were firearms officers watching the house, Harriet couldn't see them. When she knocked on the door and bellowed, 'DS March!' it was opened by DC Freddie Kuang, who was very pleased to see her, presumably because that meant he could now go home.

As she entered the great hall, put down Caesar (who was desperate to explore) and went to warm herself by the fire, Freddie explained that the firearms team had left around the same time as her last night, but there were a couple of armed officers still patrolling the grounds. The cleaning crew had arrived this morning after CSI had said it was OK to proceed. Peony had cheerfully told them to send the bill to Giles Weston, who was the legal owner of the house.

Drake had left his laptop behind on a coffee table between the two sofas in front of the fire, still helpfully linked to all the motion sensor cameras he'd installed, but it'd gone into sleep mode and no one knew the password. Knowing Drake, it wouldn't be his birth date. They could call in Tech, but unfortunately that wouldn't be legal. Lady Rose never seemed to leave her bedroom, content to watch old Jane Austen adaptations, but Lady Peony had begun packing, so that was something.

Pete and Freddie weren't quite so pleased when Harriet explained that they'd all be working shifts at the house until the Weston sisters moved out, and she expected to see the two of them back tomorrow morning, promptly at eight. After they'd left, muttering under their breath, she phoned Sam and assigned him to help her with the night shift. He wasn't happy either, considering how much he loved ghost films.

After ensuring all the windows and doors downstairs were locked and bolted, Harriet went in search of Lady Peony. She found Lady Rose instead, lying fully dressed on top of her enormous four-poster bed, watching a black and white version of *Pride and Prejudice*. Rose was no help at all, despite her delight at having a visitor.

'I'm looking for Lady Peony,' Harriet said, slowly and clearly, in case Lady Rose was hard of hearing.

'Lady Peony,' Rose agreed, smiling and nodding happily. 'Let me ring for tea.'

Harriet noticed a fraying bell pull beside the fireplace and wondered what would happen if she actually rang it. Would it fall off in her hand?

'Dear little doggy,' Rose was saying, patting the bed to encourage Caesar to jump up, and then trying to coax him with one of the sweets. 'Up! Up!'

Caesar immediately backed away, deeply suspicious, and sat on Harriet's foot.

'I'm afraid the bed is too high for him, Lady Rose,' Harriet said, 'and he's not allowed treats.'

Shrugging, Lady Rose unwrapped the brightly coloured sweet and popped it into her own mouth. 'My mother always said one never hurts.'

Harriet could have explained that chocolate was toxic to dogs, but it was easier to say nothing. She backed out of the room, Caesar keeping close by her side, but Lady Rose's attention had already drifted back to the TV, so it was doubtful she'd even remember Harriet had been there.

After checking all the bedrooms on the first floor, Harriet found Lady Peony on her hands and knees in the downstairs study and ran forward, followed by an over-excited Caesar. 'Are you alright?'

'*Obviously*, darling.' Peony sat back on her heels and glared at her. 'I'm sixty-five, not a hundred and five.'

'I thought you'd fallen over.'

Peony humphed. 'Living in this house, running up and down stairs all day after Rose, I'm probably fitter than you.'

'Yip,' Caesar said, bouncing up to Peony, assuming they were playing some kind of game.

Peony smiled and stroked his little head. 'Aren't you cute?' Then, teasingly, 'Are you a police dog? Have you come to guard me?'

'Yip,' Caesar said seriously, and they both laughed, so at least that was the ice broken.

Peony was wearing a flouncy white dress, yellowed with age, which might have started life as a Victorian petticoat. Over that she wore a cricket sweater and a black sequinned dinner jacket that Harriet had a horrible suspicion was vintage Yves St Laurent. On her feet were brown riding boots. Nothing matched. It made Harriet feel twitchy just looking at her.

Peony hauled herself up off the floor by grabbing the desk. It was hard not to offer to help, but Harriet knew that wouldn't be well received.

'You're packing?' she said, realising, too late, that the only boxes in the room were empty and had *Kieran Drake Investigations, c/o Blackheath Hall, Raven's Edge* written on them.

'Sort of...' Peony looked guilty. 'I'm going through each room, checking for personal things that belonged to my parents and separating them from items owned by the estate (meaning Giles), which have to stay with the house. Sadly, there's not very much and either Giles or his solicitor will have to approve what I'm taking, in case I'm pinching the family silver. Not that there *is* any silver to pinch. Everything of value was sold long ago, when my father died, to pay his astronomical bills.' She sighed sadly. 'Dear Papa, he did love to party.'

Harriet hadn't reached the rank of detective sergeant without being able to tell when someone was lying. Peony was trying to find items of value and Harriet couldn't blame her. Still, there was that pesky thing known as the law.

'Would an inventory help?' she suggested.

Peony laughed. 'The only inventory I've ever seen is dated 1832.'

'Could your solicitor compile one? This all seems like a lot of work for you.'

'Our solicitor is also Giles's solicitor,' was Peony's dry reply.

From what Harriet had seen of the house so far, the study appeared to be the only room not swathed in dust sheets. It was smallish, cosy and square, with bookcases on each wall and even around the window and fireplace. The books, unfortunately, appeared to be mainly about estate management and were old and dusty. It was a great aesthetic though, despite the desk in the centre, far too big for the space it occupied. On one corner were three leather-bound albums.

Peony, noticing Harriet's interest, pointed to the albums and said, 'That's as far as I've got – rescuing the family photo albums for Rose. Legally, I suppose they belong to Giles too but, as he's not in them, I wouldn't have thought he'd be interested.'

'May I?'

'Help yourself.' Peony shrugged. 'Lots of boring dead people. I never want to see any of them again, but I thought they might help with Rose's memory.'

Harriet flipped through the pages. The album seemed to date from the 1930s and through to the late 1950s. There were lots of photos of young, glamorous people having fun. She put it down and picked up another that appeared slightly newer. These photos were in colour but could be dated to the 1960s and 70s by their neat square shape and the fashions. Again, they showed young, glamorous people having fun, although the locations were slightly more exotic. No wonder the Westons had run out of money. Had they spent *all* their time partying or on holiday?

Harriet couldn't remember the last time she'd even *had* a holiday abroad.

She pointed to a photo of two young girls, one small and dark-haired, one tall and blonde, building sandcastles on a beach. Judging from the turquoise sea and golden sand, it hadn't been taken in England.

'Is this you and your sister?'

Peony took hold of the album and squinted at the photo. 'I think that was Corfu in the late 1960s. Papa thought it would be fun to go rustic for the summer to save money. Needless to say, my parents were bored by the end of the week, but Rose and I had fun.' She sighed, closing the album and placing it back on the desk.

'It's not safe for you to live here,' Harriet said gently. 'You don't need to pack everything, just take an overnight bag for you both, until this haunting business is cleared up.'

'I keep forgetting you're so young,' Peony said. 'Do you really think Giles would let us come back once we've walked out that door? The entailment states that we only have the right to live here until we marry – which, technically, already rules out Rose as she's a widow – or move out. He'd be perfectly within his rights to change the locks and shove poor Rose into a home – and that would kill her. No idea where *I'd* end up. I have no money. No income, apart from a small allowance. Everything went to Cousin Jasper – Giles's grandfather – when Papa died.

'Perhaps Giles will let me have one of those boxy little houses he plans on building here once he's torn the place down. Number 12, Blackheath Avenue. Or maybe they'll call it Castle Gardens. That would have more cachet, wouldn't it?' She wiped her sleeve across her eyes. 'To think a Weston should come to this.'

Personally, Harriet thought Peony would be extremely lucky if Giles gave her a house – a nice new *modern* house – in exchange for this one, which was literally falling down around her ears.

She knew better than to say so though.

Dakota would have given Peony a hug.

Harriet said, 'How about a nice mug of coffee?'

Peony stared at her as though she were crazy. 'To make me feel better?'

Put like that, it did sound crass.

'I know you mean well' – the older woman patted Harriet's shoulder – 'but at this time of day it's *tea*, darling. I might be struggling to keep a roof over my head, but I still have my standards.'

'Sure, let's have a cup of tea,' Harriet said, even though she hated the stuff.

As they left the study, Caesar zigzagging behind them, sniffing excitedly at everything, Harriet was distracted by a distant tapping sound, far above their heads, echoing around the gallery.

'What's that?'

Peony grimaced. 'My cohabitees, the rats. At least they haven't deserted the sinking ship, so perhaps there's hope for us all yet.'

SIXTEEN

If Kat Davenport was surprised to see Ben walk into The Witch's Brew for the second time that day, she didn't show it. Instead of heading for his usual table – the one by the window where he and Harriet often had lunch or just a catch-up over coffee – he collected a menu directly from the counter and ordered carrot and coriander soup, with a freshly-baked granary roll. As Ruby, the barista, rang it up on the till, he turned around to see who else was here.

The Witch's Brew was the most popular café in the village. It was where the famous 'witch', Margaret Lawrence, had lived in the latter part of the seventeenth century. A well-known healer who was tolerated at first, the villagers' distrust had soon turned to outright hostility and, depending on the version of the legend, Meg had been drowned in the pond, thrown from the bridge, or had run off to hell with her demon lover.

Ben had always suspected the third version was the most plausible, particularly if you swapped 'hell' for somewhere equally mysterious to the seventeenth-century villagers, such as the New World, and 'demon lover' for the regular kind. Hopefully, Magik Meg had lived happily ever after – although not long enough to witness the irony of her accusers' descendants cashing in on her tragic backstory to sell Raven's Edge as a popular tourist destination.

Kat's husband, Jake Davenport, was a direct descendant of another of Raven's Edge's larger-than-life characters: a highwayman named Jacob Lewis, who was the hero of Jake's bestselling historical thrillers.

Ben had often seen Jake working in a quiet corner of the café, usually the little nook beside the fire. He was here today too, scowling at his laptop screen, so Ben ordered coffee for them both and walked over to the fireplace, pulling out the only other chair at the table.

'That seat's taken,' Jake said, without looking up. He didn't look like a copper, ex or otherwise. He wore unfashionably small wire-rimmed spectacles, which were currently sliding down his nose. Long brown hair had been neatly tied back from his thin face with a narrow strip of leather, and all his clothes were black. He could have time-travelled from the mid-1700s, which was probably the point.

Ben sat down regardless, belatedly noticing a pot of ballpoint pens with the title of Jake's latest book written along the side, and several copies of the same hardback book stacked beside it.

'Why are you still here?' Jake's fingers flew over the keypad without pause.

'I'm sorry to interrupt you while you're working—'

'No, you're not.'

'Perhaps I'd like to buy a book?' Ben picked one up. There was an image of Raven's Edge on the cover, put through several dark filters to make it appear gloomier and more sinister than usual.

'No, you don't. You're DI Taylor from the Murder Investigation Team. Do you even have *time* to read books?'

'Good point.' Ben put the book down.

Jake's typing stopped abruptly. 'Now you're making me feel guilty.' He spun the uppermost book around, flipped it open and signed the title page with a big, swirly signature before handing it back. 'There you go. Enjoy.'

'Er, thanks.' Ben flicked through a few pages. He liked reading crime novels, provided they weren't police procedurals – the inaccuracies in *those* drove him crazy. He'd thrown the last one at the wall. This one seemed fast-paced and well-written, and any historical errors would go completely over his head. And, hopefully, it would take his mind off wanting to check up on Milla every five minutes the next time she was out on a job with Drake. Although, at the moment, she was saying she never wanted to work with him again. 'How much do I owe you?'

'First one is free.'

'I don't mind—'

'Wait a minute...' Jake frowned over the top of his spectacles. 'Ben *Taylor*? Have I got that right? Because you look an awful lot like—'

Drew Elliott.

Fortunately, at that moment Ruby sashayed over with a tray containing two coffees and a plate of mini cookies.

'Your coffee is from Ben,' she told Jake, placing one cup in front of him, 'and the cookies are to share – a gift from Kat. Your soup will be a couple more minutes, Ben.'

As Ruby walked away, Jake raised his cup in a toast to Ben and said, 'Thanks. Let me guess, you want to talk about the man previously known as Detective Sergeant Kieran Drake.'

'How did—?'

Jake chuckled. 'Former detective inspector, remember?' He took one of the cookies and bit into it, closing his eyes in bliss. 'Mmm, peanut butter. Heaven. You should try one.'

'Perhaps after my soup.'

'Full disclosure, they might not last that long.' Jake took another. 'OK, where should I begin?' As he spoke, he waved the little cookie around. 'This is a small community, people love to gossip. The fact that our local private detective was shot at Blackheath Hall last night, particularly as no one likes him very much, is all over the village. Why do you think I work in a busy café? I hear all sorts of interesting gossip and rumours I'd never even get a sniff at if people knew I was an ex-cop.'

Ben sighed. 'Kieran Drake set up a fake haunting at Blackheath Hall last night. The object was to frighten the occupants into leaving but it came back to bite him when, right on cue, the resident "ghost" shot him. The ghost was authentically dressed as a Parliamentarian soldier and although Drake didn't get a good look at the weapon, he believes it was a flintlock pistol. Milla Graham, who was with him at the time, remembers seeing smoke coming from the gun, which looked old, and a burning smell, but she doesn't remember much detail about the pistol itself, or the person firing it – their face was masked by a helmet with bars across the front.'

Jake whistled. 'That's a lot of trouble to go to. What if the pistol had misfired? They were taking a huge risk that Kieran might have retaliated.'

'At this point, we're unsure whether the intended victim was Drake or either Lady Peony or Lady Rose Weston.'

'Because someone wants Peony and Rose out of the house?'

'It would've been my first theory, except the person who wants them out of the house is the same person who paid Drake to fake the haunting in the first place.'

Jake regarded him thoughtfully. 'Your cousin, Drew Elliott?'

As Milla had said, whatever the question, the answer was always Drew Elliott.

'Probably.'

'Then my theory is that Kieran was always the intended victim. The ghost, if you'll forgive the cliché, was only smoke and mirrors to divert your attention – and resources.'

Ben felt the same. In his line of work, Drake was always going to have enemies.

'I can't imagine him as a police officer. What was he like?'

Jake laughed. 'You *know* what he's like: tricky, stubborn, troublemaking, mocking everything – a complete pain in the arse. Do I need to go on?'

'Was he always like that?'

Jake regarded him thoughtfully. 'There are things I can't tell you, due to confidentiality. Those details you'll have to get from Kieran yourself.'

'I've tried. You know Drake. He's not... chatty.'

'Even when his own life is on the line?'

'He believes he can sort it out himself. He doesn't like me – long story – but any member of the MIT would've been given the same response.'

'Sadly, that sounds just like him. Incredibly quick-witted, with an original way of thinking, he'd often be streets ahead of everyone else during an investigation – and that was also his problem. He didn't like working as one of a team and in our business that never ends well.'

'I believe he was shot on duty and invalided out?' That was a matter of public record due to the court case that followed. 'And there was something about becoming romantically involved with a suspect?' Ben winced as he said it. Hadn't he met Milla the same way?

Jake sighed. 'Kieran wasn't invalided out and he wasn't fired. A case went badly for him. Everything happened at once. He was betrayed by his childhood friends and became disillusioned with the Force. He resigned. Simple as that. It was a sad waste of his talent. For a few months I heard nothing from him, and then we had some intel about a new private investigator in Port Rell. Doing very well, but causing us a lot of headaches. To set up that kind of business, on that scale, that quickly? Kieran must have had financial backing – and not from the local bank.'

'Drew Elliott?'

'I'll let you confirm that.'

Ben could imagine how *that* conversation would go.

Drake would laugh in his face.

'What did you think of Drake personally?' he asked instead.

'I thought very highly of him,' Jake replied, without hesitation. 'Top bloke. Hardworking, honest, determined to get the job done.

I'd have recommended him for a detective inspector's role, except he plainly wasn't cut out for the job. With Kieran, it was all about the investigation: the puzzle and the chase. Collecting the kind of evidence we could actually use in court to secure a conviction? Not so much. A desk job like yours would have driven him crazy. Perhaps it was for the best that he did resign.'

Ben grimaced at 'desk job', knowing exactly how little time he spent at his own desk or even in his office. Perhaps he and Drake had more in common than he'd like to think? Not that he'd ever admit it.

'Any enemies?'

'The usual suspects – and he did have a gift for rubbing people the wrong way – mostly those in authority. I often thought he'd have been best suited to a role where he could be his own boss, but it sounds as though he's worked that out for himself.'

Ben's soup arrived then, and the conversation turned to more mundane subjects, such as the difference in policing when Jake had been in charge of CID. When they parted, it was with a mutual respect. Jake Davenport was an easy man to get along with. It was a shame he no longer worked for the Force. The MIT could do with another detective inspector on the team. They'd been one short since it had been created, almost a year ago.

Ben finished his lunch and let Jake get back to his work before walking back to the police station with plenty to think about.

He could see glimpses of past Drake in the man he knew, but 'honest'? A 'top bloke'? That wasn't any description Ben recognised.

What the hell had happened to Kieran Drake to change him so completely?

SEVENTEEN
TEN YEARS PREVIOUSLY

Kieran waited until the bitter end but didn't learn any more about why Arlo Fisher had decided to stage a psychic performance at the local museum. Phyllis Halfpenny was escorted from the premises by her minders as soon as the show finished, and Fisher didn't even turn up.

'Nothing suspicious at all,' DC Carina Field had said cheerfully, practically dancing back to the police station. 'I don't know what the boss was worried about. Can we come again tomorrow? It was such fun.'

Kieran and DC Carl Nicholls exchanged pained glances over the top of her head. The fact that the show hadn't appeared suspicious made it *highly* suspicious, yet Kieran was still wondering what on earth he was going to put in his report to DI Davenport; it was going to be very, very short.

So what did he know?

The Halfpennys were a well-known family in Port Rell, where Kieran had grown up. While Phyllis was a few years younger than him, they'd been at the same school together. Phyllis had always been an enigmatic character, considered harmless but strange; a girl who never socialised with others her own age – never socialised with *anyone*. The only other thing he remembered was that she'd left home at eighteen, to run off to London with a man her parents didn't approve of. Had that man been Fisher?

He didn't plan to pass any of this information on to DI Davenport though.

He wasn't sure why. Loyalty to those who'd once been his friends? Or, more likely, he didn't want his colleagues to learn of his own less than respectable family background.

Early the following morning he parked his car outside his grandmother's house. Esme Merriweather had recently retired, but she still lived in the same thatched cottage, high on the cliff above Port Rell. It was next-door-but-one to Smuggler's Cottage, where the Halfpenny family still lived, but he walked past that too, up to the very top of the cliff, where there was an old, abandoned church. The local children had always played here and, somehow, he knew *she'd* be there, waiting for him.

Sure enough, as he walked through the gap in the little stone wall, he saw a woman sitting on one of the ancient chest tombs overlooking the sea. She was dressed completely in black – presumably this was in keeping with her 'image'.

His lip curled, his mood crashed and he hadn't even spoken to her yet.

Although he'd made no noise she turned to watch his approach, waiting until he was standing in front of her so he could hear her words before the wind snatched them away.

'Have you made your choice, Kieran Drake?'

Was she seriously going to start with that?

'You don't need to spout that rubbish with me,' he said. 'I've known you since you were a baby.'

She blinked, apparently taken aback.

He had to say, she was a really good actress.

'Your friends need to pack up and leave,' he said, ignoring the fact that, technically, they'd once been his friends too. 'There's no place for people like you in the King's Forest. Go back to...' – where was it she'd moved to? Oh yes – 'London.'

She shrugged. 'We're booked to perform at the museum for one more night. The tickets have sold out.'

We?

She *was* working with Fisher. Surely she knew what kind of man he'd become? How about her family? Did they know what she was up to now? The Halfpennys were famed for being hard-working and honest – sometimes, a little *too* honest. Sure, they were slightly eccentric, but everyone liked them.

And then there was Phyllis.

'How can you live with yourself?' he found himself snapping. She really did bring out the worst in him. 'Conning people out of their life savings? It's despicable!'

'I've not conned anyone out of their savings,' she said patiently. 'Every performance is completely free.'

'Don't be naïve. How can Fisher put on these performances without paying for the hall, the refreshments, someone to *serve* the refreshments? He's not doing it for charity.'

'I don't know. He takes care of that. I don't charge anyone and the people coming to the show aren't charged either.' When Kieran didn't reply, Phyllis pulled off one boot and held it up for him to see the sole. There was a large hole in it.

He felt a shiver of guilt. It'd rained this morning. The long grass that surrounded them was soaking wet and the path leading up to the old church was potholed because no one used it. Her sock was soaked, which would not be pleasant in this bitter cold.

'Don't you think that if I was making any money, I could at least pay for new boots?' she said.

Somebody was making money, and he'd bet it was Fisher.

'Stay out of my way,' he told her. 'Stop conning little old ladies or—' He broke off, frowning. The stormy sky was tinging her eyes that strange golden colour again. She didn't even have the decency to look straight at him. Her gaze was strangely unfocused, as though watching something play out behind him. It gave him the creeps.

She gave him the creeps.

He glanced behind but saw nothing other than a space in the stone wall where the gate should have been, and the little path leading down the hill to the hamlet of thatched cottages.

When he looked back, her eyes were a perfectly normal swirl of green and brown, and her expression was one of pity.

It was the same look she'd given DC Nicholls.

'Out with it,' he said. 'Whatever quote you've stolen from a fortune cookie—'

'Kieran Drake,' she said, in such a low, quiet voice he had to step closer to hear her. '*Never* underestimate little old ladies...'

EIGHTEEN
PRESENT DAY

Saturday

Drew Elliott was one of the most powerful men in the county. Like Kieran Drake, he'd taken over his father's failing business at a young age and completely regenerated it. *Unlike* Drake, Drew Elliott lived in a beautiful art deco mansion called Orion House, worth several million pounds. Drake, meanwhile, lived in a flat above his office, sometimes falling asleep at his desk and waking the next morning with the imprint of his keyboard on his face.

Knowing Elliott would not appreciate a taxi driving up to his house, Drake kept his sling in his pocket and hired an automatic car, driving it very carefully from Norchester to Calahurst, cursing every time he went over the slightest bump.

The wide but simply styled wrought-iron gates of Orion House were designed to be easily missed along a road full of other houses with similar gates. Even though Drake had visited the house several times before, he still found himself muttering, 'look for the lamppost, look for the lamppost'. And then there it was. No name, no number; Drew Elliott only wanted a chosen few to ever find the entrance.

On top of each gate post was a security camera, partly hidden by the abundant foliage. There was an intercom too, but as soon as Drake approached, the gates opened automatically. On his left was a bank of rhododendrons; on the right, a large expanse of lawn broken up by several ancient cedar trees; and ahead was a magnificent white house, all tinted glass and curving lines. It looked like a 1930s ocean liner.

Drake parked his car beside the double doors, which opened on his approach. He didn't recognise the dark-suited security guard, but Elliott kept a large team to protect himself and his young family. He was more paranoid than Dermot Graham, but Elliott had annoyed a great number of people over the years.

The entrance hall was vast, taking up the entire central block, with huge windows and a central staircase leading up to a wide gallery. As Drake was escorted towards it, his footsteps echoing on the black and white stone tiles, he realised that the house resembled the centuries-older Blackheath Hall. How strange. Perhaps house design hadn't changed that much in five hundred years?

Unlike Blackheath Hall the air was warm, almost stiflingly so, yet there was no fireplace. Underfloor heating? There wasn't any art on the walls, not even mirrors, only those vast windows with beautiful views of the extensive garden behind the house and the wide expanse of open sea to the front. It was a room designed to impress by its sheer size.

On either side of the staircase were full-size lemon trees in metallic pots. Waiting at the top of the staircase was another impassive-faced guard, who escorted Drake along the passage to Elliott's office overlooking the front of the house. He must have seen Drake arrive.

The door to the office was already open. Inside was a wide desk with an array of monitors and keyboards, but no chairs other than Elliott's. This was his inner sanctum that few were invited into – and apparently none of them got to sit down.

Drake had always suspected that Drew Elliott relied on his youth and good looks as a distraction, allowing his competitors to seriously underestimate him. His height, dark-blond hair and green eyes made him attractive enough not to require the added allure of massive wealth – but it couldn't hurt. Officially, his portfolio consisted of a nightclub in Norchester and several hotels around the country, as well as a livery stable here in the King's Forest and a multitude of properties that he rented out. Plus a whole bunch of other stuff that was unlikely to be on the books.

Drake knew from a previous visit that one flick of a switch would illuminate the row of glass display cabinets along one wall of the office, revealing a collection of archaeological finds that Elliott had discovered during his many dives on the wrecks in Rell Bay. Was Elliott yet another fool seeking the monks' lost treasury? Is *that* what he wanted with Blackheath Hall? Or was it as simple as wanting to make another fortune building on its land? Wasn't he rich enough?

In Drake's experience, no wealthy man ever felt he was rich enough.

As always, Drake was struck by Drew Elliott's resemblance to his cousin, DI Ben Taylor. They could've been twins, except Taylor had a beard and seemed permanently exhausted, whereas Elliott looked like he regularly had eight hours sleep. His conscience, if he even had one, was apparently undisturbed at the thought of making two little old ladies homeless.

Drake wanted to tell him to stuff his job.

But, as his grandmother would have said, 'Beggars can't be choosers.'

(She might have made an exception when it came to Drew Elliott though.)

Drake sighed. Exactly how many bad life choices had it taken to bring him here, subservient to this man?

'*I'll tell you this. You always have a choice.*'

Did Phyllis ever remember what she'd told him that day?

'Well?' Elliott asked, almost making him start, he was that deep in thought. 'That was an unmitigated disaster.'

Not, 'Sorry you got shot, mate. How are you?'

As Elliott obviously didn't require an answer, Drake remained silent.

'I thought we'd agreed to a few bumps in the night, not a physical manifestation?'

What?

Elliott thought he'd engineered *this*? That he'd got shot on *purpose*?

Just what kind of—

Yeah... Best not to go there. No one had a high opinion of Kieran Drake. As far as the men who hired him believed, he was a mere rat, far beneath their notice, scuttling about in the gutter, doing their dirty work.

Choice. What a bloody stupid word. No one like him ever got to make a choice. His father had been right. His fate had been mapped out from the moment he'd been born.

Elliott snapped his laptop shut, finally looking at him, those green eyes regarding him contemptuously. 'Or perhaps the "ghost" wasn't there for the Weston sisters?'

Drake had been trying not to think about that. Did someone really hate him enough to want him dead?

'A few party tricks to frighten a couple of little old ladies out of their house,' Elliott said, 'and suddenly we have a murder, an attempted murder, and a *lot* of interest in a house that everyone had forgotten existed. Now the place is crawling with police. The press will soon be all over it, lots of speculation about the ghosts and the monks' lost treasury, and the price will shoot up when other parties become interested. Right now, I have Giles Weston squirming on a pin, desperate to accept any offer I care to make. But in a few days' time...? You've probably cost me a few extra million.'

Elliott wouldn't drop out when the price went up?

Interesting...

'We could have gone for structurally unsound,' Drake said, 'but it would have been harder to pull off: "experts" to bribe and so forth.'

'Easier to control than ghosts,' Elliott mocked.

'Yes, but someone could have been seriously hurt. A house like that? A little bit of "subsidence" and the whole thing could collapse in on itself.'

'Someone *was* hurt,' Elliott pointed out, which was the closest Drake was likely to get to an apology. 'But enough about that. Tell me about this "ghost". What did they look like? Male or female?'

'I couldn't tell. They were wearing a Civil War costume – a Parliamentarian soldier – complete with helmet with bars across the front, hiding their face. It was also dark outside...'

He frowned. *Why* was it dark? Had the exterior light been disabled? How had they done that? Knocked out a few light bulbs? He hadn't even noticed...

Something that had apparently occurred to Elliott. He raised an eyebrow.

'The lighting inside the house was also dim,' Drake continued. 'At the time it didn't seem important. I was expecting to find a couple of kids outside, larking about.'

'It was definitely an adult, then?'

'They were the same height as me. Taller, perhaps, because I was standing at the top of the steps. The soldier – ghost – was at ground level. I managed to catch some of the attack on camera, but it wasn't a good enough angle. Not for a detailed image. The other camera – the main one over the door – had been disabled.'

By the same person who'd knocked out the lights?

Why hadn't he noticed?

Elliott regarded him thoughtfully before turning back to his laptop. 'You've made a statement to the police.'

It wasn't a question.

'They have a description of the person who attacked me and a copy of the camera footage.' Thank *you*, Milla. 'They know exactly why I was there and who hired me.'

Elliott's fingers paused. 'You *told* them?'

'My associate let it slip.'

'By "associate", you mean Camilla Graham. I don't know why you hired her. That woman is nothing but trouble.'

Maybe it hadn't been smart but, 'She has a certain skillset.'

'Breaking and entering,' was Elliott's dry reply.

Milla was also the girlfriend of DI Ben Taylor – the man investigating Drake's shooting – and the daughter of Dermot Graham, Elliott's main business rival.

'She's talented at what she does,' Drake said.

Even to himself he sounded defensive.

'Causing trouble?'

It was easier to change the subject. 'One good thing's come out of this,' Drake said. 'Because of the shooting, and the murder by the Gateway to the Dead, the police are now really keen to get the ladies out of the house. They can't afford to keep a presence there for more than a couple of days. They'll do our job for us. We just have to wait.'

'I wish I had your confidence,' Elliott said, his attention sliding back to his monitors. 'In the meantime, Giles Weston is proving elusive. I may need you to track him down for me, remind him of our agreement.'

Did he look like hired muscle? 'That's not my job—'

'Keep me updated,' Elliot spoke over him. 'And see yourself out.'

NINETEEN

Harriet went to put the kettle on in the kitchen at Blackheath Hall, trailed by Lady Peony who wanted to grumble about Pete and Freddie; she hadn't warmed to them at all. Sam arrived, reluctantly declined a coffee, collected one of the radios Pete and Freddie had left on the table in the great hall and began to methodically check each room before it got dark.

As Harriet and Peony returned to the hall with their hot drinks (Harriet surreptitiously checking her phone for any messages from Misha), the remaining radio crackled into life.

Harriet picked it up. 'DS March.'

It was the firearms officer who'd been left on duty in the court-yard. 'I have a visitor for Lady Peony Weston.'

Harriet glanced back at Peony. 'Were you expecting anyone?'

'No...' But instead of being pleased Peony seemed anxious, glancing nervously towards the door and looking ready to flee at any moment.

But if you'd spent your life isolated from everyone in a semi-ruined house, an influx of unexpected visitors would seem terrifying.

Harriet spoke into the radio. 'Who is it?'

'Mrs Brianna Graham,' the officer said.

Brianna was the matriarch of the wealthy Graham family, Milla's grandmother, and widely considered to be the Queen of Raven's Edge.

Harriet turned to Peony. 'Brianna Graham? Why would she visit? Is she a friend of yours?'

'Certainly not,' Peony snapped. 'Dreadful woman: patronising and bossy. She'd have poor Rose put into a care home as soon as look at her, when Rose is quite capable of looking after herself.'

That wasn't entirely accurate. Physically, perhaps, but mentally?

Harriet thought about how she'd feel to be forced out of her lovely flat and into a care home, and was inclined to agree with Peony. If Rose was loved and cared for here, why couldn't she stay?

'I keep away from the village to avoid women like Brianna,' Peony added. 'Interfering busybody.'

Harriet sighed. While she'd never met Brianna Graham, from what she'd heard in the village, the wealthy widow was considered excellent at organising events and very kind-hearted, which could explain her presence here. Plus, wasn't she Peony's neighbour? *If* someone who lived two miles away could be considered a neighbour...

Peony was now creeping towards the window, perhaps in the hope of spotting Brianna, but it was too high to see anything other than bits of the surrounding wall and the top of one of the towers over the gatehouse.

'You should open the door,' Sam said, leaning over the gallery railing. 'You don't leave someone like Brianna Graham waiting on your doorstep.'

'Good idea,' Peony said, gently pushing Harriet forward. 'Tell her I'm indisposed – shock and so forth – and not receiving visitors.'

Didn't that excuse depend on how well Brianna knew Peony, who – so far – didn't seem the type to be shocked by anything?

But Harriet was the senior officer on site, so she told the firearms officer to allow Brianna to approach before opening the door. The courtyard outside was sheltered from the wind and sunny, and an elderly lady was waiting at the foot of the steps, slightly confused. She was immaculately and expensively dressed, her grey hair wound around the top of her head like a coronet. There was a large hamper beside her – the kind of thing expensive stores advertised on TV at Christmas – along with someone hidden behind what appeared to be half a flower shop.

'Oh,' Brianna said, looking her up and down. 'DS March?'

Harriet was impressed Brianna knew who she was.

'Where's Lady Peony?'

Harriet braced herself for the lie. 'I'm sorry, Lady Peony is feeling indisposed. Shock, you know...'

One of Brianna's eyebrows hitched in disbelief. 'Shock?' She laughed. '*Peony?* That girl's never been fazed by anything.'

It seemed Brianna knew Peony *very* well.

Damn Peony for putting Harriet in this position. She should've sent Sam out. He could charm anyone.

The large bouquet of flowers beside Brianna lowered, revealing a man slightly older than Harriet, with a short, half-hearted pony-tail, brown skin and distinctive grey eyes.

Oh no...

Without realising she was doing it, Harriet took a step back into the house.

Mal Graham.

What was *he* doing here?

Supporting his grandmother, presumably, because he was just as surprised to see her.

He smiled uncertainly. 'Har... er, DS March. Good to see you again.'

The last time she'd seen him, the night of her mother's Christmas party, she'd told him in no uncertain terms to leave her alone. And he had. She hadn't even seen him around the village.

'Is it?' came out before she could stop it. 'Or are you just being polite?'

He blinked. 'Er...'

Brianna slowly swivelled her head, staring incredulously at him.

He swallowed, but still didn't speak.

It wasn't often Mal Graham was lost for words. Where was the sharp-edged banter he was known for? Or was he happily envisaging a scenario where he could sprint off down the drive, never to see her again?

She smiled at the thought of the indolent Mal running anywhere...

Mal smiled back.

Damn, he was beautiful. A woman could quite lose her head. Not *her*, obviously, because *she* was Harriet March and made of much sterner stuff and—

Brianna made little throat-clearing noises.

'Where are my manners?' Mal said. 'Granny, may I introduce Detective Sergeant Harriet March? She works with DI Ben Taylor at Raven's Edge Police Station.'

At least he'd said 'with' and not 'for'.

'I *know*,' Brianna said, but she seemed amused and held out her hand anyway.

'Harriet, this is my grandmother, Brianna Graham.'

'Um, hi?'

Brianna was still holding out her hand, so Harriet felt obliged to walk down the steps to shake it, at once feeling disadvantaged. Both Brianna and Mal were tall, like Peony and Rose, but then most people were taller than Harriet.

'Pleased to meet you,' Brianna said.

'Yes. I mean, I'm pleased to meet you, too.'

She would have shook Mal's hand as though they were in a receiving line at a wedding, but he lifted the mass of flowers he held. 'Sorry, hands full.'

'They are... eye-catching,' she said, regarding the clashing yellow daffodils, purple irises and pink tulips. 'Very... spring-like.'

And not at all like Foxglove & Hemlock's usual gothic posies.

'Indeed,' Brianna said. 'One has to be very firm with Amelia

Locke. If not properly supervised, she runs amuck with the gloomiest of colours.'

Oh dear. Poor Amelia.

Harriet held out her arms. 'Shall I take them?'

'Why?'

'To pass them on to Peony and Rose? I'll let them know they're from you.'

'No, that won't do. I want to give them to the girls myself.'

The girls?

Was she going to have to repeat the lie?

'I'm afraid Lady Peony hasn't recovered from last evening's… incident.'

'Yes, I heard about that.' Brianna slowed her voice, as though Harriet didn't understand English. 'It's why I'm here; to cheer them up with a few treats.' She indicated the hamper by her feet.

This was becoming more awkward by the minute.

Why hadn't she sent Sam out?

'I'm sorry, Lady Peony's not up to seeing anyone.'

'Lady Peony, *not* receiving visitors?' Brianna replied. 'That doesn't sound like her at all but I'm sure she'll make an exception for me. I haven't seen her for at least three years – or Rose, come to think of it, since she came back from Australia. I never understood why she felt she had to run off like that…' Brianna shook her head, adding more briskly, 'But it'll be good for us all to catch up. I think the last time I saw Rose it was at her wedding!'

She climbed the first step, putting Harriet in the uncomfortable position of having to move in front of her.

'I'm sorry, Lady Peony was quite adamant.'

Brianna's eyes narrowed, and at that moment Harriet could quite easily imagine her on a chariot, waving a spear about.

'Granny,' Mal warned.

Harriet could almost see the exact moment when Brianna collected herself.

'Well, I'm sure the poor girl is still in shock. Perhaps tomorrow?'

Did she *have* to make it sound like a threat? Did she honestly believe Harriet was holding the ladies hostage or something?

'In the meantime,' Brianna said, 'be sure to tell Peony and Rose they're welcome to stay with us at Hartfell for as long as they wish.'

It took a couple of seconds for Harriet to realise what she'd said. 'Stay at Hartfell? *Really?* That'd be brilliant!'

Perhaps said with *slightly* too much enthusiasm but, after a confused pause, Brianna added, 'I've already had two lovely rooms made ready. Just say the word and Dermot's chauffeur, Sidney' – here she paused to wave vaguely behind her, presumably to where her car was parked out of sight behind the turreted gatehouse – 'will be happy to collect them and their luggage, and any belongings they wish to bring to help them feel at home.'

Harriet couldn't believe her luck. DCI Cameron was unlikely to agree to moving Peony and Rose to a 'safe house' as there was no evidence they were the ones at risk rather than Drake. Surely it would be easier to persuade the ladies to move in with Brianna at no cost to themselves, rather than force them into a hotel? Peony and Rose didn't seem to have much money, despite the size of the house.

Although Harriet did wonder what Dermot Graham would think when he found his home overrun by elderly ladies.

But what did she care about Dermot Graham? The ladies would soon be installed at Hartfell, and she and Sam could return to their normal duties. It would be the perfect result. DCI Cameron would be delighted.

Unfortunately, Mal seemed to have followed her thoughts exactly because he grinned and said, 'Would you like me to carry the hamper inside?'

'That won't be necessary.' Unexpectedly, Sam appeared on the steps beside Harriet. He took the bouquets from a surprised Mal and dropped them on top of the hamper before sweeping every-thing up as though it weighed nothing. 'We'll take it from here. Thank you, Mrs Graham. A very thoughtful gift.' He turned and walked back inside.

That's what *she* should have done. Tackle bad guys? No problem. Make polite conversation with local dignitaries? Utter failure. And, if she didn't move quickly, she'd have to make more polite conversation because Sam would likely shut the door on her in exasperation.

Quickly, she repeated her thanks, resisted the urge to curtsey to Brianna Graham, and hurried up the steps after Sam.

When she glanced back before closing the door, Mal Graham winked.

And Harriet had to quell an unexpected tingle of excitement that she'd never felt with poor Misha.

TWENTY
TEN YEARS PREVIOUSLY

Kieran returned to work the following day with a renewed determination to catch out Phyllis and her boss, Arlo Fisher. He and his team interviewed everyone Phyllis had spoken to when she'd performed in Norchester, and confirmed that no money had changed hands.

As unlikely as it seemed, Phyllis was telling the truth.

He stared at the statements in front of him, flicking through and then flicking through again, trying to find a link. Phyllis would be performing tonight and then she'd move on to another town. Whatever she was up to, she'd get away with it.

Fisher would get away with it.

Kieran dragged a map out of his drawer, spreading it out on the desk. OK, he'd try again. Cast the net wider. Send a request for help to every other CID in the county.

So he did.

By the end of the day, there'd been no response.

Surely they couldn't *all* be too busy?

He was just drafting another message when he was summoned into the DI's office and reprimanded for not sending his request through the proper channels.

Kieran regarded his boss with ill-disguised exasperation.

Honestly, the man had no idea how modern policing worked. Was Kieran expected to seek approval for everything he did? He was a detective *sergeant*, for heaven's sake!

'Sir' – he kept his voice level – 'we don't have time to go through—'

'*Yes*, you do.' DI Davenport didn't even glance up from his laptop. Apparently, he could talk and type at the same time. 'Unless you want to find yourself on a discipline? I've just been thoroughly' – the DI paused, presumably searching for a politer word to the one more commonly used in the station – 'berated by the Detective Chief Superintendent. It was a deeply humiliating experience, which I have no intention of repeating. Please don't assume my laissez-faire approach to policing means I don't know exactly what goes on within this department.'

'But—'

'What were you *thinking*?' DI Davenport stopped typing and glared at Kieran over the top of his spectacles. 'No crime has taken place! We'd be taking officers away from more important tasks for no good reason.'

'More important than...?' Kieran was so enraged he couldn't get the words out.

'*Yes*,' the DI said.

One glance at those hard brown eyes and Kieran realised he'd made a similar mistake to many other officers before him.

He'd assumed the DI's relaxed attitude was a sign of weak character.

'You're a good lad.' Somehow the DI managed not to sound condescending. 'Don't let this become a personal vendetta.'

'No, sir,' Kieran said automatically. It was expected. He knew how this worked.

'I'm aware of how important it is to you that we arrest Arlo Fisher.'

What? Did he mean...? But how would the DI have found out? His father had never pressed charges against Fisher after the assault. There'd be no point, Francis had said. The Fishers were a respectable, middle-class family. The Drakes... weren't. Who were people going to believe?

But the DI had already gone back to whatever he was tapping into his laptop, confident that he'd got his point across, so Kieran left before he thought of something else to nag him about, careful to close the door behind him.

When he returned to his desk, DC Carl Nicholls was waiting.

'Is there a problem?' Nicholls glanced back at the DI's office.

Kieran rolled his eyes. 'I've been thoroughly "berated" for over-stepping my brief.'

Nicholls was smart enough not to comment, saying instead, 'This'll cheer you up.' He slid a photocopied newspaper article across the desk. 'My mate over in Calahurst remembered reading about this in the national press six months back, so I dug it out for you. It happened in Surrey, so not our jurisdiction, but apparently the curator at one of their museums was recently sacked for theft. It came to light when the museum changed from being run by the local authority to a community not-for-profit organisation. Anyway, the woman taking over responsibility demanded a thorough audit by an outside party and several items – several *valuable* items – were found to be missing.'

Kieran speed-read the article. 'Do we know if Arlo Fisher arranged for Phyllis Halfpenny to do her show there?'

'I double-checked and they *did* stage a performance – but it was a full year before this happened.' Nicholls tapped the article.

'What was the curator's defence?'

'He argued that he couldn't have done it because the items in question were kept in a locked vault.'

'They had a *vault*? A local museum?'

'I've been doing some research and yes, many museums keep items not on display in a secure room.'

'Who had access to this vault?'

'Everyone, but there was a system in place where they'd access it in pairs – not so much for security, but in case someone was acci-dentally locked in. It sounds like a comedy sketch, doesn't it? The curator was able to prove he'd never accessed the vault alone, which is why he was found innocent of all charges and sued to get his job back. Now the museum's solicitors are trying to get him for negligence instead. They've not been able to trace any of the stolen items either. They failed to reappear on the market.'

'Stolen to order, in other words, or broken up. What was taken?'

Nicholls checked his notes. 'Low-value items dug up by a local detectorist and bought by the museum. Jewellery, bits of a sword, lots of coins—'

'Jewellery?'

'A selection of gold torcs, possibly Bronze Age. It's believed the items were hugely undervalued. The detectorists are given a "reward" for finding this sort of thing, but it's usually in favour of the museum. Ironic, really, when you think that if it wasn't for the detectorists, some of this stuff would never have been found.'

'Why wasn't it on display?'

'They were planning a themed exhibition but hadn't got round to it.'

'If the theft had been from one of the public rooms, it would have been caught on security camera. If not an inside job, did someone just walk in, take the key and help themselves? The incompetence is breath-taking.'

'These are small, rural museums,' Nicholls said. 'They'd only have one CCTV camera, if that, and their security routine would consist of checking they'd locked the front door every night.'

'And then hidden the key under a flowerpot? The thieves knew those items were there. Someone must have done a shedload of research, both to locate the items and then find a buyer.'

'Was it Fisher, do you think?'

'I don't know,' replied Kieran, 'but what better scam than to rob someone who won't even notice they've been robbed?'

TWENTY-ONE

PRESENT DAY

Brianna Graham's hamper was a huge success. Lady Rose actually left her bedroom to view it, making her grand entrance into the hall from the top of the staircase, waiting until she had everyone's attention before walking slowly down as though she were wearing a ballgown rather than flared white trousers and a holey striped sweater that looked older than Harriet.

The two ladies disappeared into the kitchen to unpack the hamper together, gleefully exclaiming over the contents and dancing around with pots of jam and pâté as though it were Christmas. It was lovely to see. They then spent another hour arranging the two enormous bouquets into a series of small glass vases and arguing happily about where to display them around the house.

Although Peony did sigh mournfully when she opened the vase cupboard – 'Of *course* the silver rose bowls have gone. Mama must have sold them first' – the spring flowers did bring splashes of colour to the gloomiest corners of Blackheath Hall.

Peony insisted on using the contents of the hamper to make tea for everyone, adding dainty pâté sandwiches and traditional jam and cream scones to a colourful three-tier stand in the centre of the kitchen table. She even allowed her sister to make a large pot of tea, under supervision (which Harriet and Sam politely sipped at, because neither of them liked tea), while Peony regaled them with tales of her and Rose growing up at Blackheath Hall.

Harriet had already noticed the multitude of scratches and marks on the kitchen table. How many people had sat here to eat over the centuries? Perhaps the question should have been, how many people had used this table to prepare food for *others* to eat, because it *was* in the kitchen.

Peony noticed Harriet tracing the etchings on the table with her finger and smiled, pointing to a large 'P' carved along one edge, surrounded by ornate swirls. 'That's my handiwork. I was an abominable child, but my parents didn't care what we did. They were madly in love, flying around the globe, spending the family money. Poor Cousin Jasper – and later his grandson, Giles – didn't inherit a bean.'

For a moment her expression turned bitter, but then she tossed her head and pointed to a pretty rosebud in one corner. 'Rose left her mark there, and our cousins, Jasper and Theodora, there.'

Harriet could only see a large 'J' but then realised the two letters had been entwined and decorated with tiny ivy leaves. All the Westons seemed to have been skilled artists – but she could only imagine her grandmother's reaction if she'd carved her name into *their* kitchen table!

'Blackheath Hall was a fabulous place to grow up,' Peony sighed, 'but we were basically left to run feral with our cousins – completely untrained for anything and totally unemployable.'

The evening and night passed uneventfully and, in what seemed like no time at all, it was eight in the morning. Rose was fast asleep in her room, but Peony was making breakfast (a little too cheerfully for the hour), and Harriet and Sam were completing their final check of the house.

DCs Pete Kershaw and Freddie Kuang arrived to take over, banging on the door and shouting their names, as Harriet had done yesterday.

She noticed they were fifteen minutes late, with no good excuse other than vaguely muttering about rush hour traffic. In Raven's Edge? They weren't even bothering to hide the fact that they didn't want to be here. Neither did she; the difference being she got on with it without whinging.

'You're late,' she said.

'We can't just walk here like you,' Pete said. 'We live in Port Rell.'

'If you don't want to be here, give your sergeant a valid reason and he'll send someone else.'

Judging from their sulky expressions, they'd already tried that.

'Doesn't Calahurst have any other DCs?' Sam asked.

'Funnily enough, no one likes working in Raven's Edge. I can't think why.' Pete waggled his fingers and added, 'Wooooo.'

'So you're stuck with us,' Freddie said. 'Sorry.'

Harriet left Sam trying to think of a comeback. Lady Peony was now tidying away the breakfast things. Harriet couldn't help seeing there was hardly anything in the enormous larder, yet the ladies had happily shared their hamper with her and Sam.

'Hi, Peony,' she said. 'Sam and I will be leaving now. DCs Kershaw and Kuang from Calahurst have arrived to take over. Sam's currently updating them.'

Peony frowned. 'But I don't want anyone else. I want *you*.'

'You'll see me again tonight.'

'Why can't you stay?'

'I have other responsibilities,' Harriet said gently, 'and I'll need to update my boss.'

'You can do that over the phone. You young people are always calling and messaging on your phones.'

Not in Raven's Edge, where the signal was almost non-existent.

'My dog needs to be fed properly and taken for a walk,' she said.

Caesar had been thoroughly spoilt, with Peony giving him the end of the pâté jar, and he'd spent most of the night snuggled into the nest of blankets on the sofa in the great hall.

'There were some sausages in the hamper,' Peony said. 'I put them in the fridge. He could have those. We both could. I have an excellent recipe from a darling Spanish *marqués* I met in Madrid. He wanted to marry me but of course Papa said no. He was always spoiling my fun. I'll need peppers and olives, turmeric and paprika...' She trailed off, sighing heavily. 'None of which I have. *Bother*. I suppose I could go to the shops. If I really had to...'

It was hard not to smile. Did Peony truly believe Harriet could be wooed with a sausage bake?

Although it would probably work on Caesar.

And definitely on Sam.

'Why not take Brianna Graham up on her offer?' she said instead, although Peony had been distinctly underwhelmed when Harriet had passed the message onto her yesterday. 'Hartfell is a fabulous house in the centre of a lake surrounded by beautiful topiary, with views towards the sea. The Graham family even have their own chef. You'd love it there, I know you would.'

Peony's eyes narrowed. 'I have visited Hartfell before. I know *exactly* what the place is like. It's one of those horrible modern glass and steel cube houses, which I'm sure Giles is going to build here as soon as he's razed this place to the ground. I never thought you'd take *his* side, darling. I thought you understood how much this house means to me?'

'Peony, it's not safe for you to be here. And Lady Rose needs expert care—'

'Nonsense! She's perfectly fine, just a bit absent-minded. You saw her dancing around the kitchen with me. She's happy here. Too many people want us out of this house and they're being very creative about it. Well, stuff them! I'm not leaving here until I'm dead. They can take me out in a box.'

Not helpful, Harriet thought, wondering how she was supposed to reply to that. Why on earth had DCI Cameron chosen her for this job, when everyone knew she had the tact of a breeze block?

Before she could say anything, a loud crash reverberated around the house.

What the hell?

Both women stared at each other in shock.

'Oh no!' Peony cried. 'Not the great hall! That's virtually the only ceiling left intact.'

Harriet's blood chilled. She'd left Caesar asleep in the hall, and Sam sparring with Pete and Freddie. If something had happened to them...

She sprinted out of the kitchen and into the hall, which appeared much the same as usual, although the three police detectives were now staring at each other in confusion.

The deafening crash came again.

It was loud enough to vibrate the floorboards – and yet it was coming from... the *door*?

Was that a *knock*? It hadn't sounded like that when Pete and Freddie had knocked earlier.

'It's not nine o'clock,' Sam said. 'It's not even night-time.'

Harriet was only half paying attention, glancing across to the sofa to check on Caesar, but he was still sound asleep, his legs in the air, yipping softly, completely oblivious. 'What difference does that make?'

'He's early.'

The ghost?

She stared at him. It was as though she'd stepped into a parallel universe. It was all very well to announce that she didn't believe in ghosts, but when faced with something that felt very much like reality...

Fortunately, reason won out.

'It's a trick,' she said firmly.

'Of course it's a *trick*,' Sam said, striding across the hall to the door. 'But someone has to open it. We can't stand here clutching our pearls like little old ladies. No offence,' he added to Peony.

'None taken,' Peony said, although she looked as stunned as

everyone. 'I'm five foot ten, sixty-five is *not* old, and I've never worn pearls in my life.'

'Sam, *wait*!' Harriet said. 'There could be a gunman on the other side. Maybe even a sniper.'

'A *sniper*?' Sam repeated scornfully. 'In *Raven's Edge*? I thought I was the one who'd seen too many movies.'

To her surprise, Pete said, 'The boss is right, let's do this properly.' He put a call out to the firearms officer outside.

They all heard the reply.

'I don't know what you're talking about, mate. Sure, I heard a crash, but I'm standing right here in the courtyard with a clear sight of the door.'

Harriet's skin prickled into goosebumps. She'd heard it! They'd all heard it! Someone had knocked on that door!

Pete spoke into the radio again. 'Can you repeat?'

'There's no one out here, only me.'

'Right,' Sam said, but didn't move.

Harriet pushed past him to grab the handle and wrenched the door open. The steps and the courtyard beyond were empty. She checked left and right. Nothing.

Sheltering from the drizzle beneath the crumbling gatehouse opposite was the firearms officer. He gave them a sarcastic 'jazz hands' wave with his free hand.

She wasn't sure whether to be relieved or irritated, but closed the door, took a calming breath and turned to face everyone, walking back into the centre of the hall.

'New rule,' she said. 'The next time this blessed "ghost" knocks on the door, we'll ignore it. Agreed? Maybe he'll get bored and go haunt someone else.'

At which point every light bulb in the great hall exploded and the huge iron chandelier dropped from the ceiling and smashed into the floorboards, a metre from where Harriet was standing.

TWENTY-TWO

For several moments there was silence, then Sam said, 'Why doesn't the ghost write us a helpful note? You know, the usual thing, on a mirror, in a steamy bathroom. It would be *so* much easier.'

'Sam...' Harriet warned. 'I'm not in the mood for—'

'A *note*?' Pete Kershaw's brow furrowed. Apparently, he wasn't as clued up on horror films as Sam.

'To tell us what it wants,' Sam said cheerfully. 'You know: "Leave Now Or Bad Things Will Happen".'

Harriet massaged her forehead. She had the start of a headache. Was this how Ben felt? All the time?

'Please don't tell me you *believe* in this rubbish?' she said, waving her hand towards the chandelier. 'This is a *scam*. One of Drake's nasty little tricks. We must have set it off somehow, with a keyword or movement too close to a sensor, or—' She broke off as Sam raised an eyebrow. '*What?*'

Having known Sam since they were in kindergarten meant he wasn't remotely intimidated by her.

'Or maybe the house *is* haunted?' he suggested. 'Have you considered that?'

Her eyes narrowed. 'I'm considering a *lot* of things at the moment, none of which being that there *is* a ghost, because that would be *bloody stupid*.' She took a deep breath, trying to regain her calm. Sam was her oldest friend, she had to remember that. He was also a good officer and always had her back, and sometimes that meant she had the benefit of his 'advice', despite her higher rank.

She tried again. 'Don't you think it's extremely suspicious that the light bulbs exploded the exact same moment I suggested we ignore the ghost?'

'Yeah,' Pete agreed. She'd almost forgotten he was there. 'How could he have pulled that off? Someone must be watching us – or listening to us – *all* the time.'

'A comforting thought,' Sam said.

Harriet turned on the spot, scanning the great hall, hoping to spot something out of the ordinary. Something *technical* that could have triggered this. Wires where they shouldn't be; little black boxes – that kind of thing. Although Drake would have designed it to be invisible.

She could call Tech to come down from Headquarters and check the place out, but that would make it look like she couldn't do her job.

It was a *prank*, for heaven's sake! Just a (admittedly very clever) prank. If she called out Tech, she'd never live it down. She'd be forever known as the officer spooked by a 'haunted' house. Being nicknamed something like 'Ghost Girl' for the rest of her life would be the very least of it.

Think *logically*. Could the electrics be at fault? It was an old house – a *very* old house – yet Lady Peony had been standing right next to Harriet when the chandelier fell. Could *she* have been the target? Instead of trying to frighten the old ladies out of the house, was someone now actively trying to kill them?

She looked around. Peony was standing less than a metre away, completely still, mouth slightly open. She couldn't take her eyes from the chandelier, lying at an angle on the floor. The decorative spikes had stabbed through the floorboards and the whole thing was haloed by a thick ring of shattered glass. Some shards had landed on Peony's boots and she slowly lifted each foot to shake them off, then looked up at the ceiling.

Harriet followed her gaze. The only evidence the chandelier had ever been hanging there was a small round hole and a few centimetres of exposed cable. Had it been deliberately cut? She couldn't tell from this distance.

'Lady Peony?' Harriet said, in her best 'police officer' voice. The one that usually brooked no argument. 'Do you *still* want to stay here?' This last bit came out slightly more sarcastic than she'd intended, but she was being paid to ensure this woman's safety – and a chandelier had almost fallen directly onto her head!

She shuddered at the thought of that metal... no, she *wouldn't* think about it. She'd shove it to the back of her mind, along with all the other things she didn't like to think about.

There are no such things as ghosts.

'You're right,' Peony said, slowly shaking her head. She was the most subdued Harriet had ever seen her. 'Of course you are. We can't stay here – but I need time to explain the situation to Lady Rose and pack all our things. We don't have much...' Her voice turned bitter. 'Legally, everything belongs to Giles – probably even this dress.'

Harriet thought that unlikely but knew better than to argue.

Was Lady Peony genuinely agreeing to leave? Was it really that easy?

'You'll leave today? We can take you to Hartfell?'

'No!' Peony closed her eyes and rocked back on her feet before opening them again and staring directly at Harriet. '*Please*, I couldn't possibly... Give us two days. This is our home. We've never lived anywhere else. It has so many memories... I don't think I can leave it... and as for Rose... Oh, poor Rose! What am I going to tell her?'

The indomitable Lady Peony Weston began to cry.

Harriet had an unexpected urge to hug her, as she would have her grandmother, but that wouldn't have been professional, so she patted Peony on the shoulder instead and said, more gently this time, 'Tomorrow? We can't give you any more time than that. We don't want anything to happen to you or Lady Rose. When we find out who's doing this, you can come back.'

Peony cheered up a little. 'Do you think so?'

Harriet thought it unlikely – the wretched Marquess would probably change the locks the minute Peony and Rose crossed the threshold – and was therefore unable to utter the lie.

Sam must have come to the same conclusion because his expression had turned disapproving. 'We'll have to work in a stricter shift pattern,' he said, 'and keep the firearms unit here. The boss won't be happy. It'll make a hell of a dent in the budget.'

And they all knew DCI Cameron's views regarding frivolous demands on his budget.

Harriet sighed. No one wanted to see Peony and Rose forced to leave, especially if their lives were in danger, but it was unfair to spend so much on them when others out there needed that same level of protection – others who hadn't been offered an indefinite stay in the local billionaire's mansion.

Why was it taking Peony so long to pack? It wasn't as though she seemed to have very much – and she constantly grumbled that Giles owned everything – but there was definitely *something* here she was determined to take with her. Harriet really hoped it wasn't anything of value, because that would create a whole load of new problems she didn't feel she could cope with on top of everything else.

As usual her feelings must have shown on her face because Pete quickly said, 'Let's have a nice cup of tea,' and herded Peony towards the kitchen.

'Coffee for me,' Harriet said automatically, before walking into the study to phone Dakota and ask her to arrange a call-out from an emergency electrician. There *had* to be a logical explanation for those light bulbs exploding – a system overload perhaps? But when he arrived, less than an hour later, he couldn't find anything wrong, not even any electronic 'trickery' – although he glanced at Harriet very strangely when she suggested that.

'Nothing,' he said decisively. 'And someone's done an excellent job on rewiring the place, which must have been a *nightmare* to do – glad it wasn't *me*.'

He even checked the mounting for the chandelier – beneath the floorboards in what must have been a nursery in the old days, where the dust sheets over the furniture were mouldy and toad-stools were growing unchecked across the carpet.

His verdict? The chandelier had managed to unscrew itself.

Or, as the electrician put it, with another suspicious glance in her direction, the mounting had 'failed'.

He took care of the exposed wiring but said someone else would need to reinstall it and they should check with their insurers before parting with any cash.

Harriet wondered if Blackheath Hall even *had* insurance.

While Pete and Freddie kept Peony and Rose distracted – it was officially their shift after all – Harriet and Sam searched every room in the house, including the attic. There was no sign of any intruder.

'He'll be long gone,' Sam said flatly.

'Do you believe someone might have broken in?'

'Hard to see how he'd have got past the guys out front,' he replied. 'They're not as relaxed as us.'

By 'relaxed' did he mean 'sloppy'?

Goaded, Harriet marched back down the stairs and into the kitchen, where Pete and Freddie were having far too much fun drinking tea with Lady Peony while she regaled them with her scandalous romance with a famous rock star. It was bizarre enough to be true.

'Does Blackheath Hall have any secret passages?' Harriet demanded.

Pete and Freddie laughed, but Peony hitched up her long skirt and strode back into the great hall, shoving at the panelling beside the fireplace with the flat of her hand.

To everyone's stunned amazement, an entire panel spun around vertically. As one, they bent to see what was on the other side: a small dark space with an ancient wooden ladder propped up against a stone wall – presumably the chimney breast.

'Bloody hell,' Sam said. 'That was there, all the time?'

'For nearly five hundred years, I should think,' was Peony's blithe reply. 'My grandfather found it by accident, falling against it while completely sloshed. My grandmother was furious. I think she'd have happily shoved him inside and left him there.'

Somehow, Harriet managed to squash down her fury. They were being plagued by a prankster, and no one had thought to tell her about the *bloody secret passage*?

She glanced at Sam.

'Oh no,' he said, raising his hands and taking a step back. 'Don't look at me. I'm not going in there.'

'I'm too tall,' Pete said.

Freddie nodded. 'Me too.'

'Bunch of cowards,' she muttered, getting down on her hands and knees, and shining her torch into the gap. As much as it pained her to admit it, the gap *was* only large enough for the ladder and a smallish person to climb it.

As usual, she was that smallish person.

Harriet crawled into the gap and shone the torch around. She could just about see a narrow opening above her head.

Tucking the phone into her pocket, she climbed the ladder, which, despite its age, was surprisingly robust.

She had to angle her body to squeeze her shoulders through the gap, emerging into a narrow passage that took her around the chimney breast (shuffling sideways) and into a tiny space that was more prison cell than secret room. There was no window or light of any kind, and it was warm and stuffy, but a cold draught in one corner meant fresh air must be coming in from somewhere.

She took a few photos on her phone before returning the way she'd come and crawling back into the great hall.

'Empty,' she told her colleagues, brushing the dust from her trousers before turning to Peony and, by supreme effort, managing to keep the sarcasm from her voice. 'Do you have any *other* priest holes or secret passages you'd like to tell us about?'

Peony shrugged. 'The house must be riddled with them. My father could have told you where they all are but Rose and I were never interested.'

Harriet didn't believe her. What small child growing up in a house like this wouldn't find secret rooms and passages thrilling?

But there was nothing to gain from forcing it.

'Do you have any plans of the house?' she asked.

'Just the one dating from the 1930s, but it doesn't mention secret passages. Only the head of the family is supposed to know about them. Giles might, or perhaps there's an older plan in the County Archives? I don't think there's anything else here. If there were, they'd be in my father's study and I've never seen anything like that.'

Peony *had* been systematically searching the house over the past few days, so presumably she'd have found a plan if one existed. Unless that was something else she wanted to hide? It was dispiriting that Peony thought she could be so easily fooled.

It would be easier to ask Dakota to contact the County Archives and check if any original plans of the house were kept there. Although, from what Harriet remembered of her history lessons, priest holes would have been built during Tudor times and this house was much older than that.

Why was nothing *simple*?

Feeling the need to take out her frustration on someone, Harriet phoned Drake's office.

The call was answered by his secretary, Esme Merriweather, but (allegedly) Drake was still on sick leave.

After giving her name, Harriet came straight to the point. 'Did

Drake leave any "equipment" behind at Blackheath Hall, operating on a timer?'

'Equipment?' Esme repeated dubiously.

She didn't sound as though she was prevaricating. Perhaps Esme was oblivious to what her boss got up to?

Yeah, right.

'The kind that might be accidentally triggered by movement or sound,' Harriet said, 'causing distress to anyone who witnessed it?'

There was silence on the other end of the phone.

'Technical trickery?' Esme said doubtfully. 'Is that what you mean?'

So she *did* have an inkling of what her boss got up to.

It wasn't much consolation that Esme sounded disapproving.

'Something like that...'

Esme sighed. 'I'll ensure that Mr Drake returns to collect any equipment remaining at Blackheath Hall as soon as possible. Thank you for your call, DS March. Goodbye.'

Harriet stared at her phone in disbelief. Esme had hung up on her?

Could Drake have primed the light bulbs to explode?

But how would he even *do* that?

The electrician couldn't find anything out of the ordinary.

It didn't make sense!

And Harriet *really* hated things that didn't make sense.

TWENTY-THREE
TEN YEARS PREVIOUSLY

'Always happy to help the police,' said the curator of the Raven's Edge museum (in a voice that implied that, actually, he'd rather go boil his own head), and reluctantly introduced himself as Alaric Gilbert.

'Thank you,' Kieran replied, pretending not to notice the snide tone. It wasn't anything he wasn't used to.

He followed the curator through the panelled hall of what had once been a large seventeenth-century manor house and home to the influential Buckley family, who'd lost most of their money and all of their influence over the following centuries, until neither they nor their fortune was left. Even the village no longer bore their name.

The central hall appeared much as it had done the night before. The glass display cabinets were still pushed to the sides, leaving scuff marks on the dusty floor, and the plastic chairs, no longer in neat rows, remained in place for this evening's 'performance'. Fisher's minions must have been responsible for setting up, because the curator looked at least a hundred years old and about as sturdy as candyfloss. The mulish set to his jaw, however, suggested Kieran shouldn't push him too far.

Kieran indicated the rows of chairs. 'Shall we sit down?'

Gilbert seemed to consider this a personal insult. 'No, thank you.'

Kieran was certain he was the same elderly man who'd held the job when he'd visited as part of a school trip, which would have been at least fifteen years ago.

'Perhaps a coffee?' Kieran suggested, attempting a friendly smile.

Gilbert's scowl darkened in return. 'We don't have a café here. You'd be best off visiting The Witch's Brew.'

A mug of instant would have been fine, but it wasn't worth pressing the point.

'Let me explain why I'm here. We believe your museum is about to be targeted by thieves.'

'The museum belongs to everyone,' Gilbert said coldly, 'and there's nothing here worth pinching.'

Kieran was willing to bet there was plenty here worth pinching, for the right collector.

'It can't all be rubbish,' came out slightly blunter than he'd intended, but he was growing tired of being treated like an uneducated fool.

'Some things you can't put a value on,' Gilbert said. 'You'd have to be an expert to appreciate them.'

Implication? Kieran wasn't.

'What kind of things?' he asked.

'Do your own research. I don't have time for—'

'Neither do I,' Kieran said mildly, 'but here I am, still trying to help you. Don't you care that you're about to be robbed?'

'Fine. Have you a notebook to write all this down?'

Kieran tapped his temple. 'Yep.'

'The entire history of Raven's Edge is kept within these walls. We have the grimoires of Magik Meg, some of her potion bottles and her furniture – that was donated by Miss Lily when she inherited Raven's Cottage. The journals of Professor Clement Wainwright, who lived at Raven's Hollow, are very popular. He was the one who believed in fairies.'

Fairies? Kieran was beginning to see why the only visitors to the museum were school children who had very little choice in the matter. How on earth did this place keep going? And was Gilbert the *only* member of staff?

'I was thinking more along the lines of old jewellery, coins, works of art...'

'Works of art?' Gilbert snorted. 'This isn't the National Gallery.'

'What's your most valuable item?'

A shadow crossed the elderly man's face. 'It used to be the sword of Matthew Elliott – the highwayman? But it was only on loan and the family wanted it back.'

None of this sounded promising. What was here that could *possibly* be of interest to Fisher? He'd gone to so much trouble, booking the hall and providing free entertainment for the village. The payback would have to be huge. But this was a tiny rural museum...

It didn't make sense.

'Do you have a storeroom, where you hold items no longer on display?' he asked. 'Perhaps only of interest to researchers?'

Gilbert's expression shifted. For the first time, he actually looked worried.

'There's the muniment room,' he admitted. 'It was built in Victorian times for the Buckley family to store estate documents. It's in the basement. They paid for the best, ensuring it was fireproof and impossible to break into, but unfortunately it soon became apparent the room was susceptible to damp. That collection is now stored at the County Archives.'

'The room is empty?'

'Not... exactly. Like every museum, we have "donations" from local residents; we don't have room to display them, but we keep them secure.'

'You mean Aunt Mildred's collection of seventies kitsch?'

'Something like that.' Reluctantly, Gilbert smiled. 'Anything sold as "collectable" usually isn't.'

'But you don't want to turn anything down in case one day it rockets in value?'

'Fashions do have an inconvenient habit of changing.'

'Could I see this muniment room?'

'I can show you where it is,' Gilbert said, 'but we won't be able to look inside. I don't have the key.'

Strange, but... 'Fair enough.'

The steps to the basement were in a small room on the other side of a massive Victorian kitchen, now forming part of the museum. The room might have once been a scullery but was now a modern kitchen, with a kettle and microwave, presumably for use by the staff.

The stone steps leading into the basement were worn but easily navigated and well-lit. Kieran had been expecting something like a dungeon with a vaulted ceiling and spooky atmosphere, but it was surprisingly warm and apparently used to store furniture. In one corner was a normal-looking wooden door which, when opened by the curator, led to a second, inner door with a large brass lever in its centre, along with a keyhole.

Kieran recognised the name of the manufacturer, founded in the early nineteenth century and famous for their 'unpickable' locks.

'Yes, it's basically a giant safe,' Gilbert sighed. 'I don't know what the Buckley family owned that was worth so much and, sadly, they've almost all died out, so I guess we'll never know. There's nothing of theirs left, as I said before.'

'What's inside?'

'No idea. I don't think it's been opened in twenty years.'

'Why not?'

'No point.'

'You mean it's empty?'

'I don't think so... I remember coming across a comprehensive audit once. I'm sure I can dig you out a copy. I believe there are some items that were found during an archaeological dig in the village forty years ago. And, in a village this ancient, there's always broken pottery and old coins turning up in gardens. They usually end up here. We have a lot of broken pots thanks to the Romans, who had several kilns in the forest during the third century. People believe they're doing us a favour bringing it all in.'

'You called it a muniment room. Does that mean it's an actual room?'

'Oh yes, there are shelves and a worktop around the sides, and a big old table in the middle. It's been a while since I was inside, but I remember that much. The shelves used to hold files and paperwork. Now they're used for boxes and crates. Rubbish, I expect, or the county museum would have taken them. I suppose I really ought to look for the key and get someone to go through it with me.'

'How many keys are there?'

'There's one here but I've no idea where it is. It's been so long since we've needed to access the room. As I said, there's nothing of value in there. It's just another storeroom. Junk.'

'But with a very fancy lock...' Kieran ran his fingertips over the door. It was a thing of beauty. Protected by the outer door, the woodwork gleamed and the brass shone, with only a few tarnished patches. 'Are there any other keys that you know of?'

'Just one other.'

'Who keeps that?'

Gilbert seemed to think that was funny. 'You do.'

'*Me?*'

'Well, not you *personally*,' Gilbert laughed. 'The police station has always kept a copy. After all, what's safer than a police station?'

TWENTY-FOUR

PRESENT DAY

Sunday

After receiving a very tetchy call from Esme, Drake returned to Blackheath Hall to collect his technical equipment and apologise profusely to Lady Peony. He even bought a posy of pink roses from Foxglove & Hemlock, which turned out to be eye-wateringly expensive. And, to gain sympathy, he put his sling back on.

A firearms officer, lolling against one of the ruined towers of the gatehouse, waved him through, tilting his head to radio to the house. Drake was surprised he was still on duty but perhaps Peony and her sister would be moving out tonight and the police presence could withdraw.

As he walked across the courtyard, DS Harriet March opened the door. That wasn't a surprise. If the police believed Peony's life was in danger, they'd hardly let her open it herself.

He grinned up at her, remembering the trick he'd played with the doughnuts, but she didn't appear to have taken it in good part because she was now looking at him as though he was something she'd found stuck to the sole of her shoe. It was disappointing because he'd thought she had a good sense of humour, but the police had never paid him much respect. After all he'd sacrificed for them, he found that especially bitter.

At least her words were polite. 'May I help you?'

He started up the stone steps but heard Peony shouting from somewhere inside.

'Tell him to bugger off! He's had plenty of time to make his apology. He's only here because he wants his equipment back.'

All of which was true.

Harriet winced but, before she could speak, a male voice replied, 'The poor bloke *did* get shot...'

'Which he brought on himself!'

Also true.

He stopped halfway up the steps. 'I guess that's a "no" to coming inside?'

'Sounds like it.' Harriet's expression was carefully blank.

'I came here at your request,' he pointed out. Actually, he'd been nagged to within an inch of his life by Esme, who'd not been impressed by his plan to con a couple of elderly ladies out of their house – even if they would receive a cosy cottage of their own in exchange. 'The message I received was to remove all technical equipment: cameras, speakers, motion detectors—'

Immediately she was on alert. 'You admit it? You rigged up some special effects to make it sound as though someone was knocking on the door?'

Why was she pleased by that? Was he about to be charged with something?

'There are hidden speakers set up around the gallery,' he said carefully, 'linked to my laptop.' It hadn't been difficult to set up. Surely the police had worked that out for themselves? They weren't stupid.

'On a timer, set to go off at nine every night?'

'No, operated manually by my phone.' He took it out of his pocket and held it up. 'I can show you, if you like?'

Maybe that would earn him some goodwill points from DI Taylor.

It was completely the wrong thing to have said.

'It *was* you earlier, frightening poor Peony half to death playing your stupid pranks! Someone could have been badly hurt. That chandelier missed us by centimetres. I should arrest you right now.' She glared at him.

Saying, 'I'd like to see you try,' would not go down well.

Did she mean it? She certainly seemed serious.

'What happened with the chandelier? Has there been another attempt on Lady Peony? Is that why the Tactical Firearms Team are still on site?'

'You think I'm going to tell *you?*'

If there was one thing his time in the police had taught him, it was how to talk to people in a calm, reasonable way.

'It would be helpful to know what I'm accused of,' he said. 'From my point of view, I only arrived in Raven's Edge thirty minutes ago, most of which I spent at Foxglove & Hemlock waiting for Amelia to make this posy.' He held the flowers up, adding in a confiding tone, 'And I had a devil of a time persuading her to use pink roses instead of ones that were such a dark red they could have been black.'

There was a definite twitch to Harriet's lips.

He'd got her.

Taking a further step up, he coaxed, 'Tell me what happened this morning. Perhaps I can help?'

As her expression frosted over, he realised he'd (literally) taken a step too far.

'Sure you can – because you were the one who caused it in the first place!'

Denial would be futile, so... 'Was there another knock on the door?' Whoever it was, they must be getting desperate. According to legend, the ghost always knocked at nine in the evening. 'Let me remove my equipment. Then, if it happens again—'

'You think I trust you? You'd leave something behind and still blame the ghost!'

Cautiously, he took yet another step up. She took one forward and then they were standing eye to eye, albeit with him two steps lower.

'There *was* another knock on the door,' he said.

'You should know – you did it!'

A chill ran through him. 'No, I was in Raven's Edge this morning, you can check with Amelia Locke. And I was in Calahurst and Norchester yesterday.' Calling on anyone with a motive to kill him – and there'd been far too many of those. 'You saw me yourself.'

'You used a timer or operated it remotely.'

'Now you're twisting the facts to suit your theory.' He gave a short laugh. 'I'm not that good and neither is the equipment I use. It's basically a sound effect looping on my laptop, sent wirelessly to the speakers.'

'Using an app on your phone?'

'Yes, that too, but I have to be within about fifteen metres for it to work.'

Her eyes narrowed. 'And the light bulbs? How did you get them to explode?'

'Ex—' he began, before, '*What?* The light bulbs *exploded?* That's... not possible.'

'It was one of your special effects, like everything else.'

'No...'

What the *hell?* How many people were *after* this house? How many had infiltrated it, as he had? Could someone have bribed a police officer? Not DS March, obviously, but there'd be others on duty. Could DI Taylor vouch for all his team?

'No,' he said again. 'That... wasn't me. I don't mess with electricity. It sounds bloody dangerous. The whole house could've gone up. You need to speak to your boss – and get an electrician in.'

'Tried that. He said there's nothing wrong. He even admired the rewiring.'

Drake cursed beneath his breath. 'Tell me, from the beginning, what happened. There was a knock on the door—'

'This is an ongoing investigation. I can't share that information with you.' Harriet retreated into the house and moved to close the door, but he jumped forward and caught hold of it.

'Was anyone hurt?'

'That's the thing about tricks and pranks,' she said, 'someone always gets hurt. Fortunately, this time we all came out of it unscathed.'

'Then you were lucky. If you allow me inside, I'll start taking everything down. But the only thing I was responsible for was that first knock on the door. It was a simple sound effect from my laptop to the six speakers I positioned around the hall. I can show you where they are—'

'List them. We can disconnect them ourselves.'

'OK...' He reeled off the locations. 'Can I at least have my laptop back? I left it on the table in front of the fire.'

Had someone else accessed it? They'd need his password, and he was always very particular about that. No one would be able to crack it easily.

'Probably not,' she replied. 'We'll need it as evidence.'

'Now you're just being mean.' He hoped Drew Elliott had a good lawyer – and that he'd be willing to pay for Drake's defence, because he certainly didn't have the spare cash for that. 'The equipment was expensive.' Frustration made his words sound like a threat. 'If you won't allow me to remove it, it'll need to be done by a professional.'

'I'll arrange for everything to be returned to you within the next few days.'

That didn't sound too bad. 'Will you call in Tech?'

'To take down a few speakers? No, we'll use a civilian contractor. Don't worry, we'll still send the bill to you.' Harriet smiled sweetly before firmly shutting the door, leaving him staring at the large brass knocker. The lion seemed to sneer at him.

From the other side of the door, he clearly heard Peony say, 'That's my girl! Odious little twerp. What a cheek, thinking he can just turn up. I've a good mind to chuck his stuff into the courtyard and set light to it.'

'That would be *illegal*,' he heard DS March sigh.

Drake turned and walked back down the steps. *Little?* OK, so he didn't quite match Ben Taylor's lofty height, but he was five foot eleven, which must put him at least an inch above Lady Peony.

As he walked across the courtyard, past the smirking firearms officer and between the ruined towers of the gatehouse, a pretty Black girl, wearing spectacles and a beanie hat, headed towards the house from the opposite direction. She was carrying a bucket of cleaning materials and had parked her van beside his hire car. It sported a generic mop and bucket logo but no company name or contact details.

Odd...

He glanced back at the house.

DS March had opened the door again, but this time she was smiling. 'You must be Cally?'

The woman nodded and said something Drake didn't quite catch.

'Lady Peony has no need of you this week,' DS March said, 'but she'll be in touch with you very soon, and told me to tell you that you'll still be paid.'

The woman nodded again and turned away, but Drake saw her friendly expression harden to one of frustration – before her mask descended again when she spotted him watching her.

The door to Blackheath Hall closing behind her, the cleaner marched back across the courtyard, her head down, intent on ignoring him.

No chance.

He stepped in front of her before she could reach the van.

'Hello, Bailey,' he said softly so the firearms officer didn't over-hear him. 'How long have you been working undercover here?'

'I could say the same to you.'

'Is that why you arranged to have me shot? To get me out of the way and leave the field clear for you?'

'As I've already said, I had nothing to do with that. Maybe you should be more careful who you upset?'

'Me?' He laughed. 'Everyone gets on with me.'

She rolled her eyes at that and moved to step around him.

He blocked her path again, mainly because he could, but found his gaze drifting over her head to the dilapidated manor house.

'What *is* it about this place that has everyone so riled up?'

'Poor Kieran,' she said, patting his shoulder, 'always a step behind everyone else.' Then she gave him a hard shove and strode past, getting into her van and driving away.

He got into his own car before glancing back at the house. Blackheath Hall *was* smack in the middle of a plot of valuable real estate, but why would Bailey be interested in that? She was a *jeweller*.

Oh no...

He chuckled to himself.

Surely she wasn't hoping to find the monks' lost treasury?

And, if she did find it, what would she do with a crate of old silver? Melt it down?

Perhaps he should do her a favour and tell her...

No.

The tiny piece of him that still thought like a detective sergeant (and occasionally moonlighted as his conscience), decided it would be far better for the monks' long-lost treasury to stay exactly where it was.

For now.

That left the matter of the alleged ghost.

Kieran Drake started the car and headed back into Raven's Edge, his expression turning grim because, unfortunately, he knew *exactly* who he was going to have to call.

TWENTY-FIVE

Thirty minutes later, Ben drove up to Blackheath Hall at the exact moment the front door was flung open and Harriet stomped down the steps carrying Caesar. She'd had an eventful night, that was for certain, and was absolutely filthy. He parked his car and stepped out to greet her, but knew better than to ask how her shift had gone.

There was no sign of the precious sports car she'd nicknamed 'Little Red'.

Therefore, his best opening would be, 'Can I give you a lift somewhere?'

'Yes please, but why are you here?'

'I came to see how you were getting on. No point in staying if you're not either. You can update me in the car. Where would you like me to take you? Did you have plans?'

'Yes' – she crossed the courtyard and got into his car – 'bath, pizza, bed.'

She slammed the car door so he was already talking to himself when he said, 'I'll take you back to your apartment.'

He slid back into the car. It felt off kilter for Harriet to be in the passenger seat. In the almost eighteen months they'd worked together, this was only one of a handful of times he'd driven.

As he steered the car in a loop around the courtyard and out beneath what was left of the gatehouse, Harriet said, in a slightly calmer tone, 'I've persuaded Lady Peony to leave tomorrow morning, but that's the earliest she'll agree to. I believe it will be detrimental to the health of Lady Rose if we force it. I've asked Dakota to find a medical professional for advice, and for Lady Rose to talk to if necessary.'

'Excellent work.'

'Thanks.' But Harriet was staring out the window as they drove towards the main road, her fingers tapping on the door handle, another clue to her frustration. 'Peony's in denial. If she never finishes packing, she has an excuse not to leave.'

Ah...

Harriet, who'd always been task-focused, would find that exasperating.

'And I suspect she's also searching the house for valuables to sneak out.'

'Which would rightfully belong to Giles Weston.'

'Making it even more awkward,' Harriet sighed.

'I'm sorry you were lumbered with this,' he said, 'but DCI Cameron was right. You are the best person for the job.'

She side-eyed him. 'Only because no one else would do it!'

He decided to concentrate on the tourist traffic.

She continued the conversation without him.

'There've been no more intruders. Sam and I thoroughly searched the house less than thirty minutes ago. We found a "secret passage"' – she used her thumb to point to her general grubbiness – 'and somehow triggered one of Drake's little magic tricks, which, as DCI Cameron might say, livened up the proceedings somewhat.'

Harriet attempting an imitation of Cameron's sarcasm made Ben laugh – and he received a reluctant smile back. That explained her scowl, the dust and the cobwebs, and the—

Should he tell her she had a little spider in her hair?

He reached out and flicked it away.

'That better not have been a money spider,' she grumbled. 'They're supposed to be lucky, and I need all the luck I can get. Oh, and then, for a grand finale, Drake himself turned up, demanding his equipment back. Can you imagine? The cheek of the man!'

'Did you let him in?'

'I told him we'd send it on to him,' she said, 'and charge him accordingly.'

Ben winced. 'It's not a great idea to upset Kieran Drake.'

'Or he'll do what? He has no power over me. He's only a private detective.'

'You're right, but occasionally, as unlikely as it sounds, the man can be useful.'

She didn't reply to that, but folded her arms and glared out of the window at the little thatched cottages, half hidden by the forest, so Ben knew she wasn't happy.

He let a few minutes pass before saying, 'Harriet, I know it's the end of your shift, and you're shattered, and that you'd rather be using your investigative skills—'

'Than babysitting a couple of eccentric old dears in a haunted house? Sure, you could say that.'

'I thought you might like a treat.'

Suddenly, she was all smiles. 'Breakfast at The Witch's Brew?'

'OK...' He'd already eaten but would never refuse a coffee. 'But, after that, would you like to visit Kyle Hayward's house with me?'

She regarded him suspiciously. 'Is it haunted?'

'I don't believe so!'

'Then count me in.'

Kyle Hayward had lived in one of the crooked medieval cottages that Raven's Edge was famous for, down a little dark alley that led from the main street. This one was called Church Lane because it was an ancient path to the churchyard, and Hayward lived at number six. It was a cosy little place, with two rooms to each floor, but seemed even smaller because each room was lined with old wooden shelves crammed with books on local history. In front of those, piled high on the dusty floorboards, were transparent plastic crates filled with scrunched-up newspaper.

'Great, a hoarder,' Harriet sighed, stepping over a pile of uncollected post — far more than one would expect to see in the house of a man who'd barely been deceased for two days. 'I'm glad we dropped Caesar off first. If he got lost in here, we'd never find him again.'

Ben picked up a handful of envelopes. They appeared to be bills. Had he been ignoring them? Did he have financial worries? Hence the need for 'that one big find that would make his name — and his fortune', as Adam Buchanan had put it?

It was something else for Dakota to research.

In addition to the crates and the shelves, paperwork had been scattered on every available surface. There were letters (either accepting or refusing Kyle access to private land, including Blackheath Hall), both old and modern maps, and lots and lots of cuttings from newspapers and magazines — usually concerning finds by other detectorists. It was a huge collection which would take some poor soul weeks, if not months, to sort through.

It was hard not to knock things over as they moved methodically through the house, having first taken the precaution to snap on gloves. They hadn't suited up because it wasn't a crime scene.

At least, Ben hoped it wasn't.

In the sitting room were two glass display cases, similar to the one Adam Buchanan owned. They weren't as fancy, and the items within weren't labelled or arranged on cloth. It was almost as if they'd been randomly shoved in wherever there happened to be room — as though Kyle took pleasure from finding the things, but then he'd lost interest.

Ben wiped the dust from the nearest cabinet with his sleeve.

Inside were piles of coins, buttons, and strange bits of twisted metal that could have just been junk. He remembered Buchanan's joke about collecting enough ring-pulls to fill a house.

Harriet's attention had been caught by some misshapen rings set with plain opaque stones. 'Do you think these are real?'

'Gold, you mean?'

'That one, for instance.' She pointed to a small ring that wasn't quite as scratched as the others. 'Do you think the blue stone is a sapphire?'

Ben's knowledge of rings extended to the two he'd bought for his ex-wife – an engagement ring and a wedding ring, both of which she'd kept after their divorce and occasionally still wore as dress rings – which he thought was odd but wouldn't dream of commenting. He assumed she was keeping them for Sophie, and—

'Ben?'

'I suppose it could be,' he said. 'We'll need to call in an expert to catalogue this. If Hayward was the kind of person to metal-detect illegally, presumably he wouldn't have reported his finds.'

Harriet moved closer to the cabinet, almost pressing her nose against the glass. 'They could be super valuable?'

'Perhaps.' Ben moved into the kitchen, which was just as crammed with crates, and found a modern map of Raven's Edge rolled out on the table and held in place by rusty baked bean tins. The tins had left marks on the map, so they must have been there for some time. 'Or perhaps it's a load of old junk. If any of this was valuable, wouldn't Hayward have sold it on?'

'Good point.'

He walked around to the other side of the table to look at the map the right way up. He could see The Square and the church, and the larger buildings such as Foxglove & Hemlock, where Harriet lived, and the museum, all clearly labelled. He followed the main street with his finger, past Raven's Cottage (also known as The Witch's Brew), and along a lane to a large rectangle made up of dashes. The dashes represented bits of broken wall because the rectangle was labelled 'Buckley Abbey' and the area to its side was marked with red crosses; the pen was still lying beside the map.

'X marks the spot,' Harriet said, coming to stand beside him. 'Buried treasure.'

'Hayward certainly thought so.'

'If he did find anything, do you think it might be in these crates?'

'It might,' Ben said cautiously, 'but equally, his finds could be from anywhere in the King's Forest – or even further afield.'

'I hope he kept a record of what he found and where he found it, because that's our history he's messing with. It belongs to everyone.'

'I'll ask Dakota to contact the County Archaeology department. Perhaps they could send someone.'

'They'd love to get their hands on all this!'

'But do they have the time?' Ben took down the nearest crate and opened it. The newspaper inside was five years old, which didn't bode well, wrapped around some unglazed, roughly made pottery that looked like something his seven-year-old daughter might bring home from school. 'I believe this is Roman.'

Harriet wrinkled her nose. 'It looks like the kind of thing you'd find at a garden centre. There are pots like this at Blackheath Hall.'

'Adam Buchanan said there were Roman kilns throughout the forest, because of the fort at Norchester,'

Harriet peered into the crate. 'How do you find pottery with a metal detector?'

He knew she was joking but... 'I have a horrible feeling that Kyle might have been dealing with something larger than night-hawking.'

'Do you think it's valuable?' She watched as he wrapped up the pottery, returning it to the crate. 'What shall we open next? It's like Christmas!'

'We'd better let CSI go through it properly,' he said, but she'd already opened a smaller crate sitting by the back door – and promptly shrieked, dropping the plastic lid.

Ben hurried over. 'What is it?'

Harriet grimaced and pointed into the crate.

A very old skull, encrusted with damp soil, grinned back at him.

'That *is* real, isn't it?' she said. 'Do you think it's a monk or a soldier?'

'Or a murder victim.'

'Nice.' Harriet glanced round at the crates, which suddenly seemed more sinister. 'There are so many things we could've charged this guy with – if he hadn't already been murdered.'

It wasn't a crime to fail to report finding human remains, but Ben was sure he could have found *something* to charge Hayward with.

'We need to stop right now,' he said, 'in case there are more bones in these boxes.'

'That's fine by me.' Harriet took out her phone and snapped a photo of the skull, then used her fingers to enlarge it. 'It's covered in loose soil, which looks damp, and there's more at the bottom of the crate. Do you think it came from the Gateway to the Dead?'

He really, *really* didn't want to say it, but... 'Yes.'

'How old do you think it is?'

'More than a hundred years old and hopefully not our problem.'

Harriet forwarded her photos of the skull to Frank McAllister, the forensic anthropologist at Norchester University, who immediately messaged back:

> Human skull 💀

He added an emoji to hammer the point home.

Harriet rolled her eyes and showed Ben the message. 'No kidding!' she said before sending another:

> How old?

> Box it up and send it to me

Harriet replaced the lid and picked the crate up. 'At least it's already gift-wrapped. Have we ever seen Dr McAllister at a crime scene?'

'You'd know better than me. I've worked in Raven's Edge for less than eighteen months and I've never met him. How about you?'

'I'm starting to wonder if he even exists.'

TWENTY-SIX

TEN YEARS PREVIOUSLY

After visiting the museum, Kieran should have returned to the station and updated DI Davenport on his conversation with the curator. Instead, he drove out to Port Rell and up the hill to the little hamlet once lived in by the smugglers and outcasts of the village. Smuggler's Cottage was two doors along from where his grandmother lived. He parked outside and went up the path, knocking hard on the stout oak door.

It was opened by Joseph Halfpenny, a large man with a mane of curly, grey-streaked hair and a solitary gold ring glinting in his ear, who looked as though he could have been part-pirate himself. He had the same hazel eyes as Phyllis.

Joseph's unfriendly glower cleared as he recognised the man standing on his doorstep.

'Kieran Drake!' he boomed. 'Esme's grandson.'

Kieran inclined his head. 'Yes, that's—'

Joseph didn't let him finish. 'You're a detective now, over Raven's Edge way?'

'*Police* detective, yes. I'm a DS.' He held out his hand and Joseph enclosed it in his own meaty fists and shook it vigorously.

'Come in, come in.' He almost dragged him into the cottage. 'Good to see you again. How many years has it been? It doesn't seem like five minutes since you, Arlo and Bailey were running in and out of here.' He turned to bellow, 'Put the kettle on, Hilly! You'll never guess who it is!'

His wife entered the hall from the kitchen, wiping her hands on a tea towel. 'Hello, Kieran. Lovely to see you again. Your grandmother was telling us only the other day how well you're getting on at Raven's Edge.'

Kieran tried not to cringe. Many of his grandmother's friends who'd watched him grow up treated him as though he were still twelve, not twenty-four.

Footsteps on the staircase made him turn his head. Phyllis was standing halfway up, confusion evident on her face. She must have heard her father shouting.

'Kieran?'

'We need to talk,' he said, before she could launch into, 'What are *you* doing here?'

She glanced towards her parents and hurried down the last few steps. 'Sure, let's go for a walk.'

But as she turned to grab her coat from the rack on the wall, he heard her mother say, in a far too audible undertone: 'You didn't tell me you had a boyfriend!'

Was it the dim lighting in here or did Phyllis appear mortified? 'Mum! He's *not—*'

'A friend then! You have a *friend*!'

If he'd had less on his mind he might have found the whole exchange gut-wrenchingly sad. But he grabbed her hand before she'd even put on her coat and pulled her out of Smuggler's Cottage into the lane leading up the hill.

Once out of earshot of the cottage, she yanked her hand back.

'Whatever you feel about me,' she said in a low voice, 'do *not* involve my parents. They've done nothing wrong and don't deserve the police harassing them.'

'*Harass?* Why on earth would you think—?'

But she was already marching on up the hill, slipping through the broken stone wall and into the abandoned churchyard.

He hurried after her, exasperated. '*Phyllis!*'

But before he could catch her up, she'd turned to confront him. 'I'm warning you, Kieran. I'll make an official complaint!'

He'd never seen her so furious. Why, when nothing else he'd done or said had rattled her?

It was obvious, really. He'd involved her family.

Was that why she was working for Arlo Fisher? Had he threatened them?

Kieran held up his hands. 'Calm down,' he said. 'Whatever you've done, I can help you.'

Belatedly he remembered it was the worst thing to say – it invariably had the opposite effect.

'*Calm down?*' she repeated, as though she were now contemplating actual bodily harm. 'You have the nerve to barge into my parents' house and tell *me* to calm down?'

'What's he got on you? How is Fisher blackmailing you to work for him?'

'Why would you think that?' She glared at him. 'Maybe I enjoy the work.'

If she did, it wasn't the point. He tried again, using a gentler tone. 'Is Fisher forcing you to work for him? Has he threatened your family?'

Reluctantly, her gaze slid towards the cluster of thatched cottages down the hill. 'Maybe it's not *my* family you need to worry about,' she said softly.

'Fisher wouldn't dare threaten me. I'm a detective sergeant.'

Phyllis raised an eyebrow. She was calmer now, but her mood didn't appear to have improved.

'Why are you being so arrogant?' she said. 'No one can stop Fisher once he's set his mind on something. It's pointless even trying.'

'Fisher is targeting museums,' he said. 'We know that. He blackmails the curator into handing over the key or code to gain access to whatever storage facility they have. He helps himself to anything valuable and no one notices for weeks or even months, if ever.'

She didn't appear as shocked as he'd hoped. In fact, she hardly seemed to be paying attention, glancing again down the hill.

He frowned. What had caught her attention? The lane was empty.

'Let me have your full cooperation,' he said. 'Make a statement and I'll put in a good word for you.'

'Generous of you,' but her mocking tone was back.

'It's over,' he said. Why couldn't she understand that? What was that hold Fisher had on her? 'If you're worried about your family, we can protect them – Fisher can't do anything from a prison cell – but only if you help us.'

He hated that he had to add the caveat, but he had little choice in the matter.

Choice. There was that word again.

Had he got through to her?

She was regarding him sadly. 'Don't you get it? I'd do anything to keep my family safe.'

'I understand that, which is why—'

She'd taken her phone from her pocket, and Kieran saw Fisher's name on the screen.

'You *called* him?'

And then he saw the man himself walking up the hill. No, not walking, *swaggering,* and he was taken right back to his teenage years and a youth stamping on his hand: 'You're a *rat*' – stamp – 'from the *gutter.* How *dare* you date my sister?'

'This has all been to catch you,' Phyllis was saying. 'The only key to the muniment room at the museum is kept at the police station. We needed a police officer to help us, and that police officer was you. Forget about me and mine. Worry about your own family.'

The irony.

'I don't *have* a family,' he said. 'No wife or girlfriend, and I'm an only child. I've not spoken to my father since I joined the police, and I've no idea where my mother is or even if she's still alive.'

Phyllis didn't comment, just waited for him to work it out himself.

'Oh, no...'

Phyllis nodded. 'Esme.'

'He's got her? Why didn't you *say* anything earlier?' Kieran watched Fisher walking through the broken wall, wondering if he had time to call the station, call anyone, but what good would that do if they already had Esme? 'Bloody hell, Phyllis! All that rubbish about choices? *You* had a choice! And you chose *him*? Why couldn't you have trusted me?'

She shook her head. 'You didn't trust me.'

Now within earshot, Fisher was grinning.

And Kieran, for the first time in ten years, felt overwhelming panic.

How had he fallen for this, the most basic of scams? *How?*

'Drake,' Fisher said, tipping his head in acknowledgement. 'Long time no see.' And then he grinned. 'How's the hand?'

TWENTY-SEVEN

PRESENT DAY

Sunday

Dropping Harriet off at her apartment to catch up on her sleep, Ben arrived in the MIT office to a message from Caroline with the results of her post-mortem on Kyle Hayward.

The cause of death had been the pike, which didn't come as a surprise to anyone. The pike would have originally been attached to a wooden shaft but, despite a search of the clearing, there was no sign of it. Left buried in the soil for almost four hundred years, the shaft would have rotted away.

He didn't need to be a historian to know the pike would have belonged to a Civil War soldier, either accidentally dropped or abandoned after the 'skirmish' in the woods. It made for a convenient murder weapon, unearthed at just the right time.

Or the wrong time, depending on your point of view.

He fetched himself a black coffee from the machine and settled down to read his notes on Hayward's murder and try to make a connection to the attempt on Drake's life at Blackheath Hall.

Despite the exhaustive search, none of Hayward's personal belongings had been recovered. There was no sign of his metal detector, no bag to collect his finds, or any tools to help recover them. No phone, no wallet, only an old watch, worn loose on his wrist.

Was that significant? Hayward's features had looked gaunt; had he lost more weight recently? Stress? Perhaps related to money worries? There'd been bills still lying on the mat at his cottage. Could desperation have forced him to behave recklessly? To go night-hawking at a legally protected site without permission?

Drake's theory, that Kyle Hayward had been in costume to enable him to blend in with Oscar's ghost tour, was not entirely far-fetched. How long had these ghost tours been going on for? Oscar had told Harriet he was authorised to take his tour through the Gateway to the Dead and into the clearing beyond, but had he been telling the truth?

Ben got up to call DC Dakota Lawrence in from the outside office, and she'd stepped through the door before he'd even had a chance to return to his desk. She was the sharpest of the three detective constables working out of Raven's Edge but was often overlooked due to her quiet demeanour and creative way of thinking outside the box, which, unfortunately, often clashed with traditional policing. It also meant she tended to be lumbered with the more technical aspects of their investigations.

When Ben indicated that she should take a seat, she sat bolt upright with her notebook on her lap, eager to impress. Harriet had told him that Dakota was keen to spend more time out of the office. Well, now was her opportunity.

'Tell me about the ghost tours Oscar Montgomery's been running. I'm assuming he doesn't need a licence. How old is he anyway?'

Dakota's face fell a little at the banality of the question and she fumbled a little finding her place in her notebook. 'He's an enter-prising lad who I found very intelligent and knowledgeable about the history of Raven's Edge.'

She must have interviewed him when he came to the station with his mother. Presumably Oscar's statement was buried somewhere in the pile on his desk, waiting for him to have time to read it.

'He's only eighteen,' Dakota was saying, 'and I received the strong impression that his mother would have preferred him to go to university.'

Ben, having met Oscar's mother, had no trouble imagining how that conversation had gone.

'He's been running them for about six months, after organising the first one – originally as a one-off – last Halloween. They proved to be very popular, and he's been making a good living. He's always careful to include the various local businesses – his tours often end up at one of the pubs or cafés – so he's not treading on any toes. All the villagers seem to like him because he brings in extra custom, although everyone agrees that sometimes his ideas are a little too ambitious.'

'The Gateway to the Dead is on council land,' Ben said, 'but did he have permission to access the field beyond, which is part of the Blackheath Hall estate?'

'I phoned Lady Peony Weston, and she said she remembered receiving a letter from Oscar requesting permission to access the field for his ghost tour, but forgot about it and never replied. Lady Peony was very chatty and also said that her father sold the Gateway to the Dead – officially known as "the ruins of Buckley Abbey" – to the local council shortly before he died in 1983 so that they could look after it properly. The council organised an archaeological dig with indecent haste, which took place that summer. The media had a fine time accusing them of only being interested in finding the monks' legendary long-lost treasury, with reports that it would be worth several million "in today's money" – although that would have been in 1983.'

'I can imagine,' Ben said dryly. 'Those press reports must be responsible for the detectorists who've descended on the site ever since.'

'Lady Peony repeated that "the battlefield", as her family have always called the clearing, is still owned by the Weston family and she's never given permission for anyone to dig or excavate the area. There are signs warning people they'll be prosecuted if they do so, because the battlefield, like the abbey, is protected as a scheduled monument, but of course she doesn't have the time or finances to enforce that.'

Ben remembered the holes and trenches criss-crossing the battlefield. 'You said the archaeological dig didn't find anything?'

Dakota consulted her notes. 'It was mainly concentrated around the abbey ruins. The lead archaeologist's name was Bruce Ogilvy. He was able to identify the original walls of the abbey, hidden just below the surface soil. There were no human remains. He believed the monks removed the bodies of their brothers and benefactors to an unknown location – possibly the Priory over at Myra's Peak. However, they did find a mass grave in the far corner of the abbey land, right on the border with the battlefield, containing about twenty skeletons of men aged between mid-teens and middle-aged who'd died violently, presumably during the battle here in 1645. They were re-buried in the village graveyard, and the church holds a special service every year to commemorate them.'

'Definitely no treasure?'

For that Dakota didn't even need to look at her notes. 'Only the odd coin and buckle, but lots of lead shot. Bruce Ogilvy was quoted in the local newspaper at the time as saying, "Statistically, there should have been more to find, but sometimes that's how it goes." He's retired now but lives here in the village, if you want me to interview him?' she added hopefully. 'I think he liked Raven's Edge so much he stayed.'

Ben didn't miss the enthusiasm in her voice. 'That's useful to know, but there'd be no point interviewing him at the moment. Have you had any luck contacting the current Marquess of Blackheath, Giles Weston?'

Dakota shook her head. 'Lord Blackheath isn't at his London office or apartment, and his secretary, Jorge Alves, is worried because that's not his usual behaviour. Mr Alves was thinking of contacting us when I called him, and is planning on travelling down today to check out Lord Blackheath's country house in case something happened to him when he visited last week.'

'Lord Blackheath's "country house"?' Ben repeated before he could stop himself. 'How many does he have?' From the state of Blackheath Hall, he'd assumed the Weston family were hard up for cash.

Taking his comment literally, Dakota rifled through her notes. 'Lord Blackheath owns a London apartment, a sixteenth-century manor house in the north of the county, which he inherited from his maternal grandmother, and a villa in the South of France, which he inherited from his maternal aunt.'

Why would he want the responsibility of another house? It was probably why he was so keen to sell.

'How long has Lord Blackheath been missing?' he asked Dakota.

'Possibly a week? Mr Alves said the Marquess intended to meet with a property developer and spend some time freshwater fishing up at Raven's Glass.'

'Do we have a name for this property developer?'

When she regarded him blankly, he sighed. While he hated to always think the worst of his cousin… 'Could it have been Drew Elliott?'

'I don't know but I can find out?'

'It might be worth contacting Drew and asking if Lord Blackheath had an appointment.'

Assuming that Drew would tell them the truth.

There was a distinct pause before Dakota said, 'Yes, sir.'

He sighed. 'Don't worry, I'll do it. When did Lord Blackheath's secretary say he was visiting the county?'

'Today. Lord Blackheath has a cleaner who visits once a week. She went to the house yesterday, as usual, but was surprised to find it empty, with no sign of Lord Blackheath being in residence apart from some food in the fridge. Mr Alves said he wanted to check the house personally, to see if Lord Blackheath had left a message, or any clue as to where he could have gone. Mr Alves has the keys to the property and often works there with Lord Blackheath. I had the impression their relationship was more than just employer and employee. Mr Alves is *very* worried.'

'Call him back and ask if we could meet him there.'

'*We?*' Dakota's eyes lit up hopefully, even if the rest of her face remained professionally impassive.

'Yes, Dakota. Today's the day you finally leave the office.'

'Um, I do occasionally leave the office during working hours, just not as much as I'd—'

He raised an eyebrow.

She gathered up her notebook and pen and slithered quickly out of her seat. 'Going to make that call now, sir.'

The Marquess of Blackheath lived in a cosy medieval manor house, surrounded by a pretty garden filled with spring bulbs and blossom, but obviously not in the same league as Blackheath Hall. As Dakota parked her pale green electric Mini Cooper outside the front door, Giles Weston's secretary was already waiting for them – hovering, in fact. He was a slight, dark-haired man, who smiled shyly at Dakota but seemed intimidated by Ben.

Ben tried to relax his tiredness-induced frown but couldn't do anything about his height. He certainly wasn't going to slouch his way around the manor.

Once they'd introduced themselves, Jorge Alves admitted that he was reluctant to enter the house without a police presence.

Although he could just be saying that, Ben thought, as they waited for Alves to unlock the door. The default of any detective was to immediately assume guilt, but if there had been a bloody crime scene inside, the cleaner would have spotted it.

Alves led them into a small, sun-warmed hall, where paintings hung on every wall and the floorboards gleamed with wax polish. Again, the contrast with the rotting Blackheath Hall was stark. This house was also a much-loved home, but it'd been regularly maintained and modernised whenever necessary. Blackheath Hall looked as though it was stuck in time, somewhere about 1536.

'I was about to report Giles as a missing person,' Alves admitted, in an American-tinged accent. 'He doesn't usually go silent and always responds to my messages immediately. This is very unusual behaviour.' His voice wobbled on the last sentence.

In which case, Ben thought irritably, why didn't you contact us before?

'When was the last time you heard from Lord Blackheath?' he asked, wandering through into a sun-dappled sitting room, where crowded bookshelves lined the walls and family photos covered every surface. Giles Weston's home was certainly very welcoming.

'A week ago,' Alves said.

Ben watched him straighten a couple of pictures and check one of the houseplants to see if it needed watering. Even before he'd asked the question, he knew the answer.

'Does Lord Blackheath have a significant other, or children?'

Alves's brown cheeks took on a rosy hue. 'Um, that would be me. That is, I'm the significant other and he doesn't have any children. He's said, quite often, that the title will die with him and seems quite unbothered by it. He tells everyone to call him "Giles". He's a lovely man...' This was accompanied by a distinct sniff.

While Ben was still wondering whether this was a calculated performance, Dakota patted Alves's shoulder soothingly. At least she didn't hug him. Damn, he missed Harriet.

'Don't worry,' Dakota told Alves, 'we'll find him for you.'

Ben tried not to sigh. He'd forgotten to have the 'Don't make promises you can't keep' talk with Dakota.

Alves rallied, apparently expecting great things from them, and gave them a tour of the house, taking them up the wide wooden staircase to the upper floors. Even the boards beneath their feet creaked in a friendly way. Ben kept an eye out for signs of a break-in, a disturbance or any kind of altercation as they checked each room. There were none. It was very odd.

Alves led them back downstairs.

'How was Lord Blackheath's relationship with his family?' Ben asked, more for something to say than anything else.

'He was very attached to his grandfather, Jasper Weston, from whom he inherited the title,' Alves said. 'His father died of leukaemia when he was ten, and his parents had been through an acrimonious divorce, so he was raised by Jasper and his wife, Ariella. This was originally Ariella's family home and nothing to do with the Westons. Jasper was the old Marquess's nephew and not expected to inherit...' Alves shrugged. 'But the title and estate always go through the male line. I think Jasper felt sorry for his cousins, Peony and Rose. He was always bailing them out financially.'

That was worth knowing. 'And the current Lord Blackheath? How's his relationship with Lady Peony and Lady Rose?'

'Oh, that's very good. He likes them and they often spoke on the phone – until about three years ago, anyway. Peony had always been very friendly but, as she got older, she became a little more reclusive and said she didn't like talking on the phone. Giles didn't want to just barge in on them at Blackheath. He paid for the Hall to be rewired a couple of years ago. It also needs a new roof, which Giles can't afford at the moment, and yes, he *was* trying to persuade them to move out, perhaps into a smaller house in the same village if they wanted to stay near their friends, for which he was perfectly happy to pay.'

'Giles wants to sell the house?' Dakota asked, even though they knew that. 'Does he have a buyer lined up?'

'There are a few people interested. Have you visited the Hall? I've only seen pictures but it's more of a mini castle than a house – far bigger than this place. Giles told me it's just outside the boundary of Raven's Edge, and therefore the planning regulations are a little more relaxed.'

'Did he mention any names?'

Dakota, Ben had to admit, was far better at pretending to be guileless than Harriet.

Alves frowned. 'It's something Giles is dealing with personally, but this week I've been fielding calls from someone called Elliott – Lou Elliott? – who's being very... persistent.'

Ben hid a smile. '*Drew* Elliott?'

'Yes, that's him! He's quite... a force of nature.'

'Has he threatened Lord Blackheath?' Ben knew his cousin could be ruthless – he'd hardly get to his level of business if he wasn't – but, as far as he knew, Drew had never resorted to threats or violence.

Unless he paid someone else to do that for him?

'No, no, nothing like that,' Alves said hastily. 'Quite personable, really. I just got the impression he's... er, not used to people saying "no" to him.'

He had that right.

'Did Lord Blackheath mention what Drew Elliott intends to do with the property?'

'Giles joked that Drew would tear the old place down and build a housing estate. He pretended to be unaffected, but I could tell it would have made him sad. He's never cared much for his title; it's more about the history of his family. He'd love to sell to someone who'd care for it, like Peony's father, the old Marquess, but, realistically, he knows the house is too far gone to save.'

They continued their tour of the house but there was no trace of Giles. The cleaner couldn't be sure if he'd slept in his bed since he'd arrived from London – he always made it himself and wasn't a messy person. There was food in his fridge, but the milk had gone two days past its sell-by date. There was a train timetable lying on the desk in his study, with the Norchester train times highlighted.

'Giles often travelled by train,' Alves explained. 'He said it gave him time to catch up on his work. Not sure why he'd want to go to Norchester though...'

Norchester was the station to change at if you wanted to go to Raven's Edge, Calahurst or Port Rell – where Drew Elliott lived.

Ben exchanged an uneasy glance with Dakota.

'Mr Alves, I think we need to consider that Lord Blackheath may be a missing person...'

TWENTY-EIGHT

Drake had spent an eye-opening couple of days, narrowing down the list of people who wanted to see him dead. It had been worryingly long but, when he'd begun calling on them, he'd found them oddly sympathetic – once they'd stopped laughing.

'Wear a *costume*?' was what usually set them off, followed by a helpful explanation of how they *would* kill him should the need ever arise.

There was one last person on his list.

The one he'd been putting off until DS March had let slip the recent events at Blackheath Hall.

Now he stood in the north-west corner of The Square in Raven's Edge and stared at the village's least favourite café: Spellbound.

It was a mystery to him why it should be so unpopular. The coffee machine was the latest and most expensive brand on the market, and the cakes and pastries were delicious and delivered fresh every day. There was even a sign: 'Free fortune telling with every pot of tea'. Who else offered that? He'd have thought the visitors to Raven's Edge, in search of their supernatural thrills, would have lapped it up. Yet still the place was empty.

At least there'd be no witnesses.

He shoved open the door. Unlike the other colourful, half-timbered houses on The Square, the café had been painted navy-blue and the ancient stone steps went down instead of up. The interior was so gloomy he almost cracked his head on the low door lintel as he went inside.

He automatically headed towards the back, his preferred place to sit. There was a pretty inglenook fireplace, but it looked strangely uninviting despite the warmth radiating out into the room. He did an about turn and chose a seat beside the window.

The waitress, who was also the barista, appeared beside him. She had dark-blonde hair, tied back in a stubby ponytail, and wore head-to-toe black, relieved by thin strands of silver chain wound around her neck and wrists.

'Are those to ward off evil spirits?' he said without thinking.

Phyllis Halfpenny did tend to have that effect on him.

'If so, they're not working,' she replied, completely deadpan. 'Can I take your order or would you like a few more minutes?'

'That all depends...' He made a show of picking up the menu. 'Are you likely to try and poison me?'

'*Poison* you?'

'Because shooting me didn't work.'

'I...' For a moment he thought she was going to admit to it, but then the colour drained from her face.

'I had no choice,' she whispered. 'You know that.'

Really? She was going with *that*?

She was such a hypocrite. Didn't she remember that time when she'd warned *him* about choice?

'You'll always have a choice,' he mocked, and then noticed her fingers were clutching a neighbouring table for support and she seemed on the verge of being sick.

He'd forgotten his number one rule.

Pay attention.

What was the *other* thing she'd said?

You know that.

She'd thought he was talking about their past, not their present.

It *hadn't* been her.

But who did that leave?

As Phyllis swayed on her feet, Drake swore beneath his breath, then got up and shoved her into his seat, taking the one opposite. 'I'm talking about *two nights ago*, when someone dressed as a Civil War soldier tried to kill me, *not* the good old days.'

Her eyes widened. '*What?* But that wasn't me!'

'So I gather,' was his dry response. 'Any idea who did do it? Because I'm running out of suspects here.'

She regarded him blankly, her eyes that curious hazel colour, but at least they weren't glowing gold. It was too dark in here. Perhaps if they were in daylight...

Her expression turned suspicious. 'Why are you staring at me?'

He told her the truth. Why not? What did he have to lose?

'I was wondering if you could do that' – he wiggled his fingers in the direction of her eyes – 'thing you do, and tell me who *did* shoot me.'

It was the wrong thing to have said. She closed down immediately, pushing back from the table and getting up, walking back towards the counter.

'I think you'd better leave.'

'Do you remember Carl Nicholls?'

She paused, but didn't turn around.

'He was the detective constable the night of your performance at the museum. You told him some tall tale about a car hidden in the forest and not to trust a friend, and you were right. He was murdered a few years later.'

'I'm sorry,' she said.

Perhaps if he laid it on thick?

'Carl had been promoted, was about to propose to his girl, and was murdered by someone he knew.'

'I saw the story on the news. I recognised him immediately. I'm sorry for your loss. He seemed kind.'

Kinder than *him*, at any rate. Was that what she meant?

'Was it luck?' Drake asked. 'A guess pulled out of thin air? How did you *know* someone would kill him?'

'What's the point in me telling you anything?' She finally turned, her expression unexpectedly hard. 'Your heart is closed, remember? I can't help you. You don't believe.'

'Make me.'

'I'd be wasting my time.'

But the hesitation was there.

He pounced on it. 'That night at the museum, you saw it happen... somehow. Am I right? Whatever it is that you do, inside your head you saw Carl's death and tried to warn him.'

She dropped eye contact, staring at her hands instead. She still held the little notebook to take his order, and was turning it over and over.

'I try to be vague,' Phyllis said, her voice low, as though worried they'd be overheard, 'but Carl kept on pushing. I knew you were with the police and it was some kind of test. Fisher saw you both in the audience and warned me beforehand. When I saw you sitting there, with your supercilious attitude, I was annoyed and I lost my temper. I'd never normally tell someone something like that. I'd tell them some nonsense—'

He couldn't help it. His eyebrow went up.

She slammed the notebook down on the counter, walking around it to the other side.

Putting it between them like a barrier?

Excellent. He was getting to her.

'I think you'd better leave,' she said.

Drake forced a more conciliatory tone. 'So, how do you do it?'

'Do what?'

'You know what I'm talking about. How do you talk to dead people?'

'I don't talk to dead people,' she said.

'Don't lie to—'

'They talk to me.'

What could he say to *that*?

Phyllis's lips quirked, as though reading his mind. 'No one ever believes me, so I keep it to myself. It's easier that way. People already think I'm weird, so I play up to it. I put on a performance, the kind of thing everyone expects. I add a lot of waffle about names beginning with "A" or whatever, because that's what everyone wants, and then I slip in a truth when no one's paying attention. Hopefully, the person I speak to remembers it when it becomes relevant.'

'OK... How do the dead talk to *you*?'

(He was *so* glad no one could overhear this conversation.)

'Sometimes I'll hear a tiny snippet, perhaps just one sentence, but it'll be as clear as anything inside my head. Like tuning in to a radio station. Sometimes I can sense a presence, usually limited to an emotion: happy, sad, benign, evil. Sometimes I'll catch a glimpse of something, a shadow or echo of the past... But you still don't believe me,' she added sadly.

'I'm *trying* here, it's just... Well, I don't believe in ghosts.'

Unexpectedly, Phyllis smiled, tilting her head to one side. 'And how's that working out for you?'

He returned the smile, but it took effort. 'Not great, actually.'

She slid a cup beneath the coffee machine and turned it on. 'Kieran Drake, why are you *really* here?'

Had fate led him?

He got up and went over to the counter, leaning on it.

She didn't move away.

'I suppose I need your help,' he said.

'*My* help?'

'Have you heard of Blackheath Hall?'

She gave him an old-fashioned look.

'OK, I can see that was a stupid question. There are lots of ghosts in residence, I take it?'

'It's the Gateway to the Dead,' she said, as though that explained everything. 'The area around the abbey was a peaceful place, even after the monks left and King Henry's men destroyed it. But then the soldiers came and fought each other...'

'That was centuries ago and they moved all the bodies to the churchyard.'

'Fear and pain have imprinted themselves on the land. It draws other spirits there. It's a horrible place.' She shook her head. 'I never go near it.'

It wasn't a favourite of his either but... 'What about the *house*?'

'The house hidden behind the wall?'

'That's the one.' He regarded her dubiously. 'What can... er, you tell me about it?'

Phyllis closed her eyes and took hold of his hand.

'Blackheath Hall is not a happy house. Awful things have happened there.'

'Awful things happen everywhere.'

And this was getting him nowhere.

'Brother shall deliver up the brother to death,' she was saying.

'Yes, I know that bit.'

'And the father the child; and the children shall rise up against their parents.'

'OK, that bit's new.'

'It's from the Bible,' she said, opening her eyes.

'I didn't know that.' Churches had not been a regular port of call for the Drake family. 'Are you talking about Peony and Rose?' he ventured. They'd been getting along fine whenever he'd seen them, and were noticeably affectionate towards each other. 'Or some other family that lived there? I don't want to sound critical, but this isn't very helpful.'

'That was the message.' She sighed and closed her eyes again. 'I see a woman in a red dress...'

Also not helpful but it made a change from a woman in black. Or white. Or grey. Every big old house seemed to have a grey lady haunting it.

He kept that to himself.

'She's dancing,' Phyllis said. 'She's happy.'

'Is she the one who's haunting Blackheath Hall?' Something he *never* thought he'd say. 'What about the Civil War soldier who knocks on the door every night? Major Lord John Weston?'

'There are many souls trapped at Blackheath Hall.'

Of *course* there were.

'This is hopeless.' He pulled his hand away. If she was offended, she didn't show it. 'I don't even know why I'm here.'

'You're trying to find out who wants you dead,' she said, practical as ever.

'I know I wasn't shot by a ghost!'

'Then why *are* you here, Kieran Drake?'

For closure? The thing about Phyllis Halfpenny was that she'd known him since he was a child. She knew everything about him. He couldn't pretend or put on an act, the way he did with everyone else. It was such a cliché but, basically, he could be himself.

He found himself telling her the truth. 'I'm worried I've started something I can't finish. Like my old dad, I went into this job unprepared and stirred something up, something that should have stayed in the past. I'm worried someone's going to get hurt – and it'll be because of me being my usual smartass self. Do you know what I've been doing these past few days? Going around my competitors and asking which one of them tried to kill me. They think it's hilarious. Kieran Drake, caught at last – by a ghost!'

'You don't believe in ghosts,' Phyllis reminded him.

'No, I don't.' He sighed and took a five-pound note from his wallet for the coffee he hadn't ordered but that she'd made and then left cooling in the machine, apparently forgotten. He placed it on the counter. 'Thanks for humouring me. I won't hold you up any longer.'

'Hold me up?' She looked pointedly around the café. 'From what?'

He'd forgotten her sense of humour. *That* was the Phyllis he remembered.

Playing tag amongst the headstones in the old churchyard as children, with Arlo and Bailey.

How long ago had *that* been?

Those days were *long* gone.

As he stepped out through the door, Drake realised she was following him. Perhaps she was planning on locking up and going home? It wasn't as if she had any customers.

'Goodbye,' he said and turned away, almost missing her reply.

'You don't have to *believe* in ghosts, Kieran Drake. You just have to know when to duck.'

What?

'Wait!' He placed his palm against the door to prevent her closing it on him. 'Was that one of your... you know, "predictions"?'

Her eyebrow quirked again and he noticed her eyes were still hazel. Had he imagined the gold that night? He took his hand away from the door, feeling slightly stupid.

'Maybe,' she said, in that distant way he used to find so irritating. 'Or maybe it's just good advice?'

She shut the door.

And Drake walked away, wondering what the hell had just happened.

TWENTY-NINE

TEN YEARS PREVIOUSLY

Kieran's first reaction was to punch that self-satisfied smirk from Arlo Fisher's face. It was why his father had paid for those boxing lessons after all. But punching Fisher as a civilian would have fewer consequences than punching him as a detective sergeant, so Kieran side-stepped him instead, intending to not give him the satisfaction of a response.

Fisher held up one finger. 'Wait,' he said, scrolling through his phone.

Like he was a *dog*? Well, Fisher could whistle.

'Your investigation has put a huge dent in my profit margin,' Fisher said, without looking up. 'Your spiteful little circular to every police station in the county has raised suspicions about the motivation behind our performances. They're no longer seen as altruistic, so the venues are being cancelled one after the other, for the most transparently petty reasons, and I'm not happy about it.'

'I don't care,' Kieran said.

'You will.' Fisher turned his phone so that he could see the screen.

It took a second for him to understand what he was supposed to be looking at. He recognised the background first. A cast-iron fireback, carved with an oak tree design, surrounded by herring-bone brickwork and a stone mantelpiece. As his brain recognised each part of the familiar fireplace, he realised there was a slight figure slumped on a wooden chair beside it.

It was Esme, wearing her full-length white cotton nightdress, her grey head bowed.

Was she sleeping?

Was she *dead*?

His stomach curled in on itself, the contents wanting out.

Instead, he threw himself on Fisher without care or thought.

But Fisher was a head taller and several stones heavier and, for the second time in ten years, Kieran's face made contact with Fisher's fist. Hard.

The blow sent him reeling but he staggered back to his feet, raising his fists. 'If you've hurt her in any way—'

'You'll do what?' Fisher mocked. 'Come on, street rat. I could do with a laugh. You're a bit slow, to be honest. We were expecting you to pick up on this *much* earlier.'

Was that why Esme was in her nightdress? She usually rose at seven, even at the weekend, and only stayed in bed if she was ill.

Fisher glanced back at the screen. 'Game old bird, your grandma. Put up quite a fight. I couldn't go myself because she'd have recognised me and given me an earful, but one of my lads is going to be sporting a black eye for a while.'

Good for Esme, but Kieran kept his voice neutral. 'What do you need me to do?'

'Haven't you worked it out?'

Kieran sighed. 'You're targeting museums up and down the country as part of some "history comes alive" initiative. Phyllis puts on her melodramatic performance and while the audience's attention is otherwise engaged, you break into the safe or vault, or wherever they keep the valuable and forgotten stuff, and then you help yourself while the alarms are switched off. Am I right so far?'

'Very good.' Fisher tucked the phone back into his pocket. 'Best of all, whatever we take won't be missed for weeks, months, even years. It's the perfect crime – and it was working very well until you shoved your nose in it.'

'Sorry,' Kieran said, bracing himself for another punch, but Fisher merely smiled.

'Still, every cloud, blah, blah, blah. The muniment room at the museum in Raven's Edge is proving harder to get into than usual. There's a key, of course, but the senile old curator can't remember where it is.'

The curator had seemed alert enough to him, but one frail elderly man standing up against however many Fisher had working for him...

It wasn't good odds.

Again keeping his tone neutral (politely interested rather than frantic, as his carefully constructed new life dissolved around him), 'What did you do to him?'

'Nothing – yet,' Fisher said. 'This is where *you* come in. It's your chance to be a hero and save the day.'

It wasn't hard to work out the direction this was going to take.

'There's a second key,' Fisher said, 'held at the police station for "safekeeping". I need a police officer to retrieve it for me – and I remembered my old friend, Kieran Drake.'

It was as though he'd regressed to the age of fifteen. 'I'm not your friend.'

Did it matter what he said? He'd stepped right into Fisher's trap. What couldn't he do with a cop in his pocket? Why stop at museum theft?

Except, for that to work, he'd have to hold Esme indefinitely.

Another wave of nausea hit.

'What if I refuse?' he asked, more to keep Fisher talking while he formulated a plan. The man appeared to be on his own and—

Fisher stepped closer, bending his head so that his mouth was level with Kieran's ear, as though they were in a packed club rather than an abandoned graveyard. 'One, two, three. Retrieve the key,

open the muniment room, help us load the boxes into the van –
then Grandma goes free.'

'What boxes?'

'There are six cardboard boxes in the muniment room.
According to my research, they've been there since 1924, when
they were donated by the Marquess of Blackheath. He thought it
was a worthless assortment of Victorian knick-knacks and holiday
souvenirs. I suspect it's a collection of the usual chalices, croziers,
and monstrances donated by various wealthy benefactors to
Buckley Abbey, from at least the fourteenth century right up until
that land grab known as the Dissolution of the Monasteries.'

Kieran stared at him. Was he *serious*?

'The lost treasury? That's a myth – like every other story in
Raven's Edge. There's no hidden room, no buried treasure.'

'It's very much real. I've cross-referenced some old
photographs in the County Archives with the surviving records
from the abbey. That stupid Marquess had no idea what he owned.
Strapped for cash and he gave it all away without even bothering
with a valuation. The museum was just as bad. Any jeweller could
have told them how valuable that stuff was.'

'And instead of doing them a favour and telling them they've
got a fortune locked away, you're going to steal it from them?'

How the hell had Arlo Fisher, a man from a good family and a
comfortable background, ended up as a common thief? He'd had
every opportunity and this was what he did with it: researching
long-lost valuables and the museums they were likely to be held in.

Now he wanted Kieran to help.

And Kieran couldn't see any way out.

How could he take the risk that Fisher would carry out his
threat to harm Esme?

The alternative would be to confide in DI Davenport – but
how far could he trust a man he barely knew? Wouldn't it be safer
for Esme if he agreed to what Fisher wanted? Stealing a bunch of
old silver from a museum that didn't even know of its existence?
Who would that hurt?

Fisher was watching him closely. 'You'd better not be trying to sneak your way out of this, street rat. Because if I'm caught, I'll make sure you take the fall. But you're going to do your very best to ensure we won't fail, aren't you?'

'Yes,' Kieran said without hesitation.

What choice did he have after all?

THIRTY

PRESENT DAY

Sunday

The call from Ash came as Ben and Dakota drove back to Raven's Edge.

'Hi, boss.' Ash's perpetual cheerfulness was even evident over the crackly signal. 'We've found another body.'

Ben exhaled, counting to five. Ash made it sound as though he'd accidentally tripped over it on his way to The Witch's Brew.

Knowing Ash, perhaps he had.

'Where?'

'The Gateway to the Dead,' Ash said.

Wonderful.

Before he could comment, Ash added, 'It's skeletonised, and Dr Serrano says it could be several hundred years old.'

That was something. A corpse that old was not his problem.

'It's missing the skull,' Ash was saying, 'but Dr Serrano is sure it'll turn up.'

On its way to Frank McAllister at Norchester University, no doubt. How many other random skulls were likely to be floating around Raven's Edge?

It was probably best not to think about that.

He also knew the answer to his next question but asked it anyway.

'Where exactly was the skeleton found?'

'Directly beneath the body of Kyle Hayward, after Dr Serrano continued to excavate.'

It was not hard to work out what had happened. Hayward must have been in the process of digging the skeleton up – he'd already found the skull, now he wanted the rest – when someone had stabbed him with the pike and shoved him into the same grave – only to be disturbed by the ghost tour before they could bury him.

So what *had* Hayward found that was worth killing him for?

Jewellery? Coins? Ben tried to remember what else Kyle Hayward and Adam Buchanan had proudly displayed in their cabinets.

One big find that would make his name – and his fortune.

But, as a detectorist, why was Hayward interested in a centuries-old *skeleton*? That wouldn't be worth anything.

'Hello?' Ash said. 'Are you still there, sir?'

'Thanks, Ash,' he said automatically. 'Good work.' Even though Ash hadn't done much more than turn up and report back. 'I'll be along shortly.'

Ben asked Dakota to drop him off at the Gateway to the Dead and he walked the rest of the way down the little overgrown lane, turning his collar up against the bitter wind following behind him. He hoped it wasn't going to rain but the sky to the west was already dark enough to blend seamlessly with the surrounding forest.

Compared to his last visit there were very few CSIs remaining on site and the only police officers were uniformed: one beside the ruined arch and the second on the other side of the clearing, standing next to the path that led up to Blackheath Manor. There was, however, a small crowd of interested onlookers who murmured excitedly as he approached and ducked beneath the tape. They included Oscar Montgomery, who'd discovered Hayward's body with Harriet, and Oscar's friend, Stuart Huntingdon. They were no longer in costume but wore jeans and hoodies, like any other teen. Although, Ben realised suddenly, Stuart hadn't been in costume when he'd turned up late for the ghost tour. Something about a dry cleaner?

He called Dakota. 'I need you to check something for me,' he said. 'Contact all the local dry cleaners and find out whether Stuart Huntingdon left a Royalist Civil War costume with them – more commonly known as a *Cavalier* costume, I should think – and, if so, whether he's collected it. The dates are particularly important.'

'Right on it, sir,' was her cheerful reply.

He slid the phone back into his pocket and, careful to watch his step, headed for the tent. Lucia Serrano was the only person inside, crouched in the bottom of a trench that was larger than he remembered. In there with her lay a skeleton in surprisingly good condition, although the bones were no longer articulated.

Lucia smiled when she saw him, immediately climbing out of the trench and brushing herself off. 'Ben! I wasn't expecting to see you here again!'

'Dead body,' he said, thumbing in the direction of the skeleton. 'It's my job.'

She laughed. 'But it's a very *old* body.'

'Found in the same grave as a *new* body.'

She frowned. 'Strange that.'

'I believe my sergeant and I found the skull earlier, in the house of Kyle Hayward – the previous occupant of this trench.'

If he'd been talking to Caroline, his ex-wife and the Force's forensic anthropologist, she'd have told him off for making assumptions but really, the chances of *two* skeletons being linked to the same person?

Slim.

'Anything left to identify him?' he asked. 'I'm assuming it's a "him"?'

'I believe so, but that kind of thing is really Dr McAllister's area. I just do the digging. No clothes remaining. They could have rotted away but soldiers from the Civil War were usually stripped of their clothing and other valuables before burial. It's unusual that he wasn't tipped into a mass grave with his compatriots though...'

'Could he date from a different time period? I'd assumed he was the original owner of the pike.'

'Possibly... According to the soil samples we took from the pike it was definitely found here, although not necessarily in this specific grave. You could ask for carbon dating for the skeleton, but that'd be expensive.'

'If it's not a modern corpse, it's all irrelevant anyway.'

'I know,' she said sadly. 'It would be nice to give him a name though. Perhaps if there was some press interest, the university might make a project of him. As I mentioned, soldiers from the Civil War were usually stripped before burial but there are traces that he *could* have been clothed – and in those days, clothes were considered too valuable to bury. The pike was a wonderful find but in the grave itself we've found shoe buckles, possibly silver, and some gold coins, meaning he might have been of high status—'

'Or a thief.'

'Yes, but look at this.' She went over to a long collapsible table where she'd set up several transparent plastic containers for the bones and related evidence. She picked up the smallest box and handed it to him, adding, '*Don't* open it and *don't* drop it,' as though he was a small child.

Intrigued, he held the box beneath one of the lights. Inside were two dirt-encrusted yellow lumps, which didn't look like anything much.

'Erm...?' he said, glancing back at her.

'Rings!' she said. 'Gold rings set with semi-precious stones. They might even be *precious* stones! We won't know for sure until we remove the dirt properly.'

'So his clothes were too valuable to bury him in but the gold rings were OK?'

'Exactly! Meaning it's more likely he *was* clothed.'

'And buried in a hurry.' Murdered, in other words. 'Can't you...?' He waved in the direction of the skeleton.

'No, not my area of expertise. For that you need Frank McAllister, and he'll need to examine the entire skeleton. And if the skeleton *is* almost four hundred years old—'

'No one's going to be in a hurry to identify him – or pay to have him identified. Shame,' Ben said, handing her back the box.

'There *could* be interest,' Lucia said, 'if the skeleton is someone of status. From an archaeological point of view, it would be a huge find.'

But it was becoming increasingly obvious that the skeleton wasn't the original owner of the pike. Were there other weapons still hidden beneath the clearing, waiting to be discovered, or had the night-hawks found them all?

Ben remembered this grave had originally been uncovered by Kyle Hayward. He'd seen similar rings in Hayward's display cabinet. Aside from the skull, what *else* had Hayward taken from the grave? And had the murderer then stolen them from him?

'DI Taylor?' One of the uniformed officers stuck his head through the entrance to the tent, and Ben's first thought was that another body had been found, but instead, 'There's a man waiting by the Gateway to the Dead who'd like a word with you.'

Ben glanced across the battlefield to see an elderly gentleman, perhaps in his early seventies, wearing boots, cargo trousers, T-shirt, and leather jacket, accessorised with a wide-brimmed hat. While Ben would hate to stereotype anyone, it wasn't hard to work out who he was.

'Hi there,' the man said in a very faint Scottish accent as Ben approached. 'I'm Bruce Ogilvy. I understand you've found an old skeleton, and I wonder if I can be of assistance?' He showed Ben his driving licence as proof of ID. 'You see, forty years ago, I was the archaeologist in charge of the Buckley Abbey dig.'

THIRTY-ONE

When Harriet walked into the courtyard of Blackheath Hall later that afternoon, a silver Audi was parked outside the door, with a small removal truck next to it, where two men were struggling to load old-fashioned trunks into the back – the kind of thing wealthy passengers would have taken on a cruise about a hundred years ago. Where on earth had Peony *found* them?

More to the point, where had Peony found a removal van?

Harriet walked faster, only to almost collide with Mal Graham coming down the steps with a crate labelled 'books'.

'Hi, Harriet.'

'Um... hi?' What was *he* doing here?

Sam appeared on the steps behind him. 'Brianna Graham sent a removal van,' he said. 'Genius move on her part. Lady Peony found a lot of things that she decided belonged to her and Rose – mainly clothes and books. I suspect the books legally belong to the Marquess, but I can't see him missing Jane Austen and the Brontës, even if they are first editions. He'd probably gift Peony and Rose his entire library if he thought that would get them out sooner.'

'I heard that, young man!' Lady Peony's voice wafted from the great hall behind him.

Sam rolled his eyes but added, 'The boss went to visit the Marquess earlier, but no one's seen him for a week, so he's officially a missing person.'

'We're doing all this for Giles, yet he doesn't even have the manners to show up!' Peony shouted.

'That's not good,' Harriet said in a hopefully quieter voice, so that Peony wouldn't overhear. 'And coming so hard on the back of a murder and attempted murder in the vicinity of Blackheath Hall...'

'It's going to look like we posted a guard on the wrong people,' Sam finished.

Didn't it just.

Sam stepped aside to let her pass, but she was distracted by Mal handing up the crate of books to one of the removal men as though it weighed nothing. For someone who normally spent all day in an office, he seemed very fit...

And she was very shallow. Swiftly she turned away before he could spot her ogling, only to find Sam regarding her in a very judgy way.

'Malcolm Graham is the Managing Director of Graham Media,' he said, so laconically it took a moment for her to realise he was making a point. 'Why is he supervising a house move for two little old ladies?'

'Erm... For his grandmother? Brianna did say she was worried about the ladies' safety.'

Sam thumbed in Mal's direction. 'Him, care about two little old ladies he's never met? More likely he cares about *you* and needed an excuse to see you again.'

'*Me?*' Hopefully she didn't appear too pleased. 'Really? Why?'

He gave her an old-fashioned look. 'Would you like me to use shorter words? Harriet, he *likes* you.'

'No, he doesn't,' she said, far too quickly. 'As you said, he's Mal Graham. I'm only a detective sergeant. We have nothing in common.'

'I've never, in my *life*, heard you refer to yourself as "only" anything, Harriet March, and I've known you since you were five years old.' His eyes narrowed. 'Your mum really did a number on you, didn't she?'

'What does my mother have to do with this?'

'Nothing "in common"? What rubbish! It's exactly what *she* would have said. You only need to have *one* thing in common, and from the glances you two are trying *not* to send each other, I suspect you already have it.'

'Sam!'

But he'd already turned back into the house as Mal materialised beside her with the speed of a vampire, somehow conjuring two coffees with The Witch's Brew logo on the side.

Where had he got *those*?

He handed one over. 'Cappuccino, right?' he said. 'Isn't that what you like? I ordered it from The Witch's Brew when I heard you were on your way, and they deliver. Isn't that great?'

How had he known she was on her way? Unless Kat had spotted her? And since when had The Witch's Brew delivered?

Maybe they did – if you were Mal Graham.

He tugged an orange paper bag from his pocket and shook it under her nose. 'I have muffins...'

She spoke without thinking. 'Are you seriously trying to seduce me with cake?' And then wanted to sink through the ground.

'Maybe.' He grinned. 'Is it working?'

She glanced towards the open door to the great hall, hoping Sam was no longer in earshot.

'I asked Kat what kind you liked best,' Mal said. 'She recommended the gingerbread and the apple crumble.'

Kat would be right.

Meanwhile, Sam, Peony, Pete and Freddie were probably listening through the open door, not to mention the two random removal men hovering by their van. The juicy titbit that Mal Graham had bought Harriet March coffee and cake would be all over the village by tomorrow, if not sooner.

'I'm not due to start my shift yet,' she said, adding, more brusquely than she'd intended, 'Walk with me.'

Mal regarded the darkening sky dubiously. 'If you like. Er, where did you want to go?'

'The garden.' *Well* out of earshot of those in the great hall. There ought to be some kind of bench to sit on, and then they could drink their coffee. In *private*.

The garden at Blackheath Hall had been a seventeenth-century afterthought, planted on the far side of the original medieval wall surrounding the house. It must once have been quite formally laid out, perhaps with little gravel paths, low box hedging and an enclosing wall of its own. But now...

'It's very overgrown,' Mal said, as he unsnagged a dead spiral of bramble from what were probably very expensive jeans without complaint. 'It must have been beautiful in its day.'

This wasn't one of her better ideas, Harriet thought, but at least the wall sheltered them from the howling wind.

'Peony told me her father was mad keen on gardening,' she said, 'and liked to open the garden to the public. I suppose that stopped when he died and Peony found it all too much to cope with.'

'My grandmother said Peony was a lot of fun when she was younger, and quite indomitable.'

Was that a polite way of saying 'stubborn'?

'She's still like that now,' Harriet agreed. Mal held back a thick branch of camellia to allow her to continue along the path. It had fat pink buds, about to burst into flower. 'I bet this place was stunning twenty years ago.'

'It's quite spectacular now.' He pointed to the swathes of primroses and daffodils peeping out from beneath the deciduous shrubs. 'I guess nature takes care of itself.'

They followed the length of what had once been a flagstone path rather than trying to force a route through the undergrowth. As they walked, Mal told her about the books his family's company were about to publish, and she listened with interest, sipping at her coffee, which was exactly how she liked it, and thinking how nice it was to talk to a man like this, rather than have to pretend to be interested in something she wasn't, like baking.

Mal had already seen her at her worst, too. She grinned, remembering the first time they'd met, at a masquerade ball when she thought he'd been about to jump into his father's lake. And then later, when they'd argued across the unconscious body of a murderer.

Was Sam right? *Did* he 'like' her?

But where did that leave her and Misha?

Although, if the lack of replies to her messaging was anything to go by, there was no 'her and Misha'.

The path came to an end at a decorative wrought-iron gate – although the wall on either side had collapsed. It was the same gate she and Ben had walked through the night she'd found Kyle Hayward's body.

The night of the ghost tour.

The night of her ill-fated date with Misha.

Mal pushed open the gate. 'After you.'

She hesitated. 'This path leads to the Gateway to the Dead. My colleagues are still working there.'

And nothing said 'romance' like an open grave.

'Oh, OK,' Mal said. 'Should we head back?'

Yes, because that sky was becoming blacker by the minute, but then she saw another path leading past the garden and further up the hill, and said, 'What about that way?' because she was enjoying herself and the only thing waiting for her back at Blackheath Hall was the thankless task of trying to persuade two very obstinate old ladies to leave it.

'Are we *sure* that's a path though?' he said, but took it anyway, holding back some of the larger branches for her.

No one had been here for a very long time. The path was so narrow even she had to turn sideways to scrape through the bushes.

A single raven watched their progress disdainfully, before issuing a discordant croak and flying away.

Was that a warning?

'I hope you have a map app on your phone,' Mal called back. 'It would be embarrassing to become lost.'

Particularly if you were a police officer.

'Have you ever *tried* to use a map app in the King's Forest?' she asked. 'Most of the time you're just a blue dot on a green splodge, and that's if you can even get a signal.'

Suddenly, the trees cleared to reveal a neat grassy hill with a little stone house built into the side. Around the top of the house were miniature battlements and, squatting on each corner, a stone raven.

'It's a little castle,' Harriet said.

Mal stopped but she continued towards the entrance, intrigued.

'Is it a summer house?'

He grimaced. 'I believe it's a mausoleum, perhaps early or mid-nineteenth century, going by the gothic style.'

Fabulous. Her first date with Misha had been on a ghost tour, now her walk with Mal had ended up at a mausoleum.

She hoped it wasn't a sign.

Steps in front of her led directly into the hill, to a large, studded door set in a stone arch, much the same as the one back at Blackheath Hall. Had it also come from Buckley Abbey?

Above the arch, a carved stone panel said:

BLACKHEATH

1853

Mal stood beside her. 'That'll be where the coffins are, with the monuments on the level above.'

'How many members of the family do you think are in there?'

'Hopefully just the dead ones.'

She snickered and, having no desire to meet any of them, walked around the hill to the back, where another set of steps led to the top storey. Perhaps there'd once been a view over the top of the trees, but now they were too tall.

A path led around the mausoleum, past another door and a glass window above the front entrance. Harriet shielded the light with her hands to peer through the window but could only see a single marble statue in the centre of an otherwise empty room. Was all this grandeur just for one person?

'Do you want to go inside?' Mal indicated the door.

She shuddered. 'Ugh, no.'

'Scared there might be ghosts?' He moved closer.

'I have enough ghosts to be going on with, thank you.'

He seemed puzzled by that but then she noticed he was doing that head tilt thing, and leaning towards her, and Harriet was just wondering whether she should close her eyes (because that had gone so well last time) when there was a flash of light so bright it felt as though it had seared her eyeballs, accompanied by a violent crash that echoed around the forest and vibrated beneath their feet.

'A thunderstorm,' Mal muttered, taking her hand. 'Perfect timing. We'd better make a run for it. Any minute now those clouds are going to burst.'

Harriet was too busy trying to analyse what he meant by 'perfect timing' – good/bad? – to notice he was still holding her hand as they ran back through the garden and into the courtyard of Blackheath Hall, when the heavens opened and it poured down.

There was no sign of Pete or Freddie, but Sam was waiting on the steps like a disapproving father. When he saw her, he turned and headed back inside.

What was up with him? Her shift hadn't even started yet!

'I'd better go,' Mal said, lightly touching her shoulder to get her attention. 'I'll call you.'

But as he ducked into his Audi and drove away, the removal truck following closely behind, she remembered he didn't have her phone number or even know where she lived.

But she was sure he'd work it out. She wasn't exactly hard to find.

As she ran across the courtyard, a vein of lightning split the sky over Blackheath Hall, followed by another rumble of thunder.

They were about to have one hell of a storm.

THIRTY-TWO

TEN YEARS PREVIOUSLY

The key to the museum's muniment room, unsurprisingly, was kept, helpfully labelled, in the key cabinet at the police station.

It took several visits to the admin office until Drake found it empty, and he had to pick the lock of the admin officer's desk to get hold of the key to the cabinet, but when he finally headed back outside into the corridor, the muniment room key clutched in his hand, he felt very pleased with himself.

Whereupon he found DI Davenport leaning against the wall sipping a coffee, peering at Kieran over the top of the cup.

'Hi, boss,' Kieran said.

Davenport sighed. 'My office, DS Drake. *Now.*'

Should he make a run for it?

In a police station?

Yeah... that wouldn't work.

With Davenport following, he returned upstairs to the CID offices. Fortunately, this late in the day they were practically empty.

Davenport nodded towards his office. Kieran entered and then waited for permission to sit down.

He didn't get it.

Why was DI Davenport still here anyway? Didn't he have a home to go to?

'It's the last performance at the museum tonight,' the DI said, walking around his desk to calmly sit in the chair. 'I wondered who Fisher would send to collect the key to the muniment room. I never thought it would be you.' He placed his coffee on the desk and leant back, surveying Kieran thoughtfully. 'I never thought it would be you,' he repeated sadly. 'How much is he paying? It must be a lot if you're willing to risk a promising career for whatever the museum has stashed away.'

Davenport knew about the muniment room?

Possibly because Kieran was holding an over-large key with a label that said: *Muniment Room, Museum*.

What should he do now?

Resign? That wouldn't achieve anything.

Confess? Attempt to talk Davenport round?

Could he *trust* him?

What did he know about him?

Other than he hated his job and would rather be somewhere else.

Should he try to blag his way out? Tell Davenport that he only wanted the key to check what was in the muniment room as part of his security assessment?

At six in the evening?

He might as well ask Davenport if he believed in Father Christmas.

What would happen if he told Davenport the truth?

A clumsy rescue attempt could result in Esme's death.

Would Fisher *really* kill her though? An elderly lady he'd known all his life?

Oh, yes.

Kieran's fingers clenched around the key.

Davenport noticed, the same way he noticed everything, his dark-brown eyes rising to meet Kieran's. 'Something beyond price?' he said softly. 'Who's he threatened? Your fa... No, your *grand-*

mother. She'll be the person you care about most in the world. Am I right?'

Kieran stared at him. How the hell...?

Davenport exhaled. 'You're wondering if you can trust me. A reasonable question. As much as you can trust anyone, I suppose. Perhaps more than others in this station, unfortunately. The reach of some unsavoury types has permeated even Raven's Edge – something I hope to eradicate while I'm here. We'll talk about that some other time. So, Arlo Fisher is holding your grandmother hostage and, in return for her safety, you've agreed to steal that key for him?'

Before Kieran could reply, Davenport added, 'Although you didn't *really* steal it, did you? You remembered the curator had lost his own key, and you spotted a spare and thought you'd help him out by having a copy made. Am I right?'

Again, at six in the evening?

Where was the boss *going* with this?

'You'd been so busy with the Fisher case, you'd quite forgotten until it was the end of your shift.'

This story *almost* sounded plausible.

What was the right answer? Should he agree? Would Davenport really let him hand over the key to Fisher? Where was the catch? *Where was the scam?*

And what about *Esme*?

Davenport sighed and picked up his coffee. 'I thought you were smart, Kieran.'

Was he disappointed Kieran hadn't taken the lifeline he'd offered? Or, more likely, the bait?

Why couldn't Davenport *say* what he meant? Alternatively, what would happen if Kieran agreed, turned on his heel and left with the key? Would there really be no repercussions?

All this second-guessing was doing his head in.

He'd thought working for the police would be like stepping into a safe black-and-white world, now it appeared to have murky shades of grey like everywhere else.

He glanced behind, through the little window into the CID office. It was empty. Unless someone was hiding beneath their desk – *unlikely* – they wouldn't be overheard.

He took a step closer to the desk, rested his hands against it and leaned towards Davenport.

'Maybe I'm being stupid, but you'll have to spell it out for me, boss.'

'Tell me,' Davenport said, 'where's Esme?'

Kieran took a deep breath. 'At her cottage, I think. Fisher showed me a photo of her tied to a chair in front of her fireplace.'

'It would be the most sensible place to hold her. She wouldn't have to be moved. She wouldn't be seen by a third party. What's the plan?' He nodded towards the key Kieran still held. 'You take that to Fisher in exchange for your grandmother? Tonight? While the show's taking place?'

'In theory.'

'But you don't trust him?'

'No.'

'You don't trust me either.'

Kieran remained silent.

Davenport sighed. 'Give me time to get a team together to extract Esme. I'll message you when it's done. I'll have another team on standby at the museum. No one will get away.'

A team? Where the hell was he going to get *that* from?

'You want him to go *ahead* with the robbery?'

Davenport shrugged. 'The easiest way to convict him will be to catch him in the act.'

That was his plan? There were so many holes in it, Kieran hardly knew where to begin. 'What if Fisher gets away?'

'He won't.'

Kieran wished he had his boss's confidence.

Then again, it wasn't *his* grandmother's life at stake.

'OK,' Kieran said, 'I leave here, head to the museum and hand over the key.' It was hard to hide the derision in his voice. '*That's* your plan? That's *it*?'

'Pretty much.' Davenport picked up his phone, presumably to set everything in motion.

Kieran turned to leave, unsure whether to laugh, cry or punch the DI's wall as he left. Or, better still, punch the DI.

'One last thing,' Davenport called after him. 'Try to stall for as long as possible. It's going to take time to get this arranged.'

THIRTY-THREE

PRESENT DAY

Sunday

'Archaeology and crime-scene investigation are not dissimilar,'
Bruce Ogilvy said cheerfully as he and Ben picked their way
between the holes and hollows that littered the old battlefield. His
clothes were far more suited to the terrain than Ben's, whose
trousers were already mud-splattered and snagged by brambles. He
should have worn his wellington boots.

'I assume it wasn't your team that left these holes?' Ben said.

'From forty years ago? Oh, no. Our dig was concentrated
around the abbey ruins and we always tidied up after ourselves. I
suspect these holes were caused by night-hawks.' He paused,
giving Ben the chance to ask what a night-hawk was, but he had
heard enough about metal detectorists over the past few days and
remained silent. It didn't stop Ogilvy continuing with, 'The detectorists will tell you they're doing you a favour, finding artefacts that
could've stayed lost for another couple of centuries, but sadly, not
all of them are upfront and honest about what they do, and the odd
bad apple causes real damage to historical sites like this one.' His
lips pursed as they detoured around another hole. 'Although it

must be very tempting, if you're broke and have just unearthed a hoard, to go home with it and keep quiet.'

As Kyle Hayward had done. But why take the skull too? Was he hoping to identify it before going public? Was he trying to retrieve the rest of the skeleton when he was murdered? But surely moving it away from the battlefield would make it harder to prove its identity?

By now they'd reached the tent and Ben gestured for Ogilvy to enter first, before following him in and introducing him to Lucia. It turned out Ogilvy and Lucia knew each other very well, and Ben soon felt like a spare part as Lucia excitedly showed Ogilvy the skeleton and the finds table – mainly ancient bits of metal, and nothing to do with the Hayward investigation at all – except she let Ogilvy take a gold ring out of the box to examine more closely.

Ogilvy held it to the light. 'My old eyes aren't as good as they used to be,' he began, but Lucia shoved a magnifying glass at him. 'Ah, thanks...'

Ben was tempted to leave them to it. He had work of his own to catch up on, but, technically, this was a crime scene. Was Ash still on site?

He returned outside to check the field. The sky had darkened and the wind was beginning to get up, shaking the trees opposite and flapping at the tent. He hoped it was securely fastened. There was no sign of Ash but Oscar and Stuart and the small crowd were still there, watching him. Apparently, the crime scene had swiftly become as big an attraction as the Gateway to the Dead itself. Natural curiosity, he supposed, but it seemed morbid. Why would you want to see the site of a murder? Some were even taking photos.

'This is the crest of the Marquesses of Blackheath,' Ogilvy was saying as Ben returned. He held the ring out to Ben, indicating a flat oval on top. The ring was in surprisingly good condition, not at all bent, although the crest was very faint. He offered Ben the magnifying glass.

Why did everything loop back to Blackheath Hall?

Ben waved it aside, uninterested. 'This *was* his estate.'

He should have known better than to argue with an archaeologist.

'The ring would have been worn by the head of the family,' Ogilvy said, 'and handed down through the generations. It was their seal.'

'Could it have belonged to Major John Weston?' Lucia could barely contain her excitement, her Spanish accent becoming more pronounced. 'Do you think this could be *his* skeleton? But why wasn't his body stripped of valuables and dropped into the pit like all the others?'

'Because someone wanted to hide it,' Ben said. Was that only obvious to him? 'And they were in a hurry.'

Lucia took a step back to the trench, gazing down at the jumbled bones now carefully brushed clean of soil. 'Contemporary reports say Major Weston was murdered by his brother, although there's no record of what happened to his body afterwards. Whereas there's evidence the Marquess abandoned his men and disappeared for the next fifteen years, only to return in 1660 when King Charles II reclaimed the throne.'

'But did he?' Ogilvy's blue eyes were gleaming with excitement. 'What if it was the *Marquess* who was murdered and the *Major* who vanished?'

'What would be the motivation?' Ben said. 'The Major was on the winning side. Why would he give all that up to impersonate his brother, risking death or imprisonment?'

'The Marquess was sole owner of a considerable fortune,' Ogilvy said. 'Estates like this weren't shared; everything went to the eldest male.'

'And this one would have been seized by the Parliamentarians anyway after their victory,' Lucia said. 'You're right, Ben. It doesn't make sense. If the Major shot the Marquess, he wouldn't need to hide. He'd have been celebrated.'

'If the Marquess had been trying to surrender when his brother killed him,' Ogilvy said, 'it would have been murder.'

'There was a war on,' Ben said. 'No one would have cared.'

Ogilvy held up the ring. 'This signet ring was always worn by the head of the Weston family, meaning that skeleton is the Fifth Marquess of Blackheath and the Major stole his brother's title, his house and his life.'

'Or the Marquess dropped his ring when he buried his brother,' Ben couldn't help pointing out.

The pair of them turned to stare at him.

He sighed. 'And after three hundred and eighty years, does it really matter?'

'*Yes!*' Lucia took the ring from Ogilvy and returned it to the box. 'It matters.'

'You're right, of course.' Ogilvy grinned at Ben. 'We should examine all the evidence before coming up with a theory. Archaeologists have more in common with detectives than historians, you know, but it's easy for us to get carried away.' A loud crack of thunder caused him to glance outside at the darkening sky. 'I believe it's going to tip down. Anyone fancy coming back to my place for a brew? I only live five minutes away and I've got photos of the original dig, way back in 1983, if you're interested?'

Regretfully, Lucia turned the invitation down. 'I need to remove the skeleton from the grave, otherwise it'll have to be covered again overnight – and that looks like quite a storm on its way.'

Ben, however, accepted. It was a twenty-minute walk to the station and he was wearing his wool coat rather than a more sensible anorak because it had been cold this morning. There was the chance he might learn something from Ogilvy's photos of the dig, but mostly it appealed more than the alternatives: being trapped in a tent with two archaeologists or getting soaked on his way back to the station.

When he and Ogilvy crossed the field and ducked beneath the police tape, most of the villagers had already left. The rain started as they exited the lane onto the main road, and began to positively pour down once they were past The Witch's Brew. Ben cast a longing look through the little lattice windows and tried not to think about hot soup and freshly baked granary rolls.

They were soaked by the time they reached Ogilvy's tiny terrace cottage down one of the side alleys. It was similar in age and style to Kyle Hayward's, but fortunately without the hoarding. It was a welcoming place, with lots of photos of Ogilvy and his family, and older ones of various digs. There were books and pot plants and ornaments, some of which had obviously been made by a small child. It was definitely a home rather than a pseudo museum with creepy display cabinets filled with ancient broken things.

Ogilvy switched on the lights and arranged their coats on chairs in front of the fire, which he stoked up before heading to the kitchen to make coffee. Ben sat on a well-worn but comfy sofa as the lights dimmed and flickered, followed by an ear-splitting crack of thunder. Rain began hammering at the tiny windows in earnest. He hoped Lucia was safe and dry in her tent.

Ogilvy returned with two mugs of coffee and a plate of chocolate and praline brownies, which he placed on a table beside Ben. They tasted very familiar.

'They're great, aren't they?' Ogilvy beamed. 'My granddaughter brings them round as a treat. She works at The Witch's Brew.'

Did he mean Ruby, the barista?

Ogilvy rummaged in a cupboard and dumped an old photo album on the sofa. 'Here you go, as promised. My wife suggested I make albums for all my digs. It's been a while though. I retired five years ago. Got too old. Scrabbling about in freezing mud for a few bits of stone suddenly lost its appeal.'

Ben opened the album. The first photo was of a jumble of skeletons piled into a pit.

Ogilvy grimaced. 'Sorry, I should have warned you. I never had the patience to put them in chronological order, to "tell a story", as my wife put it.'

'Were these the Civil War soldiers?' The ones alleged to haunt the forest around Raven's Edge.

'Yes. We excavated nineteen skeletons, all piled on top of each other, as you can see. We suspect they were the Marquess's men, probably local lads, massacred after the siege. No care was taken with their interment. They died of the usual wounds synonymous with a battle and were re-buried in a corner of the graveyard at St Francis Church. There's a monument there now that marks the spot.'

Ben grew up in the village, so he already knew this. The local school children would lay flowers on the anniversary of the siege and the vicar would hold a special service.

He took another sip of coffee and began flicking through the album. The old archaeological dig had absolutely nothing to do with his current investigation, but Ogilvy's coffee was good, the brownies were delicious – and the weather was atrocious, so he intended to take his time.

Although the photos were old and yellowing, amongst the happy faces posing around the abbey ruins he recognised a girl with pink bobbed hair, wearing denim shorts, a white T-shirt and a wide grin: Lady Peony. The woman beside her was smaller, with dark hair and eyes, and much less flamboyant: Lady Rose.

It was hard to reconcile the photos with the ladies currently in residence at Blackheath Hall, but then Ogilvy didn't look much like the gangly twenty-something with the scrappy beard and eighties indie-band T-shirt crouching beside them, doing a double thumbs up.

Spotting the photo of Peony and Rose, Ogilvy said, 'Great girls. Lots of fun, although they argued a lot. Complete opposites in personality. Lady Rose invited us all to her wedding but then they didn't seem to have many relations or friends. Their parents had died a few months earlier, after selling the abbey to the council. It was a car crash, I think.'

Ogilvy turned through several pages at once and there were Rose and Peony again, this time posing together at the foot of the staircase at Blackheath Hall. They were both wearing what appeared to be full-skirted ballgowns, in complete contrast to the grubby clothes they'd worn during the excavation. Rose's dress was crimson; Peony's was a shimmering white. Rose wore a diamond tiara in her dark-brown hair and a matching necklace, whereas Peony had wide diamond bracelets on her wrists and a single strand of pearls around her neck.

'*Rose* was the bride?'

Ogilvy grinned. 'Yes, and she wore red, as you can see. It caused a lot of fuss amongst the old biddies and a bit of an argument with the vicar, who wanted to cancel the whole thing, citing disrespect. Her boyfriend put him right. White dresses for brides only became a thing in the mid-nineteenth century. I liked him. He was a braw lad – the gardener, you know. Can't for the life of me remember his name. Both girls had a huge crush on him, but he only had eyes for Rose. Apparently, her parents hadn't approved but they were no longer around to object. Rose had a traditional ceremony at St Francis, with Peony as a bridesmaid, and then a rip-roaring party in the old mausoleum.' Ogilvy sighed. 'Those were the days.'

Ben turned over a few more pages, but there were no more photographs, so he flipped back to the one of Peony standing beside Rose at the foot of the staircase. They didn't look alike. Rose was small and had light-brown skin, whereas Peony was tall, pale and freckly. She hadn't changed much. She even had the pink hair, cut in a short bob.

'I'll always remember that summer,' Ogilvy said. 'I fell head over heels with Peony. She was a lovely lass. I asked her to marry me at least twice, but in those days my work took me all over the country and she said she didn't want to leave the house. Once she did, it would be lost to her forever – an entail her father had added when they'd been children, in case anything happened to him.

'Rose didn't care about the house. She and her husband were emigrating to Australia the day after the wedding. I always thought it was strange that Peony didn't go with them. It seemed terribly mean to leave her behind but then things had become frosty between them once Rose announced her engagement. I'm surprised Peony agreed to be bridesmaid, to be honest.'

'They left Peony on her own? How old was she?'

'Twenty-three, but she had a large allowance from her cousin Jasper, the new Marquess.' Ogilvy sighed again. 'When Peony was left alone in that big old house, she became terribly eccentric; a shadow of herself. She hardly left the place; she was that terrified she'd lose the only home she'd ever known. It was so sad.'

Ben, remembering his encounter with Lady Peony, thought that 'shadow' was the last word he'd use to describe her, but it did go some way to explaining her obsession with the house.

As though realising he'd become maudlin, Ogilvy gave a cheery grin. 'In the end, I married the barmaid from The Lucky Cavalier! We had a daughter – Jenny – and then our granddaughter, Ruby. Occasionally I see Lady Peony in the village. She still has that bright pink hair and those fabulous vintage clothes! Although the last time I met her, about three years past, she stared straight through me as though she didn't recognise me.' Shaking his head sadly, he took the album from Ben, smoothed his hand over the cover, and then carefully placed it back on the table.

'It was more than forty years ago, but I'll never forget that summer,' he sighed. 'A few years ago, we heard Lady Rose's husband had died and she'd returned to live with Lady Peony, due to early-onset dementia. Such a shame. She was a lovely lass. They both were.'

Outside, the rain had begun to slow and Ben's phone pinged with a message from Dakota, asking him to return to the station as a matter of urgency. He finished his coffee, made his excuses and left. It *was* a sad story. Two elderly ladies rattling around in a tumbledown house that was far too big for them to cope with, terrified they were going to be ruthlessly evicted by the current Lord Blackheath.

No wonder they were seeing ghosts.

THIRTY-FOUR

Thirty minutes earlier

The interior of Blackheath Hall was as cold and unwelcoming as Harriet remembered, despite the warmth from the fire. Without the added light from the missing bulbs, a perpetual gloom hung over the great hall, while the flickering flames created eerie shadows that chased each other around the walls.

Or maybe she'd read too many ghost stories.

She arranged her dripping coat over the back of a chair and placed it in front of the fire, where it began to steam gently. It would smell of smoke by the end of the night, but she was past caring.

One more shift to go...

Sam didn't comment or even say 'hello', just picked up one of the radios from the table, presumably to start the check and lock-up of the house. Was he unhappy that she'd gone for a walk with Mal instead of starting work? But she was *early*!

'Where are Pete and Freddie?' she asked, purely to get a conversation going. 'It's not even 6.oo pm. Their shift wasn't due to finish until 8.oo pm.'

'We had news that one of the tributaries into the River Hurst was likely to flood,' Sam said without looking at her. 'It would block the road out of the village.'

'The one next to Ben's cottage?' That one flooded regularly, but fortunately never high enough to damage his house. 'But it's only just started raining!'

'It's been raining heavily in Norchester all afternoon, but I wanted to be rid of them, to be honest. I was fed up with their whinging.'

'Me too!' Lady Peony called, lifting her head above the sofa. Swathed in multi-coloured blankets and clutching a book, she'd been perfectly camouflaged.

Harriet turned her attention back to Sam, lowering her voice. 'We're police officers. We stay on the job for as long as it takes. How can we call ourselves one of the emergency services if we leave at the first sign of an actual emergency?'

'I'm sorry,' he said, 'I didn't feel it was important. The danger to the ladies has obviously passed and—'

'If the danger's passed, *we* wouldn't be here and we wouldn't be moving the ladies out. For goodness' sake, Sam! Use your common sense!'

His sulky expression turned mutinous.

She still couldn't stop herself adding, 'As long as you realise we're effectively working an extra couple of hours this evening, unpaid, because DCI Cameron won't sanction overtime.'

'Totally worth it to get rid of Pete and Freddie,' Sam grumbled. 'Didn't you get that message from DCI Cameron? I thought that's why you were here early.'

'What message?'

Sam glanced in the direction of Peony, who thankfully was pouring herself a shot of whisky into one of her chipped porcelain cups and not paying them the slightest attention. 'Maybe check your phone?'

She slid it out and, sure enough, DCI Cameron had messaged to say he'd withdrawn the Tactical Firearms Team and they were to get Peony and Rose out of the house by lunchtime tomorrow, because then he'd be pulling her, Sam, Pete and Freddie off the case too. If Peony and Rose insisted on staying on at Blackheath Hall, he could no longer guarantee their safety.

She quashed a surge of anger. Damn DCI Cameron and his stupid budget.

Her thoughts must have shown on her face because Sam said, 'We did tell him we hoped to move the ladies out tomorrow. We always knew we were against the clock.'

She ignored him, walking over to Lady Peony who regarded her warily.

'Bad news, darling?'

'I'm afraid so. We'll need to pack you up and move you to Hartfell by twelve tomorrow. My boss will be withdrawing all police support.'

'But that's good, isn't it?' Peony brightened. 'It must mean he believes Mr Drake was the gunman's target and not us? That means we'll be able to stay!'

A throbbing started behind Harriet's left temple. 'Lady Peony, it's not safe for you to continue living here, even without the threat of a gunman. You know that.'

'I've lived here for sixty-five years without a single mishap.'

'Two nights ago, a man was shot on your doorstep, and this morning *you* were almost hit by a chandelier.'

Peony's shoulders drooped. 'But I don't *want* to leave.'

'Would you like me to help you pack?'

'Even if I want to take items that don't belong to me?'

Harriet closed her eyes and rubbed her temple. 'Please don't put me in that position.'

'In that case, it shouldn't take long. What do I truly own, after all? A few photo albums? The clothes I'm standing in?'

'Lady Peony, you know that isn't true—'

'Bloody well is.'

When this was over, Harriet thought, she'd put in for some leave, stay in bed, catch up on her reading and eat nothing but takeaways from Pizza at Cosimo's. It would be *bliss*.

Sam cursed loudly, shocking her out of her daydream.

'What the hell, Sam?' She rounded on him. 'Aren't we jittery enough?'

He pointed towards the staircase. 'I saw... That is, I thought I saw...' He lowered his hand, muttering, 'But that would be ridiculous...'

Due to the missing chandelier, the great hall was not well-lit. There was the fire, of course, and electric lights around the walls on both floors, but they didn't have enough replacement bulbs and more than half the sockets remained empty. She was surprised he could see anything in this gloom.

'*What* did you see, Sam?'

'Nothing, sorry.' He started towards the staircase. 'I've spent too long in this house. It's starting to freak me out. Damn ghosts.'

'Sam,' she started patiently, 'there are no such things as—'

The lights went out with a dull fizzle, leaving only the flickering firelight, but at least this time the bulbs didn't explode.

In the dark, Sam tripped over what was presumably the bottom step of the staircase and swore again.

So did Peony, who'd apparently spilled her drink down her front. 'Bother. That was the last of Papa's '63 Finlayson's.'

Harriet took a calming breath and then held her phone out to use as a torch. 'Lady Peony, could you tell me where the fuse box is please?'

'Don't worry, I'll do it.' Peony put her mug down and shoved her nest of blankets onto the floor to enable her to get up. 'One of you will need to come with me. I don't have a phone like yours. I won't be able to see where I'm going.'

'Use this.' Sam reached into his pocket, took out a small torch and switched it on. It was far brighter than his phone. 'I brought a spare after the fun we had this morning.'

'*Fun?*' repeated Peony. 'Is *that* what you're calling it?' But she took the proffered torch and strode off into the study.

Harriet waited for the study door to close before turning to

Sam. 'If the power's out, the landline won't work. What signal have you got?'

'In Raven's Edge?' Sam held up his phone. 'Zero, as usual. Sometimes I wonder why I bother to carry the thing.'

'Try a text.'

Sam did as she suggested, then held his phone up to show the text hadn't been sent.

'How about the radio?'

'I tried that yesterday. It's OK talking to each other in the house but it doesn't reach the station. We're too far out.'

'It's two miles away! They have a range of six!'

'Yeah, well, Raven's Edge. Need I say more?'

'This is the twenty-first century and you're saying we're completely cut off from the outside world?'

'Until the power comes back on, yes.'

Harriet lowered her voice further. 'Do you think it could be deliberate?'

'Nothing wrong with the fuses,' Peony announced, coming out of the study and making them both jump. 'And the landline's dead too. Don't worry, darling.' She patted Harriet's shoulder. 'We're *always* having power cuts here. There must be a line down somewhere due to the storm. I'm sure it will come back on soon. We could play cards or something?' She smiled hopefully.

Harriet was about to remind her that she was on duty when a plaintive wail came from upstairs.

Peony sighed. 'Poor Rose. I'll go upstairs to be with her. She hates being on her own and will be more unnerved by the power cut than the storm. She used to love storms. She'd go outside and dance in the rain. Mama was quite convinced she'd catch her death. You'll find candles in the kitchen,' she added over her shoulder as she started up the staircase.

'We need to check the house again,' Harriet told Sam, 'and make sure it's securely locked down.'

He held up the radio. 'I *was* on my way to do that.'

'When you said you saw something... What was it?'

He grimaced. 'Do you really want to know?'

'Yes!'

Even in the dim light from the fire, she saw his cheeks redden. 'I'm sure it was a trick of the light – or rather the shadows – but I thought I saw a person going up the stairs.'

'And you've waited until *now* to tell me? Bloody hell, Sam!'

'It wasn't real!'

'How do you *know* it wasn't real?' She paused, regarding him suspiciously. 'Please don't tell me you saw a ghost!'

'Fine,' he snapped back. 'I won't tell you I saw a ghost.'

They regarded each other uneasily.

Then Harriet said softly, 'What did it look like?'

'Nothing, really.'

'You mean it was see-through, like in a film?'

He folded his arms. 'If you won't take me seriously, I'm not telling you.'

'As your senior officer—'

'Don't pull that crap on me, Harriet March! I've known you since you were five.'

'Then tell me what you saw!'

'A woman! Is that good enough for you? I saw a woman and she was as solid as anything. One minute the stairs were empty, the next she was there, and then she wasn't. It was a split second, less than the time it takes to blink. I thought she was a shadow caused by the flickering fire, but she looked directly at me and smiled. And then she wasn't there.'

Harriet stared at him, hardly knowing what to say. 'It must have been a trick of the light.'

'*That's* what I keep telling you.'

'Is everything all right down there?' sang out a familiar voice. Lady Peony was leaning over the banister of the gallery above them.

'We're fine here, Peony,' Harriet lied. 'How's Rose?'

Peony humphed. 'Getting herself in a state as usual, so I'm going to stay up here until the power comes back on. Could one of you bring me some candles? They're in the kitchen drawer, along with the matches.'

'No problem. I'll be right up.' Harriet waited until she heard Rose's bedroom door click, and then said to Sam, 'We should check the priest's hole.'

Sam nodded grimly.

They went over to the fireplace and Harriet hit the panel on the side. Watching it swing round so easily still unnerved her.

'You'll have to go inside,' he said. 'I won't fit.'

'Whatever.' It took her less than five minutes to climb the ladder and shimmy around the chimney breast. She held her breath as she rounded the corner, but the little space was empty.

She returned to the great hall, covered in cobwebs again.

Sam pulled a strand from her hair. 'Anything?'

She shook her head. 'Do you think the power cut was deliberate? If someone's watching the house, they'll know the police presence is being scaled down.'

'If they wait until tomorrow afternoon,' Sam said with some feeling, 'we'll have gone and they *and* the ghosts can have the house to themselves.'

'What do you suggest?'

'We're cut off from the station and with that storm the power could be out for hours. We could wait it out, but it's only a twenty-minute walk into the village – ten if I run.'

'You know I can't let you do that.'

'To be honest, I'd rather face the storm than stay in this creepy house a second longer.'

'You *like* films about ghosts…' Harriet couldn't help teasing.

'But not in real life!'

She sighed. 'You'd be leaving me alone with Peony and Rose, and possibly an intruder. Perhaps we should all leave. Stay together.'

'How? None of us has a car and we can't drag Lady Rose out in weather like this. She's in her seventies and has dementia.'

'I know, I *know*.'

He regarded her speculatively. 'What's your gut instinct telling you?'

'This *must* be a coincidence but—'

'It wouldn't stop someone taking advantage of it.'

'Do you really think we're in danger?'

'Sitting ducks.'

'There are no lights over at The Witch's Brew,' Peony called. 'I thought you'd like to know.'

Harriet wished she'd stop doing that – or at least move about more noisily. There were enough squeaky floorboards in the house. Couldn't she find a few to step on?

Sam recovered his equilibrium first. 'You can see The Witch's Brew from upstairs?'

'Only their lights after dark,' Peony said. 'The rest of the time it's trees and more trees.'

'I've an idea,' Sam said to Harriet. 'Why don't I run to The Witch's Brew and tell them what's happened. Jake Davenport can drive over to the station to pass on the message that we need back-up, and I can come back here. That way, you'll only be left on your own for ten minutes. Jake used to be a detective inspector. He'll know what to do.'

'*I* know what to do,' Harriet snapped. 'We lock everything down and wait it out, not panic after five minutes.'

'If there's a threat, we need back-up.'

Somewhere in the distance, Rose was shouting.

'I'd better go to her,' Peony said. 'I just thought you'd want to know about The Witch's Brew.'

'That could mean the whole village is out,' Harriet said, 'and one of our team is already on their way here.'

'We can't rely on that. You know, I could have been there and back by now.'

'*Sam.*'

'I need those candles,' Peony shouted over the banister. 'Rose is becoming very upset.'

'I'm on it,' Harriet called up to her. 'Go,' she told Sam in an undertone. 'Be as quick as you can.'

He ran to where he'd left his coat by the fire, pulled it on, muttered, 'I wish I'd brought my car!' and disappeared out through the door, which was promptly caught by the wind and crashed back against the wall.

Harriet ran over to force the door shut. She had to shove her shoulder against it. This was some storm. Surely they'd have heard if anyone had entered the house this way?

Ensuring the door was locked and bolted, Harriet crossed the hall to the kitchen. According to Peony, in the old days there'd been a complete servants' wing, now demolished, including a servants' hall and a housekeeper's room, a still room and a brew house, a laundry and a lamp room. Now there was only the main kitchen, the larder and the scullery, with a tiny boot room beside the servants' staircase.

Harriet paused on the threshold of the kitchen. There was a large cast-iron range with all kinds of copper saucepans hanging from hooks around it, as well as a bed-warming pan. Several wooden dressers lined the walls, displaying pretty but cracked plates. They all had drawers. Which one did Peony mean? She started with the nearest, sliding each one open. They contained the usual things: cutlery and cooking utensils, tea towels and cloths, and some items Harriet didn't recognise because she'd never cared much for cooking.

There were no candles, however.

She checked the larder – depressingly empty – and then the scullery, which had a large sink and not much else, unless you counted the spider crouching by the plug hole. She should have told Sam to bring the floodlights they normally used for crime scenes. That would stop them seeing 'ghosts'.

There was one room left. Peony called it the boot room and whatever it had been used for in the past, there was now a row of rotting wellington boots in every size, along with a rack of coats, stiff with age and white mould, and decorated with the ubiquitous cobwebs. Harriet wrinkled her nose. Why hadn't Peony thrown them away?

She was about to return to the hall when she noticed a plain wooden wardrobe at the opposite side of the room. When she opened the door, she saw around ten sets of shapeless brown and beige uniforms. Had these belonged to the staff?

She pulled one out, knocking something shiny onto the floor. It rolled across the flagstones with a metallic rattle, and she stopped it with her foot.

It was a helmet, with three vertical bars across the face.

Heart thudding, she stared at the tunic in her hand and the buff-coloured trousers hanging in the closet.

Realisation dropped into her stomach like a stone.

These weren't *staff* uniforms.

They were Civil War costumes.

And there was a cupboard full of them.

THIRTY-FIVE

TEN YEARS PREVIOUSLY

Kieran entered the museum with the rest of the villagers, shortly before the show began at seven thirty. While they excitedly took their seats, he stood at the back and tried not to be conspicuous as he waited for Fisher's signal. Surprisingly, as the show moved well into the second half, it was the curator, Alaric Gilbert, who beckoned him into the room behind where Phyllis had been sitting.

Kieran hesitated, then followed. Why had he assumed the curator was being held hostage like Esme? Was he working for Fisher too?

Gilbert didn't speak to Kieran but led him into the kitchen, where he pointed through the scullery to the staircase that led to the basement. 'This is what you call "helping me", is it?' he said, glaring at Kieran.

There was nothing Kieran could say to that.

If Gilbert knew their identities, Fisher must have a plan to disappear following the heist, perhaps overseas. Did he honestly believe there was a fortune in medieval silver lying forgotten in the basement of a rural village museum?

What would happen to Esme if there wasn't?

Maybe he and Esme would be the ones to disappear...

He furtively checked his phone, but there was nothing from DI Davenport.

Two men were waiting for him in the basement standing either side of the muniment room door, their arms folded as though they were bouncers at a nightclub.

Kieran took the key from his pocket and waved it. 'Who wants this?'

One of the men shook his head. 'We wait for Fisher.'

He'd assumed the plan was to leave the museum at the same time as the audience, but Phyllis's performance had little in the way of stage props. Wouldn't the villagers think it odd if they saw a van being loaded up when the museum was supposed to be closed?

But the longer he had before the muniment room was unlocked, the longer Davenport had to rescue Esme.

The DI had already had nearly two hours. Why hadn't he heard anything?

There were footsteps behind him and Fisher appeared in the basement, his gaze switching from his men to Kieran.

'All good?' he said.

Kieran, unsure whether Fisher was talking to him, didn't reply.

Fisher frowned. 'Key?'

He held it up. 'Key,' he agreed.

Kieran heard more footsteps and felt a flicker of hope. Was that Davenport's 'team'? Was Esme finally safe?

But it was Phyllis who walked into the room, followed by another of Fisher's men.

'Sorry, boss,' the man said. 'I couldn't stop her.'

Fisher sighed. 'You were supposed to go home to establish an alibi.'

'I know,' she shrugged. 'But it's more important for me to be here.'

'Those psychic vibes of yours playing up again?' He turned back to Kieran. 'Open it,' he said, nodding towards the door.

Kieran swallowed. This had better work. When had the door last been opened? Twenty years ago? What if the lock jammed?

He opened the outer door.

'Wait,' Fisher said, holding out his hand.

Did that mean he wanted to unlock the vault? Weird but whatever. Kieran held out the key.

Fisher rolled his eyes. 'Not *that*. Your *phone*.'

As casually as he could manage, Kieran said, 'Why do you want my phone?'

'Why do you think? Hand it over.'

Reluctantly, he dug into his pocket and gave it to Fisher. He'd set it to vibrate so he'd know as soon as Davenport had Esme.

Unfortunately, Fisher would now know, too.

Esme's safety was the main thing. It didn't matter what happened to him, which was easy enough to say, but when faced with the reality...

'What are you waiting for?' Fisher grumbled.

The inner door to the muniment room had an ornate, brass lock. The company that had made it, almost two centuries ago, had marketed it as 'unpickable'. Kieran knew that if the key failed, it would trigger an automatic jamming system and they'd never get it open.

He held his breath and carefully turned the key, waiting for that nudge of resistance.

(He may have closed his eyes.)

There was a satisfying 'click'. Hardly daring to believe his luck, he opened his eyes, tried the lever and the door swung noiselessly open.

Despite losing his phone, this was all going suspiciously well.

He'd assumed Fisher and his cohorts would surge past him, grab what they'd come for and then leave.

Instead, Fisher shoved him through first. 'So I can keep an eye on you.'

'Fair enough,' Kieran said, 'but could you let Esme go now?'

'Not until the job's finished.'

Would he though? Esme could identify him. It would be easier for Fisher to...

But no, he wasn't going to think about that.

It was pointless pleading for himself, so he said, somewhat desperately, 'What about Phyllis? Why don't you let her leave?'

Fisher laughed. 'Phyllis *wants* to be here. Didn't you hear her? She can leave any time she likes.'

'This is where I'm supposed to be,' she nodded. 'Don't worry, Kieran Drake. Everything will be fine.'

Oh, Phyllis...

Fisher shook his head and turned his attention back to the muniment room.

The door might have resembled the entrance to a bank vault, but the inside was exactly as the curator had described, and a lot like the evidence room up at Police Headquarters. Each wall was lined with shelving. There were some plastic crates but mostly it was cardboard boxes that had contained things like crisps and orange juice, and everything smelt musty. Most of the boxes had softened and sagged with age, some were spotted with mould, some were spilling onto the floor. No wonder Gilbert had put off tackling it. It would take several weeks' work to catalogue it all.

'Stall for time,' Davenport had told him.

Well, that wasn't going to be a problem...

He glanced towards the open door. In theory, he could make a dash for it and then slam the door shut. Fisher and his friends would be trapped. Mobile phones had never worked well in Raven's Edge and they certainly wouldn't work in an underground vault.

Fisher grunted. 'Don't even think about it. If my men don't receive a message from me every ten minutes, that's the end of Grandma.'

Kieran's fists tightened. Beside him, Phyllis slowly shook her head.

Fisher, however, was becoming more and more irate as box after box was torn down, spilling random artefacts across the floor. Fortunately, as Gilbert had implied, there were more kitsch knick-knacks than anything of true value.

'Hurry up!' Fisher snarled. 'Open every box if you have to. You're looking for silver, but black with age. If it didn't look like rubbish, it wouldn't be here. Come *on*, guys!'

Were other valuable items being missed thanks to Fisher's obsession with the monks' treasury? Was it actually valuable at all? Historically perhaps, but the resale value of the silver wouldn't be worth *this* much effort, surely?

What was Fisher's hurry? There was no alarm, no security cameras. No one knew they were here. Surely they had all night?

When he caught Fisher watching him, he froze.

Fisher *knew*. He was sure of it. He'd been so anxious about checking his own phone it hadn't occurred to him that Fisher would be checking his.

Did that mean he'd lost contact with his men at Esme's cottage? That a rescue was in progress?

He dipped his head in case Fisher saw the hope in his eyes.

Until now, Kieran hadn't noticed most of the boxes had been stacked in alphabetical order. Fisher's men were concentrating on the 'B' section, ripping through the cardboard and tossing the contents across the floor.

'B' for Buckley Abbey or 'B' for Blackheath?

But the family name of the Marquesses of Blackheath was Weston...

Kieran's gaze reluctantly slid along the shelving to the far end, which was near the door and less than one metre from where he was standing. A solitary stained cardboard box on the floor had been inadvertently shoved further into the recess than its neighbours because of its smaller size. On the front was a peeling label that read 'Weston'.

If it hadn't been for the desperate seriousness of the situation, Kieran would have laughed. Such a basic mistake, especially when you considered how much research Fisher must have undertaken in tracking the silver down.

If he told Fisher he was looking in the wrong place, would he release Esme? No. Would they release him? Definitely not.

In which case, why not keep quiet and appreciate the entertainment value of Fisher becoming more frustrated, more furious...

On the central table Kieran's phone lit up with a one-word message.

He could read it from here:

Safe

Fisher snatched up the phone and laughed, albeit without humour, before tossing it to the ground and stamping on it, taking Kieran right back to the terror of his schooldays.

Two strides and Fisher was beside him, thrusting his face into Kieran's. 'You think she's safe? I'll snatch her again. I've got a lifetime ahead of me. You, however...' He turned away and said, so carelessly that at first Kieran didn't catch it, 'Kill him.'

THIRTY-SIX
PRESENT DAY

Sunday

Alarmed by the message he'd received from Dakota, Ben hurried back to the police station. He arrived, thoroughly soaked and frozen, to find her and Ash waiting for him in the MIT office, incredibly pleased with themselves because they had Stuart Huntingdon in custody.

Ben glanced from one to the other. 'Er, why?'

'I did as you suggested, sir,' Dakota said. 'I checked the local dry cleaners to see if anyone had handed in a Cavalier fancy-dress costume. No one had. I even checked the ones in Norchester, although Mr Huntingdon lives here in Raven's Edge.'

'And?'

'I decided to call on Mr Huntingdon to ask him to clarify his statement, but he wasn't at home. I was on my way back to the station when I spotted him walking east along the high street towards me, with his friend Mr Montgomery. I called out to Mr Huntingdon, but he took one look at me and ran in the opposite direction. I gave chase—'

'I caught him,' Ash said. 'He ran straight into my arms. Sucker.'

Dakota shot him a sideways glare. 'Otherwise, I'm sure *I* would have caught him.'

Ben massaged his temple. 'And you arrested him because...?'

'He's obviously guilty of *something*, sir. Or he wouldn't have run away.'

It would be a waste of time telling them they couldn't arrest someone purely on suspicion of something, because legally they could. He'd have liked a *little* more in the way of 'reasonable grounds' though.

'One more thing, sir.' Dakota held up an evidence bag. 'When Mr Huntingdon was booked into the custody suite and had to hand over his personal belongings, this was amongst them. He was *wearing* it.'

Ben took the bag and held it up to the light. Inside was a small gold ring set with a flat, orangey-red stone, carved with a man's head in profile. He felt a flicker of excitement. Was this really the kind of thing a student would wear?

'I sent a photo to the Art & Antiques Unit at Headquarters,' Dakota said. 'They told me they don't have anything like this on their list, but that it *could* be a couple of centuries old. The stone, however, might be an intaglio, and they were often found in Roman ruins. There was a fashion, around three hundred years ago, for rich men to collect these carved stones and have them made into jewellery. The Art & Antiques Unit suggested taking the ring to a specialist for evaluation. It wasn't something they could do.'

Ben remembered the gold rings Lucia had found in the grave of the skeleton by the Gateway to the Dead. They'd been nothing like this. Had Huntingdon found it first? Had he killed Hayward for it?

'You're right,' he said. 'We should have the ring properly evaluated by an expert. In the meantime, we need to have a little word with Mr Huntingdon...'

. . .

By the time they'd organised a solicitor for Stuart Huntingdon and arranged for him to be taken to one of the interview rooms, he'd been in police custody long enough to look suitably worried.

His solicitor, Olivia Greenwood-Fitzpatrick, was rather more composed and calmly announced, 'My client is willing to cooperate fully with your investigation,' as they took their seats and Dakota started up the recording machine.

Olivia had already informed Ben of this when they'd met outside the interview room. It would make his job far easier if Huntingdon was happy to admit everything in exchange for the possibility of a reduced sentence.

But he was getting ahead of himself.

Ben placed an evidence bag containing the ring on the table.

'This is very unusual,' he said. 'It looks old. How did it come into your possession?'

'I found it,' Huntingdon said. 'On the ground, just beyond the Gateway to the Dead.'

Ben skipped over 'Why didn't you hand it in?' and asked instead, 'What were you doing there?'

Huntingdon gave him a confused glance, as though he suspected it was a trick question. 'I was waiting for my friend, Oscar. He has a ghost tour business. Me and some of his other friends from college dress up in old-time costumes and pretend to be characters from village history.'

'Is Kyle Hayward part of this tour?'

When Huntingdon regarded him blankly, Ben added, 'The man in the Cavalier costume, found half-buried by the Gateway to the Dead?'

'Don't ask me, mate. I'd never seen him before.'

'But you did see him alive, earlier that night?'

Huntingdon glanced uneasily towards Olivia, who nodded encouragingly.

'Um, yeah. Sure. Don't know why he was all dressed up. Thought he might want my job! I said something like, "Oi, what you doing, mate?" and he turned around and randomly attacked me!'

'He punched you?'

'No, he had this spiky prong thing in his hand and he lunged at me with it.'

Dakota pushed a photo of the pike across the table. 'Do you mean this?'

'Maybe. It was dark, I couldn't see anything much, only that it was sharp and pointy.'

'What did you do when he attacked you?' Ben asked.

'I got it off him, didn't I?' Huntingdon smirked. 'He wasn't expecting me to fight back, he just waved it threateningly as though he couldn't believe I was there.'

'Hayward thought you were a ghost,' Ben said softly. Huntingdon was well-built for an eighteen-year-old. Dressed as a Cavalier soldier and suddenly appearing through the mist, Kyle Hayward must have been terrified. Perhaps already on edge, the fear of discovery had overridden the logic that Huntingdon was part of the ghost tour, and he'd struck out with the nearest thing he had to hand – the remains of the medieval pike he'd just unearthed.

Huntingdon, however, chuckled at the suggestion that he must have been mistaken for a ghostly soldier. 'I suppose so, yeah. What an idiot. The guy was shaking so hard I was able to grab the pike off him. Surprised myself, to be honest.'

No empathy, no pity.

Ben exchanged a glance with Dakota, who was doing her best not to look shocked, but then she'd not been in the job for as long as him.

'What happened next?'

Huntingdon met his gaze without hesitation. 'He fell on it.'

'He... fell on it...?' Ben glanced towards Olivia, who shrugged.

'How do you account for the fact that the pike was found protruding from Kyle Hayward's *back*?'

'He fell *backwards*,' Huntingdon said, adding, so that Ben was clear on this point, 'It was nothing to do with me. He did it to himself. It was an *accident*.'

Of *course* it was.

This was not going to be as straightforward as Ben had hoped.

'Let me see if I've understood this,' he said. 'Last Friday evening you walked through the Gateway to the Dead, ready to play your part in Oscar Montgomery's ghost tour, but instead of him, you found Kyle Hayward in the clearing and asked why he was there—'

'There was no *asking* about it.' Huntingdon leant back in his chair, completely at ease. 'I told him he was trespassing, that he had no right to be there, and what the hell did he think he was doing, digging a bloody great hole on a protected site. Seriously, man. These metal detectorists have no respect for history.'

'How did you know Kyle Hayward was a detectorist?' Dakota asked.

Huntingdon glanced towards her, slowing his speech as though he thought her a fool. 'Because he had a metal detector.'

Yet no detector had been found at the scene.

'What did Hayward say when you challenged him?' Ben asked.

'He didn't *say* anything, just waved that pike at me.'

Because he was terrified.

'That must have been very frightening for you,' Dakota soothed.

'*Frightened? Me?* Not likely! I snatched the thing off him, easy as anything. He didn't even fight me for it. Damned coward couldn't get away fast enough.'

Ben waited for the admission of guilt that would surely follow, but unfortunately Olivia interrupted.

'Er, Mr Huntingdon?'

Huntingdon checked himself. 'The guy was scrabbling over the dirt to get away from me, trying to hide what he'd done, but it turned out we were standing on the edge of a grave.'

'How did you know it was a grave?'

'There was a skeleton in it – in pieces, but with no skull – and it had gold rings on its fingers.'

This confirmed Ben's theory that Hayward had discovered the skull first, taken it home, and returned the following evening to excavate the rest of the body.

Poor Hayward. He thought he'd discovered the one find that would make his fortune, but instead...

'A skeleton?' Dakota sounded awe-struck. 'That must have been a surprise!'

Huntingdon winked. 'You have no idea.'

'*Mr Huntingdon,*' Olivia tried again.

Huntingdon ignored her. 'Obviously the man was a grave robber. When I came across him, he was standing in the bottom of the grave, picking up these gold coins that were scattered all around and shoving them into his bag as fast as he could.'

The finds bag that'd *also* gone missing from the crime scene. What was the betting that it was stashed somewhere in Huntingdon's house?

'Perhaps we should take a break?' Olivia interjected, giving Huntingdon the benefit of a raised eyebrow and a meaningful look.

Huntingdon was too busy preening to notice. 'I couldn't let him get away with it, darlin',' he told Dakota. 'I grabbed his collar and yanked him back, but the side of the grave caved in and I fell on top of him. I forgot I still had the pike in my hand...' He grimaced, for the first time showing some emotion. 'It slipped in so easily. It was kind of horrible.'

Finally! An admission of guilt – to manslaughter, at any rate. Would he now utter a few words of regret over Kyle Hayward's death?

'I did you guys a favour,' Huntingdon said.

Apparently not.

'If I hadn't stepped in, the thief would have gotten away with it. He'd have stolen the rings and the gold coins, covered up the skeleton, and no one would ever have known.'

'Why didn't you tell someone what'd happened?' Ben asked.

'Didn't you think about Hayward's family and friends, how worried they'd be when he didn't come home?'

'I wasn't certain he was dead. He could've been unconscious and might've attacked me again when he woke up. I chucked some soil over him to slow him down. I didn't want anyone else to steal the gold, so I buried the skeleton again, then ran off through the forest.'

Did he honestly expect Ben to believe this? He'd picked one ring up but was happy to re-bury the others? Ben's seven-year-old daughter could've come up with a better story. More likely, he'd been planning to come back later and search the grave more thoroughly.

Huntingdon wouldn't have been the first person to panic after inadvertently causing someone else's death. But he *hadn't* panicked, had he? He'd calmly collected this ring from the grave and then attempted to re-bury the skeleton – and Hayward, too. Had he been in shock? Maybe, but he'd spotted Ben at the crime scene earlier today and could've easily confessed then.

Like many before him, Huntingdon thought he could bluff his way out of trouble, but now he'd been formally arrested the police would be able to search his home for evidence. He'd probably dumped the heavier items as he'd run home, but perhaps they'd get lucky; find Hayward's bag and possibly a blood-stained Cavalier costume?

Glancing down at his notes before pausing the interview, Ben's attention snagged on something.

'You say you ran off through the forest?'

Huntingdon seemed to be considering whether an honest answer would further incriminate him. 'Yes...?'

'Instead of returning to the main road via the Gateway to the Dead – where you might have bumped into the ghost tour – you continued across the clearing to the path that leads up the hill and through the forest?'

'Yes, there's a ruined house hidden behind a huge stone wall. Oscar talks about it as part of the ghost tour. The path comes out at a wrought-iron gate; it's usually kept locked but the wall on either side has collapsed, so I stepped over the rubble and ended up in the garden.'

'You'd been there before?'

'No, but the garden was so overgrown there was only one clear path. I followed it beneath an archway and into a courtyard in front of a big old house. There were security lights above the front door and an old guy was on a stepladder trying to fix them.'

'An "old guy".' Not what Ben had been expecting to hear. Did Huntingdon mean Drake? Perhaps to the younger man, Drake *was* old. 'In his thirties?'

'Ha! More like seventy! He had grey hair and was all dressed up in a Civil War costume, like Oscar's.'

'A *costume*?'

'Uh huh. He couldn't get the lights to work, so he gave up and went round the side of the house. I thought he'd gone, so I stayed in the shadows and ran around the courtyard. But before I could make it to the gatehouse, he returned, wearing a helmet and carrying an old-fashioned pistol. He went up to the front door and banged on it with that creepy old knocker.'

'What happened next?'

'No idea. I ran for it, like any normal person would. I'm not going to hang around when there's a guy with a gun, even if it was an antique. Bloody odd, if you ask me. Why come out the back door, just to bang on the front door all threatening like?'

Didn't Huntingdon realise what he'd witnessed?

'Did you see anything else? Hear anything?'

'I...' Huntingdon glanced warily towards Olivia, who nodded. 'I didn't see anything, but I heard a woman shout "No!" and then the gun went off. I thought they were talking to *me*! I thought they were shooting at *me*! I ran like mad all the way home.'

'The person with the gun was the same one who'd tried to fix the lights?'

'Yes.'

'Tall, male, grey-haired—' The person who'd shot Drake had

come from inside the house, presumably a side entrance leading to the kitchen. Drake had said that the security lights hadn't been working properly when he'd opened the door. What if this 'old guy' had disabled them – and Drake's camera – before coming back to shoot him – unaware there'd been a witness watching from the shadows.

There was only one problem with this.

There were no elderly men living at Blackheath Hall.

There were, however, two elderly *women*, one of whom was desperate to stay in that house, despite a marriage proposal, despite her sister leaving the country, despite the house falling down around her, despite a fake haunting from a very plausible conman, and despite the police doing their best to encourage her to leave.

Desperate people often did very desperate things.

Ben abruptly pushed away from the table and said, 'I'm terminating this interview.' Dakota quickly realised what was going on and he heard her formally finish the interview as he ran out into the corridor, pulling his phone from his pocket to call Harriet.

Only to hear a recorded message telling him his call couldn't be put through.

THIRTY-SEVEN

Drake's would-be murderer had been caught on camera wearing buff-coloured clothes and a surprisingly shiny helmet with vertical bars across the face. Now Harriet had found three or four sets of identical clothes *and* the same helmet. No boots, but Lady Peony habitually wore brown riding boots around the house, although she called them 'field boots' and they had lacing around the ankle.

What kind of boots had the 'ghost' worn?

Harriet took out her phone and checked her copy of the video Milla had forwarded to Ben, but the footage was too dark to see anything more than the top half of the 'ghost'.

She shoved the phone back into her pocket. There was still no signal, so it was not as though she could tell anyone until Sam got back.

What motivation would Peony have to shoot Drake?

It hadn't been so long ago that Civil War re-enactments in the village had been a regular occurrence. It would make sense for the Weston family to have their own set of costumes. Maybe it was just a coincidence?

No police officer believed in coincidence.

OK... Peony had the opportunity. She'd been on site, along

with her sister Rose. They'd both been upstairs in Lady Rose's bedroom.

But how could Peony have run downstairs and around to the front of the house so quickly without being seen, bearing in mind the only staircase led from the gallery directly into the great hall.

Except, it wasn't the only staircase...

There was the second staircase, the *servants'* staircase, which led from the kitchen, past the gallery and up to the second floor. Peony had told her it was too dangerous to use.

Well, she would, wouldn't she?

Each piece of the puzzle slotted into place.

It was a sound theory, but did Harriet seriously believe *Peony* had shot Drake?

She was fit enough to have run down the servants' staircase to the front of the house. She'd said it herself: she spent most of her days running up and down the main staircase fetching things for Rose.

But what was Peony's *motivation*?

Had she found out that Drake was part of the conspiracy to frighten her out of Blackheath Hall? Had she decided to give him a fright back?

That *did* sound like the kind of thing she might do.

Had she intended to hurt him or kill him?

Reluctantly, Harriet suspected the latter.

Damn.

She *liked* Lady Peony.

Harriet carefully tucked the costumes back into the wardrobe and closed the door. She'd stay quiet for now. She was alone in the house with Peony and Rose, with no back-up and no power. Her phone signal, which was nearly always non-existent in Raven's Edge, had finally given up completely. The landline was down because of the storm, and many of the roads leading into the village were likely to be blocked because of flooding or fallen trees.

Hopefully Sam would return soon with a couple of their

colleagues. Between them they should be able to overpower one little old lady.

If only Pete and Freddie hadn't left.

There was a flicker of torchlight behind her.

'Sam?' She spun delightedly. 'You're ba—'

'You've been gone for an awfully long time,' Peony said. 'I was worried about you.' She walked into the boot room, wrinkling her nose in distaste. 'Gosh, it smells terrible! You won't find any candles in here, darling.'

Harriet stood awkwardly in front of the wardrobe, wishing she'd taken the opportunity to move away. 'I don't think you *have* any candles, Lady Peony. I've searched everywhere.'

For a moment she thought she'd been believed. Then Peony's attention slid towards the wardrobe.

'Yes, you certainly have.' Her expression turned calculating. 'But what *did* you find, DS March?'

Harriet, as everyone *always* told her, was hopeless at lying, so she didn't even try. 'Some very interesting fancy-dress costumes. Were they used during the re-enactments?'

'Costumes?' Peony approached her. 'Is that all? You ought to have looked harder.'

Harriet instinctively took a step sideways, but Peony opened the wardrobe and groped along the bottom.

'Ah, here it is!'

As she turned, Harriet saw Peony was holding an old-fashioned pistol. Was it a reproduction, like the costumes?

Harriet thought she'd rather not hang around to find out.

She took another step towards the door.

Peony didn't appear to notice. 'It's pitiful,' she was saying, 'that it should take you so long to work it out.'

Harriet sidled away a little further.

'I've given myself away so many times, reminding you that I have as strong a motive to get rid of Giles as he has to get rid of me.'

What had Sam said? That the Marquess had disappeared and was about to be officially listed as a missing person?

'You... you've *killed* him?'

'Not yet. I'm tempted though.' Peony raised the pistol. 'Meanwhile, what should I do with *you*?'

'Lady Peony,' Harriet began carefully, taking another subtle step towards the door.

'*Lady* Peony?' the other woman mocked. 'I must be in trouble.'

'If you come with me to the station and confess to everything, I'll be sure to put in a good word for you.'

Peony glanced towards the rain pounding on the window, but not long enough for Harriet to make a dash for the door. 'In this weather?'

'My superior officer will be here very soon. He'll bring his car.' (One more step.)

'That's a shame,' Peony said, 'because he'll be too late.'

Harriet swallowed. 'Could you lower the pistol? You're making me anxious.'

'That's entirely the point.' Peony pulled back the hammer.

And Harriet bolted, straight into the kitchen. There were two exits. One led into the great hall, the other into the courtyard. Harriet sprinted towards the back door, but she was moving too fast, the flagstone floor was worn and uneven, and she immediately tripped.

Above her head something hit the door, creating a shower of splinters.

Bloody hell!

From the sound of footsteps, Peony was drawing closer.

How long did it take to reload a flintlock?

The door was too far away. Harriet would never make it. Instead, she rolled across the floor, scrambling for the nearest cover, which was the servants' staircase.

Now would be the opportunity to discover just how dangerous it was.

Trying not to think of all those films where the idiot chase-victim chooses to go *up* a building instead of getting out, Harriet ran up it, jumping over each missing step.

'You're wasting your time!' Peony called after her, perfectly politely. 'If you don't break your neck, the only way out of the house is right here.'

Or via the main staircase which would lead her to the front door, and she'd won prizes at school for sprinting. Peony would never be able to keep up with her.

Peony didn't even try.

As Harriet yanked open the door onto the gallery, Peony had already run into the hall.

Something cracked into one of the gallery banisters, splintering it.

Harriet did an about turn and almost fell into the nearest bedroom, closing the door quietly behind her in the hope Peony wouldn't have seen which room she'd gone into.

As with most of Blackheath Hall, the furniture had been shrouded by those creepy dust sheets – easy to hide beneath or behind, but equally easy for Peony to rip off and find her.

Harriet headed for the window but, like the others at Blackheath Hall, it was tall and thin: a mullion window with stone columns dividing it into three.

Beneath the nearest dust sheet, she found a dressing table and stool. The stool was too small, but she dragged the dressing table beneath the window and climbed onto it, flipping up the window catch and shoving it open.

She'd forgotten about the storm. Even though the window overlooked the side of the house, which was more sheltered, the wind still howled through, tearing off more dust sheets and sending them flying around the room.

Harriet carefully stepped onto the stone windowsill and peered outside. The ground was a dizzying distance below. It would be a hard, painful fall.

Why was she even *considering* this?

She searched for an alternative and spotted a wooden trellis within grabbing distance. Maybe it had once held some kind of climbing plant but right now it would make an excellent ladder.

She squeezed through the narrow gap, grabbing the trellis and swinging onto it as the bedroom door opened and a projectile shattered the window beside her.

Peony muttered something that might have been a curse, but Harriet didn't bother to listen. She half-climbed, half-fell down the trellis, splinters jabbing into her fingers, until about halfway, when, with a loud 'crack', the trellis snapped from the wall and crashed to the ground. She only fell a couple of metres, but it was enough to knock the breath right out of her.

It took a couple of moments for her to force herself to her feet and stagger around the corner, only to go headfirst into a bedwarming pan that had Lady Peony on the other end of it.

As Harriet was knocked back, tripping over the stone steps leading up to the main entrance of Blackheath Hall and sliding into unconsciousness, the last thing she heard was, 'Sorry, darling, but it's for the best. You'll see...'

THIRTY-EIGHT

TEN YEARS PREVIOUSLY

'Wait,' Phyllis said.

The men in the muniment room turned to look at her.

'You're going to plead for his life?' Fisher sounded amused. 'This should be entertaining. Not sure I have the time though. Can we skip to the end?'

'I'll do it,' she said.

'Do what?'

'Kill him,' she said, and held out her hand.

Fisher burst out laughing. 'A fan of yours, is she?' he said to Kieran.

But Kieran was staring at Phyllis.

What the hell?

'Er, Phyllis?' he said.

Fisher glanced between them and smiled. 'Adorable.' He held out his hand without taking his attention from Kieran. One of the other men handed over a gun and Fisher gave it to Phyllis.

Kieran looked at her in disbelief. They'd played together as kids. At one time he'd even suspected she had a crush on him. This was a double-cross. It had to be. She'd point the gun at Fisher and tell him to...

Except Phyllis was now pointing the gun at *him*.

Did she know what she was *doing* with that thing?

'Er... Phyllis?' he said again.

She winked – then casually shot him in the shoulder.

It was like being stung by a very large, very angry wasp. His legs gave way and he collapsed straight onto the pile of rubbish littering the muniment room floor. Something stabbed his knee and the pain was so excruciating he almost passed out. When his vision cleared, it was to see Fisher directing his gang to grab anything of value and get out of there.

It was too late.

There were heavy boots outside, shouts of 'Armed police' and orders to throw away their weapons and lie on the floor.

This meant Kieran was now indistinguishable from Fisher and his men.

It was hard to see how things could have gone more wrong.

Any moment now, he was going to be yanked to his feet and lined up with the rest of them, except he didn't think he could stand.

He closed his eyes. This was going to hurt...

'Wait! He's with me.'

Kieran opened his eyes to see DI Davenport crouched beside him, his thin face creased with worry. 'Is she safe?' Kieran asked.

'Esme's fine,' Davenport said. 'She told the man left guarding her that she needed the loo, and then hit him with a chair. She was tying him up with a pair of stockings when we arrived. Seemed quite disappointed to be interrupted, actually. An impressive lady, your grandmother.'

She certainly was.

'How about you?' Davenport asked, speaking in that cheery voice people often used when they were trying to hide bad news. 'You look like you've been through the wars...'

'I'm fine,' Kieran said. 'Although it's a bit cold in here...'

He couldn't stop shivering and shut his eyes again as a wave of tiredness rolled over him.

'Medic!' he heard Davenport shout. 'I need a medic!'

Had someone been hurt? Was it Phyllis?
He should help but he couldn't even sit up.
It was so hard to stay awake...

THIRTY-NINE
PRESENT DAY

Ben exited the interview room to discover the storm had taken out the power and the emergency generators had kicked in. The rest of the village was in darkness, apart from the streetlights. Roads were flooded and trees were down, taking power cables and telephone lines with them. Although the worst of the storm had passed, Raven's Edge had been completely cut off from its neighbours and was likely to remain that way for some time.

A Major Incident had been declared and the station was emptying fast, as his fellow officers headed out to help the other emergency services. He was just wondering how to warn Harriet and Sam about Peony and Rose at Blackheath Hall, when, as though he'd conjured him up, Sam ran through the public entrance to the police station, leaving a trail of water and mud across the floor, without seeing Ben standing just inside the door.

Ben grabbed him before he could run past. 'What's happened?'

'The power's out at Blackheath Hall. I called at The Witch's Brew to get help from Jake Davenport, but the place was deserted, so I ran here. We need back-up, if you can spare...' Sam trailed off, realising everyone was leaving. 'Although I can see you can't. Don't worry, we'll be OK. The house has stood for – what, five hundred years? It should be good for a while longer yet.'

Having seen Blackheath Hall, he had to admire Sam's optimism.

'Wait, there's been a development.' He turned to Dakota, who'd followed him. 'Call in CSI to search Stuart Huntingdon's house once the roads reopen. Specifically, I need them to search for the missing metal detector, Kyle Hayward's bag and any tools, and Huntingdon's Cavalier costume, which probably has blood on it. Once confronted with solid evidence, Huntingdon might be more honest with us. If I'm not back within the hour, resume his interview. Have Ash sit in with you. He needs the experience. We need to decide whether to charge Huntingdon with manslaughter or murder. If we run him through his story again, some elements might change enough to clarify that.'

Dakota beamed. 'Yes, sir!'

He turned back to Sam. 'Call out an armed response vehicle to Blackheath Hall and follow me in your car. Harriet's in danger. I believe Peony might have shot Drake.'

'*Peony?* Bloody hell! I've left Harriet alone with her!' Sam turned, as though about to disappear back into the storm.

Ben yanked him back. 'Armed response vehicle; follow me in your car,' he repeated. 'We need to check Harriet is safe before charging in with sirens blaring. We don't want to panic Peony into doing something stupid.'

'Right away, sir.' Sam disappeared up the stairs to the MIT office.

Ben grabbed a police-issue anorak and headed out into the storm.

Although the streetlights along the main road were lit, Blackheath Hall was in darkness like the rest of Raven's Edge. Ben parked on one side of the courtyard, grabbed his torch from the glove compartment, pulled on the anorak but left his wellington boots in the back.

Expecting his sergeant, he was unsettled when Lady Peony answered the door. Did that mean something had happened to Harriet?

Keeping his voice and expression neutral, he inclined his head. 'Good evening, Lady Peony. Do you remember me? I'm Detective Inspector Taylor. I'm glad to see you're in good health. I hope this power cut isn't causing too much inconvenience for you?'

'It's a damned nuisance,' Lady Peony muttered, turning her head away to yell 'I'm coming!' before stepping back to allow him to enter the great hall. 'I'm sorry, Detective Inspector. My sister is playing up because of the power cut. She doesn't mind thunderstorms but she's terrified of the dark. Do come in. I'll make you a nice cup of tea.'

Ben entered the hall, taking care to wipe his feet, conscious he was dripping all over the floor. 'No, thank you. I've just called to have a word with DS March, if that's possible? Where is she?'

Lady Peony frowned and glanced at her watch. 'That's a very good question. Harriet thought she saw an intruder outside and went to investigate. I've been so busy, I hadn't realised it must have been a good twenty minutes ago. Oh dear... I do hope nothing's happened to her.'

'Harriet went outside on her own?'

Leaving the two ladies to fend for themselves? That didn't sound right.

'She's been gone for such a long time...' Lady Peony trailed off, anxiously twisting her hands together. 'Parts of the house are in ruins, as you know, and not safe at all, particularly with this awful weather. Do you think something might have happened to her?'

In this storm? Very likely! What the hell had Harriet been *thinking*?

'She's definitely not in the house?' Ben glanced towards the staircase leading up to the gallery. Unlike outside, the house was almost supernaturally still and quiet. It was easy to believe Peony was alone in the house, but hadn't she mentioned that her sister was upstairs?

'I would've heard Harriet come back inside.' Peony lowered her voice confidingly. 'The door has a habit of slamming in this wind.'

Back into the storm it was then. 'Which direction did DS March take?'

'If she's not in the courtyard, she must have gone into the garden. There's nowhere else to go.'

'Don't worry, I'm sure I'll find her.'

'Thank you! You know, Harriet might have taken cover in the old mausoleum, beyond the garden wall? It's not kept locked.'

Why on earth would Harriet shelter in the mausoleum when Lady Peony and her sister could be in danger here at the house? None of this made any sense but Peony was regarding him anxiously. If she was playing a part, she was doing so very convincingly. Could Stuart Huntingdon have made a mistake – or even spun him another web of lies? What about Peony's sister Rose? Could she have shot Drake? Should he search the house before the garden?

But for that he'd need back-up and there was still no sign of Sam, let alone the armed response vehicle.

'I'll be right back,' he told Peony. 'DC Sam King will be returning very shortly. You won't be on your own for long.'

'Thank you!' Peony said, looking absurdly grateful.

Still conflicted, Ben stepped back into the torrential rain, yanking up the hood of his anorak, not that it made much difference. It would be impossible for him to get any wetter.

The courtyard was surrounded by a high stone wall, with the main gatehouse opposite and a small arch on the east side that led into the garden. It was the same route, in reverse, that he and Harriet had taken when they'd first arrived at Blackheath Hall.

'Harriet!' he yelled into the dark, but the wind whipped his voice away.

The garden was so overgrown there was only one useable path, leading through the tangled bushes towards another gate on the opposite side. He followed it, calling Harriet's name again and again, swinging the torch around in the hope of finding her.

The more he considered the idea of Harriet abandoning two (allegedly) vulnerable, elderly ladies, the more ridiculous it seemed. She was nothing if not tenacious. Even if she'd gone outside, she wouldn't seek shelter. She'd walk through the storm regardless of how wet she got.

If she'd not returned to the house, that meant she'd met with an accident.

With the help of Lady Peony?

Her concern for Harriet had seemed genuine, but had this all been a ruse to get him out of the house?

And he'd fallen for it? What had happened to his default, always assuming guilt? Had he really been swayed by the pleas of a little old lady? If she'd been a man, and the same age as him, would he have believed her? Not a chance!

He was an utter *fool*!

But he'd better check Harriet *wasn't* out here before he turned back.

He took out his phone to warn Sam to be on his guard: no signal. He almost threw the thing into the shrubbery. *Why* hadn't he picked up a radio before he left the station?

Because he'd been in a hurry, allowing his emotions to overrule logic.

He typed out the message anyway, giving an update and explaining where he was going, hit 'send', then slid the phone back into his pocket before any error message appeared.

'*Harriet!*'

Where are you...?

He'd give it five more minutes and then head back. By then, Sam should have arrived. They could take Peony into custody and thoroughly search the house. Do the job properly this time, as DCI Cameron would have said.

Five more minutes...

Reaching the far side of the garden, he stepped through the gate and into the woods, which gave him some shelter from the storm. The path leading to the right and down the hill would end up at the battlefield and then the Gateway to the Dead. That meant the left-hand path must lead to the mausoleum. It was overgrown to the point of being non-existent. Had Harriet really come this way?

He shoved his way through the bushes, falling out into a clearing where a short, squat structure had been built into a low, manmade hill.

The mausoleum, as Lady Peony had said.

Illuminated by his torch were mossy stone steps leading down to a door very similar to the one at Blackheath Hall.

He banged on it. 'Harriet! Are you in there?'

There was a rusted key in the lock. He turned it. The door opened outward and he took a step inside. Curiously, the air was warm and musty, not damp and cold as he'd expected. Perhaps because the room had been built into a hill?

'Harriet?'

He ran the beam of the torch in a wide arc. It wasn't a large room and there were no coffins, for which he was *very* grateful. The mausoleum had been plainly decorated, with a bare stone floor and walls, and a solitary chest tomb in the centre. Little pools of wax showed someone had placed a multitude of candles there a long time ago.

He walked towards it. How strange, to have an entire mausoleum dedicated to one person – although it would explain why 'Blackheath' had been carved on the lintel over the door rather than 'Weston'. This must be the last resting place of one of the Victorian Marquesses. Perhaps the last one with money.

There was a movement behind him and he quickly turned. 'Harriet?'

It was only the door slamming shut, blown by the wind.

This was hopeless. Harriet had never been here. He was wasting his time, perhaps as Lady Peony had intended.

He returned to the door and turned the handle.

It was stuck.

He yanked at it and then ran his torch around the edge to see if anything was blocking it. The key had been in the lock. Could it have locked itself with the force of that slam? Or was something more sinister in play?

He checked for a phone signal, knowing he was wasting his time. The message to Sam hadn't been sent either.

Could there be another way out?

He swung the torch around again. There were no other doors or a staircase to the room he knew was above, only a long table at the far side, covered in curious black lumps, with two shadowy shapes behind it.

At first his mind couldn't process what he was seeing.

A person? A woman?

Was it *Harriet*? Was she... dead?

'Hello?'

He moved closer but the woman remained perfectly still. Brown hair tumbled around her shoulders, but her eyes were closed and her cheeks sunken. As he drew closer, he knew she was dead and had been for some time, reclining in an ornate chair that must have come from the Hall. She looked like a queen, with diamonds in her hair and around her neck, and was wearing the faded remnants of a full-skirted gown that must once have been a beautiful dark crimson.

Lady Rose Weston?

And she was still wearing her wedding dress.

FORTY

Drake spent most of his day trying to catch up with everything he'd neglected while on the fool's errand of searching for his assailant – and trying to forget his conversation with Phyllis.

He'd almost succeeded when Esme entered his office and caught him with his feet up on the desk, a coffee cradled against his chest and his eyes *briefly* closed.

'Kieran Drake! How can you *sleep* when there are two vulnerable old ladies at the mercy of every con artist in the King's Forest?'

The front legs of his chair hit the floor, jarring him awake.

'Wha—? Oh, damn, Esme! You made me spill my coffee.'

'I'll tip it over your head if you don't return to Blackheath Hall and sort out the mess you've created. Speakers? Motion detectors? *Holographic projections?*'

'*Speakers*,' he protested. 'That was all. Designed to recreate the knock of Major Lord John Weston. Holographic projections are not in my skillset, budget or even *possible* in a place like Blackheath Hall. You *know* all this, so...' He broke off, eyes narrowing. 'What's happened?'

'DCI Cameron is withdrawing all police support by twelve tomorrow.'

'I'm surprised he kept them there for so long, to be honest.' He took a sip of his coffee and, finding it cold, grimaced. He held it out to Esme hopefully.

She glared at him. 'Get back to Blackheath Hall and sort out their ghost problem or you can find another receptionist. I don't have to work here, you know. I was having a lovely retirement—'

'Rubbish. You were bored out of your mind.'

'Kieran, these are two defenceless old ladies. If you could find out who's been terrorising them...?'

'OK, OK' – he dropped the coffee onto his desk – 'I'm going.'

Esme beamed. 'Excellent. And if you could call in at Pizza at Cosimo's on the way home? I don't feel like cooking tonight.'

Drake might not have been so quick to agree if he'd realised how much the weather had worsened while he'd been asle... *working*. The road through Calahurst was closed due to flooding, and there was another 'road closed' sign along the cliff road, which he completely ignored and just drove around. The streetlights seemed to be OK but Blackheath Hall was in darkness when he pulled up beside the gatehouse.

The force of the wind almost knocked him off his feet as he got out of the car. He was about to run across the courtyard, bang on the door and demand to be let in, when he caught movement in the garden beyond the east wall and hesitated. Was that a *person* or had some piece of junk been caught by the wind?

He sheltered beneath the gatehouse while he considered the situation. The garden was in darkness but so was the house. Was someone taking advantage of that?

The lightning flashed again, making him jump. This time he saw the figure more clearly, before he was plunged into darkness.

With horrible clarity, he remembered what Phyllis had said to him.

'*I see a woman in a red dress.*'

Was *this* what she'd meant?

He wasn't even sure he'd seen a *woman*, let alone the colour of her clothes. Why would anyone be outside on a night like this? He must have imagined it.

He had *imagined* it...

Lightning tore through the sky.

There you go: *nothing*.

Except... He squinted against the light. A woman in red, looking directly at him, disappearing before the flash had even faded.

He leant back against the wall, heart racing uncomfortably, too stunned to even curse.

The rain hadn't affected her.

It was as though the rain wasn't *there*.

Or rather, *she* wasn't.

Oh *hell*...

Had he actually seen... a *ghost*?

No, no, no. It was a figment of his imagination, brought on by painkillers, lack of sleep, too much caffeine – take your pick.

There are no such things as ghosts.

Curse Esme for bringing him out on a night like this. Now he was seeing things. Curse Drew Elliott for setting him up, curse Ben Taylor for interfering, and curse the entire Weston family for being so terrible with money they'd landed themselves in this mess in the first place, dragging everyone else along too.

He risked another look around the gatehouse. Thunder cracked so loudly the ground seemed to vibrate beneath his feet.

House or garden? Where should he go first? The house would be drier, but...

You always have a choice.

'I can't believe I'm doing this,' he muttered, turning up his collar and sprinting for the garden, remembering at the last moment to take out his phone to use as a torch before he tripped over and broke his neck, which would really complete his day.

He kept to the narrow path, seeing nothing more. There was nowhere for his 'ghost' to hide. There was nothing beyond the garden gate but the forest and the Gateway to the Dead. Had this been an elaborate attempt to lure him away from the house? Was this an ambush?

Here on the hill, the gale forced the trees to bend almost double. Drake caught a brief glimpse of red to his left and then nothing more, even when the next bolt of lightning lit up the forest.

Well, he'd come this far...

Forcing a path through the bushes, he stumbled out into a clearing where a small stone structure had been built into a grassy incline.

Was this the mausoleum Peony had told them about?

There was no sign of his 'ghost'.

It was certainly a strange old building. Mossy stone steps led down to a wooden door, very similar to that at Blackheath Hall but without the giant knocker.

Why would you need a knocker on a door to the dead?

He descended the steps – carefully, because they were wet.

Was he *seriously* considering entering a mausoleum after dark, during a violent thunderstorm?

No.

Decisively, he turned away – and saw a woman waiting for him at the top of the steps.

This one was real. She was as soaked as him, hair plastered over her forehead, make-up tracking her cheeks.

'*Lady Peony?* What are you doing out—'

She raised her hand.

He recognised the movement.

It sent him straight back to two nights ago and the doorstep of Blackheath Hall.

This time, instead of looking at her face, he glanced at her raised hand – and saw what she held in it.

Damn.

'*You don't have to believe in ghosts, Kieran Drake. You just have to know when to—*'

He ducked.

A lead ball ripped through the wood above his head.

She'd shot at him!

With a wall on either side, he was a fish in a barrel unless he moved *quickly*.

He groped for the handle behind him and found a key instead, turning it and yanking at the door. It was heavier than he'd expected, scraping over the uneven stone, but there was a gap wide enough for him to slide through.

The door slammed shut with very little effort and he was fumbling for a bolt, *anything* to keep her out, when something splintered the wood beside his head.

'Bloody hell!'

Sliding sideways, he hoped the stone wall would do a better job of protecting him. If she followed him in here, he'd knock the flint-lock out of her hand. It was what he should've done when he first saw her. Now he was cowering inside this tomb, waiting for her next shot.

She was taking her time. How long had it been? Twenty seconds?

Why hadn't she fired again? Had the pistol jammed? Had she run out of lead shot?

Had she taken the easier option and locked him in?

It's what he would have done.

Why hadn't he grabbed the key?

Slowly, silently, he reached for the door handle.

Not only did it fail to turn, the door didn't budge either.

He rattled it.

Thumped it with the side of his fist.

He was locked in.

How had *he* fallen for the oldest trick in the book?

He kicked the door but only succeeded in hurting his foot. That thing was *solid*.

'I tried that too,' a familiar voice said. 'I'm afraid we're stuck.'

He hardly needed to, but he lifted his torch anyway.

A tall blond man raised his hand to shield his eyes.

'Ben Taylor? *Damn*... Somebody up there must hate me.'

'The feeling, I assure you, is mutual,' came Taylor's stiff reply. 'Why don't we work together to find a way out of here? Do you have your tool kit on you?'

'I'm not entirely sure what kind of "tool kit" you're referring to – presumably something illegal and therefore not what I'd be in the habit of carrying on my person, *obviously* – but this is a very big, very old lock. Even if I *could* get inside it, the mechanism would likely be rusted up.'

'I appreciate that you're feeling angry and frustrated because you're trapped—'

'Do *not* psycho-analyse me, petal, because we've been on the same course and I *will* do it right back.'

There was silence for a moment and then... 'Why do you persist in calling me that?'

Despite his mood, Taylor's vexed tone made him smile. 'Because it annoys you.'

'Why annoy me? We're in this together for a few hours yet.'

'*Days*, mate.' Drake felt suddenly tired. 'We're going to be here for days.' *If not forever.* 'Who knows this place is here? Your lot will search the house and the forest before they even think to check in here. Dozy fools.'

There was a slight pause before Taylor said, 'They used to be "your lot" too.'

'Not for a very long time.'

If ever.

Taylor was silent again, and then he said, 'Why *did* you resign?'

'It's no business of yours.'

'What else are we going to talk about?'

'Ways to get out?' Drake raised his phone again and saw that Taylor was leaning against the edge of a large marble tomb, arms folded, far too relaxed. Also caught in the beam was the end of a long wooden table behind him and a row of chairs. Why hadn't he sat there? Although a table did seem to be a strange thing to have in a mausoleum...

Drake ran the beam along the length, which had curious black lumps arranged on it, and—

'Bloody hell!'

Taylor winced. 'Sorry, I forgot to mention we're not alone.'

Drake used his torch to outline the two figures sitting at the centre of the table. His first thought was that they were plastic skeletons, abandoned after a Halloween party. Following hard on that was the horrible realisation that the remains were human – and mummified. In a poignant touch, their clothes had been almost perfectly preserved. One wore a morning suit with a cravat and winged collar. The other...

Oh no...

The other wore a scarlet wedding dress. He could even see the remains of a long veil, held in place by a diamond tiara, glittering in his torchlight. There were more large diamonds around her throat. If they were real, they'd be worth a fortune.

Were they real? Was *this* what Bailey had been searching for?

'I see a woman in a red dress... She's dancing. She's happy.'

'I believe this is Lady Rose Weston,' Taylor said, in answer to the question Drake couldn't bring himself to ask. 'The other is her husband, whose name I don't know. According to someone I was speaking with recently, they held their wedding reception here forty years ago and... er, it appears they never left.'

'If that's Lady Rose Weston,' Drake said, 'who's lying in bed at Blackheath Hall, watching back-to-back *Pride and Prejudice* films?'

'An excellent question,' Ben said. 'Unfortunately, I don't have a clue.'

'Two random little old ladies found Blackheath Hall empty and decided to move in?'

'Possibly.'

'That wasn't the real Lady Peony who locked us in here?'

'Probably not.'

Drake put his head in his hands. 'I am *never* going to live this down. Scammed – *me!* – by two little old ladies!'

'You and me both,' Taylor sighed.

'It might be easier if we stayed here.'

Taylor grimaced. 'Perhaps.'

'Maybe someone will find *us* in forty years' time.'

'Possibly sooner, if my cousin buys the house, knocks it down and builds a housing estate.'

'Here's hoping!'

They lapsed into silence and then Taylor said, 'Why do you hate me?'

'I don't "hate" you. You irritate me, certainly, with your boy scout attitude and how everything's been handed to you on a plate, and you don't even seem to realise that.'

'Don't be ridiculous.'

'You became a detective inspector with minimum effort—'

'I worked hard!'

'You were awarded a scholarship!' Drake snapped. 'You were fast-tracked.'

'You could have done the same!'

'No, I couldn't. You're oblivious to all the opportunities you've had.'

'Opportunities!' Taylor retorted. 'I've had to fight for *everything*. My father was sent to prison for fifteen years for armed robbery. The entire village thought I was cut from the same cloth. Why do you think I left as soon as I could? It took a lot for the police to even consider my application.'

'It was my dream to become a police detective,' Drake sighed. 'Right from being a little kid.'

He'd not told anyone that before, not even Esme. Why tell Taylor?

Because they might never get out of here.

'And then you were shot on duty and invalided out,' Taylor said. 'I'm sorry.'

'What? No! That's not what happened! Is that what they're saying?' Despite everything, he couldn't help laughing.

'You were a hero,' Taylor said. Although now, to add insult to injury, he sounded doubtful.

'A hero? What does that even mean? That I was too stupid to duck? I've no idea how *that* rumour started. In my entire life, I've never saved anyone except for myself. I didn't even get the girl.'

That caught Taylor's attention. 'The girl?'

Uh oh.

'Figuratively speaking. Seriously, there was no girl. Forget I even—'

'You care for Milla...' Ben said. 'I knew it! Why else would you have risked getting involved with that business over at Ravenswood House? It was to save *her*, wasn't it?'

'I'm *not* in the business of saving damsels in distress. In fact, usually *I'm* the one—'

Taylor wasn't listening. 'And you hate that she chose me.'

His worst enemy couldn't have picked a better punishment: stuck in a mausoleum with Milla Graham's jealous boyfriend.

Old Drake would have said, 'But has she, mate?', even though he knew that Taylor was right. New Drake decided he might as well admit the truth.

'I felt sorry for Milla,' he said, 'having a father like Dermot Graham. Wealthy as hell, but he still kept finding excuses not to let her into his family – yet wanted to keep tabs on everything she did.'

And possibly because Milla reminded him of Bailey, his childhood sweetheart, who'd also been inflicted with appalling relatives who didn't seem to care about her.

He liked to wind Taylor up about 'saving the girl' but wasn't he the same? When it came down to it, the only woman who'd ever tried to save *him* was Phyllis Halfpenny – and look at the way he'd treated her.

'I see...' Taylor said slowly, although he plainly didn't.

But then the mausoleum door creaked open and both men rushed to duck behind the marble tomb.

'Um, boss? Are you in here?'

'Don't shut the door!' they shouted in unison.

(As it slammed shut.)

Really, DI Ben Taylor had an impressive knowledge of Anglo-Saxon curses despite that boy scout reputation.

Drake swung the beam of his torch towards the door, spotlighting DC Sam King, with one hand over his eyes against the glare and the other holding a large iron key.

'I'm not receiving any "pleased to see you" vibes?' DC King grumbled.

Presumably that was a joke, but Drake didn't feel like laughing.

'You're living dangerously, young King,' he said, swiping the key and inserting it into the lock. The door opened easily. 'Let's go.'

FORTY-ONE
TEN YEARS PREVIOUSLY

The only people to visit Kieran in hospital were his boss and his grandmother, who fussed over him, bringing him little treats every day, which was lovely, but did his head in.

'I'm not dead,' he told her, after the third day. 'I'm going to make a full recovery.'

The last bit was a lie. The bullet wound had given him very little bother, apart from the initial pain, but his knee, where he'd fallen on it, was agony. He'd fractured his patella and torn a ligament. Now his leg was in plaster with the prospect of more surgery to come.

DI Jake Davenport, when he came to visit, seemed equally morose. Kieran knew it couldn't be good news, but even he wasn't prepared for... 'When you're fit, you'll be expected to attend a disciplinary hearing,' Davenport said. 'The entire case has been taken over by the Detective Chief Superintendent, and he believes he has enough evidence to charge you, along with Arlo Fisher, with robbery. Fisher insists the entire plan was your idea, and the fact that you and he have known each other since childhood, as well as Phyllis Halfpenny... Well, it doesn't look good.'

Kieran was too stunned to reply.

'I am *so* sorry...' And, to his credit, the DI did look wretched. 'I did my best to persuade him otherwise, assuming that even if they charged you as an accessory, we could work with that. But you were also caught in the muniment room with the others—'

'Because they threatened my grandmother.'

'We have no proof of that. Just your word – and hers – against theirs. It didn't help that she escaped...'

Thank goodness she had, because if he'd relied on *this* lot to rescue her...

'It's up to the Crown Prosecution Service, of course, but the Detective Chief Superintendent believes he has enough evidence to secure a conviction.'

That was that then.

Kieran turned his face to the wall. 'They want to make an example of me, because of my background.'

'I'm sure that's not true. It's circumstantial evidence at best. We can fight against it.'

'What if I don't want to?'

He remembered the day he'd stood in the tin shack and proudly told his father he'd been accepted into the police.

Francis had barked a laugh. '*My* son? They'd never have you.'

Well, it had taken them six years, but they'd finally found a way to exterminate the street rat.

'The Federation are hard at work behind the scenes on your behalf...'

Kieran turned, frowning. 'Why? I didn't ask them to.'

'*I* did. You've been incapacitated. I thought they would have sent a rep to speak to you by now, actually.'

'Tell them not to bother.'

He had an idea that Davenport would tell them no such thing, but hoped he'd leave anyway. Never had he wanted to be left alone so much.

'Fisher and his associates have been arrested and charged,' Davenport said.

Did he think that was going to make him feel better?

'He was hoping for bail,' Davenport added.

'In which case, he'll be back on the streets before me,' Kieran said. The words were supposed to have sounded upbeat, like a joke. They fell utterly flat.

He couldn't bear to see the pity in Davenport's eyes.

Go away...

'I was going to put in a good word for Phyllis Halfpenny when her trial comes up,' Davenport said, as though that would cheer him up.

'What the hell for? *She's* the reason I'm in here!'

The DI glanced towards Kieran's leg. They both knew that if it hadn't been for his fall, he'd have been discharged days ago – and be awaiting trial in Norchester prison, along with Arlo Fisher.

'Fisher threatened to hurt her family, too, but she deliberately shot to miss you,' Davenport said. 'I'm surprised she didn't shoot Fisher, to be honest, but I'm glad she didn't. That would have complicated matters. This way, if she admits to everything she might only serve a few months.'

'Lovely,' Kieran deadpanned.

'She saved your life.'

It was like being told off by a supply teacher. How on earth had Davenport made detective inspector?

'Tell her not to bother next time.' Kieran closed his eyes. 'Just go for it.'

'Kieran?' Now the DI sounded worried. 'Are you feeling low? It's quite common after anaesthetic, you know. I'm sure you'll feel more yourself tomorrow.'

Kieran doubted he'd feel like himself ever again.

'Phyllis is worried about you.'

'She should be.'

'She heard my team arrive outside the museum and stalled for time. If Fisher had shot you, you *would* be dead. *That's* why she volunteered to do it. She *saved* you.'

'And you believe her?'

'I thought she was your friend? That you were... fond of her?'

'I've gone off her a lot since she shot me.'

'She cares about you.'

'Because my testimony is likely to put her in prison!'

DI Davenport studied him. 'You need time to recover,' he said kindly. 'We'll talk again, when you're back at work.'

'I'm not *coming* back to work,' Kieran said. Why couldn't this man understand? 'I quit. Tell the Detective Chief Superintendent to charge me with whatever he likes. I'll see him in court – and I'll take you *all* to the cleaners.'

FORTY-TWO
PRESENT DAY

Sunday

Harriet woke to find herself lying in a dusty attic room with a dead man.

She'd had better days.

She knew she was in an attic because the ceiling sloped and had a tiny window set into it, yet all she could see through it was the stormy sky.

Ignoring her pounding head, she stood up, albeit swaying slightly, and staggered over to check on the dead man. Her feet left prints on the dusty floorboards which were broken in several places; she had to take care not to misstep, not least because she didn't trust the floor beneath this one to break her fall either.

The dead man wasn't much older than her, maybe around thirty. He lay on a metal-framed bed that had been made up with mould-spotted sheets – probably caused by the constant drip of rainwater through the roof.

Although pale, he didn't appear to have been dead for very long. His blond hair was cut into what her grandmother would have called a pudding-basin style. His clothes were clean but well-worn – a pale-blue cotton shirt mismatched with beige corduroy trousers, and a fisherman's waistcoat with a multitude of pockets.

What would a dead *fisherman* be doing in the attic at Blackheath Hall?

Ben would have told her she was asking the wrong question.

Shouldn't she have double-checked the man actually *was* dead?

She leant over him, pressing two fingers to the side of his neck, only for him to jerk open his eyes.

It was hard to know who was more shocked.

'Who are you?' he demanded.

His accent was fancier than Peony's.

'Detective Sergeant Harriet March. Who are *you*?'

'I'm Blackheath,' he said, as though she should already know.

'Blackheath?' she repeated dubiously. 'Like the house?' Because the surname of the people who lived here was Weston.

He laughed but it turned into a coughing fit. He might be alive but did not seem well. 'My name is Giles Weston. I'm the *Marquess* of Blackheath.'

'A lot of people have been looking for you, Mr...' – how did one address a Marquess? – 'Giles.'

'Really?' He seemed anxious. 'Poor Jorge must be so worried. I was only supposed to be away for a weekend's fishing up at the lake.'

That explained the waistcoat.

'Then how did you end up...? No, forget I asked that. It's a stupid question. You trusted Lady Peony.'

He sighed. 'In a nutshell, yes.'

Harriet took another look around the attic. It was a horrible room; cold, damp and draughty. No fire had been lit in the tiny fireplace and the skeleton of a bird lay on the grate.

'How long have you been in here?' Was that the tapping she'd heard?

'I'm not sure. About a week? I thought it would be kind to call in on Peony and Rose as I was passing through the village. I wanted to tell them I'd had an offer on the house that I couldn't afford to turn down. I said I'd pay all their expenses if they moved out and I'd buy them a nice little cottage. Something that would be legally theirs, not subject to any silly trust or entailment like this one. I thought they'd be pleased but Peony was very rude to me, accusing me of kicking them out and making them homeless, which wasn't true.'

Exchange the prestige of a manor house, even a decrepit one, for a small cottage? Was he truly that naïve?

'Blackheath Hall *was* their childhood home. I expect they're very fond of it.'

Now she sounded like Ben.

'I then made it worse,' Giles said, 'because I realised the lady who'd introduced herself to me as Peony was someone else entirely.'

'What?'

'*Peony* was the woman she'd introduced as Rose.'

'Say that again.'

'Lady Rose is Lady Peony, and Lady Peony is someone else. *That's* why I'm here. I stumbled on their deception.'

It sounded so bizarre she had to ask, 'Are you *sure*?'

'I wasn't at first,' he admitted. 'Little old ladies look much the same to me: white hair, a twinkle in the eye, knitting on the go, that kind of thing.'

Giles Weston had obviously *never* met Brianna Graham.

'It was when I was introduced to Lady Rose that I twigged. She was too *tall*. Unlike the rest of us, who are blond giants, Rose was small and dark-haired. My grandfather once said, quite casually, that he was glad Rose was a girl because otherwise she'd have inherited everything and that would have been unfair to the rest of us.'

Harriet frowned. 'For a woman to inherit?'

'No – because Rose's *real* father was an Argentinian polo player! She's not a Weston at all!'

They were drifting too far off track. 'OK, if Peony is pretending to be Rose, who's Peony?'

'I believe she's my Great-Aunt Thea – my grandfather's sister. They quarrelled over forty years ago. I'd never met her, but the family resemblance is strong. I can't see who else she could be.'

'What happened next?' Harriet asked, although she had a fairly good idea.

'They offered me a rather disgusting cup of tea, which I felt obliged to pretend to drink – I much prefer coffee – and secretly poured the rest into the hearth. The next thing I remember was waking up here.'

Harriet shivered. He wouldn't have been the first person to fall for that trick. 'You were lucky it only knocked you out.'

He sighed. 'I've been shouting and banging on the door, but it's a big house so no one heard me. I thought I'd be stuck in here forever.'

'Has Thea given you any food?'

If she had, Harriet couldn't see any trace of it.

'I found a cleanish jug and glass on the table,' he said, 'and collected rainwater through the window. I had a packet of sandwiches in my pocket that I made last. No sign of my bag, sadly, because it had my phone inside, which would have been really useful.'

'Thea left you with no food or water?'

'I suppose she thought it would save her the trouble of murdering me herself. It's not easy to kill someone in cold blood.'

'But she's your *aunt*!'

'*Great*-aunt,' he said. 'I'd never have recognised her except she looks like the rest of us.' He pointed to his face. 'It's the Weston nose... I'm lucky really. She could have killed me there and then.'

Did he mean a slow death was preferable?

Well, *she* had no intention of being locked in here with only rainwater to drink!

She went over to the door and rattled it.

'I did try that,' Giles said mildly. 'It's quite sturdy, considering the rest of the house.'

'What's on the other side?'

'If I remember correctly, I believe this room is at the top of a small staircase hidden behind a painting of the Fifth Marquess in the gallery.'

'A *painting*?'

'Monstrous thing. You can't have missed it. Floor-to-ceiling affair, showing a supercilious chap wearing lots of lace and a big hat. Hard to believe we're related but, you know, the nose.' He pointed to his again.

'There's a *secret passage*? Behind the *painting*?'

'The house is riddled with them,' Giles said cheerfully. 'The staircase must have originally led onto the roof or into a tower – long demolished now – then hidden and turned into another priest's hole. There are several of those scattered around the house. We even have *fake* priest's holes – easy for the authorities to find and assume we weren't harbouring whoever it was they were looking for.'

Giles Weston sounded remarkably perky for someone who'd spent the last week locked up on his own with only a sandwich and a jug of rainwater.

'How long do you think Thea has been impersonating Peony?'

'It could have been going on for years, none of us would have known, although "Peony" sent me a letter via a solicitor about twelve months ago to say the house needed rewiring. We hadn't heard from her in years. My grandfather would have recognised Thea right away, but he was never interested in visiting. He said Peony would consider that an intrusion and it would create bad feeling between them. Someone did tell us Peony had closed up most of the rooms after her father – the old Marquess – died and my grandfather inherited. She cut herself off from the family completely. I expect that's why Thea found it so easy to impersonate her. None of us would have known what Peony looks like now. We only remember the pink hair.'

Harriet, remembering the real Peony's dementia, said, 'Did none of you *care* what happened to Peony? That she was living here all alone?'

'We did *try* to keep in contact,' he said. 'Of course we were worried, but she wouldn't answer the door to anyone. Grandpa said grief does funny things to people and we should let her be. She'd come around eventually. Sadly, she never did. After the old Marquess died, Lady Rose married the gardener and went to live in Australia, but we never heard from her again either. As you can see, we're not really a close family.'

'At least they were allowed to remain in the house.'

'I suspect the old Marquess thought Peony and Rose would move out as soon as they married, but Peony never did! They both receive an allowance from the estate, and legally Peony's responsible for any repairs while she lives here, but I had some spare cash from a good investment and paid for the rewiring myself. Peony obviously doesn't have two pennies to rub together but there was no sense in neglecting the property. It would become my responsibility again at some point and I didn't want to inherit a wreck.' He grimaced at that, the irony not escaping him.

Restless, Harriet checked the door again. *Could* she kick it down?

Presumably she'd be missed at some point – even if it was only when she didn't turn up for work – but would anyone think to search Blackheath Hall if Peony said she wasn't there?

She ran her fingers over the wood. As Giles had said, unlike the rest of the house, the door seemed fairly solidly built.

The floorboards, however...

She peered into the largest hole, but the room below was in darkness, with no furniture visible to provide a clue as to which one it was.

'What's beneath here?' she asked Giles.

He stood beside her. 'I'm not sure. I'd never actually been here before, only seen floorplans and heard my father's stories about the place. It *could* be one of the state rooms or it could be the nursery.

But if you're thinking of smashing your way through, be warned, the plaster on the other side is incredibly thick. In those days they made it with lime, sand and horsehair.'

'But it's old and presumably delicate? There's already a sizable hole in it!'

'It's also incredibly rare and valuable,' he snapped back, suddenly sounding a lot more Marquess-like. 'I'd rather you tried something else.'

She stared up at him. Had she understood correctly?

'You'd rather starve in an attic than have me put my boot through your fancy plaster ceiling?'

He hesitated. 'I'm hoping it won't come to that.'

'Well, I'm not ruling it out. Just so you know.'

'This *is* my house.'

'This is my *life*.'

They glared at each other.

'OK... How about the window?' she suggested, trying to ignore the pounding of rain on the slates above. 'I suppose it leads directly onto the roof?'

'Ye-es.'

'And then the walkway above the courtyard?'

'I suppose so.'

'Does the walkway have a parapet?'

'A parapet?'

She rolled her eyes. 'To stop me from sliding off the walkway and falling to my death?'

Unless she found a nice soft shrub to land on...

'Oh...' he said. 'To be honest, I've no idea. There's a pitched roof, but it doesn't extend over the walkway. The house was built *against* the wall at a later date, not *into* the wall. But the wall was slighted – partially demolished – during the Civil War. I wouldn't recommend walking on it. It's not safe.'

'Neither is staying in this attic,' she retorted, dragging a wooden chair across the room until it was directly beneath the window. 'What if Thea comes back with another pot of tea?'

Assuming she was serious, he said, 'I wouldn't drink it, obviously.'

'Maybe she wouldn't give you the choice!' Harriet climbed up onto the chair and shoved open the window.

She'd almost forgotten about the storm raging above. The wind snatched the window from her, lifting it up and over and slamming it against the roof. The single pane shattered instantly, the shards skittering over the slate tiles and pouring through the gap like a waterfall.

Giles cursed and jumped back out of the way.

Harriet covered her eyes and kept absolutely still.

Then shook herself.

When she opened her eyes again it was to find most of the glass had missed her and lay in a little glittering pile behind her.

Ignoring Giles's predictions of doom, she stuck her head through the window frame, only to be hit by a gust of freezing wind and rain so heavy it felt like hail.

'Perhaps if you waited until the storm passed?' Giles suggested, presumably hearing her curse. 'Or the morning?'

'By the morning we could be dead!'

Gritting her teeth, Harriet counted the seconds between the blinding flash of lightning and the rumbling crash that followed it.

'One, two, three... Damn, that one was loud! The storm must be almost directly overhead!'

'Come back!' Giles called.

Should she wait for it to pass?

And for Thea to return?

Without giving herself the chance to reconsider, Harriet levered herself onto the roof using her elbows, leaving her feet kicking ineffectually in the air, until Giles appeared beneath her, grabbed her thighs and shoved her up and through the gap – a little too enthusiastically. Fortunately, she had time to grab the sides of the wooden frame and turn around, so that she was facing the right way and not somersaulting headfirst down the roof.

As the window frame promptly crumbled into nothing beneath

her fingers, she lost her grip and began to slide down the roof, just as someone grabbed her hand.

She glanced up and saw Giles, who must have been standing on the chair because his head was now only centimetres from hers, his eyelashes stuck together from the rain, his hair flattened to his scalp, probably like hers.

'I've got you,' he said.

She smiled weakly. 'Thank you.'

'Are you coming back in now?'

She snorted. The sensible thing would have been not to come out here in the first place, but she had no intention of giving up now.

'Not yet,' she said. 'You're higher than me. Can you see what's behind me?'

'The... ah, roof?' he replied, as though it was a trick question. 'Um, the forest? I'm sure if I was taller, I'd be able to see the spires of Norchester.'

During a *storm?*

Harriet felt she really ought to win some kind of prize for keeping calm under extreme pressure.

'I meant, can you see if the walkway will break my fall or' – she swallowed – 'if I'd go straight over the edge and drop into the forest?'

Giles stood on tiptoe, but his frown didn't lessen. 'Purely from *memory*, you understand, the second floor and everything above it, including these attics, are a nineteenth-century addition, so the roof extends above the height of the walkway but doesn't cover it. It's why the rear of the house has always suffered from damp. But I wouldn't like to bet on—'

'That's good enough for me,' Harriet said.

She allowed her wet hand to slide through Giles's fingers.

And then she let go.

FORTY-THREE

The roof of Blackheath Hall was as smooth as glass.

Harriet scrabbled with her fingers, desperately trying to get a grip, to find a hand or foothold, but *nothing* slowed her fall.

Then the roof ended and there wasn't anything beneath her but air.

Was this it?

Was *this* how she was going to die?

Through sheer *stupidity*?

Then her feet hit the walkway and she overbalanced onto her rear (with enough force to knock a curse from her lips), before, for a grand finale, she smacked the back of her head on the stone parapet behind.

White sparkly stars danced between the raindrops as the stone wall of Blackheath Hall came into focus in front of her.

She'd fallen less than two metres from the edge of the roof.

Damn.

How lucky was she?

Still, better not do it again.

Or *tell* anyone.

Especially Ben.

She shoved her wet hair out of her eyes and sat up, taking a good look around. She'd been sitting on this wall for less than a minute but was already soaked and shivering, although that might have been shock from her fall.

To her left, beyond the far corner of the house, the walkway disintegrated into the garden – presumably a casualty of those Parliamentarian cannons. She could see the huge gap even through the torrential rain, and remembered the flowerpots arranged on the broken stones. There'd be no escape that way.

She turned her head. The walkway continued past the end of the house, curving around the courtyard to the opposite side and – thank *you* to whichever guardian angel was looking after her today – into one of the half-ruined towers that had once been the gatehouse.

Harriet placed her palms firmly on the balustrade and the wall of the house, and risked standing up. While the walkway felt firm enough beneath her feet, once past the shelter of the house, the rain stung her face and the wind howled along the length of the wall, tugging at her jacket and trying to knock her off balance.

This was one of the few times when being short was an advantage. Keeping her head low, she moved carefully, following the curving wall towards the first tower, checking each foothold was firm before trusting the walkway with her weight.

It seemed to take forever, but it was really only a few minutes before she was ducking through a stone archway and into the ruined tower. The steps here were long gone so she crossed over the gate and into the second tower, stepping directly onto a little wooden landing that seemed fairly new. Set in the opposite wall, another door-less arch led out onto the continuation of the walkway, but she certainly wasn't going that way. It led towards the garden and had been partially demolished.

It was such a relief to be out of the torrential rain.

Harriet turned to descend the spiral staircase—

And found Lady Peony Weston waiting for her, a distinctly unamused expression on her face.

Except she now knew this wasn't Lady Peony.

Thea Weston was as bedraggled as Harriet felt. Her pink hair hung in rats' tails around her face and her black eyeliner was smudged and streaked down her cheeks.

Harriet took a step back into the doorway.

A frozen blast of what felt like hail against her shoulders reminded her where she was, along with Thea's smirk.

Harriet stood a little straighter. 'Hello, Thea.' She kept her voice level and calm. 'I know about your deception. If you come with me to the station and provide a statement admitting to everything, I'll put in a good word for you.'

'Honestly? I don't feel you're in a position to negotiate.'

With an eight-metre drop onto the stone-paved courtyard, perhaps not.

Harriet raised her chin.

In return Thea lifted her hand, as if to help Harriet back onto the landing, but she'd been a police officer for too long.

She ducked, stepping out onto the walkway and back into the rain.

Something like an angry wasp bounced off the stone doorway, causing tiny shards of stone to splinter off and cut Harriet's cheek.

It stung, but it could have been much worse.

'Bother,' Thea said, glaring at the ancient flintlock in her hand. 'I missed. Point blank range, too. Bloody thing must fire to the right.'

Harriet decided she must be in shock. Why else hadn't she turned and fled? Although where would she have gone?

But four-hundred-year-old flintlocks took time to reload, so she still had a chance to get out of here.

Something that must also have occurred to Thea – or perhaps she hadn't brought any spare ammunition with her, because she threw the flintlock at Harriet.

Fortunately, that missed too, bouncing once on the stone threshold, once on the walkway, and then disappearing into the rain and the forest below.

Reminding Harriet exactly how far above the ground she was.

It was only when she watched it fall that she realised she'd made a terrible mistake.

She'd stepped out onto the walkway but was sheltered from the worst of the elements by the tower – which should have been a clue.

The *wind* hadn't changed direction.

Harriet was on the wrong side of the tower.

When she'd stepped away from Thea and through the doorway, she'd headed onto the walkway that led towards the garden.

The walkway that no longer existed.

There wasn't even a parapet between the walkway and the forest, only a thin iron railing, so old it had possibly been installed in Victorian times.

Thea was right. Harriet *wasn't* in any position to negotiate.

What was she going to do?

She glanced back at Thea, automatically tensing for her next attack. Thea was taller and in a better position, but she was also in her sixties and presumably untrained in self-defence.

Yet Harriet had constantly underestimated Thea.

Her chances didn't look good.

A crack of lightning, even closer this time, revealed Thea more clearly, leaning back against the doorway, eyes closed as though utterly exhausted.

'I'm too old for this,' Thea muttered.

That sounded promising. Harriet took a step forward. Maybe—

Without turning her head, Thea raised her other hand and Harriet froze.

She had *another* pistol?

What the *hell*?

Who *was* this woman?

'Stay where you are, damn it!' Thea snapped. 'I don't *want* to shoot you. I *like* you!'

'You've just *taken* a shot at me!' Harriet retorted. So much for diplomacy. If Ben were here, he'd be shaking his head. 'Do you *usually* shoot at people you like?'

'When they annoy me, *yes*.' As if the pistol was too heavy for her, Thea's arm flopped down to her side and she leant against the tower again, trying to get her breath back.

In her head, Harriet ran through the steps required to disarm Thea. As soon as she made a move, Thea would point that pistol right back at her. Harriet could step aside, grab the barrel and push it away, try to use her other hand to bend Thea's wrist back, so she'd be forced to release it.

It was what Harriet had been trained to do.

But she'd never had to do it during a thunderstorm, while balanced precariously on a narrow walkway, a dizzying height from the ground – with the assailant holding an antique pistol far larger than a handgun.

Damn...

Thea raised the flintlock with a steady hand, barely even glancing in Harriet's direction. 'Don't even think about it,' she said. 'It would be far too easy to shoot you and I'm still considering it.'

'Considering'? That was something at least.

Thea's wig was slightly askew. Of all the things to notice.

What would she look like without it?

Another little old lady: invisible, insignificant, unimportant, *underestimated*.

Harriet wasn't going to make that mistake again.

But what if she could get Thea to underestimate *her*?

'Where's the real Lady Rose?' she asked, as casually as she could manage. 'Did you kill her, too?'

'Of course not! I've no idea where she is. Still in Australia, I assume, or dead. I couldn't find a single piece of correspondence from her in the house, not even a postcard, considering she and Peony were supposedly so close. I've tried asking Peony, but she only wants to talk about Rose stealing the man she loved, and the parties they used to have in the mausoleum.' Thea sighed. 'The poor woman lives in her own reality and becomes quite cross if anyone questions it. I suppose her memories are all she has left of her former life and they're slowly eroding. Dementia is such hell.'

'Do you think she'll be alright on her own? Would the thunderstorm frighten her?'

'Not Peony. In the old days she'd have been dancing in the rain.'

'I wish I'd known her then.'

Thea sighed. 'She was a lot of fun.'

'Let's go back inside,' Harriet said kindly, 'and forget about all this. We could have a nice cup of—'

Thea snorted. 'Tea? You're lucky you only drink coffee – and even then you *would* keep on insisting on making it yourself. I did wonder if you suspected.'

Suspected? Oh no...

'The real Peony poisoned the tea,' she said out loud. Yet how many times had Thea offered to make it for them? They hadn't wanted to take advantage of her, plus Harriet and Sam drank coffee, as did Milla and Drake. But what about Pete Kershaw and Freddie Kuang? Had they got home safely?

'Giles told you,' Thea said flatly. 'Is that idiot still alive?'

'You left him locked in the attic with no access to food or water.'

'But did I?' Thea pointed up. 'What about the rainwater pouring through the holes in the roof? I even left him a jug to catch it with, and a glass. Wasn't he smart enough to work it out for himself? Yet male primogeniture is still a thing. Heaven help us all. Now don't look at me like that, darling. I had to do it. As soon as he turned up, he knew who I was. I didn't mean for him to stay there *forever*, just long enough for me to find something of value and leave.'

'I know you've not been packing,' Harriet said. 'All this time, you've been searching the house for valuables. You're nothing but a common thief.'

'Never common, darling,' Thea laughed. 'And can I really be a thief, for wanting what I'm entitled to? Do you know what it's like to watch the family fortune pass from male heir to male heir, leaving nothing for me, Peony and Rose? "To split an estate is to diminish it." How often did I hear my uncle, the old Marquess, say that? *I* was left with nothing but at least Peony and Rose had the use of this house, a house that should have been theirs by right – and would have, if they'd been men.

'I came here three years ago, hoping to blag a few antiques or jewellery, and found Peony struggling to cope on her own. She wouldn't have minded what I took. Peony never cared about money. She used to wear our grandmother's diamond bracelets to do the gardening. But no, the bloody Weston family have spent, or lost, the lot. I've searched the entire house, secret passages and all. There's no money, no antiquities, no jewellery. Rose must have taken my grandmother's tiara with her to Australia. I almost feel sorry for Giles. All he's inherited is a mountain of debts and this wreck of a house.'

For which Drew Elliott was willing to pay a fortune because of the land it was built on, but Harriet knew better than to say so – it would only inflame Thea further. Instead, she took another couple of steps forward. If Thea noticed she never said anything, just continued leaning against the door frame, completely at ease, swinging the flintlock between her fingertips...

There was Harriet's opportunity.

She lunged for the pistol.

She failed to take into consideration that the walkway was medieval and the stones were loose and worn with age.

Her foot slipped.

Harriet grabbed at the railing – one end of which promptly came loose from its base and swung out over the forest, dragging her to her knees but fortunately not over the edge.

She'd assumed the railing had been firmly cemented into the walkway.

At Blackheath Hall? The building was such a wreck it was a miracle it was still standing.

She was a *fool*.

She'd *also* assumed Thea hadn't been paying attention to her but suddenly the older woman was on the walkway beside her, holding out one hand.

'Take it, you stupid girl! I'm trying to save your life!'

After trying to shoot her first?

She'd be a fool to trust Thea Weston.

Dakota would have but Dakota was an idiot who always thought the best of people and—

The railing swung out another few centimetres, taking Harriet along with it and leaving her completely off balance. There was no way of getting back to the walkway without letting go. And if she let go...

Thea tossed aside the flintlock – Harriet watched it crash once on the walkway, thankfully *not* firing, then sliding over the edge – before grabbing Harriet, hauling her to safety, leaving both women kneeling on the walkway, arms around each other.

Self-preservation had Harriet scooting away, crawling back to the shelter of the tower before she'd risk standing up again, but she was on her own.

Thea was still kneeling on the walkway, peering over the edge.

What was she looking at? There was nothing down there but trees and bushes.

'Thea? What are you doing? Come inside!'

The older woman staggered to her feet. 'I've had fun,' she said, raising her voice above the wind. 'I suppose that's the point of life, isn't it? Like Peony? To have fun?'

'Thea, come here! It's not safe!'

'I don't think so.' Thea shook her head sadly. 'You see, I wouldn't have much fun in prison. And that's where I'd be heading.'

'Thea? *Thea!*'

'Goodbye, darling!'

'*No!*' Harriet lurched towards the other woman, grabbing for her, but their hands were wet and Thea's fingers slid straight through hers.

All Harriet could do was watch helplessly as Thea Weston disappeared over the edge.

FORTY-FOUR

NINE YEARS PREVIOUSLY

Kieran's bullet wound healed quickly enough but the injuries he'd sustained to his knee meant a series of operations over several months, each more painful than the last, that left him with a pronounced limp and the possibility of having to use a cane for the rest of his life.

His grandmother visited every time he ended up back in hospital, and the day after what he hoped was his final operation, she handed him a key and told him his father had died and left him everything.

'Everything' – once the debts were taken into account, and the loans paid back, notice given to the landlords of his childhood home and Francis's 'office', aka the tin fishing shack at the far end of Port Rell Harbour – turned out to be fifty-two pounds.

Kieran thought he'd go to the pub and drown his sorrows at The Smuggler's Inn, but apparently alcohol and painkillers didn't mix, and once he'd finished throwing up in the gents, he ended up hobbling the length of the harbour, swigging from a can of cola, to go and view his 'estate'.

Unfortunately, the owner of the tin shack had swiftly cleared everything into a skip, ready for the next tenant. This was probably illegal, but Francis *had* owed him almost six months' back rent.

Kieran had a poke about in the skip but there was nothing worth saving, although all the paperwork had been dumped into cardboard boxes, which was something. He shuddered to think how many data protection laws were being broken. He had no idea how he was going to get the boxes back to Esme's place either. He'd given up his own apartment the second he'd resigned and lost his income, and currently he couldn't drive.

He sat on the pavement, his bad leg stretched out, not bothering to consider how he was going to get back up again. He'd have liked another drink, despite how well it had gone last time, but The Smuggler's Inn was at the other end of the harbour and he was here. In the gutter. Again.

Damn.

What the *hell* was he going to do now? There were few openings for ex-coppers without extensive retraining, and how could he afford that? Apart from a civilian position with the police, a security guard, or a store detective, that was about it.

How had it come to this?

Having *principles*, that's how it had come to this.

If Francis had been alive, he'd have laughed his head off.

And it was Francis's fault he was in this mess.

And Phyllis Halfpenny's.

How could she have betrayed him like that? They'd been *friends*.

But he *wasn't* going to think about—

He scooped up the drink can from the pavement beside him and hurled it into the road, spraying cola everywhere – as a sleek black Range Rover pulled up beside him.

The can bounced off one wing, leaving a small but noticeable dent.

Terrific. Now he could add criminal damage to everything else.

He put his head in his hands, vaguely aware of the driver's door opening and a man in a smart black suit getting out.

He glanced up. The man pointedly bent to inspect the dent,

straightened, glared at Kieran and then opened the back passenger door.

His stomach went into freefall as he recognised the man who got out. Who wouldn't? He was one of the most famous – yet reclusive – businessmen in the country. Dermot Graham, owner of Graham Media, which included several newspapers and magazines, and his own broadcasting company.

'Shoot me again,' Kieran muttered, putting his head back in his hands.

'Wouldn't you rather have a job?' said Graham's smooth dulcet voice.

Kieran glanced up. 'That's a joke, right?'

He hadn't realised he'd spoken aloud until Graham replied, 'I rarely joke, Mr Drake.'

Kieran should probably get out of the gutter at this point, if only to be polite, but he wasn't sure how he was going to manage it without—

'Ouff!'

Graham's chauffeur had grabbed him under the arms and yanked him to his feet. Graham himself swiped up Kieran's cane and handed it to him.

'Er, thanks,' Kieran said, 'but to be honest, I'm not in any shape to take on work at the moment, as you can see.'

Graham's thin lips twitched in what on anyone else might have been a smile.

'In your own time, Mr Drake. I can wait.'

Kieran's eyes narrowed. 'What kind of job?'

'To be completely honest with you, too, Mr Drake, I was rather hoping you were going to take over your father's detective agency.'

'*Detective agency?*' Kieran snorted. It sounded like something from one of those old black-and-white films his grandmother liked to watch. On the other hand... Dermot Graham was extremely wealthy; he could have gone anywhere, which meant the work he had in mind would be highly... specialised.

Translation: illegal.

Kieran sighed. What was his grandmother's favourite expression? Oh yes, beggars can't be choosers. Being found sitting in the gutter was about as low as he could get. Yet Dermot Graham *still* wanted to hire him?

'What do you want me to do?'

'I'm always looking for business opportunities,' Graham said, 'and this seems like a good investment for me.'

Aware, exactly, of what the tin shack behind him looked like, Kieran waited for the punchline.

Strangely, there didn't seem to be one.

The chauffeur had become bored and was leaning against the car, his arms folded, keeping a wary eye on the street, perhaps in case his boss was recognised, but Dermot Graham was watching Kieran patiently, waiting for his answer.

'What *is* it you want me to do?' Kieran repeated.

'Nothing illegal,' Graham returned smoothly.

It was something illegal.

'Thanks, but no thanks.' He pointedly turned away – with some effort; he still hadn't got the hang of the blasted cane.

'I'm willing to invest in a... private investigative and surveillance business,' Graham said, raising his voice slightly as Kieran hobbled away. 'I'll buy the premises and pay all the bills, including at least one member of staff and your own salary, of course. You pick and choose your jobs. I won't interfere in the slightest.'

'Money laundering then?' Kieran said over his shoulder. 'Nice try.'

Dermot made a sound of exasperation and caught up with him. 'Everything is completely above board.'

Kieran stopped and turned to face him. It was one thing to hobble all the way down here on his own, at his leisure, quite another to do it with an audience. 'Then what?' he said. 'Why do you want to open an "investigative and surveillance business" with me as a front? To get stories for your newspapers?'

Graham rolled his eyes. 'For that, I have journalists. No, there is one particular person I'd like you to keep track of – at a distance – and write me a weekly report. It's something your father used to do for me.' His lip curled slightly as his attention fell on the boxes piled outside the shack. A slight indication of his head, and the chauffeur began stacking them into the boot of the car.

Should he stop him?

He decided he couldn't be bothered.

'Who?' Kieran asked bluntly.

Graham slid his hand into his inside jacket pocket and brought out his wallet. Hesitating so briefly Kieran half-thought he'd imagined it, he held up a small photograph of a pretty teenage girl.

'I'd like you to keep an eye on my daughter, Camilla Graham.'

'You want me to *spy* on your *teenage* daughter? No, thanks.'

Graham sighed. 'She's sixteen and doesn't know she's my daughter. I don't want you to spy, just ensure she's happy and comes to no harm.'

'Where's her mother? I'm not getting involved in any custody case.'

'Rosemary died when she was six. Camilla was brought up by her grandmother, who died when she was ten. Now she's living with her grandmother's nephew. It's... complicated,' Graham added, before Kieran could ask another question.

Kieran was already feeling sorry for a girl he'd never met. 'If I have to watch her twenty-four seven, I won't have time to do anything else.'

'As I said, you may hire staff.'

'How many?'

'We'll start with one, but I'll increase that if you can make a reasonable case for it.'

'And you'll provide premises?'

Graham glanced behind him, at the tin shack. With all the junk outside, it appeared even more disreputable than usual.

'Did you have somewhere in mind?'

Kieran's gaze wandered down the road and came to a stop on a tall, narrow building. The one with 'Commercial Premises For Sale' written on a sign swinging back and forth in the breeze.

'How about that one?' he suggested, only half serious.

'Done,' Graham said, holding out his hand, presumably to seal the deal.

Someone had been, and Kieran hoped it wasn't him. He'd always swore he wouldn't follow his father into the private investigation business but, with the amount Graham was offering, Kieran would be able to afford smarter premises, attract a better clientele, charge more and perhaps employ a receptionist.

An image of Esme popped into his mind. She wasn't enjoying her retirement. Why shouldn't he offer her the job?

He grinned at the thought, remembering how much she'd despised Francis's precious detective agency but, equally, she'd hate to miss out on this new adventure.

He'd forgotten Graham was still watching him.

'Is it a deal?' Graham asked.

Kieran tipped his head, as though considering it. 'What's my budget? Because I'm going to need a street team of informants before I even consider it.'

Dermot Graham, a man whose name regularly made the Rich List, said, 'I think I can stand it.'

FORTY-FIVE

PRESENT DAY

Sunday

Ben sprinted towards the house, icy rain dashing his face, blurring his vision and turning the stone-paved courtyard beneath his feet into a skating rink. He was closely followed by Sam, with Drake far behind, not even attempting to keep up with them, probably because he couldn't.

Despite pounding on the heavy oak door and shouting 'Police!' no one answered. Although, to add insult to injury, all the security lights promptly came on. 'Peony!' he tried again. 'Open this bloody door!'

'You're too polite.'

He glanced round. Drake was standing beside him, staring thoughtfully up at the house.

'Think you could do better?' Ben gestured towards the door. 'Please, have at it.'

Drake rested his palm against the battered wood. 'It was built to withstand sieges. Nothing short of a sledgehammer will get through that.'

Ben took a step back, checking the door for weak points, wondering whether he and Sam would be able to smash it open between them. But although the door appeared ancient and cobbled together with mismatched planks and rusty nails, Drake was right. It was more robust than it looked.

That didn't stop him kicking it though.

The door barely moved.

'Told you,' Drake said helpfully. 'They built things to last in those days.'

'*Harriet* is in danger!'

'*Harriet* is a highly trained police officer and can take care of herself. Stop treating your team like your family. Give them the space to do their jobs without fussing over them.'

'They *are* my family! And if anything happens to one of them...'

'Then I feel sorry for you.'

'Really? Because I'm starting to feel sorry for you. Is there no one in your life whose safety you care about?'

As Drake remained silent, Ben backed down the steps, trying to work out how else he could obtain entry. Force a window? Perhaps, but they were high and narrow. It was doubtful any of them would be able to squeeze through that way.

There was no sign of the armed response vehicle. So much for being able to deploy at a moment's notice. Although, to be fair, the storm had probably slowed them down. He could see Sam waving his phone about, trying to get a signal to call the station for back-up. At least someone was being proactive.

Thinking logically, there wouldn't be a back door because the house had been built into the surrounding wall, but surely there'd be an entrance to a kitchen or for servants? Hadn't Stuart Huntingdon mentioned seeing someone come out of a side door?

A crack of thunder broke over their heads, so loud Ben could almost feel it rattle his teeth. As if on cue, Harriet stumbled out of the ruined gatehouse behind them, filthy and soaking wet, her blonde curls plastered to her head, revealing a nasty cut on her forehead.

He ran across the courtyard, so relieved she was unhurt he

almost swept her into a hug, which they'd both have found embarrassing.

Fortunately, she dashed straight past him, pointing around the side of the house and bellowing, 'There's another door this way!' over the storm.

To the left of the house were low stone walls that might once have been outbuildings. Harriet ran between them and the three men followed, and suddenly they were out of the incessant wind and rain, sheltered by the surrounding wall, with a modern door directly in front of them.

Harriet shoved at it and they hurried inside.

The silence after the storm was disconcerting.

Ben caught up with Harriet as she entered the great hall and turned her around. 'Slow down, you're hurt.'

'Am I?' She touched her forehead gingerly, her fingers coming away bloody. 'Oh, that must have been when Thea hit me with the bed-warming pan.'

'*Bed-warming pan?* What the *hell?*'

'I *know*! It's been a very eventful evening. I hardly know where to start.'

'At the beginning!'

Drake strolled past as though he owned the place, tossing his jacket on the back of the sofa and a few more logs onto the fire.

'It was Peony who shot me the other night,' Drake told Harriet. 'That's why I'm here. She must have realised I was part of Drew Elliott's scheme to get her out of the house, and decided to remove me. Not permanently,' he added quickly. 'She deliberately shot to miss.'

'I don't think she did,' Harriet said. 'When she fired the same pistol at me, she was grumbling that it fired to the right.'

'Oh...' Despite the flickering fire, Drake's face paled.

'Where's Peony now?' Ben asked Harriet. 'Is she still armed?'

'No. She attempted to shoot me but changed her mind and deliberately stepped off the wall rather than give herself up.' Harriet shook her head, as though still processing it. 'I tried to stop her, but she knew we had enough evidence to secure a conviction, and she didn't want to go to prison.'

'No one could have survived a fall like that,' Ben said quietly.

'Also, she's not really Lady Peony,' Harriet said. 'She's Peony's cousin, *Thea* Weston. The *real* Lady Peony is the one with dementia, who watches TV in bed all day. Thea says she has no idea where the real Lady Rose is. Presumably still in Australia.'

Drake grimaced. 'Sadly, Lady Rose never made it as far as Australia. She didn't even leave the country. We met her and her husband in the mausoleum half an hour ago, still sitting down to their wedding breakfast.'

Harriet turned to Ben. 'Is he *serious*?'

'I'm afraid so.' Ben shuddered at the memory. 'Lady Rose was wearing her red wedding dress, a diamond tiara, veil and all. It was macabre. I'm working on the theory that the real Lady Peony must have poisoned them, perhaps for falling in love and abandoning her. There are no obvious injuries.'

'Oh no! Giles!' Harriet spun round and ran up the stairs. 'I can't believe I forgot about him!'

Giles who? Did she mean the Marquess of Blackheath?

'Where are you going?' Ben called, loath to leave the warmth of the fire. He watched as she approached a large painting halfway along the wall of the gallery and began pulling at one side of the frame. 'Harriet?'

He glanced at Drake, who also had no intention of moving away from the fire, because he was making shooing motions with his hand. 'Run along, Detective Inspector. Maybe there's someone for you to save after all.'

By the time Ben arrived on the landing, Harriet had managed to swing the entire painting to one side like a door, revealing an ancient stone staircase behind it, and had already clambered inside.

Ben reluctantly followed. With his height it was hard to squeeze into such a small space, and he bashed his elbow before he'd even climbed two steps. The low, narrow staircase was warm and airless, and lined with thick cobwebs. It led straight up, quite steeply. Judging from the worn stone, the steps might once have led to a tower or parapet. How far up did they go?

'Harriet?' he called, but, being a good deal shorter, she'd found the steps easier to navigate and was well ahead of him.

He heard the click of a lock and by the time he'd reached the top, Harriet had unlocked the door and accessed a small attic room.

There was a tiny sloping window set into the roof, smashed and leaving the room open to the elements, and a small Victorian fireplace. Perhaps a more modern hideaway rather than a secret room?

Lying on a mouldy old bed was a man about the same age as himself, utterly astonished to see them.

'Harriet!' The man struggled to sit up, suffering a nasty coughing fit. 'I thought you were dead!'

'It'd take more than a slide off the roof to kill me,' Harriet said, in what Ben recognised as pure bravado. 'You were right. I landed on the walkway. It led to the gatehouse, and I came straight back here to rescue you.'

Ben recognised a lie when he heard it. Something else had happened to Harriet between the walkway and returning here. Was that when Thea Weston had tried to kill her?

'Oh, Harriet,' the man groaned. 'Promise me you'll never do anything like that again?'

'It's my *job*.'

'But not to throw yourself off a roof,' Ben snapped. 'Next time, wait to be rescued.'

'*Rescued?*' She turned on him, eyes sparking. 'Like a damsel in distress? Would you say that to Sam?'

'Yes, actually!'

Harriet, perhaps belatedly remembering he was her senior officer, thankfully shut up.

Ben turned his attention to the man on the bed. Why had he been locked in here? And why did he seem familiar? That pale face, sharp features, blond hair, prominent nose...

It was the nose that clinched it.

He was the spitting image of the man in the portrait on the gallery.

'*Lord Blackheath?*'

The Marquess of Blackheath smiled politely. 'Have we met?'

'I'm DI Taylor. I've been looking for you.'

'To arrest you for terrorising two little old ladies,' Harriet put in.

'*What?*' Lord Blackheath's eyes widened.

She sent a wicked glance in Ben's direction. 'But apparently we had that the wrong way round...'

They helped Giles down the steps and into the great hall, where he took his turn to warm up in front of the fire while they waited for the paramedics to arrive. Outside, the storm was finally moving away, with the odd lethargic rumble of thunder. Like magic, the power came back on, the lights around the gallery spotlighting the elderly lady walking down the main staircase, tall and regal despite her frilly white dressing gown.

'Hello.' She beamed at Ben, who was the closest, and held out her hand. 'Who might you be? Someone important, I think. You have that look about you. Dignified.'

Was he supposed to shake her hand or kiss it?

From the other side of the room, Drake didn't even bother to hide his laughter.

'Lady Peony?' Ben ventured. Who else could it be? Her hair was white rather than pink, but cut into the same short, no-nonsense bob she'd had in 1983. She was wearing bright pink lipstick and definitely had 'the Weston nose'.

'Lady Peony,' she agreed. 'It's so lovely to have visitors. Although you are a *trifle* early. Would you like a cup of tea? No need to ring. I can make it myself. Everyone loves my tea.'

Five horrified faces turned towards him.

It was a shame, because he'd quite like a hot drink after the night he'd had, but, remembering what had happened to Lady Rose and her new husband...

'Thank you,' he said gently, 'but that won't be necessary.'

'Honestly, Ben,' Harriet grumbled sometime later, after a paramedic had checked the bumps on her head and shone a torch into her eyes; and an ambulance had taken both Lord Blackheath and the real Peony off to hospital to be checked over; and Drake had yawned widely, muttered, 'Let's *not* do this again,' and left. 'For a minute there I thought you were going to let the poisoner make you a tea!'

'*Alleged* poisoner,' Ben said. 'We have no evidence.'

'*Yet*,' Harriet said. 'I suspect the real Lady Peony has poisoned a great many people, but we might never know for sure. She certainly killed her sister and brother-in-law at their wedding. I did wonder if she murdered her parents too, but Giles just told me they died in a car crash shortly before Rose married the gardener – which probably started her off. Poor Peony couldn't bear to be left alone in this big old house – and then, because of her own actions, she was.'

'The Westons don't seem to be very good at thinking things through,' Ben said, remembering how Lucia Serrano and Bruce Ogilvy believed Major Lord John Weston had murdered his brother, taken his place and spent the next twenty years in hiding.

'Do you think we should check the mausoleum for more bodies? Perhaps dig up the garden?'

Probably, but he'd rather not think about that.

'You can file the report for this one,' he said.

They were carefully picking their way through the under-growth at the base of the wall surrounding Blackheath Hall, followed by a paramedic and a uniformed police officer, and didn't stop until they were directly beneath the ruined gatehouse.

'Thea should be here somewhere.' Harriet began pushing the undergrowth aside and almost immediately found the second flintlock. They'd already discovered the other one in the courtyard. But after another ten minutes of searching, they'd failed to find a body and Ben was wondering whether they should bring in a dog.

There were plenty of signs of where Thea *had* been – broken branches and flattened shrubs – but the elderly lady was long gone, leaving her pink wig deliberately hooked on a branch, presumably as a final 'Stuff you'.

Ben told the paramedic and uniformed officer that their services were no longer required. When he turned to Harriet, she was staring up at the wall.

'How on earth did Thea *survive*?'

'The ground is higher on this side,' he said, 'built up over the centuries, and the trees and shrubs have grown against the wall, creating a nice soft landing.'

They then stared at the flattened undergrowth.

'Do you think she's hurt?' Harriet asked quietly.

'There's no blood, and she appears to have left quite speedily. The soil is scuffed up along that little path – there are even footprints in some places – and you can see where she's broken some of the branches by grabbing at them for support.'

The track that Thea had left behind led directly into the clearing beside the Gateway to the Dead, but too many people had been this way over the past few days, and her trail soon petered out. It wasn't hard to work out where she was going though.

'She must have headed to the village,' Ben said. 'She knew we'd go straight to the house. From the village she could catch a bus or a train, even cadge a lift from someone. We can issue a warrant for her arrest, but we'll need a description. Without the wig and heavy make-up, do any of us know what she really looks like?'

'There are some photo albums back at the house,' Harriet said. 'I'll check through them.'

'Are you pleased Thea's escaped?' Ben asked as they walked back to the house. 'You seem to have formed quite a bond.'

'Why does everyone keep *saying* that? The witch tried to kill me! Twice!'

'But chose to jump instead.'

'That's not as noble as you're making it sound. Thea spent time here as a child. She must have known if she landed in the right place, she'd be fine. I saw her checking the terrain before she jumped.'

As they stepped beneath the ruined gatehouse and back into the courtyard of Blackheath Hall, Ben caught a last glimpse of the dot of pink that was Thea's wig hanging on the bushes. It was evidence, but he'd send someone else to retrieve it.

'It was quite a risk to take,' he said. 'Especially for an elderly lady.'

'*Elderly?* Pah! She's sixty-five and fitter than me. I tell you, I am *never* going to trust little old ladies again.'

FORTY-SIX

Monday

The morning after he'd been locked in the mausoleum with Ben Taylor, Kieran Drake parked his car in The Square at Raven's Edge and walked across the high street to call on his former assistant, Milla Graham, to offer a grovelling apology in person. But she still wasn't talking to him, so that was a wasted trip. He didn't even have to knock on her door, because there was already a sign pinned to it that said:

Dear Drake,
Bugger off

Oh well. He was sure she'd come around.
Eventually.
Maybe.
He crossed The Square to the chocolate shop, Something Wicked, to buy a large box for his grandmother Esme, who also had a lot to put up with. Then he headed into the café next door, going down the short flight of stone steps worn in the centre from

centuries of use, and into the gloom beyond, remembering to duck at the last minute so he didn't smack his forehead on the lintel.

It took a moment for his eyes to adjust to the dark.

Phyllis Halfpenny was watching him warily from behind the counter but, other than that, the café was completely devoid of customers.

Perfect.

Kieran Drake was about to issue another rare, in-person apology and he'd rather there weren't any witnesses.

Casually he strolled over.

Phyllis appeared to be holding her breath.

(She might also be considering braining him with a nearby teapot.)

He took a deep breath, apologised profusely for his recent behaviour and, as a conciliatory gesture, ordered a pot of tea.

'Are you sure?' she asked. 'It comes with a fortune telling...'

And they both knew how well that had gone last time.

'Do your worst,' he sighed.

Her expression didn't turn any less wary.

Maybe she'd *tip* the tea over his head instead?

She wouldn't be the first.

He went to sit at the little table in the bow window, mainly because it had the best phone signal, and stretched out his bad leg, wincing. It had a habit of locking if he sat with his knee bent for too long, which was never great if you had to unexpectedly flee for your life.

As there was no one else in the café, a mug of coffee quickly arrived on the table in front of him, along with a slice of iced, dark ginger cake.

He didn't remember ordering cake – or coffee, come to that – but the coffee was exactly how he liked it – black as night and so hot it almost burnt his mouth.

He might have moaned.

Phyllis was watching him from the counter. She seemed less antagonistic now but more confused.

'This is coffee,' he felt obliged to point out.

She tilted her head, as though considering the question. 'Shall I take it back?'

'No,' he said quickly, holding it protectively to his chest.

She grinned. 'You hate tea,' she said. 'I don't know why you ordered it. For the fortune telling? You can still have that – on the house. It'd be a pleasure.' Her eyes gleamed wickedly.

He glanced down at his coffee. 'But that's not part of the deal...'

'Not everyone likes tea, Kieran. It's better for business this way. Credit me with some sense, please. It's not as though I'm ever rushed off my feet. Why would anyone ever come here when they could go to The Witch's Brew or The Crooked Broomstick?'

'But...' He wasn't used to people arguing with him. 'If you're going to read my fortune, don't you need tea leaves?'

Phyllis sighed heavily. 'I don't need tea leaves to read your fortune because I don't actually read fortunes. I never have. I keep telling people this, but they never seem to listen. They'd rather believe I make it all up.'

'You don't?' But it's what he paid her for: read fortunes, *gather information*.

'I communicate with the dead,' she said. 'Or rather, they communicate with me. Two completely separate things. I've told you this before. They tell me things and they show me things. Brief snatches of conversation, brief slices of a person's life. I don't get to choose. For example, do you want to know why everyone sits at the table in the window, rather than the far cosier inglenook at the back?'

He assumed she wasn't referring to the phone signal, so he took a glance in that direction. *Cosy* inglenook? Sure, there was a fire, but a more gloomy, uninviting spot would be harder to find.

'Because the little old lady who died in this house, back in 1842, used to have a favourite chair, set right beside the fire, and woe betide anyone who occupies the space where it was – they'll feel a sharp jab of her darning needle. To them it won't *feel* like a darning needle, but more of a sudden, cold draught.'

'Despite the fire?' How could he take her seriously? He'd suffered rather too much from little old ladies in the last few days, but he had to admit, that inglenook did seem... uninviting, despite the flickering flames from the fire.

'The really interesting thing is that no one ever sits there,' she said. 'Even if they start to head in that direction, they'll suddenly veer away. Strange, don't you think?'

Drake found his gaze drawn in that direction again. It was a very dark, very inhospitable corner, despite being next to the fire. And if he stared for long enough, he could almost swear...

What the—

He blinked. There was nothing there. How could there be?

Phyllis had gone back to her seat behind the counter.

He felt oddly lonely, but he *was* in a café on his own. Well, alone apart from a grumpy medium and a territorial ghost.

How had his life come to this?

'What about my reading?' he grumbled.

She rolled her eyes. 'OK... Annie' – she nodded towards the corner – 'would like you to know that she's grateful the scruffy gentleman bought her house because hardly anyone visits now, so she more or less has the place to herself.'

'That's not good for business!'

'You and I aren't in the hospitality business though, are we, Kieran? We're in the business of gathering information.'

How the hell...?

She winked.

Phyllis Halfpenny actually winked at him.

He put his head in his hands. 'How did you know that I own Spellbound and I've been paying you to be one of my informants? How *long* have you known?'

'I did a little detective work of my own,' she said. 'I always thought it strange I was offered the job because not many people would employ an ex-con...'

'Why not?'

She raised her eyebrows. 'Assault with a deadly weapon?

Injuring a police officer? I was lucky to get six months rather than two years. Fortunately, I had someone willing to speak up for me. Not you,' she added, 'but Detective Inspector Davenport.'

He couldn't meet her gaze. 'I was angry,' he said. 'I behaved badly. I'm sorry. So, so sorry. If I could turn back time...'

'I know,' she said softly.

'Jake Davenport told me you'd deliberately aimed to miss.'

'I tried to tell you at the time, but you wouldn't listen. I'm a very good shot. Unexpected, I know, but there you are.'

'I'm *sorry*,' he repeated wretchedly. 'For everything, and everything I said the other day.'

She shrugged. 'I'm sorry about your knee. I thought shooting you in the shoulder would do the least amount of damage.'

'That was my own fault. I tripped.'

'You wouldn't have tripped if I hadn't shot you,' she pointed out.

'If *you* hadn't shot me, Fisher certainly would – and he wouldn't have missed.'

She smiled sadly. 'Does that mean we're friends again?'

'We've always been friends, Phyllis. Why don't you make yourself a cup of coffee and sit here and help me eat this cake – which I'm pretty sure I didn't order?'

She grinned and two dimples appeared, one in each cheek. He'd known her since they'd been children and he'd never noticed she had dimples.

Because she never smiled.

He was a pig.

'I can't do that,' she said, 'the boss might catch me skiving off.'

It took a moment for him to catch on and he frowned, confused. 'But...'

Phyllis laughed.

He'd never heard her laugh before either.

'Damn the boss,' he said, pulling out a chair for her. 'I've heard he's a complete idiot.'

FORTY-SEVEN

After a full medical check-up and a short stay in hospital to recover, Giles Weston, the Eighteenth Marquess of Blackheath, sold the house that had been in his family for six centuries to Drew Elliott at a price that made them both feel they'd got a bargain. He then returned to his (far more manageable, definitely warmer and decidedly *not* haunted) manor house in the north of the county, where he finally plucked up courage to propose to Jorge, his long-suffering secretary – and, to his surprise, was accepted.

To everyone's disbelief, Drew Elliott did not immediately flatten Blackheath Hall and its surrounding land to build a housing estate. Instead, he arranged (and paid) for the County Archaeological department to carry out another survey encompassing the land around the house, including the battlefield beside the Gateway to the Dead. All indications were that the Weston family had swiped the monks' treasury from under the nose of King Henry VIII, but the only surviving items were a few silver plates and dented chalices, wrapped in newspaper dated '1924' and stuffed in the same sagging cardboard box Drake had seen in the museum ten years previously, and finally decided to tell the new curator about.

As Ben explained to Harriet sometime later, Drew Elliott had already invested in the maritime museum in Port Rell, and was now considering restoring and opening Blackheath Hall to the public, complete with tea rooms and gift shop.

Harriet suspected that Drew, who hadn't become a multi-millionaire by chance, had noticed how popular Raven's Edge was with the tourists, and that there weren't any other historic houses in the vicinity that were open to the public.

Once the roads to Raven's Edge were reopened following the storm, DCI Cameron arrived at Blackheath Hall to take over from Ben, with DCs Pete Kershaw and Freddie Kuang happy to relieve Harriet and Sam now it was daylight, the sun was shining, and all threats (corporeal and spiritual) had been vanquished.

'Bloody cowards,' Harriet grumbled, far too audibly, as Sam hastily ushered her into his car and took her back to her apartment.

'The DCI says we can have a few days off,' Sam said as he parked outside Foxglove & Hemlock and Harriet got out.

'Good! I'm going to sleep for a week.'

Sam grimaced. 'I don't think I'll be *able* to sleep for a week!'

She laughed as she waved him goodbye and headed into the florist's.

Amelia was unpacking that morning's delivery, but Gabriel was already working at his laptop. Before he could speak, Caesar shot out from beneath the desk, obviously thrilled to see Harriet, bouncing up and down, and licking her face ecstatically when she scooped him up for a cuddle.

'I've only been gone for one night,' she told the little dog.

Gabriel was looking at her with something close to awe. 'You look...' he began, perhaps realising that to finish that sentence wouldn't be polite. Instead, he said, 'Caesar's had a walk and done his business,' and reached forward to tickle the chihuahua under the chin. 'See you tomorrow, little fella.'

'Thank you,' Harriet said, 'but I'm going to have a couple of quiet days at home.'

'Good idea!' Gabriel's reply was far too quick. 'But if you need me to take Caesar for a walk any time?'

'That would be lovely,' she agreed.

She walked upstairs, unlocked her door and went inside, placing Caesar on the floor to scamper into the kitchen in search of his food bowl. She then leant against the door as everything suddenly became too much. Had Thea *really* intended to kill her? Then why go to the trouble of rescuing her when the railing collapsed? *Should* she feel sorry for a woman who'd felt so strongly about being cheated out of an inheritance that she'd taken over someone else's identity?

Thea had obviously cared a great deal for Peony, who wouldn't have been able to continue living at Blackheath Hall without help, but then she'd kidnapped Giles and tried to poison him, imprisoned a police officer in a mausoleum and attempted to shoot another.

Harriet gently touched the bruises on her face and winced. No, she did *not* feel sorry for Thea Weston.

There was a clank as Caesar dragged his empty metal food bowl into the sitting room, dropping it at her feet with an indignant 'Yip!'

'I'm sorry.' She bent to stroke his ears. 'I'll get right on it.'

After filling his bowl, she went to soak in the bath. The hot water was absolute bliss but as she ducked down to wash her hair it turned out there were dead leaves, twigs and bits of gravel in there, along with the dried blood. Nice...

Putting on her favourite pyjamas, she risked a glance in the mirror – and almost shrieked. The paramedic had stuck a butterfly bandage over the cut on her forehead, but it was surrounded by a pale blue bruise that would be nicely purple tomorrow, in addition to several more bruises emerging on one cheekbone and the start of a black eye. Thea Weston had got her good. No wonder Gabriel had been shocked at her appearance, but it had been kind of him to offer to walk Caesar – who'd been suspiciously quiet while she'd had her bath...

She found the little dog beside the front door, his tail wagging hopefully.

'Honestly, Caesar? You want to go out *now*? Wouldn't you

rather spend the afternoon in bed snoozing? It's what I intend to do.'

She bent to pick him up and spotted a slightly chewed envelope pushed under her door – and it was attached to a ribbon.

Opening the door, she saw that the other end trailed to the top of the stairs, ending in a large bow on an orange box with The Witch's Brew logo printed on the side. Inside was a hot chocolate, a bacon and cheese panini (still warm!), two gingerbread muffins and six peanut butter cookies. It must have been delivered while she'd been in the bath.

Was it a present from Ben?

Pushing the door shut with her hip, she ripped open the envelope and found a hand-written card from Brianna Graham – the matriarch of the wealthy Graham family – inviting Harriet to her annual Spring Ball. The card was 3D and formed a lacy bouquet when opened out.

She admired the workmanship, opening and shutting the card a few more times. She'd never seen such a thing. Why on earth had Brianna invited her? Had she made *that* much of an impression?

The answer was written in an elegant scrawl across the back:

Please?

Mal

Malcolm Graham?
Was this going to be a *date*?
She'd thought he might ask her out for a coffee, but a *ball*?
Maybe rich people didn't go about dating the same way as everyone else?
She showed the card to Caesar. 'We've been invited to a *ball*.'
Was she *sure* she wanted to do this? There'd be no privacy. Her and Mal would be announcing they were together *before* they were together and, if it was noisy, there wouldn't be the chance to

talk properly. Wouldn't lunch at The Witch's Brew have been more practical?

With the entire village watching and listening in?

Maybe not.

She turned the invitation over again. The dancing might be fun... and she owned a wardrobe full of fancy clothes that she never had the opportunity to wear...

No, she should ignore it.

Go to a ball with *Malcolm Graham*?

It would be ridiculous.

(Why did that sound like something her mother might have said?)

'Am I overthinking this?' she asked the dog.

Another thought struck her. Was the invitation a way for his father and grandmother to check her out, to see if she was 'girlfriend material'? In which case, they could all get stuffed!

The bin was right beside her... She took one last look at the invitation – it *was* incredibly pretty – and dropped the card in – just as there was a knock at the door.

Instinctively she tensed.

Was she *ever* going to get over that reaction?

Misha was on the other side, stooping slightly because of the low, slanted ceiling.

'Hi, Harriet. I'm sorry I haven't been replying to your messages. I've been really busy and...' He frowned as she shifted slightly, inadvertently moving into the light. 'I can see you have, too. What the hell happened?'

'Oh...' She shrugged. 'You know... Stuff.'

I fell off a roof, got shot at by an old lady and walked into a bed-warming pan, face first. Go me.

'Just another weekend in Raven's Edge.'

Misha frowned. 'One of the officers from Calahurst said you'd fallen off the roof at Blackheath Hall.'

'Did they?' She'd bet it was Pete Kershaw, the nasty little sneak. 'I'd call it more of a controlled slide.'

There was a distinctly awkward pause before Misha seemed to remember he was holding a large paper bag with The Crooked Broomstick logo emblazoned on the side. It smelt strongly of coffee and cookies. Harriet's stomach rumbled. It was almost worth falling off a roof to get all this free food.

'I've brought you something to cheer you up,' he said, handing over the bag.

'Oh, thank you!' It smelt *wonderful*. The coffee would make her headache worse, but what the hell. She could have Mal's panini for breakfast, followed by the coffee and a cookie, and then the hot chocolate. The perfect ending to a truly terrible night. 'That's *so* kind of you.'

'I'm sorry our date ended... you know...'

With finding a dead body...

She tried not to wince. Was he going to ask her out? To be honest, she didn't think she wanted to go. She'd crushed on him since school but, now they'd spent time together, she no longer felt the same way about him. She certainly couldn't relax enough to be herself.

The way she could with Mal...

Misha was still staring at her forehead. 'You could have been killed...'

Yeah, several times, but thanks, Misha. I've been trying not to think about it.

'It's nothing. Happens all the time.' And was the reason she had a box of instant ice packs in her bathroom cupboard. 'I knew what I was getting into when I signed up.'

'You could ask to be moved to a desk job?'

She laughed – and then realised he wasn't joking. Take on Dakota's role? Become the man-in-the-van (even though they didn't *have* a van) and do all the research and techie stuff everyone else hated? She raised her chin to meet his gaze defiantly. 'Leave all the fun to someone else? I don't think so! I love my work.'

It was the wrong thing to have said.

As usual.

She'd basically flung his concern for her safety back in his face.

'I'm sorry,' she said, more gently. 'I do love my job and this' – she pointed to her face – 'doesn't happen that often. I made the mistake of trusting someone I shouldn't have.'

Misha's expression softened. 'I understand. I love baking; you love detective work – and I did have fun on the ghost tour, until...' He grimaced.

'This isn't going to work, is it?' she sighed.

'Probably not.'

'Thank you for the cookies.'

'Thank you for the date.' He bent to kiss her cheek. 'I hope you're feeling better soon, Harriet. Take it easy, OK?'

She grinned and waved the bag of cookies. 'Oh, I plan to!'

After he'd gone, she settled on the sofa with Mal's panini – and Caesar watching intently from the floor.

'Yip!'

'No, I am *not* picking you up because you're only after my bacon and you know human food is very bad for you.' She switched on the television to check if the events at Blackheath Hall had made it to the local news. They hadn't, but there was a lengthy report about the effects of the storm, which she became quite engrossed in, until there was a loud CLANG and, when she looked round, she saw Caesar had deliberately knocked over the bin and promptly disappeared inside it, tail wagging.

'There's no food in there, you daft dog,' she told him, before putting the last chunk of panini in her mouth and getting up to rescue him.

When she pulled him out (slightly dusty but very pleased with himself), he had a familiar scrap of white frilly card clamped between his jaws and was apparently hoping for a tussle over it.

'I'm not playing that game,' she told him. 'It's yours. You keep it.'

He dropped it at her feet. 'Yip!'

'I definitely don't want it *now*. You've dribbled on it.'

'Yip!'

'Oh, for goodness' sake.' Intending to put the invitation in the taller kitchen bin, well out of his reach, she picked it up by the remaining dry corner. This meant Mal's scribble was uppermost.

Please?

Harriet sighed. She'd liked Mal. *Really* liked him.

And it seemed he liked her too...

Why *shouldn't* she go to a ball? She was as good as the Grahams any day and didn't she deserve to have some fun? Ben would be there – his girlfriend, Milla, was Mal's sister – and surely there would be other people to talk to and dance with? She didn't *have* to make it a first date or any kind of a big thing. It could be... a simple invitation.

She crouched to show Caesar the card.

'What do you think? *Shall* we go to the ball?'

'*Yip!*'

'You know, I think you're right. We should.' Carefully she placed the card on the coffee table. 'After all, what's the worst that could happen?'

EPILOGUE

The jeweller had taken one look at the diamond bracelet and gone to fetch his boss, who turned out to be a stunning Black woman, aged somewhere around thirty, wearing a tailored green dress.

When she was that age, Thea Weston thought, she was happy to slob about in jeans and a T-shirt. How much she'd missed. Still, she was about to make up for that.

'Good morning,' the woman said. 'I'm Bailey Fisher. I own Wyndhurst Jewellers. How may I help you?'

Thea put her head on one side. 'Have we met?' she asked, careful to tone down her accent. 'You seem awfully familiar.'

Bailey started to deny it but then she, too, frowned. 'Possibly... Have you visited us before? Or sometimes we have exhibitions with our partners?'

Thea remembered she was no longer wearing the extravagant pink wig or the real Lady Peony's stash of vintage clothing. In fact, she probably looked just like a harmless little old lady. And right now, that was fine by her.

'I have this diamond bracelet,' she said, deciding to get to the point. She'd already noticed the security cameras and the sooner she'd achieved what she'd come here to do and left for places unknown, the better. 'It used to belong to my grandmother.'

That, at least, was true.

Unfortunately, like everything else that had been entailed, it probably now belonged to Giles – and what would *he* do with a diamond bracelet?

Bailey held out her hand. 'May I?'

Thea would rather not hand it over. What if the woman took it away into the back room and called the police? Then she'd be done for.

If that happened, Thea decided, she'd make a run for it. That bald-headed security guard might look tough but, in her experience, those kind of men seriously underestimated women like her.

She was so busy planning her escape that at first she missed what Bailey had said.

'I'm sorry, could you say that again?'

'This isn't a bracelet. It's a diamond cuff, possibly one of a pair, dating from the 1930s and worth about forty thousand pounds.'

'F... forty *thousand* pounds?'

And Lady Peony – the *real* Lady Peony – had worn it to do the gardening!

If *only* she could find the other one, and the matching tiara and necklace worn by Lady Rose on her wedding day. Presumably all that had gone to Australia too.

Bailey's eyes narrowed. 'Do you have provenance? Any paperwork to say the cuff belongs to you and that you have the right to sell it?'

Damn. She'd have to make a run for it after all.

At her age.

How undignified.

The security guard was chatting up one of the assistants so she wouldn't have to worry about *him*, but she'd still have to run the length of the shop to reach the door, which was probably locked...

She sighed and held out her hand. 'No, no provenance. I'm sorry to have wasted your time.'

Bailey's grip on the cuff didn't loosen. 'Do you still wish to sell it?'

'For forty thousand pounds?' Now it was Thea's turn to narrow her eyes. Did she look as if she'd been born yesterday? The girl would have one finger on the panic button already. Keep Thea talking until the police arrived. Like she'd fall for *that*.

Except... Bailey was still holding the cuff in one hand and her loupe in the other...

Bailey smiled – it was a rather sneaky, cat-like smile, Thea thought. Because Bailey Fisher knew exactly why Thea was here and where she'd obtained the cuff.

It did not bode well.

How far was it to the door?

'Without paperwork I couldn't give you anything like that sum,' Bailey said, still smiling that cat-like smile. 'I wouldn't be able to sell it myself without a *lot* of inconvenience. It would have to be to one of my... select clients, for a good deal less than its true value.'

Apparently, appearances were deceptive. Bailey Fisher was as big a thief as she was.

'How much?' Thea asked bluntly. What was the point of pretending?

'I could offer five...'

Five thousand pounds? She'd take it!

'But to save you obtaining alternative estimates from my competitors, and to guarantee discretion,' Bailey went on, 'I'd be willing to offer ten.'

It was what Thea had hoped to sell the bracelet for originally, but to now know it was worth forty – she could have cried. If only she'd had a little bit longer to search Blackheath Hall, maybe she could have found the original receipt. From the three years she'd spent living there, one thing had been very clear – the Weston family *never* threw anything away.

Still, ten thousand pounds...

Thea sighed, took one last longing look at the diamond cuff and said, 'You have yourself a deal.'

A LETTER FROM THE AUTHOR

Dear reader,

Thank you so much for reading *Murder at Raven's Gate*! I do hope you've enjoyed it. I have lots more mysteries planned for Ben, Harriet and their team to solve. If you'd like to be the first to hear about new releases and bonus content, you can click on the link below to sign up. Don't miss out!

www.stormpublishing.co/louise-marley

If you've enjoyed this book and could spare a few moments to leave a review that would be hugely appreciated. Even a short review (or star rating!) can make all the difference in encouraging a reader to discover my books for the first time. Thank you so much!

The Story Behind *Murder at Raven's Gate*

As with all my books, lots of different kinds of inspiration came together to create this story.

I think the starting point came when I realised how society often underestimates the elderly, which led to the creation of the indomitable Thea Weston, who soon runs rings around the younger characters.

Another influence was that I grew up reading my grandmother's collection of gothic romantic suspense novels. Published in the 1960s and 1970s, these books had fabulous covers, usually featuring the heroine running away from a big old house, often wearing a long, flowing nightdress. I am sure DS Harriet March would have been furious with me if I'd had *her* running around this story in a nightdress, but I did manage to squeeze in a ruined mansion, a few 'ghosts' and a thunderstorm!

Regular readers will know I love visiting big old houses. In this story, Blackheath Hall was inspired by several places, rather than just one. I knew I wanted to write about a fortified manor house, so a starting point was Stokesay Castle in Shropshire, which has a wall around it. Lowther Castle (Penrith) and Basing House (Hampshire) were also inspirations.

The mausoleum – for a full-on gothic, I *had* to have a mausoleum! – was inspired by the Lowther Mausoleum in Penrith.

The ghosts of the Civil War soldiers haunting the forest around Raven's Edge were mentioned in my first published book, *Smoke Gets in Your Eyes*, way back in 2002, and then went on to appear in several of my other books, so I felt they deserved to have a story of their own.

There are several entrances to former battle sites across the UK nicknamed 'the Gateway to the Dead' or 'Gate to the Dead', but they're usually the more ordinary kind of gate. Raven's Edge, I decided, needed something a little extra. Their 'gateway' is based on the ruin of Gisborough Priory.

You may have noticed that this book is dedicated to 'Betsy and Harriet'. Betsy was my grandmother and Harriet was her sister (my great-aunt). They were very close and had lots of adventures after their retirement. There's a repeated phrase in this story about never underestimating little old ladies, which definitely applied to them!

I had such fun bringing everything together for *Murder at Raven's Gate*. I do hope you've enjoyed reading it!

Thank you for being part of this journey with me. Would you like to know what happens next in Raven's Edge? Did you spot the clue to the next title and where the story will be set? Will Harriet finally get to go on a date that doesn't involve a murder? Do stay in touch. I have so many new stories planned!

Louise x

You can contact me at louise@louisemarley.co.uk. I'd love to hear from you!

www.louisemarley.co.uk

Raven's Edge: www.ravens-edge.co.uk

instagram.com/louisemarleywrites
facebook.com/LouiseMarleyAuthor
threads.com/@louisemarleywrites

ACKNOWLEDGEMENTS

Huge thanks to the fabulous Kathryn Taussig and Oliver Rhodes for taking a chance on *Murder at Raven's Edge*. I can't believe I'm now writing book five in the series! Thank you to my wonderful editor, Naomi Knox, and her very inspiring notes. And a big thank you to the terrific team at Storm for all the hard work that goes on behind the scenes – without whom you wouldn't be reading this book!

Thank you to my lovely family for their continued support and stoicism in the face of me explaining yet another plot twist and apologies to the random strangers in cafés all over North Wales, who *might* have been alarmed by overhearing: 'Do you think it's actually possible to kill someone using a...'

Thank you to Novelistas Ink for the writerly chat and pep talks. We always have the *best* fun at our book launches. Special thanks to Lottie Cardew for her encouragement and the trips to Gladstone's Library for coffee and cake!

Finally, a big hug to my lovely readers for their support across social media, their kind-hearted messages and their wonderful reviews. You are all brilliant!

9 781837 002177